THE CURSE
OF THE
IMPERIAL PAPERWEIGHTS

by George N. Kulles

Paperweight Press
Santa Cruz, California

Copyright © 1995 by Paperweight Press
761 Chestnut Street
Santa Cruz, California
All rights reserved.

No part of this book may be reproduced in any form
without written permission from the publisher.

This edition published 1995 by Paperweight Press
Printed in the United States of America

Library of Congress Catalog Card Number: 95-69055
ISBN: 0-933756-19-4

This book is dedicated to my wife Jean, who helped to refine my every word, phrase and paragraph. Without her invaluable help and encouragement, this book would still be languishing in my computer.

The Curse
Of The
Imperial Paperweights

CHAPTER I.

1.

"Good morning, Sotheby's-Chicago, Elizabeth Field speaking."

"I've got to talk to Alexandra!"

"Keith?"

"Yes—she there?"

"No, not yet, Keith. This isn't New York; it's only 8:45 here."

"Damn, we've got real trouble! Tell her to call me as soon as she gets in! It's important. Don't forget!"

"Okay, Keith, I'll—" The line suddenly went dead. His abrupt cut-off was no surprise. Keith's rudeness and changes of mood were legendary. When she worked in Sotheby's-New York, his "bitchiness" was often explained away by whispered references to probable spats with his lover, Howard. Smiling, she said aloud, "Oh Keith, you'll never change."

Each month, in a beautifully-appointed suite of rooms on the fourth floor of the Prentiss Building, Sotheby's-Chicago funneled millions of dollars in merchandise from the Midwest to New York for auction.

Elizabeth Field's desk was stationed just inside the door of the reception area, a pleasant, airy room tastefully decorated with Louis XV furnishings and over-sized Fragonard prints in elaborate Baroque frames. Three large velvet-draped windows in the adjoining room, Alexandra's office, overlooked Chicago's Magnificent Mile, a stretch of exclusive Michigan Avenue shops just north of the Chicago river. Large reproductions of French tapestries decorated its walls, and a contemporary

Chinese Oriental rug centered the polished parquet floor. But what first caught the eye of clients entering the room was a huge Louis XV bronze-mounted tulipwood desk which dominated the space. Alexandra felt that the enormous desk she "inherited" from the former director was painfully overbearing. When she first saw it she thought it was a cast-off prop from the Chicago Opera Company. To her consternation, she often bruised her shins and snagged her panty hose on the bronze winged sphinxes attached to the desk's ornate legs.

The other large piece of furniture in the director's office was a gilt-mounted marquetry display cabinet. Alexandra put this "castoff" to good use, making a show of carefully placing the clients' decorative pieces in the cabinet when she accepted their treasured consignments for auction. Soon after the clients took leave of her office, it was her usual practice to remove the objects from the cabinet and lock them in the company safe until they were prepared for shipment to New York.

A door to the left of the director's desk opened to a utility room which was off-limits to all but Alexandra and Elizabeth. A large safe, a work table, mailing supplies and a smaller table for making coffee and brewing tea crowded the small room.

As Elizabeth made a notation of Keith's call, her ears caught the familiar hurried clip of Alexandra's heels on terrazzo in the outer hallway. The door opened quickly.

Alexandra Saint George, forty-two, was strikingly attractive. She was articulate, dignified, immaculately-coifed, and dressed in stylish designer business suits—the type of magnetic person one sometimes encounters in the upper echelons of the fine-arts world. Tall, with a model-like slimness and a few fashionable strands of grey in her glossy black hair, her entry into a room mesmerized all the males present, incurring the envy of every woman in her vicinity.

As Alexandra picked up the morning mail, Elizabeth said, "You had a call from New York a couple of minutes ago. It was Keith; he sounded frantic. He wants you to call him right away."

"He can just wait," Alexandra said. "It's probably another one of his flaps over nothing. I need a strong cup of coffee, especially before I talk to him. Oh, Beth," she asked, as she opened the door to her office, "did you remember to tell the management about the dust on my windowsills?"

"Yes," Elizabeth lied. She hadn't spoken to the management; she had waited after hours to tell the cleaning ladies herself. The last time she complained to the building superintendent about paper clips under Alexandra's desk, he threatened to dismiss both cleaning ladies if Alexandra's complaints continued. Elizabeth couldn't bear to cause them trouble.

Half an hour later, Alexandra was on the telephone patiently listening to Keith's agitated and disjointed rambling. After several unsuccessful attempts to break into his frenzied discourse, she decided to sit back in her chair until the turmoil subsided. As he rambled on, she changed her desk calendar to "June 10, 1985," and then glanced at the next few pages to review her appointments for the week.

"...started to prepare the descriptions of some of the items for the paperweight sale and I can't find the three paperweights from the Edmire Estate!"

Startled, Alexandra almost dropped her cup. She quickly put it down, asking, "Not the three Imperial—"

"Yes, yes," he interrupted, "the three Imperial Paperweights! Christ, I've looked everywhere! That's why I called earlier this morning. I wanted to find out if you personally handled the paperweight shipment to us."

She became aware of Keith's sudden silence. He was

expecting a response from her. She could picture him, his eyes squinted shut, manicured fingernails rhythmically drumming on his spotless desk, and his head nervously bobbing up and down.

"Yes I did, Keith. And I know the package was received there in New York. I've got a signed return receipt."

"Yes, yes, I already know that. The package came in over a week ago according to my records. But you know, I've asked around; no one actually saw those weights. God, Alexandra, they're the heart of the auction, each one of them more valuable than any paperweight we've ever handled before!"

"Did you speak to Nottingham about it?"

"Sure I did. But you know Jonathan; he'll try to keep out of this mess. He won't get involved. Not him! You know what he said? 'I'm not worried, Keith, you'll find them.' He dropped it right back into my lap, the big shit!"

"What can I possibly do about the paperweights, sitting out here in Chicago?"

"That's just it. I wonder if the package you sent actually had the Imperial Paperweights in it. Something else might have been in that package. As I said, no one's seen those three paperweights here."

"They were in the package," she asserted, "I packed them myself."

He continued to talk, ignoring her reply. Alexandra thought to herself, he's frantically grasping at straws; he knows his twelve years at Sotheby's will come to an end if they don't turn up. She could feel sorry for him if he weren't such a difficult person. Had he been less of a professional, she thought, he would have been dismissed years ago.

Keith, unquestionably outstanding at his job, was a meticulous and demanding manager of the company's receiving department as well as one of Sotheby's experts in decorative glass. His failing was in his person-to-person relationships. Insensitive to the feelings of others, he had been involved in many confrontations, several which had unwisely included Sotheby's officials in high positions.

"And furthermore," Keith continued, "someone should check Jonathan's security procedures here. Where the hell does he get off—"

"Keith, Keith!" she interrupted.

"What?"

"There's nothing we can do here in Chicago. You'd do better to concentrate your efforts there in New York. If the paperweights are missing, they're either misplaced or stolen."

"Oh, God—"

"Hello, hello? Keith, Keith? He cut me off!"

Three years earlier, when a vacancy for the directorship had occurred in Chicago, Sotheby's governing board met to select a new director from among all those who had applied for the position. Unlike the massive New York operation, which staffed thirty-six specialty departments with one-hundred, sixteen specialists spanning fields from "American Decorative Arts and Furniture" to "Watches, Clocks and Scientific Instruments," the Chicago office staff consisted of two employees, a director and an assistant. The board members preferred someone with a general knowledge of decorative arts, antiques and antiquities. They passed over both Keith, who lived and breathed decorative glass, and Jonathan, director of security, whose passion was English silver, because they wore blinders to everything but their specialties.

Selecting Alexandra was not a difficult decision for the board. They not only felt great confidence in her general expertise, but also took special notice of the exemplary manner in which she conducted herself with the company's clientele.

Keith Parker, fully expecting to move up, was especially chagrined that a "female" with less seniority than he was elevated to that senior position. When he learned of her promotion, he rationalized to his friend Howard, "She's probably shacking up with one of the directors."

When she learned of Alexandra's promotion, Elizabeth Field, who was also employed in the New York office at the time, asked to be transferred to Chicago. She wanted to work for the woman whose poise and intelligence she admired. When a vacancy occurred in the Chicago office eighteen months later, Alexandra, who had always been impressed by Elizabeth's willingness to accept any task, offered her the position. The young girl transferred to the Chicago office where she assumed the responsibility of many duties: receptionist, assistant to the director, secretary, telephone operator, mail clerk and coffee-maker. Once she settled in, the two women became a well-meshed team, each aware of and eager to support the other's needs.

Elizabeth buzzed Alexandra on the intercom.

"Yes, Beth."

"Nick Amati called while you were talking to Keith. He said it's important. Shall I get New York for you?"

"No, Beth, I'll call him later."

"What's Keith stewing about this time?"

"He can't find those three paperweights I mailed to New York last week."

"Oh, Alex! Not the Imperial Paperweights!"

"I'm afraid so. New York must be in an awful turmoil."

"Oh, God, the three paperweights! Poor Keith! I'll bet he's worried about his job."

"He's very upset and he should be. They were his responsibility."

"But he might lose his job."

"So?" said Alexandra, switching off the intercom.

Alexandra's callous attitude surprised Elizabeth. But as she worked that afternoon she admitted to herself that she could understand Alexandra's arbitrary position. The Imperial Paperweights had been lost to the world of glass for over a century. If they were missing again, because of negligence in Keith's department, he should suffer the consequences. And yet, she couldn't help feeling sorry for him. He was so imperious, she knew that no one in the New York office would come to his aid in his time of need.

The following evening when Keith arrived at his apartment, he greeted Howard with, "Oh Christ, what a God-awful day!"

"The paperweights?"

"Yes! They're still missing."

"Why don't I mix you a drink while you get into something more comfortable?"

"Yes, a martini, Howie, please, real dry."

Returning a few minutes later, Keith gratefully accepted the drink and collapsed into his favorite wing chair. Howard sat on the floor, removed Keith's shoes and began to gently massage his feet. "You're so tense, Keith. Just try to relax. I've never seen you in such a state before."

"It's that they're so valuable."

"I've always thought paperweights were a minor art—like textiles and clocks. They don't bring the big bucks that paintings do."

"That's true Howie. But, you see, the monetary value of those missing paperweights belies their importance. The Imperial Paperweights are as significant to nineteenth-century glass as da Vinci's Mona Lisa is to fifteenth-century painting." As Howard continued to massage his feet, Keith finished his martini and leaned back in the wing chair. "God," he continued, "the awful humiliation, to be treated like a suspect after all I've done for the damn company!"

"But, surely, they can't suspect you."

"The police questioned all of us in receiving like common criminals. And then to have my judgment questioned by Baker."

"Baker?"

"Yes, Brian Baker, the V.P."

"What did he say?"

"That he'd gone over my intake procedure and found it lacking. He wasn't there seven years ago when they put me in charge. No system at all then, no security and nothing on computers, everything in ink on ledgers, like Bob Cratchet—absolutely nineteenth century!"

"Certainly, others in your department came to your support."

"The hell they did. As a matter of fact, when they questioned that bastard Amati, he told Baker my intake procedure could be improved! Amati forgets he owes his job to me."

"He's just trying to make points."

"Bullshit! He's after my job! I had it out with him. I told him off, the bastard. I ended up throwing a book at him. I told him that if I had a gun I'd have shot him on the spot!"

"You threatened him?"

"Hell yes, and I don't care who heard it. Now everyone's avoiding me. Suddenly, I'm a pariah!"

"What are you going to do?"

"What can I do. I'll report for work until they let me go."

"But you didn't take the paperweights."

"You don't seem to understand, Howie. They disappeared while they were in my department. They're so damn valuable! I wish to hell they'd never been made!"

2.

Within two days of Keith's anxious telephone call to Alexandra, the disappearance of the paperweights was no longer his own private torment. It stretched its tendrils into every office of Sotheby's-New York. Everyone was aware of the appalling fact that the company's reputation would be seriously affected if the paperweights were not recovered; the combined value of the three paperweights was estimated at over a million dollars.

The New York Police Department and Sotheby's in-house security reviewed the backgrounds of all employees. Detectives also scrutinized every step of Keith's in-take procedure and Jonathan's security system. Detectives referred the problem to the police department at the originating point of the paperweight shipment—Chicago.

Lieutenant Mulcahy, Central District—Chicago Police Department, detailed Sgt. Daniel Dobrinski and Officer Matthew Dolger to "look into the paperweight problem on Michigan Avenue." Driving through the heavy traffic, a wet stub of an unlit cigar distorting the side of his mouth, Dobrinski grumbled, "With all we got to do, we get sent out about three lousy paperweights! What the hell's Mulcahy thinking of this time? It beats all—paperweights! Next he'll send us out to find a goddamn missing pencil!"

Sgt. Dobrinski, crusty and outspoken, was an old-time cop whose tenure with the C.P.D. spanned three decades. Dobrinski's junior, Officer Dolger, recently replaced the older policeman's long-time partner, who had retired because he "had it up to here" trying to pacify the public.

Dobrinski was prone to fast decision-making and a bellicose mind-set, a style he acquired working under fire during his early years. He had lately caused problems for his superiors, especially since the emphasis in police work in Chicago had shifted from the use of the truncheon to the use of human relations techniques.

One day, while reminiscing about his early years on the force, he told his young partner, "You must of been a little kid when we battled those Commies in Lincoln Park during that Democratic convention. Hm, 1968, I think—yeah, '68. The media jumped all over old man Daley for what he said about keeping order in the streets, but we loved him for it! I busted a lot of heads that night. Some Commie bastard cut me with a broken bottle here on my arm. You won't believe this, kid, but, as busy as he was during that convention, old man Daley came to the hospital to see some of us cops who got hurt. I'll never forget him. He thanked us and actually patted me on the back. What a great guy."

"You ever run into this kind of case before, Dan—I mean, you know, paperweights and stuff?"

"Hell, yes, kid. Anything worth a couple of bucks always attracts creeps. You know, I really hate talking to those damn faggots in those art shops. They sit on their cute asses all day and sell paintings to rich old dames. It pisses me off when we got to treat them with kid gloves all the time, saying, 'yes Sir' and 'yes ma'am,' and 'please,' and 'if you don't mind.' Don't forget, kid, a lot of them got direct lines to City Hall."

Dobrinski parked the car and pushed open the car door. As he squeezed his ample bulk out from behind the steering wheel, he cautioned, "Remember, this is routine. We'll just ask a couple a questions and get our butts the hell out of there, fast. Watch what you say, and do like I do. One slip-up and we'll both get reamed! I'm too close to my pension to make waves now." He removed his soggy cigar and reluctantly tossed it into the gutter. "Can't be too careful," he muttered to himself.

They took the elevator to the fourth floor of the Prentiss Building.

"There it is Dan," said Matthew, pointing to a door to their left.

As Sgt. Dobrinski walked to the door he brushed cigar ashes off his jacket. "Hey, look at that plaque on the door, kid," he said, "'Sotheby's founded in London in 1744'! Man that's old!"

Dobrinski opened the door, removed his hat and flashed his identification, saying, "Chicago Police Department, Miss, Central District."

Elizabeth gave his I.D. a quick look. "We've been expecting the police. I'll tell Miss Saint George you're here."

As she walked to the director's office, Dobrinski directed the younger man's attention to her shifting hips, winked, gave a "thumbs-up" sign and rolled his eyes.

Elizabeth reappeared, saying, "Please have a seat. Miss Saint George will see you in a few minutes."

Alexandra quickly brought her telephone conversation to a close and went to the outer office. "Good morning, gentlemen."

"Mornin', ma'am," said Dobrinski. "We're here about those missing paperweights."

After questioning Alexandra about the shipment to New York, Dobrinski asked, "What makes those paperweights so important, ma'am?"

"Paperweights, like all art, are an affirmation of life. They show the human experience in concrete form—a form we can understand and enjoy through our senses." Dobrinski's vacant look told Alexandra that what she had said made no sense to him. She tried again. "The missing paperweights were created for an empress, Empress Carlota of Mexico. But aside from that,

Sergeant, paperweights made during the mid-nineteenth century represent the epitome of the glassmakers' art. Their creation required that all of the complex skills known to glassmakers be incorporated into an exquisite ball of glass smaller than a man's fist."

As they drove back to the station, Matthew said, "I didn't understand half of what she said about art and life."

"Yeah," Dobrinski agreed, "I got turned off too when she started spouting that arty talk. It's just farten art lingo! She sure thinks those paperweights are God's gift to man. The way she carried on you'd think the whole world'd collapse if they don't turn up."

When Lieutenant Mulcahy learned that the two policemen had made a cursory examination, he fumed, "Damn it, Dobrinski, a rookie could have done that. You spend more time on your damn racing forms! Why the hell didn't you fill out a report while you were questioning those people? What you've told me doesn't mean a damn thing, I want it on paper! Do I have to tell you two guys your job? We're under pressure from upstairs, and all you two numbskulls do is ask a few questions!"

"But, Lieutenant," Dobrinski protested, "they're just paperweights."

"Those paperweights belonged to old man Edmire! Get it? Edmire! Get your butts back over there and make out a detailed report, and I mean right now!"

As the two officers opened the door to leave his office, Mulcahy suddenly stood and yelled, "Hey, hold it right there! Another thing, Dobrinski! The motor pool's complaining that your squad car is always full of racing forms." Punctuating each word with his index finger, he shouted, "I'll have your goddamn job if I ever catch you dealing with a bookie when you're supposed to be on duty!"

As they got into their squad car, the older officer grumbled, "That jerk! Who the hell does he think he is? I was pounding a beat when his mother was changing his stinking diapers and powderin' his ass. Just because he went to college, he thinks he knows everything. Hey, no offense, kid, you ain't like that. You know, when he came to the district he was so green Captain Barootian assigned him to my squad car for a month, you know, to get the feel of the district. He acted like we was friends, calling me, 'Danny D' this and 'Danny D' that. But that didn't last long. Soon as he got behind a desk, it was like he never seen me before. I tell you, kid, things have gone from bad to worse in this damn town since old Mayor Daley died. Nobody cares about us guys on the streets no more. And another thing, how the hell was I supposed to know those damn paperweights were Edmire's?"

"Who's Edmire?"

"Old man Edmire died a couple of months ago. Rich as hell. Used to be tied in with the Democratic machine. You know—back room stuff."

"Pretty important."

"Bet your butt."

When they returned to Sotheby's, they found that Alexandra had left for a luncheon date. Dobrinski, deciding to go on a few personal errands, gave the report forms to Dolger with specific instructions to carefully question the receptionist. Matthew guessed Dobrinski's errands would include a call to his bookie and the purchase of more White Owls.

After completing the report, Elizabeth and the young officer engaged in casual conversation. To their surprise, they discovered that they spent their childhood less than ten miles apart: Elizabeth in Davenport, Iowa, and Matthew across the Mississippi, in Rock Island. She told him that after completing her B.A. at Augustana College she went to New York, where she was accepted into Sotheby's trainee program. Several years later, when the Chicago office had an opening, she took her present position. "I'm just a little over three hours from Iowa, now. How did you end up in Chicago?" she asked.

He explained that during his senior year in high school, his family moved to Chicago when his father was transferred to a managerial job there. "After graduating, I went to a city college and took classes in correctional work. A little over a year ago I took the Civil Service Exam, passed, and became a cadet in the Police Academy. After that, I was assigned as a rookie. A couple of months ago they transferred me to the Central District as Sgt. Dobrinski's partner."

By the time Dobrinski returned, Elizabeth had accepted Matthew's invitation to a movie and "something to eat, afterwards."

"Pick you up at five-fifteen," he reminded her as he and Dan left the office.

"See you," she said, thinking it might be nice to know someone from back home, but wondering if she was ready to begin dating again.

On the way to their car, Dobrinski asked, "Date with that cute blonde?"

"Yeah, tomorrow."

"Atta boy, kid. She's stacked. What'd you think of that director?"

"She's okay, but too old for me."

"Hey, you don't know much about long-legged women, do you? She's a real classy dame. I'd give my right arm—." On their way back to the station, Dobrinski said, "Funny thing, kid. Before I took the elevator back up to the fourth floor, I stopped in Walgreen's for some White Owls. When I was paying for them I saw her, that Saint George dame, making a call from the pay phone. She wiped off the mouthpiece and held the receiver in a white hanky. She looked pretty excited. I thought it was funny she didn't wait to make the call from her office—just four floors up."

"She must of had her reasons."

"Yeah. By the way, she's a southpaw."

"Yeah?"

"Uh-huh. Put the money in and punched up the phone numbers with her left hand."

The next evening, after the movie, Elizabeth and Matthew stopped at Ramona and Al's Steakhouse for ribs and draft beer. They reminisced about the Quad Cities, and mutually familiar landmarks: the Mississippi River, the big paddle-boats, the Arsenal, the levee concerts and the Bix Beiderbecke festivals. As they talked she wondered why he wasn't married. He seemed like such a good catch, tall and slim with thick curly hair and a strong chin. Elizabeth liked his small touches of humor, and especially appreciated the consideration he showed her as he opened the door for her and helped her with her chair. He made her feel feminine again. She felt comfortable with him. The prospect of dating again didn't seem as threatening to her as it once had. New York seemed far away.

Although Matthew found Elizabeth physically attractive, he did not envision her as a likely choice for a serious relationship. She laughed too often to suit him, and had the annoying habit of slightly tossing her head to one side so that her long blonde hair whisked from her shoulder to her back. But what really disturbed him most was that she seemed to shy away from him. Several times that evening when they innocently touched, he felt her stiffen and draw away. He thought to himself, why should I spend time with her and her obvious hang-ups when the others I'm dating are so responsive?

She asked, "How's your investigation of the missing paperweights coming along?"

"It's really centered in New York. There's not much we can do here. You know, I really can't understand the fuss about those three paperweights. Why are they so darn important?"

"Alex's done a lot of research on them. She discovered that they were made for royalty in 1864 by a small French company, the Verrerie de Lorraine."

3.

TRIESTE - 1863

Archduke Maximilian received Guiterrez de Estrada, personal emissary of Emperor Napoléon III, who presented him with an Imperial Invitation to visit the French Court. Carlota was stunned when her husband told her of the invitation.

"From Louis Napoléon?" she asked. "An invitation to his court? After all the grief he caused us? It's incredible! I don't believe it! Show it to me!"

Because a person of such high station carried the message, Maximilian suspected the summons from Louis Napoléon was for a more important purpose than a social visit. Maximilian might have demurred had he known he was about to be thrust once again into the demanding world of duty, honor and self-sacrifice.

Only four short years earlier he and Carlota were forced to relinquish the regencies of Lombardy and Venice. His immediate feelings of frustration and humiliation at the time of his dethronement had gradually subsided, so that he now felt content in his semi-retirement.

The ex-Viceroy and his wife had taken up residence in their enchanting castle, Miramar, a crenelated palace of white limestone and Carrara marble overlooking a sun-dappled aquamarine inlet of the Adriatic Sea. The spacious palace grounds included two enormous outbuildings: an aviary for rare birds, and because Maximilian remembered the sunny warmth of Schoenbrun's glass conservatories from his childhood during Vienna's bone-chilling winters, a large glass structure to house tropical plants.

At the relatively young age of thirty-one, Maximilian enjoyed the luxury of limitless time to devote to the many interests that duty forced him to abandon when he ruled as regent. He spent many pleasurable hours during those four unfettered years, strolling through the woods and meadows and collecting insects which he carefully prepared and catalogued. On nights when the skies were clear, he studied the heavens from the castle ramparts, pointing out its constellations and celestial phenomena to his young wife.

Carlota, restless and energetic, seethed with ambition. When they lost their regencies and returned to Trieste, she vainly attempted to occupy her newly-found leisure time with letter writing, embroidery, and music. But she quickly grew discontented. Certainly, she reasoned, she was not brought into the world to ruminate in Trieste the rest of her life. She was a royal princess, the daughter of Leopold I, King of all the Belgians. She assumed she was destined for greatness.

Although Louis Napoléon's invitation filled them with many unanswered questions, they looked forward to their visit. The recent transformation of the French capital interested Maximilian. Over the centuries, Paris had become an overgrown, dismal and unhygienic glut of old buildings on narrow, twisting streets—the natural result of its uncontrolled organic growth. When Louis Napoléon became emperor, he undertook the monumental task of metamorphosing the old Paris into a modern, beautiful city. The wide, clean boulevards, the impressive new buildings, the landscaped parks and the colorful public gardens of his new Paris opened the dark, cluttered city to the glorious light of the sun.

Carlota was especially eager to visit the emperor's palace, the Tuileries, built three centuries earlier by Catherine de Medici. Having been relegated to the backwaters of court activity for the past four years, Carlota could not help but anticipate the glitter of the Imperial French Court. She felt Paris, like an irresistible lodestone, reaching out and drawing her to its center.

Rumors which her cousin, Lady Amelia, shared in guarded confidence during a recent visit to Miramar piqued her curiosity. "Carlota, all is not well with Empress Eugenie. She is no longer the favorite flower in the emperor's garden of delight."

Anxious to learn more, Carlota asked, "What do you mean, dear cousin?"

Drawing nearer, Amelia lowered her voice to explain, "My dear, Napoléon is a philanderer. Everyone in Paris knows it. He's had many love affairs, some even with the ladies in Eugenie's personal retinue. He has become so bold he now flaunts his infidelities unashamedly, and appears in open carriages with his affairs of the heart."

"That poor woman. What a bitter cross to bear."

Amelia added, "His visits to the salon of Mme. de Castiglione, are a secret to no-one."

"The Comtese de Castiglione?" asked Carlota, surprised.

"Oh, you've heard of her. She's the most beautiful courtesan in all of France." Bending close to Carlota's ear, Amelia whispered, "They say the emperor's private sedan goes to her apartments so often that the horses find their way there without the help of the coachmen!"

"Oh dear," laughed Carlota, shielding her eyes with her fan, "I can't believe that!"

"It's true, Carlota. He showers her with pearls, diamonds and rubies while he continues to enjoy the pleasures of her bed."

"And to think I envied Empress Eugenie's power and position. Oh, Amelia, I thank God for Maximilian's fidelity."

4.

Preparations were soon completed for their journey to France. Although a storm and high seas buffeted their ship a day out of Trieste, Carlota did not complain about her nausea. It will soon pass, she thought. At least, this temporary discomfort is not as wearisome as the becalmed sameness of Miramar. Each new vista along the Adriatic coast delighted her.

After the ship safely navigated through the Straits of Messina and headed northwest, Carlota began to busy her attendants with arranging her wardrobe for the various court functions she anticipated.

When their ship docked at Marseilles, a royal delegation escorted them to the train station where three elegant rail coaches, staffed with attendants and domestics, awaited their arrival. The emperor had directed the officers of the Paris-Lyon-Marseilles Line to make the young couple's overland journey to Paris as comfortable as possible. As their train headed north through hot simmering seas of flowers, the heady scent of lavender reached Carlota. "Perfumers make the most wonderful essences from these flowers," she told her lady-in-waiting.

On their arrival at the *Paris Embarcadere d'Orleans*, Maximilian and his small entourage were escorted to Napoléon's golden carriages, where richly liveried footmen and meticulously groomed white stallions waited to convey them to the Tuileries Palace. Though not a stranger to elegance, the glitter surrounding Carlota bedazzled her. The mounted troop of Louis Napoléon's elite Cent-Guards, resplendent in golden helmets and breast-plates, escorted the carriage procession across the Seine, over the *Pont d'Austerlitz*, then west on the expansive *Rue de Rivoli*.

The clatter of iron shod horse hoofs on the cobblestone boulevard finally slowed and stopped at the Imperial Palace. There, the Grand Chamberlain received Maximilian and Carlota and conducted them to the Imperial Throne room. He struck the marble floor with his gilded bronze staff, announcing, "The Archduke and Archduchess of Austria-Hungary, Prince Maximilian Ferdinand von Hapsburg and Princess Marie Carlota Amelia."

As they advanced toward the throne, Carlota was disappointed that the enormous room contained only a handful of people—the Imperial couple, the little Imperial Prince, several men in frock coats and a scaled-down honor guard. She could not help but notice the emperor's slight stature. Even sitting, the empress towered over him. "Can this little man be the scandalous lover that Cousin Amelia described to me?" she thought.

Louis Napoléon and Empress Eugenie rose together, descended the few steps of the dais and embraced their guests. Carlota, who had anticipated a formal reception, was surprised at the casualness of their meeting. She later wrote to her mother, "Imagine my astonishment when the emperor of the French Empire received an Imperial Hapsburg Prince in the Imperial Throne Room dressed like a frock-coated merchant!"

At Louis Napoléon's suggestion, Eugenie and Carlota retired to the empress's apartments while the emperor and his advisors discussed with Maximilian the reason for his invitation.

"The emperor thought we might become better acquainted, Carlota," the empress explained. "When the emperor and Maximilian complete their discussions, you and your husband will be shown to your suite."

As white is to black, each woman was the antithesis of the other. Princess Carlota, young and eager, was slightly built. She had soft black hair and a dark, heart-shaped face. Her deep-set fiery green eyes gave her countenance a hauntingly sweet appearance. Empress Eugenie, older, possessed a voluptuous body, thick auburn hair, pale blue eyes and skin that was milk-white. Her mouth seemed fixed in a perpetual smile.

"My dear Carlota, you must be exhausted after your long journey."

"I feel quite refreshed, your Imperial Highness. Thank you for your concern. We are especially indebted to you and to his Imperial Highness for graciously providing such comfortable accommodations for our overland journey to Paris."

Touching her guest's lace-gloved hand, the empress suggested, "Please, Carlota, do use my given name, 'Eugenie.' Think of me as a sister, an older sister."

Carlota knowing full well that the empress was not as highly born as she, accepted the suggestion without hesitation, saying, "Thank you, Eugenie."

As the empress offered Carlota a place on the divan, opposite her, she said, "The emperor and I have often spoken of you and your husband and have much to ask you concerning the life you've made after Lombardy and Venice." Realizing immediately that she had made an unfortunate reference to

Maximilian's dethronement, an upheaval brought about by her own husband, Eugenie added quickly, "I'm sure you are missed by the entire populace."

Sensing Eugenie's discomfort at committing a *faux pas*, Carlota inwardly rejoiced at the empress's embarrassment. "You commoner," she thought, "it's obvious you have no breeding." Carlota deftly changed the uncomfortable situation by taking up Eugenie's allusion to happier memories. "We continue to correspond with many of our friends there. The warmth of the people reflects the sunny days and blue skies that envelope those lovely provinces. I fell in love with Lombardy and Venice on first sight. It was such a delightful change for me. You see, my own life, until then, had been spent in the pale atmosphere of the low countries. I'd never realized how the unobstructed sun could produce such vivid colors, even in shadows. Those provinces were our beautiful Elysium."

Perceiving that her selective reminiscences had served to allay Eugenie's embarrassment, Carlota tactfully shifted her conversation to the ambitions she had for her husband. "Although I've been quite happy at Miramar, Maximilian is frustrated that he is neglecting his God-given talents. He feels unfulfilled. There is a burning desire in his heart to govern, as a Hapsburg should. Surely, all descendants of royalty contain the blood of authority and rule. But, of course, he is too proud to confide those feelings to anyone, save me."

"Then, my dear little sister, we've come to the very crux of your visit with us. Carlota, I can no longer keep it from you. The emperor is going to offer Mexico to Maximilian, to rule there as emperor."

Carlota's hand flew to her breast as she gasped at the enormity of the proposal. After losing their regencies, she had feared her dreams of rule might never be fulfilled. In spite of what she told the empress, Maximilian's contentment with his imposed private life constantly frustrated Carlota. Oh, why couldn't she be present when Louis Napoléon, emperor of the French Empire, offered Mexico to her Maximilian! Would he accept? What would he say? Had she known the purpose of their visit, she would have nurtured a desire in him to take up the scepter once again. She was one of a select few who harbored the knowledge that Maximilian's imposing figure, which made him appear as a tower of strength, belied certain shortcomings which should not have existed in a Hapsburg.

As those thoughts coursed through her mind, she was brought back to the conversation, forced to respond to Eugenie's pleasantries. The empress turned from matters of state to every-day court talk. And though Carlota yearned to know more about Maximilian's immediate meeting with the emperor, she pushed her all-consuming questions out of mind.

"And just last week, Carlota, Monsieur Haussmann escorted us to the *Bois de Boulogne* to show us what has been accomplished there. The emperor ceded two thousand acres of a large dense thicket on the edge of the city to the people of Paris, and gave Monsieur Haussmann the task of transforming it into a lovely park for them."

"Were you pleased with what you saw?" asked Carlota to be polite, though thoughts of Maximilian's conference kept returning.

"Yes, we were, but there is much more to be done. The underbrush has been cleared, new trees, shrubs and flowers are being planted and the many small stagnant ponds in the forest have been dredged so that the water they now contain is crystal clear. As we inspected the work, Monsieur Haussmann indicated large open areas where he plans to create sweeping lawns and colorful plantings. The conservatories are finished and the gardeners are presently filling them with all manner of exotic tropical plants. The aviary and zoo are still under construction and a site has been selected for an aquarium."

"The park and its buildings would be of great interest to Maximilian, Eugenie. He has such a consuming interest in the biological sciences."

As they continued their conversation, Eugenie remarked that the emperor's important work allowed him little time for relaxation, but that she was fortunate to be able to manage small bits of private time in the pursuit of a few of her own selfish pleasures. Remembering what Cousin Amelia had told her about the emperor's amorous adventures, Carlota wondered if his visits to Madam Castiglione's salon were some of the "important work" that took so much of his time.

"I spend much of my leisure time admiring and examining my lovely crystal paperweights. I adore them," said the empress.

And when Carlota politely expressed an interest in the paperweights, Eugenie offered to show them to her.

Carlota was no stranger to paperweights. She possessed several Venetian paperweights which she had received as gifts when she and Maximilian journeyed by gondola to the glassmakers' island of Murano. They were small cool balls of murky glass containing tiny bits of colorful ribbon, filigree and flower-like pieces fused together in a disorganized mass. But when she examined the paperweights in Eugenie's collection, she was struck by their beauty. Her own Venetian weights seemed ugly by comparison. Lifting the empress's gleaming crystal balls from the table, she was fascinated to see that they contained beautifully crafted flowers, succulent appearing fruit, brilliant butterflies, snakes, white cameos and tiny colorful geometric disks of glass arranged in designs resembling French formal gardens.

"Oh, dear sister, these are exquisite! Such clear glass—it's like limpid water. I've never seen paperweights as beautiful as these. Where were they made?"

"Here in France—at Clichy, Saint Louis and at Baccarat. Unfortunately, these lovely objects have lost their popularity. They are no longer produced by our factories."

"You have so many!"

"About ten years ago, I began to acquire those with the cameos of Louis Napoléon imbedded in them. After acquiring so many with his likeness, I decided to gather some paperweights with other motifs. My collection has grown to what you see here. They are a constant delight to me. Do you like them?"

"Oh, yes! There is one with a cameo of the emperor. How the facets glisten!"

Because Carlota seemed genuinely interested in the paperweights, Eugenie directed her attention to the special details of many of the individual pieces. A true collector, she derived special pleasure in sharing her paperweights with others.

When they finished admiring the last of the gleaming objects, Eugenie selected one from the table and placed it in Carlota's hands, saying, "My dear little sister, I'd like you to have this Baccarat pansy as a memento of your visit with us."

Eugenie silenced Carlota's immediate protestations by touching her fingers lightly to the young woman's arm, saying, "Please, Carlota, consider this as a small gift from one sister to another. I especially want you to have this paperweight since in the 'language of flowers,' pansies are for remembrance. May it be a constant reminder of my love for you and your husband."

In their rooms, after Carlota hurriedly dismissed their personal staff, she anxiously asked Maximilian, "Did you accept Napoléon's offer?"

"Oh, did the empress mention it to you?"

"Yes, yes! You did accept, didn't you?"

"Carlota, dearest, I told him that I was undecided."

"Undecided?"

"Yes, undecided. After our humiliating experience in Lombardy and Venetia, I don't know if I have the heart to wear a crown again."

"What are you saying?"

"I certainly cannot consider reigning over people who may not want me to sit on their nation's throne. As I talked with the emperor, so many wrenching memories flooded my mind. It was this very Napoléon who led the French troops into Lombardy to defeat my brother's army. It's such a strange situation, being offered an empire by a former enemy of Austria. It was the most remote happening imaginable—but there it was!"

In an attempt to resolve Maximilian's ambivalence, Carlota said, "My dear husband, you are supremely fitted for the crown. It was only an accident of birth that made your brother emperor. If you had been born first, you'd be the emperor of Austria, and I, the empress. Louis Napoléon knows, that given the opportunity, you can make Mexico equal to any nation in the world."

"Mexico is poor," he said thoughtfully. "She has been racked by revolutions, and pillaged by most of the major nations of Europe, as well as by her powerful neighbor to the north. Do you really think that those poor hungry millions desire a European monarch on their throne—someone who represents all the foreign contact they've ever known?"

"But Maxl, you are Austrian; your line has never had anything to do with Mexico before."

"Carlota, I am European. It is we Europeans who caused much of Mexico's grief. Generations ago some of my own ancestors, the Spanish Hapsburgs, were involved in the subjugation and exploitation of the country."

"But, you must also remember, Maxl, that we Europeans were the ones who brought the Mother Church to the New World. We converted the pagans to the true faith and saved their souls from eternal damnation."

"It was also we Christians who accepted enormous land grants from European sovereigns, taking the soil away from the Mexican people, depriving them of the precious sustenance needed for their hungry families—"

As they prepared for dinner, Maximilian cautioned, "Carlota, the emperor suggested that we not openly discuss his proposal. It would be improper to generate rumors before any decisions are made."

"Even if we four dine alone?"

"Even then. We must honor the emperor's wishes. If he broaches the subject, we may respond; otherwise, we must avoid any reference to Mexico."

Carlota was disappointed that Mexico was not mentioned during dinner, nor for the balance of their visit in Paris. It was as if Louis Napoléon's offer of an empire had never occurred.

Later that night, Carlota came to her husband's bed. As she put her arms around Maximilian she whispered, "If I were an emperor, I'd have a seraglio of my own and ravish my concubines to my heart's content! No, no, don't draw away from me, Maximilian, embrace me." She stroked the inside of his thigh and pressed her warm bare breasts against his quiescent body, hungering for a flicker of response.

Carlota was seventeen years old and very much in love when she and Maximilian were married. During the first weeks of their union, she loved him all the more for the gentleness he had shown her. He had not attempted to consummate their marriage on their wedding night as they shared the same bed.

She felt he was being especially considerate of her because of her youth and innocence. However, it was not long before she saw those same qualities as signs of timidity and weakness. To others, the tall handsome bewhiskered Hapsburg Prince seemed to be endowed with strength and virility, but in the privacy of their bedrooms, it was Carlota who usually initiated their intimacies. And because their union had never been blessed with issue, she secretly blamed her inability to produce an heir on an imagined sexual defect seated in her reticent husband's loins.

That same evening, Louis Napoléon visited Eugenie in her apartments where they discussed the day's events and their impressions of their young guests.

"I was disturbed by his hesitancy."

"Didn't he accept?"

"No, but he didn't refuse, either. He wouldn't give a definite answer. I suspect Lombardy and Venice were in the back of his mind."

"They both continue to feel that loss."

"That may well be, but it's incomprehensible to me that anyone would refuse a throne. I had to control a strong urge to tell him how I struggled to gain this empire of mine. He doesn't realize that I was exiled from France, jailed by my enemies, and often close to death. It was by sheer will and determination that I survived and gained my throne. No one offered me an empire on a salver; I had to wrest it away from my enemies to make it mine!"

"If he's foolish enough to refuse the empire you are offering him, you can easily find another unemployed prince to rule Mexico."

"The point is that I want Maximilian in that position. I need someone in Mexico who is manageable—someone I can control. If I place him on the throne, his brother might also be amenable to re-establishing ties with us. Prussia would be no match for the combined might of Austria and France."

"I tell you this, Louis, if the decision were left to Carlota, they'd be on a ship sailing to Mexico this very night. She's ambitious. She craves the scepter. Her eyes sparkled with green fire when I told her what you were proposing to her husband. She's convinced she's destined for greatness. She'll persuade him."

After a long silence, Louis Napoléon said, "While we talked, an idea came to me that should win him over. It would involve General Forey who is in Mexico. A limited plebiscite there would do the trick—one which will indicate the Mexican people want Maximilian as their emperor. It can be accomplished quite easily if General Forey selects only those who will vote for Maximilian. Yes, that's the key. I'm certain the General can engineer it. If, after that, I still can't win him over, then my dear, I'll follow your suggestion and, as you so aptly put it, 'find another unemployed prince for Mexico.'"

"There are certainly enough of them around to choose from, Louis."

"I must not wait too long to gain influence over the throne of Mexico. Spain and Britain both have their eyes on that country. If I can place a prince on Mexico's throne before they act, the country will become part of our empire. Our early successes are in the past. The expansion of our commercial and cultural influence in the New World will silence our critics and once again cap our monarchy with glory."

"Never fear, Louis, Carlota will convince him."

When Louis Napoléon turned to leave the room, a familiar mocking tone in Eugenie's voice burrowed deeply into his ears. "Are you leaving the Palace again, Louis, dear?"

"Yes, I have important business to attend to."

"So late in the evening?"

Knowing full well that Eugenie had guessed his destination, he offered a simple, "Yes, Eugenie," hoping to avoid the inevitable ordeal that was about to begin once again.

"In Heaven's name, Louis, isn't it bad enough that you have your dirty little liaisons with my ladies here in the palace? The entire court laughs at me behind my back when I banish those foolish women. The reason for their dismissal is obvious to everyone. And now that you carry your sordid affairs openly, out into the streets, all of Paris knows of your lechery and my burning shame! You don't even attempt to conceal your trysts! Do you remember your jeremiads against the perversion and immorality in the land when you became emperor? You pledged to lift up France and make it Europe's standard-bearer of virtue. Don't you have any feelings of guilt, betraying those promises to the people?"

"I don't have the remotest feelings of contrition or guilt. My pleasures harm no one. Least of all, they can't mean anything to you. They do nothing more than prove my virility. Please, Eugenie, let's not have another one of those scenes."

"Why do you insist on going to her? Castiglione is just another highly paid tart! Your visits to her apartments have made her Queen of Whores!"

"Your problem, my dear, is that you perceive the act of love as a necessary evil, reserved only for procreation. Physical love is demanded by our very animal natures. Am I to blame if your Spanish blood has lost its former fire? I can't help it if tepid water flows through your veins."

"Tepid water? My blood was hot enough to produce an heir for France! How many bastards do you intend to spawn with your illicit affairs? How can you, the emperor of France, lie in bed with a woman of such low breeding? She can't know anything about you."

He thought to himself, "How little you know. She has

explored every inch of my body and I hers, a joy more than you'll ever experience. Even the act of undressing each other excites my passions. The little games we play in her boudoir unshackle my inhibitions and we do things that you in your prudishness can't ever imagine."

Deciding to break off the argument, he strode to the doorway, turned and said, "She says she's in love with me, and I believe her."

"You believe her?" Eugenie said, shaking her head, "You gullible idiot, The tart's pandering to an old fool's lecherous desires!"

He walked out of the room, muttering to himself, "You wouldn't think so if you knew how her body trembles as it presses against mine. She has an animal's passion for me."

"The devil take you both, you and your Italian slut!" she shouted after him.

As he settled back in his carriage, bound for the comfort of Virginie Castiglione's waiting embrace, Louis Napoléon brooded about this latest flare-up with his wife. "What has she done for me, except bear my son? Any woman in the world could have incubated my seed for nine months. I gave him to France! He's my son, a Bonaparte, not a Montijo! And where does she come from, this Eugenie de Montijo? Her mother, the Comtese, consorts with lovers across the continent. Where would my spiteful wife be today if I hadn't married her? I elevated her to the throne; I gave her station. She came to me with nothing, nothing—a nobody!"

5.

Several weeks after Maximilian and Carlota left Paris, Eugenie sent a letter to Monsieur Launay of the Hautin-Launay

Company, a Parisian firm that merchandised crystal. The message instructed him to arrange for the director of the Cristalleries de Saint Louis to wait upon her. Launay immediately dispatched Marcelle Follett, his assistant, to deliver the empress's command into Eugene Didierjean's hand.

"From her Imperial Highness, Follett?" asked the startled director of the Saint Louis Factory. "What does this mean?"

"Exactly what the letter states. It's a command from the Palace. Look there, Didierjean, it's imprinted with the Imperial Seal."

"But I've never had contact with the palace before," Didierjean protested. "Our crystal orders for the palace have always come from Launay."

"Monsieur Launay is as puzzled as you are. His experience is similar to yours. He has never dealt directly with anyone in the Imperial Family. He always supplies the Palace on requisitions issued by the Imperial Director of Purchases."

"But why must I go to Paris?"

"I don't know the reason, Didierjean. But, you must appear at the time you are commanded to do so. You have no choice in the matter."

"Yes, yes, I'm well aware of that," said Didierjean, reaching behind himself for his chair, then slowly sinking into it.

Follett, standing, waited silently, and after a time, began to speak again. "Monsieur Launay suggested I remain here for a day or two to allow you time to prepare for your journey to Paris. We should arrive several days early. That way, you and he can prepare for your meeting with her Imperial Highness."

In actuality, Launay had told Follett, "Didierjean is a fine glassman, but unfortunately, his background is limited; he is unsophisticated—a provincial. I confess to you, Marcelle, I anticipate his visit with a great deal of trepidation. I cannot permit him to go to court without making certain he is presentable. You must arrange for him to arrive in Paris a few days before I take him to the Tuileries. The sooner the better. I don't want him to embarrass our firm or himself by some unintentional breach of court etiquette."

As Didierjean drove his carriage home that evening, he enumerated the many reasons why he shouldn't leave Saint Louis, but, he knew they were only meaningless inventions he had fabricated to avoid the inevitable. Never in his wildest imaginings did he expect to receive an invitation to the Tuileries Palace. And here it was, at the personal command of the empress!

Throughout the long night, the anticipation of his appointment caused the director and his wife to twist and turn in bed. "Can't you sleep either, Eugene?" she asked.

"No. I get this awful emptiness in my stomach whenever I think of the empress's command. What can it be that she wants of me?"

Each time he recalled the ominous words, "the Director of the Saint Louis Glass Company is commanded—", his mind dredged up a thousand unanswered questions.

Early the next morning, Madam Didierjean began to consider more practical matters. Opening wide the armoire doors, she pointed to its contents, saying, "My dear husband, you can't go the Palace in these clothes!"

"But I only have those three frock coats, Marie. I wear them to church and to all the functions where my presence is required. There's not enough time to go to the tailors and be measured for new clothes; Follett wants to leave for Paris tomorrow. These will just have to do."

Madam Didierjean meticulously brushed, cleaned and pressed his coats, vests and trousers, a task, much too important to be left to their house maids or the local laundress. She took special pains to scrub and bleach his shirts snow-white and starch his collars bone-hard. On the morning of his departure, she packed his clothes in a newly purchased valise and placed his other necessities in a small leather travel case.

When their train arrived in Paris, Follett took Didierjean directly to Launay.

"Launay, what does this mean?" Didierjean asked.

"I can't possibly imagine, my friend. I'm as puzzled as you are. I'm not sure it's at all significant, but I've been reviewing the crystal orders we've supplied the Palace the past several months. Many of them came from your factory."

Didierjean, groping about for some connection between his crystal and the summons, suggested, "And you think there is a problem with our crystal?"

"Oh, heavens, no! On the rare occasion when there is a problem, the Royal Director of Purchases sends us a note for an adjustment. That's all there is to it." Launay thought to himself, I was right about him; he is truly provincial. Imagine, thinking that the empress would concern herself with such mundane matters. Well, I'll have to busy myself and smooth off as many of his rough corners as I can in the three days remaining before we present ourselves at court.

The Grand Chamberlain of the Tuileries Palace, Comte Bacciochi, received Didierjean and Launay on the appointed day. To Launay's dismay, Bacciochi instructed him to remain in the reception room until Didierjean's audience with Empress Eugenie ended. Launay would not be presented to her Imperial Highness; the appointment was only for Monsieur Didierjean. His nervous companion was stunned when he realized that he would face the empress without Launay at his side. As the shaken director anxiously attempted to learn from the Grand Chamberlain the reason for his summons to the Palace,

Bacciochi impatiently waved his questions aside, and gave Didierjean over to a waiting attendant, cautioning, "Do not waste precious time with questions. You must not be late for your appointment with Her Imperial Highness."

Didierjean's attendant, outfitted in black livery and wearing gold ornamental chains, escorted Didierjean in slow measured steps up the grand staircase to the ushers' room of the empress's apartments. There, the attendant ceremoniously announced the director's name and the time of his appointment to the waiting ushers. One of the ushers, resplendent in a silver embroidered maroon coat, escorted Didierjean through several grand rooms to Le Salon Vert, a large room, ornately painted and wallpapered with a pattern of green foliage and large exotic birds.

As Didierjean entered the room, the fluttering of the many-colored fans in the hands of the ladies-in-waiting who languidly lounged about the room arrested his attention. The Duchesse de Bassano, chief lady-in-waiting to the empress, rose from her desk to receive the director. She led him through several adjoining rooms to Le Salon Rose where an enormous painting of the goddess Flora decorated the pink walls. The Duchesse pointed to a richly ornamented chair and asked him to wait there until her return. Bedazzled by the increasing richness of each succeeding chamber of the empress's private apartments, Didierjean felt grateful for the opportunity to collect his senses and achieve some level of calm. He had never seen so much opulence: Sevres porcelain, marble and bronze statuary, glittering chandeliers, tapestries, paintings, gold, rich ormolu furnishings, large carved pieces of ivory and a profusion of objects cut from semi-precious stone including rock crystal, jade, lapis lazuli, amethyst, agate and malachite adorned the surroundings.

The Duchesse reappeared and conducted him to Le

Salon Bleu, the hall in which the empress officially received her guests. He stood, nervously, in the center of the room, gazing at a row of large, shield-sized portrait medallions of the Bonaparte family on the blue satin cloth-covered walls. Didierjean's escort left him once again and disappeared into Empress Eugenie's private quarters. After a few moments the Duchesse entered the room with Empress Eugenie.

"Your Imperial Highness," Duchesse de Bassano announced, "may I present Monsieur Eugene Didierjean, the director of the Cristalleries de Saint Louis."

Remembering Launay's instructions, he bowed deeply and uttered almost inaudibly, "Your Imperial Highness."

The empress asked Didierjean to accompany the Duchesse and herself to her private study to view her paperweight collection. He instantly recognized that many of the paperweights in the collection were produced a generation earlier by his own company. At the empress's request, the Duchesse went to a desk and brought Didierjean a sketch prepared by the court painter. It was a drawing of a paperweight as seen from above. Eugenie told Didierjean that she wanted the Cristalleries de Saint Louis to undertake a royal commission—the creation of three magnum paperweights, for a future monarch. She had carefully planned their design, taking motifs and ideas from the various examples in her personal paperweight collection.

Studying the drawing, Didierjean saw that the paperweight had at its center a golden shield bearing the coat-of-arms of the Hapsburgs, surmounted by an eagle. Strange, he thought, the empress has replaced the Hapsburg double-headed eagle with a single-headed eagle. And it's holding a snake in its beak! He did not realize that her design linked the Hapsburg coat-of-arms with the Mexican eagle.

The empress told Didierjean that the individual symbols

and fields on the shield were to be decorated with colorful enamels in the exact hues of the Hapsburg armorial crest. She then pointed to two cameos on opposite sides of the shield, saying, "These are profiles of Prince Maximilian and Princess Carlota." Just below the heraldic shield, the drawing included the date, 1864, decorated with tiny flowers, leaves and vines. She wanted the motif to be framed within a circle of millefiori canes, and the entire design placed above a color background. The paperweight was to be completely overlaid with a shell of opaque glass in an attractive color. A large concave facet on top and six smaller, evenly-spaced facets on the paperweight's side were to be cut through the color coating to reveal diminutive views of the internal design. As an afterthought, she suggested that the backgrounds and shells of each of the three paperweights be made in a different color: purple, green and yellow.

    Didierjean knew the folly of denying an Imperial request, but he was well aware of the near impossibility of creating such complex pieces. Paperweights of such complexity had never been created. In addition, other glass objects which were now in great demand throughout Europe had totally eclipsed the former popularity of paperweights. The continental fad for them had passed. As a result, the men who had carefully developed and honed the difficult technical skills required in their production were old now. Most were retired or had turned their efforts to less exacting glass work. And since it was no longer necessary or economically expedient for glass companies to develop the complex skills required for the production of paperweights, they were no longer taught to the younger apprentices. The last paperweights Didierjean remembered being made were created by his competitor, the Baccarat Company—a handful of poorly made weights in honor of Marshall François Canrobert. That was six or seven years ago. He remembered that they were made by an extremely old gaffer who was most likely dead by now. There was the slim possibility of a solution for Didierjean's dilemma—the Verrerie de Lorraine. That small glass factory, located near the village of Valady, employed older workers who had retired from the pressures of the larger glassworks. As Didierjean folded the empress's drawing and placed it in his coat pocket, he wondered if any of Lorraine's aging gaffers still remembered the complex processes or, more importantly, retained the skills to make fine paperweights. Keeping his thoughts to himself, he thanked the empress for the opportunity to serve her, promising, "I shall return to Saint Louis to advise my gaffers to begin work on your commission."

"Keep me informed of your progress, Monsieur."

"Yes, your Imperial Highness, I shall."

6.

The Duke de Corville established the Verrerie de Lorraine, a dim point of light in the brilliant nineteenth-century French constellation of glass producers in 1769. When the Corvilles lost their royal holdings at the execution of Louis XVI, the glass company continued to exist in the New Republic. And because the director and employees had learned the lessons of frugality and excellence well, the factory remained solvent in the face of fierce competition from the glass producing giants. Over the next seventy years, Lorraine gradually became a Mecca for glassmen too old to withstand the piecework pressures of the larger factories. This bonanza of experienced craftsmen provided the small glassworks with skilled artisans able to create glass pieces of great complexity. Lorraine specialized in short runs and individual crystal objects for its customers and the large glass companies, enabling those larger companies to satisfy their most difficult requests by secretly jobbing them out to the Verrerie de Lorraine. In this veiled arrangement, the major glasshouses continued their massive production schedules without the inconvenience or interruption caused by more technically difficult projects.

The small factory, approached by several sinuous dirt roads, stood in a large clearing near the center of a thick hardwood forest, seventeen kilometers south of the village of Valady. Gray ash-laden wooden shacks, homes of the glassworkers' families, haphazardly dotted the edges of the forest clearing. Sheds scattered among the workers' homes housed the dray animals and the wagons used to haul raw materials to the factory and the finished glass pieces to Valady for shipment to Lorraine's customers. The cooking and heating fires of the homes, the smoke and ash from the tall factory chimney and the steam and smoke from the fires of the charcoal makers combined to produce a permanent pall of layered diaphanous shrouds over the entire clearing.

From a distance, the work periods at Lorraine resembled the activity of an ant hill. Wood cutters felled trees, cut them into logs, split them and hauled the wet wedges to the charcoal makers. Here, soot-masked men heated the raw wood until the steaming sap hissed, transforming living fiber into charcoal. Wagon after wagon carried loads of charcoal, sand, lime, metal oxides, water and other material to the factory, and hauled waste as well as finished glassware out of the working compound. Flux makers, batch mixers, glass cutters, pot makers, apprentices, wives and even young children had their appointed tasks. The success of Lorraine's production rested on the shoulders of every soul living in the factory compound.

A large group of young apprentices performed all the ancillary tasks. Days before the crucial "making time" they were hard at work felling trees, making charcoal, unloading wagons, grinding oxides for coloring the glass, loading the glass tank, stoking fires day and night, cleaning the work floor areas, sorting good cullet from waste glass piles and cleaning the iron rods of their residual traces of glass from the previous work period. Their labors began long before the work bell tolled and continued after the last clear gather of glass was taken from the tank. When the good glass was exhausted and production was at an end, all of the many emptying and cleaning tasks fell to them.

  A high attrition rate, the result of glasshouse hazards as well as the advanced ages of many of the experienced workers, created a constant need for new employees. Ambitious apprentices who showed promise were given every opportunity to rise above their lowly status. Bright young boys were eagerly sought out and carefully trained with the expectation that they would one day fill the important factory floor vacancies and, if extremely gifted, eventually attain the apex of the glassworkers' hierarchy, a gaffer's chair. Those who held that honored position had absolute authority over a small group of glassworkers. They directed the work of the apprentices, gatherers and servitors through the complex steps from the hot tank to the gaffer's chair, where the gaffers' skills transformed the glowing glass into beautiful creations.

  The making of a new batch of glass began with charcoal brought into the factory to revive the dying embers that fueled the previous melt. Measured quantities of sand, potash, lime, glass cullet and lead oxide were shoveled into the tank until it was completely filled. When the temperature in the tank rose to its highest level, the mass within collapsed on itself as the liquefying materials oozed into millions of air spaces formerly trapped between the grains of sand. When the batch completely liquefied, young apprentices wearing horse blinders—protective leather shielding on the "tank side" of their faces and arms—took turns stirring the mixture with iron rods. Occasionally they paused to allow the impurities to rise to the surface. Using long hoe-like implements, they raked the floating dross to the tank sides and ladled it onto the factory floor.

The quality of the glass was determined by a precise window of time, the "making time." It began at the moment the glass melt clarified. It came to a conclusion when the aging batch of molten glass became too contaminated to use, corrupted by bits of flotsam that flaked off the interior of the holding tank, pollutants in the air and the unavoidable tainting caused by the constant immersion of iron rods into the crucible of molten glass.

When "making time" occurred, the clamoring work bell roused everyone and summoned them to the factory. The time of night or day did not matter; everyone was expected to join in and help. Until all the good glass was consumed, a small universe of toiling humanity streamed without pause out of the small huts, in and out of the forest, back and forth across the clearing and in and out of the factory.

Inside the dimly lit factory, the glassworkers juggled the white, hot molasses-like glass in a curious ballet. Each one, in his allotted space, danced his well-practiced steps, all the while bearing a long iron standard topped with a glowing ball of molten glass. The uninitiated visitor heard only a terrible cacophony of hisses and roars spewing from fiery maws—the sounds of a Dante's *Inferno*. But to those involved in the throes of creativity, those harsh sounds were the sweet symphony that invited Lorraine's performers to display their skills. After sunset, in the dim glow of the workroom fires, the dancers appeared as graceful silhouettes. Occasionally, a worker's face floated ghostlike out of the darkness lit by a hot ball of glowing glass.

There was a discernible pattern to the ballet. It began when the iron rod, topped with a gather of white-hot glass, emerged from the fiery cauldron. The "baton" was ceremoniously presented by the gatherer to the servitor, the dancer, who took center stage. The constantly turning, bright glass enveloping the tip of the baton changed magically into a hollow ball the moment it received the breath of life—a short puff of air from the lips of the dancer. As the cooling ball darkened and changed from glowing white to pink and then to dull red, the dancer thrust it into the roaring glory-hole, to have it emerge, once again, pliant and white-hot bright. He spun the baton in huge overhead arcs, elongating its appended fiery ball into a distended dim oval. After heating the glass once again, the dancer presented the standard with its glowing glass to the seated gaffer. Here the gaffer rolled the iron rod with its dimming masthead still attached back and forth on the long wooden arms of the gaffer's chair as he opened a hole in the end of the glass bubble. The rotating centrifugal force expanded the opened end of the glowing oval into a flaring vase. Using centuries-old tools, the gaffer coaxed the glass into its final rigid shape. It was then broken from the iron rod, and placed in the lehr to cool slowly overnight.

7.

Marcella Claremont lived her entire life in the shadow of the Verrerie de Lorraine. The smoke, the ash, the smells and the din of the glass factory filled her waking and sleeping hours. At the age of seventeen, Marcella married a Lorraine glassworker. Though the marriage was prearranged, she was happy with her father's choice of Emile Claremont as her husband. Four years of happiness came to a tragic end when a large clay tank burst and its molten glass contents spilled over the lower half of Emile's body, killing him instantly. Marcella did not know how she, a young widow with two small children, would survive her husband's death. But, her parents and the glass community gathered protectively about her and helped provide her with the courage and means to raise her little family. Grateful for the help, she vowed to repay everyone's generosity.

Several years later, while ministering to the birthing mothers and the new-born babies as helper to the aging midwife, Marcella found that she possessed an innate talent for healing. That discovery became the answer to her prayers. She had found a way to fulfill her promise to repay everyone. As her curative powers developed, so did her rudimentary understanding of pharmacopoeia. She raised medicinal herbs in her dusty garden and supplemented her precious store of nostrums by searching out roots and plants in the hardwood forest. Soon, many in the community ascribed magical powers to the cures she brought about with her self-taught knowledge of herbs and potions. Some preferred Marcella's amulets and charms to the prayers of the local cleric.

Her little sons grew into handsome young men, but tragically, both lost their lives fighting in Paris during the short 1848 Revolution. The loss of her husband and sons generated a terrible bitterness in Marcella. She turned away from the church and, to the dismay of the local cleric, openly denied the existence of a compassionate God. Maurice, her younger son, never married, but two year old Pierre survived Charles, her older son. At his father's untimely death, Pierre's mother sent him to Valady to be looked after by his grandmother. Marcella doted on the child. She kept an ever-watchful eye over her sole surviving relative, vowing, "Nothing, not even death, will ever take little Pierre away from me; I've suffered more than my share of grief."

In conformity with the glass tradition, Marcella apprenticed Pierre to the Lorraine Factory. She rejoiced that her grandson, so young, was soon chosen from the pool of apprentices to become a helper. The Director of the company ceremoniously fitted him with the blinder and arm-protector, pieces of leather he would wear on his arm and one side of his face to ward off the searing heat of the molten glass. He quickly rose through the highly structured hierarchy, eventually advancing to the status of gaffer, with his own chair and work-gang. As the young man refined his skills, the factory management began to call upon his talents to make many of the finest pieces. Not content with his achievement, Pierre sought out retired glassworkers to glean information from their precious store of glass knowledge. His ever-consuming obsession with glass extended to historical techniques, as well. He focused many months of study on ancient Roman glass shards unearthed by local farmers' plows, endeavoring to unravel long-lost secrets of the art.

As Pierre approached adulthood, anxious Lorraine mothers, continually seeking suitable husbands for their unwed daughters, speculated among themselves that Pierre would be a splendid son-in-law, but agreed that sharp-eyed Marcella would never permit her grandson to marry one of their "glass girls." She'd keep him sheltered in her "nest" until the day she was laid to rest.

After almost four decades, a doctor challenged Marcella's importance to the health of the glass community when he established a practice in nearby Valady. With the miracles of nineteenth-century medicine only a few kilometers away, glassworkers in Lorraine couldn't resist the opportunity to be treated by the newly-arrived university trained doctor. As she watched her patients gradually leave her care, Marcella complained to Pierre that the glassworkers were an ungrateful lot. "Even those that I brought into the world abandon me."

"*Grandmere,*" he protested, "you still help many of the people with your cures."

"Oh, yes, every now and then someone remembers me with a burn or a small cut. But for anything else, they run off to that doctor in Valady. What does he know? He's still a child!"

"My dear sweet, *Grandmere,*" Pierre said, gently cradling her face in his cupped hands, "you don't have to cure every illness in Lorraine. You deserve a little time for yourself, to rest and enjoy the world about you."

But Marcella, determined to prove her ability to her "fickle neighbors," resolved to outdo her competitor. To the store of cures she had carefully gathered over the years, she added unnatural remedies. She explored the mystical properties of spells, the evil eye, and magical potions. To the roots and leeches she understood, she added the entrails of small animals, animal droppings, spider webs, bird feathers and all manner of odd nostrums. The new malodorous fumes escaping from her ever-boiling kettles were often offensive to Pierre, but he endured them silently. He felt grateful that his grandmother's concoctions occupied her again and that she seemed to be content.

8.

When Didierjean arrived at the Verrerie de Lorraine with his charge from Empress Eugenie, the glasshouse director took him to Marcella's grandson. That Kosnar considered so young a person the most proficient gaffer at Lorraine surprised the Saint Louis director. He wondered if the skills and knowledge Pierre harvested in just a few years would be adequate to meet the challenge.

Since it was an imperial request, Director Kosnar granted Pierre a hiatus from his glasshouse responsibilities and directed him to begin work on the empress's pieces. Pierre accompanied Didierjean to the Saint Louis factory where he would have the opportunity to acquire whatever materials and tools he might deem useful to his task.

Nothing in his life prepared Pierre for the size of the Saint Louis factory. Its scope overwhelmed him. It employed more than 1500 glassworkers and 350 lumberjacks. In contrast to Lorraine's small solitary tank and its infrequent melt periods, the workers kept glass in a continuous molten state at Saint Louis in four enormous tanks. Artisans faceted finished pieces in several cutting rooms where a bank of powerful engines powered large grinding and polishing wheels. The splendid equipment and the fine accommodations provided for the workers awed him. Pierre also learned that the company had abolished labor on Sundays and was presently establishing a common fund to assist its workers should they become ill.

As Pierre carefully observed the glassmakers at work, he saw that the environment repressed individual artistic creativity. Company policy required the workers to adhere to established designs predetermined by someone other than the craftsmen. As he watched the skilled artisans monotonously produce the same article, day after day, without the slightest variation, he felt deep compassion for them.

Didierjean took Pierre to an abandoned section of one of the many warehouses and pointed to an accumulated pile of neglected iron molds. "Take as many as you wish," he said. As Didierjean poked his cane into the mound of rusty molds, he added, "I apologize for their condition, they haven't been used for years. They're so rusty! I'll see to it that someone cleans those that you select."

"How will I be using these molds?"

"To make the millefiori canes for paperweights."

"Oh, I see, for the circle of small canes around the design."

"Yes, exactly," said Didierjean as he speared one of the molds with his cane. Handing Pierre the rusted mold, he added, "Look at the shape inside this mold, Pierre, it's the type you'll need. I think that you should select several like this."

Pierre examined the large cup-shaped mold and saw that its interior wall was machine-cut with vertical serrations; the shape of its cavity resembled a large clock gear.

"It produces our company's old paperweight trademark, a fourteen-cog cane." Didierjean explained. Waving at the pile of molds, Didierjean shook his head, saying, "We must have made millions of millefiori canes with these molds." As Pierre picked through the pile of molds, Didierjean walked to a nearby workbench and picked up a small brass plate. "Pierre," he said, "take a couple of these and some of these collars. See, the collars fit around the brass plates. I think they had something to do with making millefiori canes, but I'm not exactly sure how they were used."

On the morning of the next day, Didierjean arranged for Pierre to work with an elderly glass artist who remembered how to fashion thin sheets of gold into tiny embossed shields, as well as the method for decorating them with colorful enamels. Pierre and the old glassman worked together six days creating seventeen tiny Hapsburg crests, each surmounted by a Mexican eagle—tiny armorial designs, exquisite in detail, no larger than a man's thumbnail. Pierre carefully packed the shields in a small box, telling his mentor, "I don't know how many attempts it'll take to put the empress's paperweights together, but, at least, with these I can have fourteen failures before I complete her request."

The following week, Didierjean introduced Pierre to an old glassmaker who agreed to teach the young man how to create the cameo sulphides included in the paperweights. The glassmaker learned the complex technique of sulphide fabrication from Apsley Pellatt while working in England during the 1820's.

The old man demonstrated how to make negative molds of fine plaster using two small bronze medallions of Carlota and Maximilian, struck when they were regents in Lombardy. He poured a mixture of water, white clay, and supersilicate of potash into each mold. He allowed the creamy mixture to dry in the molds until it became leather-hard. After carefully trimming away the excess material from around the air-dried profiles, he placed the two pieces in a kiln and fired them until they became fine, hard porcelain.

Pierre's first attempts to enclose the porcelain cameos in glass were unsuccessful. The glass and the cameos contracted at differing rates as they cooled, cracking under the strain. The glassworkers made numerous adjustments to the clay mixture until they finally achieved compatibility. Pierre beamed with pride as the sulphide cameos comfortably accepted their envelope of molten glass.

His study at Saint Louis at an end, Pierre returned to Lorraine to turn his attention to the creation of the millefiori canes—tiny geometric glass slices which were to ring the paperweight designs. Although glassworkers sporadically practiced the creation of millefiori canes in civilizations early as Ancient Egypt, the complex process mystified Pierre and the Saint Louis glassworkers. André Tremaine, a long-time friend of Pierre's elderly servitor, Gaspard, revealed it to him.

As a young man, Tremaine left his university studies against the wishes of his father to join Napoléon Bonaparte's Grande Armée. After Waterloo, he apprenticed himself to the Baccarat glass company. Years later, in his advanced years, he retired from the pressures of the coveted gaffer's chair and settled near the Lorraine factory. Gaspard and Tremaine shared their memories of glass in the local auberge over many pipe bowls of tobacco and an even greater number of glasses of wine. One late evening, as Tremaine refilled their glasses from a second bottle of wine, he asked, "Don't you sometimes wonder what has become of our many crystal children, Gaspard?"

"Children? Glass is glass! The pieces I made at my chair were my work, not my progeny."

"You're mistaken, my friend. Think about it for a moment. The pieces you and I created were truly unique—born of man, not of woman. God did not desire all of creation to take place only in the body of woman. In his wisdom he left the creation of beauty to us."

"I'm afraid your advancing years have addled your brain."

"Listen to me, Gaspard. A lifetime ago, when I was an apprentice at Baccarat, I fell in love with the virginal white-hot glass reposing in its fiery tank." He paused to savor another sip of wine, then continued. "I even dreamed of that liquid crystal as I slept, imagining that it beckoned me to take of its bounty. I suppose that you'd say I developed a sensual relationship with the molten glass. Oh, how I desired to be permitted to take a gather of crystal and give it life!"

"But, André, we all wanted to succeed; we all wanted to get the gaffer's chair."

"It was not the same with me. My purpose in life was not the gaffer's chair; it was to create beautiful objects out of glowing glass. The chair was only incidental, a way to an end. I saw the roaring tank of molten glass as a primordial womb."

"A womb?"

"Yes, a womb, but, one that gave of itself to those who could coax the pliable glass into children of beauty. Think of it, Gaspard, a man, taking a gather of molten crystal, an embryo, and carrying it full-term until its birth—a thing of sparkling beauty. And not, mind you, in the nine months that nature requires of woman, but in less than half an hour. Think of it! The iron rod invades the fiery womb to take a living gather of glass. The glass fetus is spun on the end of the glassmaker's rod, shaped and refined at the lover's chair. Even the act of breaking the finished piece from the iron rod is like the severing of the umbilical cord."

Tapping the cold ash from his pipe, Gaspard shook his head, declaring, "My friend, I'm afraid you've had too much to drink this evening."

Later that night, when the auberge closed, the two old friends wended their way home. As they tottered along the dark path, they used the erupting sparks of the tall factory chimney as a homing beacon.

Soon after Pierre returned from the Saint Louis factory, Gaspard brought his old friend to the factory and introduced him to Pierre. "Pierre, Monsieur Tremaine was one of Baccarat's finest paperweight artists. He has generously offered to help you master the millefiori technique."

"I've looked forward to this meeting, young man," said Tremaine. "I've heard so much about your extraordinary ability. Gaspard tells me that you have a brilliant future in glass."

"I still have much to learn, Monsieur. There are so many mysteries about glass that continue to confound me. That's why I'm indebted to you for your generous offer. When do you think you might be able to help me with the millefiori technique?"

"The white-hot glass is beckoning over there," said Tremaine, pointing to the glowing tank. "Shall we begin?"

"Now?" asked Pierre, surprised.

"Yes, now—now young man, before I grow any older. You can begin by taking a gather of clear glass on the end of a pontil and bringing it here."

As Pierre selected a long iron rod and dipped it into the glass tank, Tremaine removed his jacket and used it to wipe clean a marble slab on a nearby workbench. Tremaine lit his pipe, saying, "Now, roll that glowing embryo back and forth on this marble marver, here."

Pierre rolled the molten glass attached to the end of the pontil back and forth on the marble until the syrupy sphere hardened slightly and gradually assumed the shape of a cylinder, an inch in diameter and six inches in length.

"Keep rolling it on the marver until it cools enough to retain its shape."

"Will this cylinder be the center of my millefiori cane?" asked Pierre.

"That's correct. Now, Gaspard, you take a gather of white glass from one of the small crucibles," Tremaine instructed, pointing to the many small pots lining the interior of the furnace.

"Opaque white?" asked Gaspard.

"Yes, that's good. Now, apply it to the young man's glass. That will make a nice white layer. It'll be a good foil for the color layer."

After marvering the white glass over the surface of the clear cylinder, Pierre asked Tremaine, "And now a clear layer?"

"Of course, to give the color layers a little breathing room."

After the clear layer, Pierre marvered green glass around the expanding cylinder, then another layer of clear, and finally a layer of opaque white.

"Now, heat your piece of glass in the glory hole until it is workable again."

He rotated the glass in the roaring flames of the glory hole until the color-ringed cylinder became semi-soft. Pierre returned with the glowing glass to Tremaine who instructed him to gently force the cylinder into one of the serrated Saint Louis iron molds he had placed on the floor. "Keep it in there until it holds the shape of the mold. That's it, that's it. Now, pull it out of the mold and add another layer of glass."

Pierre withdrew the glass cylinder and saw that it now bore serrations on its side. With the help of Gaspard he added a layer of clear glass. Tremaine put down his pipe and picked up an iron rod, saying, "While I take a small gather of glass on the end of this pontil, heat your cylinder one more time and I'll attach my pontil to the end of your supple glass." Pressing his pontil onto the free end of Pierre's glass cylinder, he smiled and said, "Now, my son, the magic begins! While I stand here, you back away from me, slowly, until I tell you to stop."

The soft glass cylinder attached between the two iron rods stretched thinner and thinner as Pierre backed away. The young man began to hesitate.

"Don't stop yet, keep moving. That's it, that's it, a little more—more—more—Stop!"

The stretching cylinder had become a sagging glass rope, eight feet in length, its diameter diminished to the thickness of a pencil. It was broken off of both pontil rods and allowed to cool on the rungs of a wooden ladder that Gaspard had been instructed to place flat on the factory floor. The thin, hardened rod was then sliced into small disks, each the exact miniaturized clone of the cross section of the original cylinder. Pierre picked up one of the tiny millefiori canes, held it in his fingers and studied it for as long time. Speaking more to himself than to Gaspard or Tremaine, he said, "So that's the solution to the glass secret that has eluded me for so long." Turning to Tremaine, he gratefully said, "I've studied old Roman shards with clusters of these canes fused together and have never been able to solve the mystery of their creation. Thank you, thank you, Monsieur Tremaine! I'm so indebted to you!"

Tremaine, smiling, took the cane from Pierre's fingers, saying, "Now, I'll show you how we used these millefiori canes at Baccarat to create a circular design."

Pierre noticed for the first time that the sun had set. Concerned that the old man might be overly tired, he suggested, "We've accomplished a great deal today, Monsieur Tremaine. Shall we continue our work another day?"

"My dear boy, how can you think of stopping now? Our pallet is ready. We can't stop, we must complete the canvas!"

Tremaine carefully arranged a circle of millefiori canes in a channel cut into a small round brass template. "The channel will hold the millefiori canes in place," he explained. "We don't want them to shift their positions." He then placed a hollow metal collar around the plate. "The collar will keep your molten glass from flowing off the sides," he explained. Then Tremaine turned to Gaspard, saying, "Put this brass plate on the hot shelf of the glory hole. We must preheat the cold canes before we encase them. If the molten glass touched them now, they'd crack."

Pierre inserted a fresh pontil into the tank, withdrew it and rotated the molten glass so that its centrifugal force prevented the white-hot, molasses-like ball from dripping off the end of the rod. Tremaine then instructed Pierre to bring the white-hot glass down through the collar and on top of the millefiori-bearing template. Lifting his pontil from the template, Pierre saw that the entire circle of millefiori canes had adhered to the tacky ball of glass on the end of his pontil.

Pierre was then instructed to encase the exposed cane design with successive layers of molten glass from the tank.

The formation of the paperweight's spherical shape required repeated insertions in the flames of the glory hole quickly followed by coaxing at the gaffer's chair. There, with a cup-shaped piece of apple wood which he was told to occasionally dip into a bucket of water, Pierre forced a domed shape onto the rotating pliable glass. The water-soaked wood hissed each time it came in contact with the red hot glass.

"Keep the apple wood wet," cautioned Tremaine, "if it dries out too much it'll catch fire."

While the crystal was still pliable, Pierre was instructed to use his pucella, a large tweezer-like tool, to constrict the bottom of the paperweight into a thin neck, just above the end of the pontil.

"That's it, that's it," encouraged Tremaine, "keep rolling the paperweight back and forth until the hot ball cools enough to retain its shape. Don't let it sag."

When the glass mass became rigid, Pierre struck his pontil with a metal bar. The shock broke the finished paperweight off the end of the pontil onto a waiting box of fine sand. The paperweight was then placed in a lehr to slowly cool overnight. This final step would prevent its outer layers from cooling faster than the center, thereby avoiding the build-up of structural stresses in the finished piece—stresses which might cause it to shatter.

With the completion of the simple paperweight, Pierre acquired all he needed to know. The color ground, the overlay shell, the miniature flowers, leaves and tendrils, and the cutting of the concave facets presented few problems for Pierre; he mastered those skills previously. Now he could begin the difficult process of assembling the empress's paperweight.

9.

It was not until the dusty green of late summer changed into the chilly barren days of early winter that Pierre felt confident enough to combine all of his efforts in a paperweight. Monsieur Didierjean, informed of the test, arrived by carriage early on the appointed morning to witness the attempt. For the first time in anyone's memory, all activity around the glass-filled tank came to a standstill.

A young apprentice hurried off to bring chairs so that the two directors might observe the work in relative comfort. As soon as Didierjean and Kosnar were seated, others quickly chose their places, sitting clustered on the dirt floor about the directors' feet. Many community inhabitants whose work did not normally take place inside the factory—wood cutters, charcoal makers and drovers—came to witness the undertaking.

Pierre made three paperweights that day. After they annealed overnight in the lehr, window facets were cut through their orchid glass shells to reveal their internal designs. To Pierre's dismay, none of the pieces reached his expectations. The sulphides and coat-of-arms, although unbroken, shifted in two of the paperweights. The ring of millefiori canes became misshapen in one, while in another, the canes smeared. In all three examples, he placed the elements in the design on the brass plate face-up which reversed the date "1864" when viewed from the top so it read "4681".

Despite Pierre's disappointment, his attempts elated Monsieur Didierjean. To him, Pierre's trial run indicated a great measure of success. He believed that the remaining problems were now solvable. He would not disappoint the empress—the paperweights would be completed, and soon. He left Valady with a great sense of relief.

After many subsequent attempts, Pierre created the first successful Imperial Paperweight on the third of March; it was perfect in every detail. Pierre showed it to Marcella and then took it to Monsieur Kosnar. News of his achievement quickly spread throughout the glass community. And though everyone had been busily working for a day and two nights on a fresh batch of glass, they forgot their exhaustion when they learned of Pierre's success. Never mind that the celebrated Saint Louis factory would take credit for the paperweight. One of their own had created what seemed an impossibility. One of them produced a thing of beauty for the Imperial Palace!

Director Kosnar traveled to Saint Louis to personally deliver the paperweight to Monsieur Didierjean. Both men marveled at its fine workmanship and exquisite detail. The Hapsburg escutcheon, the perfectly sculpted cameo sulphides, the circle of millefiori canes, the regal purple background and the outer shell of pastel orchid elicited many sighs of pleasure from the two professionals.

"Her Imperial Highness will be pleased," said Didierjean, and then added effusively, "How can I ever thank you, my friend?"

"The credit goes to Pierre Claremont, he is so gifted."

"He is a true master. Tell me, when do you expect him to finish the other two?"

"Now that all the technical problems have been solved, they should be ready by the end of the month."

"Wonderful! I'll convey that information to her Imperial Highness. I'm certain she will be anxious to know."

While preparing the component parts for the second paperweight—a dark green ground to be overlaid with a shell of pastel green glass—a gather of molten glass accidentally seared Pierre's right forearm. He took no great notice of the extremely painful burn. It was a necessary hazard in glass factories. Several days later, to his consternation, the burn developed an infection. Marcella began to effect her cure; burns and infections were her particular specialty. And since it was her beloved Pierre, she fussed over his arm constantly, unwrapping dry bandages and applying new ones soaked in various earthy concoctions. Pierre suffered her repeated applications of odoriferous nostrums and poultices in silence, though they irritated and distracted him. When he became intensely involved in combining the component parts of the second paperweight, he insisted she temporarily cease her treatment. Marcella stood by and watched helplessly as the infection slowly spread along his arm. She became especially concerned when she saw dangerous red streaks radiating out from the infected area.

Pierre turned to Gaspard for assistance when his suppurating arm began to interfere with the fine detail of his exacting task. The pain eventually forced him to stop working altogether and give himself over to Marcella's care. She applied all her time-tested remedies, but his condition worsened. The massive infection, which spread at an alarming rate, more than equaled her accumulated medical knowledge. Her healing expertise with leeches, herbs, roots, and entrails of crawling and flying creatures were ineffective. Each time she unwrapped his arm and removed the poultice, panic tightened her throat.

"Compassionate Mother of God," she silently prayed, "help me. The pus and putrefaction oozing from my Pierre's arm will not stop!"

In a desperate effort to draw out all the pus, she soaked his forearm in a warm solution and then carefully lifted the edges of the encrusted scabs to release the poisonous yellow matter.

Monsieur Kosnar called on Pierre and offered to take him to Valady for medical help, but Pierre refused. Marcella realized the reason for his refusal and said, hesitantly, "My dear, I don't seem to be able to stem the infection. Maybe you should do as Monsieur Kosnar suggests. The doctor in Valady—"

"No, *Grandmere*, let's give your poultices a little more time. My arm will be better soon." Turning to Kosnar, he asked, "How is Gaspard managing without me?"

"He asked me to tell you that he added the green shell yesterday. He plans to cut the facets tomorrow. If all goes well, we'll deliver the second paperweight to Didierjean next week."

As Kosnar prepared to leave, Pierre said, "Monsieur Kosnar, I'm sorry for the problems I'm causing you."

"Causing me, Pierre?"

"Yes, I know how anxious you are about the empress's paperweights."

"All he worries about," said Marcella, "is the empress's paperweights."

"You get well, young man. That's more important than anything else right now."

When Kosnar returned to his home, his wife asked anxiously, "How is he?"

"The infection looks bad. Marcella doesn't seem to be able to stem it."

"Send for the doctor!"

"I offered to, but Pierre refused. He doesn't want to hurt Marcella's feelings."

"Send for the doctor, Eugene! There is much more than his health at stake! Have you forgotten that the empress is waiting for the other two paperweights? You don't have anyone else who can make them, do you?"

"No, you know I don't."

"What if he dies? What will you do then? Don't wait! Send someone to Valady to bring the doctor!"

"I'll wait a little longer."

Marcella anxiously fought Pierre's infection day and night. Unmindful of the roar of the factory furnaces, she was only conscious of the blood pounding in her own temples. Watching her grandson consumed by fever and sleeping fitfully, she attempted to match the rhythm of her beating heart to the pulsations of the vein throbbing in his neck, only to be distracted time and again by ominous new symptoms which caused her old heart to race. Her silent lips formed the words she could not utter, "What is this awful curse that takes away the few joys of my life? Oh, dear God, I've lost my parents, my husband and my two sons. Don't punish him because of my blasphemy; punish me instead. Don't take away my sweet Pierre. I promise I'll return to the Church; I'll honor all the Saints; I'll offer up candles and faithfully celebrate all the holy days. I'll go to confession regularly and tithe more than most. Please grant me this one request and I'll make a novena every month for the rest of my life. Dear Immaculate Mother of Jesus, intercede for me and spare my little Pierre. Sweet Sacred Heart of Mary, open up to my suffering; hear my plea."

Pierre's condition shocked Kosnar on his next visit. He was much worse. The small bedroom reeked of the putrescence in Pierre's arm. Ignoring the young man's wishes, he dispatched a company carriage to Valady to fetch the doctor.

Marcella held her breath as she watched the doctor administer to Pierre. Just poultices, bleeding and powders, she thought. It's no different than what I do. But when the doctor uncorked a large blue bottle, a strange sharp antiseptic essence flashed through the room. It didn't have the old familiar feel of her earthy nostrums; it was alien to her. Its sharp sting cut like winter ice in her nose and throat and made her eyes water. Its obvious potency gave her hope. "Oh, I pray his magic is stronger than mine," she whispered.

As the doctor prepared to take his leave, she demanded tearfully, "Tell me what to do to help my grandson!"

"You must make sure the doors and windows are shut tightly against the bad humors of the night air. Keep applying poultices. Soak the bandages in a watered-down solution of the medicine in this blue bottle and change them often. Give him this powder in warm broth twice each day, and try to keep him comfortable. If he's chilled, bundle him up; if he gets hot, bathe him with cool water."

"Will he get well? Oh doctor, he must get well!"

"I've done all that I can, madam; he's in God's hands."

Marcella wanted to pray for help, but was too embarrassed to go to the village church and face the community after so many years of church abstinence. How could she? She waited until dusk and then went out into her garden to pray to heaven. She didn't need the church nor its priest! As she implored heaven on her knees, a scythe of blackbirds slicing through the night air cut her prayer short. Taking it as an bad omen, she shook her fist at the birds, crying out, "Away with you, you damn carrion!" and returned to her hut to administer to her Pierre once again.

As Pierre's condition worsened, Marcella turned from prayer and began to focus on someone to blame. She filled her bitter watchful hours with condemnation, first, of the Saint Louis director who gave Pierre the task of fulfilling the empress's request, and then of the empress herself. But, since the Saint Louis director and the Imperial family were distant and not familiar entities on which she could concentrate her wrath, she fastened her growing hatred on the paperweights themselves.

During the final moments of his life, Pierre, delirious, struggled with the second paperweight. "...the empress's must finish it! Are the fire's hot enough, Gaspard? More glass! More glass! I'm burning—It's so hot here inside the Glory Hole! Help me, *Grandmere*, help me! Green glass, yes green. Oh, the heat, it's unbearable. Turn the pontil, mustn't sag—the empress's paperweight—hot—hot—"

Marcella held back her tears during her grandson's burial service; she would not interrupt his soul's safe passage into heaven. The roaring in her ears all but masked Father Bertrand's prayers as his words drifted in and out of her awareness, "...open the gates of Paradise to me—are my help—protection of Your wings—my soul clings fast to You, my God—Your right hand will lift—inherit the Kingdom prepared for you..."

"I'm not here, this is not happening," she thought. "Oh, my God, make it an old woman's nightmare. All my hopes lie there in that wooden box. Dear God, why, why? Oh, my Pierre."

As the pall-bearers lowered his coffin into the open ground, her muscles tensed, and a guttural curse swelled out of her bent body against all those whose lives had been or would be touched by the "evil empress's damned paperweights."

"Demons of Hell, I call on you to punish those who killed my beloved Pierre! I curse all those who have touched or will ever touch those unholy paperweights. Destroy their reason! Cut them down in the prime of their lives! Cause blood and gall to taint their offspring and their own miserable lives! Make their children and their children's children suffer the flames of the glory hole while they live, and roast in Hell after they die! Open up the ground that they may suffer the pain of an untimely death! Cast them into the void of darkness. My world has ended. There is no sun, no day, no night, only death now, the bleak abyss of death. My poor, poor Pierre."

As the mourners cast handfuls of earth on the pine coffin in a gesture of final parting, she screamed at them to stop. Her eyes wild, and spittle spewing from her open mouth, Marcella charged into the shocked mourners and shoved them away from the waiting pit. Several of the stronger men attempted to subdue her by seizing her flailing arms, but she spat at them and cursed them as she writhed to break loose. Struggling, she freed one arm and clawed at the faces of those around her. Finally, exhausted, she collapsed to the ground. Sympathetic mourners carried her limp body to her hut where a few of the older widows remained to look after her.

Having plumbed the depths of despair, Marcella gave up all desire to live. She remained in her bed taking little nourishment. She occupied her waking hours alternately grieving and blaspheming. On the fourth day she began to imagine that Pierre's corruption invaded her own body. "I feel his flesh rotting on my skin! I smell the decay of his body! The maggots are consuming his lovely eyes," she uttered, brushing away imagined worms from her face. Softly sobbing, she called out to her dead husband, "He is the last of your line, Emile. Your seed is decaying in the ground."

Marcella's condition steadily worsened until those who looked after her knew that the end was near. As she lay dying on her cot, Father Bertrand offered her absolution. But she refused, denying her own eternal salvation, choosing instead to take her hate and blasphemies to the grave. "I deny your God, false priest! Take away your crosses and holy water. I spit on them! If your God was compassionate, He would have spared His own Son. He wouldn't listen to Mary pleading for her Son's life, nor would he listen to my pleas for Pierre. Did your God have any compassion for Mary's bleeding heart when they nailed Jesus to the cross? I deny Him! I curse Him! I spit on

Him!"

As she passed into oblivion, she once again damned the paperweights and all who would ever lust after them, "...and when those they love are wrapped in their winding sheets, their shrouds of death, may their suffering be as deep as mine, knives twisting in the weeping chambers of their hearts."

During the early morning graveside service for Marcella, the day quickly darkened. Black clouds roiled in the threatening sky and rain suddenly descended in torrents. The grave diggers, assisted by the men who had gathered for the burial, furiously shoveled the dirt into her grave. All night long cracks and roars of thunder punctuated the noise of the cascading rain. The dirt of the newly plowed fields, mercilessly beaten into a river of flowing mud, swept over all the surrounding countryside, coating everything in its wake with a dismal cloak of brown.

Early the next day, insistent pounding on the rectory door interrupted Father Bertrand's morning prayers. His housekeeper answered the hysterical summons and hurried to tell the parish priest that the two grave diggers were waiting outside, begging to see him. They had a terrible calamity to report. The priest crossed himself, kissed his prayer book and directed the housekeeper to admit them. She hesitated. She had just finished scrubbing the floors and she didn't care to have the gravediggers tramping about in their muddy boots. But remembering the fear in the men's eyes, she returned to the door and admitted the mud-covered men into her clean foyer.

"Oh, Father, God protect us all! A dreadful omen! Dreadful!" They fell to the floor, kneeling with their hands clasped in supplication.

"What's happened, Thomas? Edgar? Speak up, in Heaven's name!"

"It's that witch, Marcella, Father! The earth's rejected her body! Her unholy coffin now lies on the lip of her grave! The dirt we shoveled over her has disappeared! Father, she has risen from the grave to destroy us all!"

A half-suppressed shriek escaped from the housekeeper's throat. Backing away from Father Bertand's angry glance, she crossed herself and scurried away to the safety of her kitchen.

The following Sunday morning, the glassworkers crowded into Valady's tiny church. Most of the inhabitants of Lorraine augmented the usual small Sunday flock of womenfolk and young children. Aware of the reason for their attendance, the priest assured his parishioners that Marcella's coffin came out of its grave because of natural causes. He carefully explained that a torrent of water rushing down from the hill flushed the loose dirt out of her newly dug grave, filled the cavity, and floated the wooden coffin over the edge of ground. But the Lorraine inhabitants, in a state of mortal dread, refused to accept their priest's logic. They remembered Marcella's blasphemy and believed that her soul, denied admittance into heaven, would never be allowed to rest.

For years after Marcella's reburial, the two grave diggers told all who would listen, that the second time they buried her, they covered her coffin with large field boulders which they then covered over with earth. They assured everyone that Marcella would never climb out of that deep hole, even on the Day of Resurrection.

From the time of Marcella's second interment, the Lorraine workers recounted every detail of Pierre's burial and Marcella's "unholy resurrection," especially when a death occurred within the community. To allay the persistent fear that Marcella was summoning members of the community to premature deaths, Father Bertrand opened the church records in a futile attempt to convince his parishioners that the death rate in their community had not increased after Marcella's death. But his efforts fell on closed minds; superstitious fears continued to plague the factory workers. Each time a death occurred, the members of the Lorraine community scrupulously searched their memories to uncover the link which bound the newly deceased to the cursed talismans.

"Yes, I remember. Old Abraham used his dray to bring in the white sand for the melt six days before Pierre was burned with molten glass. It was Marcella's curse that caused his horse to bolt yesterday. They say that as old Abraham lay dying, his eyes widened in terror and he whispered, 'Marcella,' with his final breath."

"Bernard hauled the charcoal to the fires for that melt, remember? That congestion in his lungs, the coughing up of blood, it had to be Marcella's curse!"

"Yes, I remember it was our poor Maurice who cleaned the molds after Pierre used them for the first paperweight."

"Philippe was so young and strong, but he was the one who..."

"Pierre asked Hugo to mix—"

"Marcella's curse—"

"The paperweights!"

"Marcella's curse is wrapping us in our death shrouds!"

"Marcella—"

"God preserve us!"

They remembered her horrible invocation:

Demons of Hell, I call on you to punish those who killed my beloved Pierre! I curse all those who have touched or will ever touch those unholy paperweights... Cut them down in the prime of their lives! ... Open up the ground that they may suffer the pain of an untimely death...

CHAPTER II.

1.

Matthew bounded up the steps and punched in two minutes late. Looking up from his cluttered desk, Sgt. Dobrinski removed his cigar and waved it at Matthew, saying, "Hey, kid, you look beat this morning. Out bumming last night?"

"Yeah, had a date."

"With that Linda?"

"Nope."

"Paula?"

"No, I was out with Beth."

"Again?"

"Uh-huh."

"You been seeing a lot of that Michigan Avenue cutie this week."

"We've gone out a couple of times."

"Made it in the sack with her, yet?"

Matthew shot back, angrily, "That's none of your damn business!"

"Whoa, buddy! Nothing personal," said the older man, taken aback by Matthew's sudden reaction. "What the hell," he thought, "he never got pissed like that when I ask about all those other dames he's been fooling around with. Wonder why he's so ticked off? Hey, what do you know, maybe he's getting serious about that little blonde." After a few minutes of aimless shuffling through report sheets, Dobrinski continued, "You know, Matt, you ought to start thinking about settling down and getting married. You could do a lot worse than that little blonde. She looks like a pretty nice kid."

"She's O.K."

Dobrinski carefully balanced his cigar on the lip of a rusty ash tray. He leaned back in his squawking chair, locked his hands behind his head and crossed his ankles. Matthew thought wearily, oh no, not another one of those fatherly lectures again.

"Don't know if I ever told you before, kid, but in early days, when I was a punk rookie, I did some whoring around. There's a lot of temptation put in the way of a young cop. But that ain't news to you. Right? Where do they usually send us? Think about it—not to some damn college, or some church social. They still put us in some of the dirtiest parts of town. When I pounded a beat, I never seen no rich assholes, no preachers, no college professors. All I ever got to know was drug pushers, drunks, and whores. What a young cop really needs is a good family life with a nice little wife and a couple of kids to prove to hisself every night that the whole world ain't a dirty shit-house.

"Man," he continued, "I don't remember how many times I kicked the hell out of those pimps. And not 'cause they made broads and kids do their dirty work for them—I was pissed at all the dirty money and sex they got. All the time I sweated my balls off for a living, that bunch of scum had diamonds on their 'pinkies' and drove around in Lincolns and Caddies picking up chicks. I was really messed up 'til I married Josie. That little woman turned my life around. Sure, I got my share of good times, especially after World War II when we occupied Japan. Did I ever tell you I was an MP there, with the First Cavalry?" Not waiting for a reply, he continued, "There was this small Japanese hotel in Nikko, a temple town ninety miles north of Tokyo, and this girl, Sumiko. Boy, I could tell you stories—" His voice trailed off as he retrieved his cigar stub from the ash tray, stared at it and silently dredged up old sweet memories, layered even sweeter by the passage of time.

Matthew was beginning to enjoy the lull when Dobrinski suddenly broke the stillness, asking, "So, what are you gonna do, kid? Gonna marry that cute little blonde?"

"Come on, Dan, we're just friends."

"When you two going out again?"

"Tonight. We're meeting at the Art Institute right after work. It's open on Tuesday nights."

"Art? Boy, ain't you getting cultured, all of a sudden."

"Beth said there's a paperweight collection there; she's going to show it to me. Maybe I'll get a better idea why everybody's so steamed about those missing paperweights."

"Have fun, kid. I'm going home after work and park my butt in front of the TV with a couple of cans of cold brew."

As the older officer eased his bulk out of the complaining chair and ambled across the small room to the files, Matthew, watching him, thought to himself that a steady diet of beer had left its mark on his partner's stomach. Dobrinski often bragged to Matthew that his belt size was the same as it was when he was in the army. "It ain't changed one inch," he'd say, cinching in his constricting belt another notch. Over the years, Dobrinski gradually moved the top of his trousers down below his ballooning belly so that his belt now dipped down to his groin. Matthew had been with him during the heat of a recent argument when Lt. Mulcahy shouted, "Damn it, Dobrinski, lose some of that gut and get some clothes that fit! You look like a slob!" His silhouette reminded Matthew of a cigar-chewing bullfrog.

While waiting in the museum lobby late that afternoon, Matthew caught sight of Beth pushing her way through the revolving door. Seeing him, she pointed to the public checking room, indicating he wait where he was until she checked her packages. They walked past Rodin's embraced lovers on their way to the Rubloff Gallery.

"Bet old man Rubloff paid off the museum to get his name on a gallery," said Matthew, a hint of sarcasm in his voice.

"He didn't have to, Matt. He gave the museum money to build the gallery. It was created over railroad tracks where a gallery never existed before."

"Probably cost a fortune."

"I guess so. But the real gift was his paperweights, more than fourteen hundred of them. They're just ahead, up those stairs. See the glass shelves there, on the right?"

"Wow!" exclaimed Matthew, as they entered the large rectangular gallery. Opposite the doorway, an oval arrangement of myriad glistening paperweights studded a large lighted wall panel. Paperweights also filled four additional panels, one in each corner of the room. Tiers of lighted shelves containing hundreds of antique and contemporary examples lined the walls between the large panels.

"Come on," said Beth, pulling at his arm, "let's get close to the cases."

As they approached the large central case, he asked, "What are the designs inside these paperweights made of?"

"Glass. Everything you see inside them is glass."

"I see flowers in some of them. Did they make them in molds?"

"Actually, they were created at a lamp."

"Made by hand?"

"Right. The glassman used a thin glass tube to blow a sharp needle of air through the flame of a lamp. He pinpointed the heat on the ends of colored glass rods. And then, with small tweezers and flatteners he worked the softened glass and shaped it into all the individual little flower parts—every single petal, every leaf, the stems, the buds. Then he joined all those pieces together, one-at-a-time, into a flower like that delicate yellow dahlia there."

"Wow! And then he encased it in molten glass?"

"Right."

"Why didn't the designs melt or smear when the molten glass hit them?"

"Sometimes you find a paperweight where the design is distorted. I don't know why they didn't all have that problem. The glass flowers had to be very fragile. It's just part of the artistry, I guess."

"Yeah, I guess—Beth. I know they cost big bucks, but I don't have any idea what any of these are worth."

"See that large one there in the center?"

"The ugly one with the worms in it?"

"Yes, that one. Those are silkworms on a mulberry leaf. Experts think it was made by the Pantin Company in France during the last century. We sold it to Mr. Rubloff a year and a half ago in our New York auction rooms for $147,000."

"Holy cripes, I had no idea! What do you suppose all these in here are worth?"

"I've heard over five million."

"Jesus!"

"Some people call them 'millionaire's marbles'."

"Yeah, I guess! Millionaire's marbles! And he gave them all to the museum?"

"Sure did."

"Five million." After a pause, Matthew turned to Elizabeth and said, "Rubloff heads a big real estate operation; his name's plastered on billboards all around the city. Where did he get his money? Rich parents?"

"No, it wasn't old money. He's one of those self-made men you hear about. His family left the Mesabi Iron Range and came to Chicago when he was just a little boy. He only had a grade school education when he started as a cabin boy on Great Lakes ships. Now he's probably a billionaire."

"God, what a brain to come this far; drive, too. Do those three missing paperweights look like any of these?"

"Most of their elements can be found somewhere in these, but not all in one paperweight. There're none as complex as the Imperial paperweights. See that large blue one over here?"

"Uh-huh."

"The Imperial paperweights are about that large, and have windows cut in them like that one, over there. And inside—come over here and look at this one—see that cameo?"

Elizabeth and Matthew talked paperweights until the museum closed. As they walked the two blocks west on Adams Street to Berghoff's Restaurant, the hot, moist oppressive air oozing in from the west immersed them in the pollutants of innumerable streets and automobile exhausts.

"It's so humid, even breathing is an effort. Alexandra told me that she doesn't ever remember being so uncomfortable. She was perspiring today, even though the air conditioner was on full-blast. While I froze at my desk, she had a big sweat spot on the back of her blouse. Even her hair was disheveled. It's so unlike her. I think it's her concern about the missing paperweights rather than the heat."

"Any more news about those paperweights?" Matthew asked.

"Yes, in a way, but I doubt if its really significant. Alex got a call from the New York office today. They said that the police questioned the director of the in-take department, Keith Parker. They consider him a suspect. They went to his apartment to question him. But, I'm sure he had nothing to do with it."

"They must have had a good reason."

"They found out that he's been spending a lot of money recently—a new car and some art glass."

"They want to know where he got the dough, right?"

"Yes, but he claims that a friend gave him the money."

"Could be money from the paperweights."

"Not Keith. He's got faults, but he's no thief!"

2.

PARIS - 1864

The months following Maximilian and Carlota's visit to Paris inspired a flurry of correspondence between Miramar, Brussels and Vienna. Letters from Carlota's father, King Leopold, and Maximilian's brother, Emperor Franz Joseph strongly advised Maximilian to insist that French troops, funds and written guarantees be included in any agreement with the French emperor before accepting his offer of the Mexican throne.

Receiving word that the Mexican plebiscite overwhelmingly favored Maximillian's enthronement, as well as the French emperor's assurances to honor requests for troops and funds, Maximilian and Carlota once again traveled to Paris. Maximilian's humble acceptance of Louis Napoléon's offer of the empire the crown of Mexico was the antithesis of the pride that Carlota openly exhibited. Her haughty self-importance at the prospect of her elevation in status embarrassed everyone in court.

As Maximilian and the French emperor met to finalize the terms of their agreement, Carlota and Eugenie visited together in the empress's private rooms.

"Carlota, Louis Napoléon and I knew that the people of Mexico would choose your husband to be their emperor. About that we had no doubt. It was surely God's will."

"Maximilian will prove to be a worthy choice for Mexico, Eugenie. He'll not betray your husband's trust." But even as Carlota spoke, a feeling of anxiety nudged at her. Her husband's preoccupation with Louis Napoléon's true intentions started her apprehensiveness. Lately, whenever she and Maximilian discussed Louis Napoléon's offer, their conversation invariably turned to the Battle of Solferino. Louis Napoléon, the victor in that engagement, caused their dethronement. And yet, this same Louis Napoléon, their former enemy, now offered them an empire. Maximilian found the circumstances of his offer to be inexplicable. What could his motives be? Why had he chosen them? No one knew Napoléon for his benevolence.

Eugenie interrupted the young woman's unsettled thoughts, asking, "Did you enjoy your visit with your family?"

"Oh, yes! When we arrived in Brussels, we found the street lamps, the royal residences and all the major buildings decorated in yellow, black and red! The entire city was festooned with bunting in our honor."

"I'm not surprised. Everyone in Belgium should be delighted at the elevation of their princess."

"My parents and I had many tearful moments together during our short stay. Only heaven knows when we will ever see each other again. From now on, our lives shall be lived an ocean apart."

"Will you be returning to Trieste when you leave us?"

"Not directly. We plan to travel to Windsor to spend a few days with cousin Victoria."

"Poor Victoria," said Eugenie, "my heart goes out to her.

She mourns so for her prince."

"It's been almost three years. I'm afraid she'll mourn her Albert until her dying day. She was so much in love with him."

"It's all so sad."

"After we leave Windsor, Maximilian wants to go to Vienna, to pay his respects to his family. Then we'll return to Miramar to prepare for our journey to Mexico."

"With God's help," Eugenie said, crossing herself, "I pray your journey will be completed successfully." Placing her hands on Carlota's arms, she continued, "Carlota, I want you to know that I've been in communication with advisors from the Vatican and with some of the leading monarchists in Mexico. They are, to a man, supportive of your new empire. It may be of comfort for you to know that my friends in Mexico have assured me they will be available to you if you desire their advice. Do not hesitate to avail yourself of their counsel if you have a need."

"How thoughtful, Eugenie."

"The emperor and the Holy Father are hopeful Maximilian will support the church in Mexico and assist the clergy in God's work."

"But, of course he shall, dear sister," said Carlota, surprised at any doubts Eugenie might have to the contrary.

Eugenie continued, explaining, "Much of the church's property was seized by the Mexican radicals. That unconscionable act incurred the wrath of the Holy Father. Juarez's soul is eternally damned, and rightly so! Imagine, Carlota, stealing from the mother church! The lands and properties he seized should be restored to the church as soon as possible."

Their conversation eventually drifted to the current social happenings in Paris, activities which were such an important part of court life.

"And, Carlota, when young Johann Strauss conducted his

newest waltz, 'The Beautiful Blue Danube', the dancers were so taken by the beauty of the music, they stopped dancing and listened, as tears welled in their eyes."

"My sister-in-law, Empress Elizabeth, wrote me about that new waltz. She said everyone in Vienna plays it. It can be heard from behind doorways, in music halls and in the parks. But, I've yet to hear it."

"We must have it played for you while you're here."

A lady-in-waiting entered the room and curtsied, "Excuse me, my lady, you asked that tea be served at this time."

The woman left the room to return moments later accompanied by two servants who brought in an elaborate tea service. As the lady-in-waiting poured tea, Eugenie instructed her to inform the wardrobe mistress to assemble carriage outfits for the following day. "Nothing too warm," she cautioned.

Carlota secretly wished she could watch. Her cousin Amelia described Eugenie's wardrobe to Carlota on one of her visits to Miramar.

"The empress's wardrobe is a large room directly above her boudoir. It's lined with a profusion of closets, armoires and chests of drawers. The wardrobe mistress and her helpers outfit several mannequins in that room, depending on the function the empress will attend. The mannequins, completely clothed, are then lowered by means of ropes and pulleys through openings in the wardrobe floor, down into the empress's boudoir below! After she chooses an outfit, the other mannequins are raised back up through the ceiling to the wardrobe room. The wardrobe mistress and her assistants then descend to the Imperial Boudoir, remove everything from the selected mannequin and clothe the empress."

As they took their tea, Carlota said, "Before we left Miramar, Maximilian gave me a crystal flacon of that new essence the Guerlain perfumers created in your honor."

"Yes, the *Eau de Cologne Imperiale*. It was quite a surprise when they presented me with a new perfume. It has such a lovely fragrance."

"Indeed it has. It is very popular, even in far-off Trieste. I'm certain it's no secret to you that your personal preferences are eagerly adopted by legions of women everywhere."

"It's flattering to know that my preferences are so widely emulated."

"We copy your coiffure, your crinolines, your hats and your perfumes. The emperor may have created a new Paris, but you, Eugenie, you've set the styles for the women of the entire world!"

After their tea, Eugenie went to a cabinet and returned with a lacquer box which she offered to Carlota. "This my dear sister, is a gift for you. After you and Maximilian left us last year, I had one of our glasshouses create a crystal piece especially for you. I hope it will be a constant symbol of a long and happy reign."

Carlota opened the box and took out the empress's gift, Pierre's magnificent paperweight. "Oh, how lovely!" She exclaimed, excitedly cradling the sparkling orb in both of her hands, turning it to catch the light of the afternoon sun. As she studied the cameo images, she thought to herself, how beautifully it captures my profile. She took special notice that the paperweight's background was deep purple, the color of royalty, and saw the Hapsburg crest surmounted by the Mexican eagle as a prophetic sign that their reign would be as glowing as the ball of crystal.

"It's a wonderful gift, Eugenie! I'll always treasure this first symbol of our new empire, especially since you had it created for me! Thank you, dear sister."

"I'm pleased that you like it."

"Oh, Eugenie, I do!"

The following day, Louis Napoléon and Eugenie took their young guests on a carriage ride through the streets of Paris. As Carlota's attention was drawn to the parasol-shaded confections that capped the coiffures of the smartly dressed Parisians, her husband excitedly viewed the sweeping changes to the city. Filled with admiration for the improvements Louis Napoléon had made to Paris, Maximilian expressed his feelings to Carlota, later that afternoon.

"Like the pure 'A' the oboe sounds to tune the varied instruments of the orchestra, Louis Napoléon's singleness of purpose has combined all the disparate elements of old sprawling Paris into a harmonious whole. Would that God might grant us the wisdom to do the same in our new empire!"

That evening, the couple accompanied Louis Napoléon and Eugenie to the newly built opera house. In honor of the emperor's young guests, the orchestra prefaced the opera with Mendelssohn's overture, *A Calm Sea and Prosperous Voyage*. At the conclusion of the overture the conductor turned and bowed to the royal box with the applauding audience following his lead. Maximilian and Carlota graciously acknowledged the ovation.

On their final evening in Paris, the Grand Chamberlain of the court appeared at Maximilian's rooms to read the emperor's official invitation to a dinner of state. Maximilian and Carlota, symbolically protected by a small retinue of palace guards, accompanied the Chamberlain who escorted them through the palace.

At the columned entrance to the Grand Salon, the Chamberlain struck his staff on the floor and formally introduced the young monarchs, "Archduke Maximilian and Princess Carlota, the future emperor and empress of Mexico."

Eugenie and Louis Napoléon met their entry with warm embraces while the assembled guests politely applauded. The

Chamberlain announced with great flourish that a dinner of state was being given in honor of Maximilian and Carlota, and led the entire company to the banquet hall. As the procession paraded through long colonnaded galleries, Maximilian marveled at the heroic appearance of the Cent-Guards lining both sides of the passageways, statuesque sentinels—each over six feet tall, garbed in shining thigh-high black boots, white breeches and blue tunics—standing motionless, eyes fixed straight ahead, their polished metal helmets, swords, buttons and breast plates reflecting the quivering lights of thousands of flickering candles.

The massive doors of the Grande Salle des Fêtes slowly opened, revealing seven enormous crystal chandeliers whose myriad twinkling candles seemed to exceed the light of day. Carlota gasped when she saw the vast banquet hall. Its sculptured ceiling appeared to float so high that its exact limits were lost to her eye. Clusters of tall Corinthian columns, rivaling those of the temples of Greece and Rome, anchored the immense arches supporting the ceiling. Iridescent white satin covers festooned with garlands of colorful flowers and centered with floral bouquets overlaid the sea of tables filling the room. The entire space glimmered and shimmered with reflected color and light from an abundance of silver and crystal. Ladies, resplendent in billowing gowns of rainbow-hued satins, brocades, lace, tulle, and ribbon, swept in on the arms of their escorts, further enhancing the splendor of the room.

The conversation filling the room ceased the instant Louis Napoléon rose to toast the future emperor of Mexico. The assembled guests, in a sudden rustle, rose to their feet and simultaneously raised their glasses, toasting, "Long live Emperor Maximilian."

At the end of the sumptuous dinner, the Grand

Chamberlain invited all of those present to accompany the emperor and empress and the honored guests to the concert hall for the evening's entertainment. Carlota marveled at the decorum of the assembled company, one moment chatting, eating, and laughing; the next, as the Chamberlain rose to speak, a quiet attentive group. She thought, "How civilized this court is. We shall certainly emulate these customs in our new empire."

The entertainment provided that evening was an aural delight. Adelina Patti's lovely voice enchanted everyone with a program of elegant bel canto arias from Bellini's opera, *La Sonnambula*. Carlota's heart rejoiced to enter the world of brilliant court life. She drank in the pomp of that dazzling night quenching her thirsty ambitions. "This," she said to herself, "is what my destiny was always meant to be."

That night she fell asleep with the purple Imperial paperweight clutched tightly in her hand. The next morning, she and Maximilian left Napoléon's court to begin their own journey into history.

3.

Four months later, a courier arrived in Brussels bearing a letter addressed to "Their Royal Highnesses, Leopold I, King of the Belgians and Queen Louise of Orleans." The closure of the envelope bore a large beribboned red wax wafer impressed with the newly struck seal of Empress Carlota of Mexico.

"My beloved mother and father," it began, "I pray this letter finds you in the best of health. We are both well.

"Please accept my sincere apology for not writing sooner. I intended to write you upon our arrival here in Mexico, but due to many unforeseen circumstances, I have been unable to do so until now. So much has transpired since we left you last April.

"When we arrived in Paris, we were pleasantly surprised by the Parisians who, having heard of our elevation, lined the boulevards cheering our procession with cries of *'Bonne chance, l'Archduke et Archeduchesse!'*

"As you have no doubt learned from the Belgian representatives who were present during the conference in Paris, Louis Napoléon, true to his promise, satisfied our requests for troops, funds and written guarantees in support of our reign.

"Our short stay in France was a whirlwind of exciting activities, filled with receptions, the opera, and visits to many cultural and historic sites. On our final day in Paris, the emperor presented us to the court and other dignitaries, offered toasts to our new empire and celebrated our elevation with an elegant dinner of state. I shall never forget that night.

"From Paris, we traveled to Windsor to pay our respects to Cousin Victoria. She still grieves for her Albert. We felt so sorry for her. My dear father, she speaks so gratefully for the support you offered her during her time of terrible distress. She said that she could not have survived Albert's demise had it not been for Uncle Leopold's help.

"Before returning to Miramar, Maxl and I visited his family. We quite naturally expected a pleasant visit; however, had we known what was awaiting us there, we should have avoided Vienna like the plague. When we arrived, the Imperial family had already left the Hofburg and taken up their usual summer residence at Schoenbrun Palace. We carriaged through Schoenbrun's elaborate palace gates, through acres of lovely formal French gardens, and stopped at the sweeping staircase that flows up the palace facade. The expansive view, across the colorful gardens and fountains and up to the pillared Gloriette, never fails to leave me breathless.

"Empress Elizabeth, 'Sissy,' met us informally as we entered the palace. What a joy she is! She is everything that is light and gay in Vienna. When I think of her, I picture her in chandeliered and mirrored halls, swirling with complete abandon to Strauss waltzes. She is such a bright light in that austere family.

"After a joyful reunion, Sissy led us to the royal residential apartments. On our way there we walked through one of the most magnificent rooms in the entire palace, the Great Gallery. The gilt-embellished room has a long wall of mirrors that reflect the windows overlooking the formal gardens. Maxl said that the frescos decorating the ceiling were painted by Gulielmi.

"Maxl's brother and mother were awaiting us in the emperor's sparsely furnished rooms. There I discovered that Franz Joseph cannot abide the trappings of royalty. Maxl told me his brother considers himself a soldier of the realm, first, and an emperor of the realm, second. As a result, he prefers personal accommodations that are mean and spare. Can you imagine, he prefers an army cot to a bed! Taking the few short steps from Franz Joseph's unadorned rooms into Sissy's drawing room is like a sudden journey from the dwelling place of a clerk into a celestial chamber.

"Except for Franz Joseph's private rooms, the residential apartments in Schoenbrun are luxurious and charming. They have brown and white paneled walls, gold-ornamented ceilings, intricately designed parquet floors, sparkling crystal chandeliers, glossy porcelain stoves, and are furnished with elegantly carved and upholstered furniture. The walls are hung with rich tapestries, ornamented mirrors, paintings and ancestral portraits of the Imperial family.

"Although Franz Joseph seemed pleased about the

Mexican crown, their mother, the Archduchess, reminded us that it was our French benefactor, Louis Napoléon, who defeated her Franz Joseph at Solferino and forced us out of Venice and Lombardy. Peering out from hooded eyes, she warned, 'Do not trust that shifty Frenchman'. She added, shaking a bony finger at Maxl, 'Since you have chosen to rule as emperor of Mexico, you must comport yourself as a Hapsburg at all times. Do not under any circumstances rely on that French Napoléon, on advisors, on churchmen or on any other outside influence when ruling those uncivilized pagans on the other side of the world. I expect you to remember that the life which has issued from my body must bring only honor to our family name.'

"But, my dear parents, what really distressed us was Franz Joseph's insistence that Maxl disclaim his hereditary succession to the Austrian throne. He said that, under the present arrangement, in the event of his own demise, Maximilian would serve as Regent of Austria until little Crown Prince Rudolph reached the age of majority. 'And how, dear brother,' he demanded of my husband, 'could you possibly reign over two empires half-way around the globe from one another?'

"The Archduchess, siding with Franz Joseph, pointedly asked, 'And if a terrible calamity befell both Franz Joseph and little Rudolph, how could you possibly be emperor of both Mexico and Austria?'

"Maxl struggled to keep his God-given birthright, but could not resist the two of them. He finally acquiesced to their pressure and signed the 'Act of Renunciation', giving up all rights of his succession to the Austrian throne. My poor husband might have withstood his brother, but he was no match for his thorny mother. Maxl's gentleness is inherited from his kindly father; Franz Joseph's gritty character stamps him as his mother's son.

"It was a bitter pill for both of us, but as Maxl reasoned later, we have the unique opportunity to build our own destiny in the new world, a land devoid of the restraints and inhibiting traditions of an aging continent.

"After three uncomfortable days, we left Schoenbrun and returned to Miramar to make ready for our voyage. The arrangements completed, we boarded the Novara and sailed to Rome to ask the blessing of the Holy Father. Our visit there proved to be almost as unpleasant as Vienna.

"Immediately on our arrival, His Holiness insisted that my Maxl assure him that all church property previously confiscated by the Mexican Government be returned to the church at once. Maximilian promised the Holy Father he would consider his suggestion, but could not make any decisions until he personally examined the situation in Mexico. The Pope and his Cardinals argued their position, quoting the anathemas which His Holiness had heaped upon Benito Juarez when he stripped the church of its properties. But, my gentle Maxl somehow found the strength to stand his ground.

"When our audience came to an end, Pope Pius begrudgingly gave us his blessing. As we parted, he insisted once again that Maxl give his request immediate attention.

"On May twenty-eighth, after six weary weeks at sea, our ship finally reached the port of Vera Cruz. Many of our older retainers, those who have been with us since Lombardy, wept, but this time, my dear parents, they wept for joy!

"Our arrival date seemed to be unknown to the local authorities for there was no one awaiting us there. We thought it extremely strange that no one in an official capacity was at the dock to receive us. I have since surmised that the absence of a reception was an intentional rebuff encouraged by those who oppose our rule.

"We boarded a small train which took us away from the

hot steamy coast and ascended a great plateau. Our first stop was the dusty town of Solitude. There, a messenger from Benito Juarez had left a disquieting personal note for Maxl. It read, in part, '...when a man attacks the rights of others, seizes their goods, assaults those who try to defend their country, makes their virtues a crime and makes his own crimes a virtue...he will reap the judgment of history.'

"This was our first indication that Maxl is looked upon by a few as Juarez's usurper and Mexico's enemy! On questioning the local officials, we were shocked to learn that the plebiscite which had requested Maximilian as emperor did not involve all of the people. The town officials of Solitude said they were not aware such an election had taken place! We suddenly realized we had been falsely led to believe the Mexican populace had truly elected Maximilian. But, what were we to do? The world knew we had accepted the throne. I told Maxl that I was unwilling to return to Europe and face ridicule. I would never go through an embarrassment like Lombardy and Venice again!

"We boarded the waiting train and traveled to the end of the line at Tomalto. From there our transport changed to large coaches pulled by sure-footed mules. The road, which took us through canyons, forests, jungles, and along high ridges, was so primitive that several of our coach wheels splintered on jagged rocks and bogged down in the ruts of muddy roadbeds. I must admit I had several anxious moments, especially when one of the carriages overturned. Fortunately, no one in our party was seriously injured.

"At noon, on the seventh day of June, my twenty-fourth birthday, the entire entourage mounted horses to cross the high Cordilleras.

"When we reached the French garrison at La Puebla de los Angeles, we received our first official welcome. Before our arrival, people had traveled there from Mexico City to bedeck the entire town with fresh flowers and colorful bunting. As we entered the town gates, cheers of *'Viva Napoléon, Viva el Emperador Maximiliano'* greeted us. After the problems and disappointments we had encountered since arriving in this land, their enthusiasm enveloped us in a wonderful feeling of euphoria.

"Reluctantly taking leave of La Puebla, our flower-bedecked carriages took us to Guadalupe where we attended High Mass in the Church of the Miraculous Image of the Virgin of Guadalupe. As we emerged from the basilica, we were delighted to see a large cluster of carriages filled with elegantly dressed Europeans and Mexicans who had arrived and were waiting to escort us in a triumphal procession to the main plaza of Mexico City. There, on the steps of the Great Cathedral, with the acclamation of the crowd ringing in our ears, we were given our crowns.

"Maxl has decided to make Chapultepec, the summer castle, our permanent residence. Unfortunately, it has sat unoccupied for many years and is in a shocking state of disrepair.

"Presently, our most pressing concern is Benito Juarez and several other recalcitrants who are attempting to set the populace against us. But, that is a temporary problem we will quickly resolve. General Bazaine and Colonel Dupin have assured us they'll soon have the few rebels in hand.

"You will be pleased to learn that we have adopted a young child, Augustin, the grandson of Iturbide, a former emperor of Mexico, as the heir to our throne. Since we have no children of our own, Maximilian thought it proper to select a child of Mexico to assume the empire as our heir. I've enclosed a small painting on ivory of your new grandson, Augustin, in this letter.

"With God's help, we pray we will one day lift our new empire to an important position in the family of nations. Maxl says, 'Like the phoenix, Mexico will rise out of the ashes of poverty and ignorance to become a shining example for the entire world.'

"My dear parents, you are constantly in my thoughts. I pray nightly for your continued health and happiness. My heart aches to see you. I yearn for the day when my arms may once again embrace you. I humbly ask for your prayers that Maximilian and I may rule this new land with wisdom and strength.

"Please give our love to my beloved brothers, Leopold and Philippe. I kiss each of you, your loving Charlotte."

As Carlota wrote, others neglected the eighteenth-century castle for many years; the military used it for a time as a barracks and a stable. While Carlota and Maximilian resided in temporary quarters, artisans quickly gathered from around the world to restore Chapultepec into a residence worthy of an emperor. The fine new marble they installed throughout, the newly chandeliered magnificence of the rooms, the ornate salons and the imported furnishings transformed the dilapidated structure into a palace to rival the opulence of the major palaces of Europe.

The Imperial couple thoroughly enjoyed their restored residence, often giving lavish state dinners and sparkling balls for the diplomatic corps, international emissaries, prominent Mexican officials and military officers of high rank, all accompanied by their finely dressed ladies. The formerly abandoned castle, at least for those who held positions of influence and power in Mexico, became a glittering, exciting European court. And to allay the uncertainty of the indigenous officials unfamiliar with European court etiquette, Emperor Maximilian himself carefully wrote a six hundred page guide detailing court protocol and ceremonial formalities.

4.

A royal courier from the French Imperial Court arrived at Chapultepec Castle in mid-March with dispatches for Maximilian and a large package for Carlota. The package, secured with seals bearing the embossment of Empress Eugenie, contained one large and seven small black lacquer boxes. Each box nested a paperweight wrapped in fine silk and tied with a golden cord. When Carlota unwrapped the contents of the first box, her curiosity was well rewarded.

"Look, Maxl! It's a paperweight with a cameo of Czar Nicholas!" The next two boxes contained sulphide cameos of Pope Pius IX and her father, King Leopold.

"Here is His Holiness—and look, look—here is one of my father!"

Quickly opening another box, she excitedly said, "Oh, look at this; it's a double portrait of Cousin Victoria and Albert! They're both on a single cameo; Prince Albert's profile shows just behind hers. It's so beautiful! How she must miss him."

Remembering the deep sadness in Queen Victoria's eyes and the long uneasy silences when they sat with her, he said, "She still keeps closeted away from her people." Putting down the dispatches, he added, "I felt so sorry for her when we visited her in Windsor. How long has it been now—Albert died of typhoid the winter of '61—over three years ago. I don't think she'll ever—"

"Oh, look, Maxl," Carlota exclaimed, "a butterfly!"

Taking the paperweight from her outstretched hand,

Maximilian marveled at the brilliantly colored wings of the insect frozen in flight inside the paperweight's exact center. Unable to classify it under any of the known lepidopterous groups he knew, he said, more to himself than to his wife, "The maker of this fanciful butterfly could teach the creator a lesson or two." Turning to Carlota, he asked, "May I have it for my desk, Carlota?"

But she did not acknowledge his request, for at that very moment she had just unwrapped the *"piece-de-resistance,"* the exquisite second Imperial Paperweight. "Oh, how beautiful! What a lovely shade of green! Look, Maxl, it's faceted exactly like my purple one. It's as beautiful as the first. What a wonderful addition to my collection!" As she carefully studied her profile in the paperweight, Maximilian put down the butterfly paperweight and opened the last two boxes. Both contained flowers: one centered with fuchsia blossoms hanging from an orange branch, and the other, a fluffy white pompon placed over a curving pink lattice background. Maximilian discovered a brief note from Eugenie in the bottom of the package and gave it to Carlota.

"My Dear Carlota," it read, "with the exception of the beautiful green paperweight, which captures the exact hue of your dark green eyes, all of these paperweights were made a generation ago. Because they are so elusive today, I sent word to my favorite antiquarian dealer and asked him to search for paperweights with cameo sulphides of important personages. As you can see, he did not disappoint me. I was especially delighted that he found one with your father's profile.

"The butterfly is a gift for Maximilian. I remember his special interest in those insects. The two flowers are from my own collection; I send them to you with my love.

"I wish you to know, dear sister, that Louis and I include you and Maximilian in our daily prayers. The papal nuncio has told me that the Holy Father looks with extreme favor on your reign. I assured him that you and Maximilian deserve his prayers and support. You will not fail to do whatever is possible in matters concerning the church.

"Your sister, in God, Eugenie"

Carlota handed the note to her husband. As he read the final paragraph, he recalled his uncomfortable audience with Pope Pius before sailing for Mexico. He perceived Eugenie's last paragraph as a veiled reminder to return the confiscated Mexican properties to the church, an impossible request for him to act on, especially during these troubled times. It would be strategically foolish for him to alienate those who presently benefited from the distribution of the church lands. He already had many enemies who were not of his own making—the followers of Juarez and other leaders who openly rejected his empire.

Benito Juarez, who fled Mexico City on Maximilian's arrival, denounced Maximilian as his usurper and declared himself the true President of the Republic. Before long, Juarez and other charismatic Mexican leaders organized small, ill-equipped guerrilla bands in the countryside for the purpose of expelling the "unwanted Europeans" from their land. The revolutionary leaders attracted recruits slowly at first, but as partisans met with successes in minor skirmishes, increasing numbers of volunteers joined their ranks.

Maximilian, growing apprehensive about the mounting unrest in his empire, attempted to eliminate the resistance to his regime by offering Juarez a cabinet post in the government. When Carlota questioned Maximilian about his curious offer, he explained, "My dear, Benito Juarez was once a poor Zapotec Indian who ran away from home when he was a child. Before our investiture here, this self-educated man rose through the legal system of Mexico to become its Chief Justice, and eventually its President. Think of the achievement—a poor uneducated Indian waif rising to the Presidency of a nation! I'm convinced, all indications to the contrary, he truly believes his opposition to our regime is for the good of the country. Gaining his support would be a decided asset to our rule."

To Maximilian's disappointment, Juarez refused the appointment.

Carlota did not share her husband's high opinion of Juarez; she saw him as a troublesome peasant. She disliked him intensely, telling Maximilian, "I mistrust that round-faced pagan. In letters to her parents, she described Benito Juarez as, "brooding, dour and dark." In one of her letters she wrote, "I've been told that he always smells of stale sweat."

To the consternation of Maximilian's generals, their efforts to eradicate the insurgents proved ineffective. General Bazaine eventually approached Maximilian with what he felt to be the perfect solution to the growing insurgency. He suggested that a proclamation be issued declaring that all captured guerrillas be classified as bandits rather than combatants. The chief-of-staff explained, "As captured soldiers, the revolutionaries are prisoners of war and cannot be dealt with harshly. But, if categorized as bandits, they can be put to death." Bazaine was certain his proposal would stem the alarming growth of the revolutionary forces and help bring about the much desired pacification of the nation.

Maximilian resisted what he felt to be an unconscionable suggestion, but Bazaine's persuasive arguments and the growing opposition to the empire weakened his resolve. On October 3, 1865, the emperor issued Bazaine's proclamation. It stated, in part, "...criminals who are members of armed bands and unauthorized societies...shall be tried by a military court and, if found guilty of such membership, shall be...executed within twenty-four hours after passing of sentence..."

Many captured soldiers were executed, including General Arteaga, Commander-in-Chief of Juarez's Army. To Maximilian's dismay, the barbarous decree, derisively named "The Black Decree" by his enemies, produced results opposite to those originally intended. The cold-blooded murder of captured soldiers created hundreds of martyrs for the revolution and proved to be a catalyst for the guerrilla cause. Within six months of "The Black Decree" the small rebellious bands had swollen into large armies of avenging volunteers.

5.

MEXICO CITY-1866

The communiqué Maximilian read dropped out of his hands onto the desk. "My God! I can't believe this!"

"What is it, Maxl?" Carlota asked, anxiously.

"How can he do this to us?" said Maximilian, shaking his head in disbelief.

"What is it?" she asked as she picked up the paper. "What does it say?"

"Read it for yourself." Maximilian said, cradling his head in his hands and sinking into a chair.

The shattering communiqué from Louis Napoléon advised Maximilian to redouble his enlistment of Mexican recruits because he intended to recall his thirty thousand French soldiers from Mexico, in the near future. "I don't understand," said Carlota. "We have written assurances of his continued support. This must be a mistake!"

"It's no mistake. Look at his signature, there above the seal."

The French emperor had not made his decision easily. He

was painfully aware he was breaking his covenant with Maximilian. But, Louis Napoléon faced a two-pronged problem. The United States, its Civil War at an end, demanded that the Monroe Doctrine be honored. In a show of determination, President Johnson began to move army units to the Mexican-American border. The American insistence convinced Louis Napoléon his ambitions for Mexico had passed their time. In addition to the American pressure, the growing Prussian divisions on France's borders made the return of Napoléon's troops an urgent necessity.

Maximilian agonized over the potential loss of the well-disciplined French troops. He knew that the balance of military power would inexorably shift to the rebels when Napoléon's combatants embarked for France. Faced with that dilemma, Maximilian began to explore the idea of abdicating in favor of his adopted son, Augustin. If the child, the grandson of former Mexican Emperor Iturbide, would be acceptable to both sides as a successor to the throne, Maximilian speculated that Augustin's enthronement might bring about a rapprochement of the various factions and end the war, as well as preserve the empire. He could offer to act as regent until the child reached the age of majority.

When he shared his thoughts of abdication with Carlota, she flew into a rage, screaming, "You will not give up our empire! I won't face the humiliation of being deposed a second time? Maximilian, for God's sake, don't panic! Call on the strength of your Hapsburg blood! Steel your will and act as an emperor should!"

Later, after she regained her composure, she attempted to convince Maximilian that all was not lost; they would win out over their enemies. "Look to your maps, Maxl. Juarez's rabble hold only uninhabited lands to the north; our own loyal troops are in complete control of the seaports, most of the major cities and here in the capital. The resistance will dissipate as soon as its misguided followers realize the benefits they shall gain through the benevolence of our rule!"

"Carlota, that pacification requires the luxury of time, and time is a commodity which we no longer have—especially now that Emperor Napoléon plans to recall his troops."

The following morning Carlota declared her intention to sail to Europe. She intended to reverse Louis Napoléon's decision.

"Carlota, my dear," Maximilian asked, "how can you think of going to Europe? You didn't attend the coronation of your brother after your father's death. It makes no sense!"

"I was needed here, at the time. My family is well aware of my love for my father and my brother. They'll understand."

Try as he might, Maximilian could not dissuade Carlota from her resolve; she was firmly convinced her efforts would preserve their empire.

As her ladies-in-waiting undertook the necessary preparations for the long journey, Carlota chose several personal mementos of her husband and adopted son to take with her. At first, she selected both of the Imperial paperweights. Later, she decided to take the purple one, telling Maximilian, "I'll leave the green paperweight here with you as a remembrance of me until I return."

She also took a newly minted gold coin struck with a likeness of her husband. After completing her business with Louis Napoléon, she planned to visit the Saint Louis Company and commission its director to use Maximilian's profile on the coin to create one-hundred sulphide paperweights as fitting gifts for those who perform outstanding service to the realm.

Before boarding the ship at Vera Cruz, Carlota confidently assured her husband, "I'll not fail our empire. After all," she reasoned, "it was Louis Napoléon who placed us on the throne. He cannot in good conscience strip us of the support he promised. He has no other recourse than to reverse his absurd decision!"

"Carlota, I wish you wouldn't go."

"I'll be back in less than four months."

Empress Carlota boarded the ship with the self-assurance she always exhibited at public functions. As the ship left the dock, she stood next to the ship's rail waving her lace handkerchief at her husband until the diminishing figures of the well-wishers on the dock finally became indistinguishable from one another. She then turned her gaze on the long stretch of ocean that lay ahead, determined to return with the answer their empire needed so desperately. She was confident she would set all matters right.

Carlota hadn't discussed with Maximilian what she would say to Louis Napoléon. She gave little thought to the line of reasoning she would use when she met with the French emperor. Whenever thoughts of the impending meeting crossed her mind during the long voyage, they invariably wandered to the gowns and jewelry that her ladies had included for her stay in Paris.

Louis Napoléon fully expected Maximilian to object to the recall of his French troops from Mexico. He was painfully aware that his decision would make Maximilian's position untenable. But, he also assumed that Maximilian's personal involvement in the daily struggle against the Mexican insurgents would prevent a face-to-face confrontation with the young monarch. He thought Maximilian's protests would arrive in official communiqués or through talks on a ministerial level. When the newly laid transatlantic cable brought him word that Carlota might travel to Paris to question his decision, he confided to Eugenie that he would much rather face

Maximilian than Carlota. He never imagined that Carlota would undertake the long voyage to face him personally. Later, when a cable advised him that Carlota had embarked for Europe, the French emperor confessed to his wife that their approaching encounter troubled him greatly.

6.

When she arrived at the Tuileries, Carlota's self assurance was slightly shaken; Louis Napoléon did not personally appear to receive her. After palace attendants showed Carlotta to her rooms, Eugenie appeared, saying, "Carlota, dear, the emperor sends his regrets. He will try to arrange a time to receive you sometime tomorrow afternoon."

"I must talk to him as soon as possible, Eugenie. What I have to discuss is of the utmost importance. I wouldn't have made the trip across the ocean if it were not so."

"We'll let you know when the emperor is free."

During their brief encounter, Carlota felt that Eugenie acted overly formal and distant. Had she mistakenly imagined Eugenie's coolness toward her? Their short visit left Carlota unsettled.

That night in bed proved to be a fitful one for the young empress. Her mind ferreted out certain disturbing connections, a half-hidden design—patterns hinted at an orchestrated series of events that had lately disarranged her life. As the night deepened, small waves of panic caused her breath to catch and nervously flutter. The few times that she momentarily lapsed into a half-sleep, she awoke with a start and wished for an end to the long night.

In the early light of the new day, her nagging demons faded. The morning with its yellow brightness, the cheerful opulence of her rooms and the excited bustle of her handmaidens, all combined to crowd the previous night's ferment out of her consciousness. Later that morning, a lady-in-waiting appeared at her apartment to leave word that the emperor and empress scheduled an appointment to see Carlota in the early afternoon.

As Carlota anticipated a formal audience with the emperor, her spirits rose. After much deliberation she chose a gown of soft ivory chantilly and jewelry of deep green emeralds and flashing diamonds. She took great pleasure admiring her reflected image in the mirrored boudoir as her handmaidens deftly clothed her. Each additional piece of luxurious raiment strengthened her resolve for the task she was about to undertake.

To Carlota's disappointment, the emperor and empress received her privately in the Imperial apartments, not in an audience of state. Several of the emperor's advisors accompanied Louis and Eugenie, who embraced Carlota and invited her to be seated opposite them on a divan.

Louis began, saying, "My dear Carlota, I regret that I was unable to receive you yesterday; urgent matters of state kept me occupied until late into the evening. Eugenie and I are grateful that God has granted you safe passage and brought you to us. We are most pleased to see you once again."

"Maximilian sends his greetings and pledges his undying fidelity, your Imperial Highness."

"And how did you find your long voyage?" he asked.

Anxious to attack the problem, she replied, "It was pleasant enough, but every day at sea seemed an eternity. Now that my journey has finally come to an end, I must speak to you about our most pressing concern."

Sensing an impending confrontation, Eugenie quickly entered the conversation, saying, "Carlota, my dear, Louis has just received extremely favorable cable dispatches from Mexico. General Miramon has taken the stronghold at Zacatecas and almost captured that rebel, Juarez!"

"That is precisely why I am here, Eugenie. With the continued help of the French troops, the rebellion will soon collapse and the country will be at peace."

Carefully emphasizing every word, Napoléon said, "Carlota, Prussia is an ever-growing menace to us. It is no secret that Bismarck intends to unite all the states of Germany. He routed Denmark, and in seven weeks, defeated the armies of your brother-in-law, Franz Joseph. Unfortunately, I unwisely assumed the role of a detached observer during those conflicts. Hindsight now tells me that I should have joined forces with Denmark and Austria; together we would have laid Bismarck's ambitions to rest. Now, France is the only obstacle to the Prussian's plan to dominate the entire continent. As much as I want to continue to help Mexico, my priorities must, of necessity, be for France. With such danger at our doorstep, we can no longer allow our soldiers to remain scattered throughout the world. Our armies must return to us, and without delay."

To her horror, Carlota realized her mission was doomed. A roaring in her ears drowned out the emperor's voice. His lips continued to move but she did not hear his words. She and Maximilian were to be abandoned! As she sat immobile, the color drained from her face, she felt faint. Suddenly, Carlota's clasped hands left her lap, her fingers entangled in a Gordian knot. One finger explosively freed itself and pointed at the emperor. Wild eyed, she hissed, "Oh, my God, Eugenie! Make him change his mind! Maximilian can't be cut off! Don't let him forsake us! What have we done to deserve such monstrous treatment?" Turning to Louis Napoléon, she insisted, "We have your word in documents, in written promises. You have no choice but to honor your pledges to us!"

The emperor raised both hands in an effort to shut out her words, all the while shaking his head in silent refusal.

Her heart pounded in her chest as if it would explode. She shouted, "You won't, you won't! Oh, you charlatan, you hypocrite! I should have known you'd turn on us again. What, after all, could we expect from a Bonaparte! You deceitful tyrant!"

Carlota's hands flew to her throat. Her eyes glared at Louis Napoléon, who by now was visibly shaken. Eugenie nervously motioned Napoléon's startled advisors to leave the room. As the door closed behind them, Carlota collapsed to the floor. Louis Napoléon stood quickly, and hurried to help the prostrate woman who appeared to have fainted. As he approached her, her arms shot out and clutched at his legs. Emotionally caught up in her agony, the emperor turned to his wife, silently appealing for help. Eugenie knelt beside Carlota and unlocked the young woman's arms from around Louis Napoléon's legs. Freed from her grasp, the emperor hurried out of the room.

Although no one informed the members of Carlota's entourage Louis Napoléon denied her request, they guessed his answer when they saw Carlota helped to her rooms by the French empress and members of the court.

That evening, Carlota refused to take any sustenance. She demanded that her ladies-in-waiting occupy the rooms adjoining her apartment, and charged them to stay awake and to remain vigilant throughout the night. Her concerned physician persuaded her to take a sedative powder with tea, but she failed to keep the concoction down.

All of the premonitions and doubts Carlota experienced the night before were but a quiet prologue to this night. Waves of suspicion, fear and hate convulsed her. Leaving her bed, she sat at a desk, and later, after many attempts, finally gained a semblance of control over her emotions. Alone in the black void, her nebulous suspicions of the previous night assembled into a definite form. Recalling the many distressful events that occurred since her marriage to Maximilian, she physically recoiled at the conclusions that emerged from her anguished mind.

"It is Louis Napoléon who has been at the vortex of all our grief," she said aloud. "He has manipulated our lives over the years! He defeated Franz Joseph at Solferino so that we would be cast out of Lombardy and Venice—he created a doomed empire for us thousands of miles away from our family and friends. And, yes, it was Louis Napoléon who engineered that fraudulent Mexican election—he tricked us into going to that hateful country. His treachery has even lost us the succession to the Austrian throne! And now he is recalling his French troops! After all his promises, he is withdrawing his help from us at the time of our most desperate need. Why? Why? And Eugenie, that Janus-faced liar who feigned love for me, calling me her 'dear little sister', I see through her treacherous scheming! Oh yes, I hear them. Listen, they mean to do me harm! I will leave this place before they imprison me, or worse yet, attempt to take my life! Oh, that tea I had last night—it must have been poisoned! That's why my body rejected it! I must keep my wits about me and refuse any food they serve me. It may be poisoned. Calm, calm, they must not know that I've detected their monstrous plot. Do I hear them conspiring against me, or is it the leaves rustling in the night wind? I'll go to Rome at once! I'll not stay here another day! I'll leave in the morning; I'll escape from them! Sanctuary, sanctuary, sanctuary!"

At daybreak, Carlota summoned Señora del Barrio, her chief lady-in-waiting. "Señora, inform the emperor's people that we are leaving for Rome this morning."

"Today? But, my lady, we are not scheduled to leave for Rome for three days."

"I've changed my mind! Do as I say! Tell my wardrobe mistress to begin preparations for our departure, at once!"

At Carlota's insistence, her domestics and Napoléon's startled court officials made hurried preparations for the immediate departure of her entourage. As Carlota paced aimlessly about her rooms, her handmaidens busied themselves with their duties, strategically working within protective distance of Carlota as they completed the final details of the journey. Her agitation and pallor did not concern them as much as her strange ramblings of that morning. In the years they served her, and especially at times of great stress, her orderly mind always exhibited an unwavering sense of purpose. This morning they served a confused wild-eyed empress.

Empress Eugenie made several overtures through her ladies-in-waiting to see Carlota, but attendants informed her each time, that her "little sister" was indisposed.

Finally, Carlota's servitors brought word that they completed arrangements for royal coaches to convey her and her party from the Tuileries to an early afternoon train bound for Rome. During the strained farewells, Carlota's entourage noticed the emperor's downcast eyes, Eugenie's overly solicitous concern and their own empress's tense demeanor.

As Carlota boarded the train, she crossed herself and gave thanks for quitting an unholy place. If she remained, she would certainly come to harm. She alarmed Señora del Barrio when she said, "With God's help we have escaped the evil that surrounded us in Louis Napoléon's Court."

"What evil, my Lady?"

"Our very lives were in jeopardy there! Surely you felt the danger! I thank God we are on our way to sanctuary and into the protective arms of the Holy Father."

As the train carried Carlota toward the "safety" of the Vatican she asked Madam del Barrio for the Imperial paperweight. Rocking back and forth, Carlota cradled it in her hand for hours at a time, quietly speaking to her husband's image, "...no, don't worry, Maxl, my dear, they'll not harm me, I've escaped Napoléon's Tuileries. Yes, I know. I see through their treacherous masquerade. I'm too cunning for them. Their evil thoughts come to me like sudden flashes of lightning. What? Yes, yes, I understand. I'll be extremely careful, my dear husband. Don't fret about that devil, Napoléon. Soft, soft, my dear, they'll hear you. Yes, I've seen his agents. When the train stops, more and more of them slither aboard."

In Carlota's crumbling mind, passengers boarding the train at various stops were Napoléon's secret agents. And once aboard, those supposed agents quickly metamorphosed into demons. In her fright, she clutched her jeweled cross in one hand and her paperweight in the other; God and Maximilian would protect her from Napoléon's forces of darkness.

Later, when she was brought food, Carlota looked at it knowingly, and refused 'Napoléon's poisoned plates.' "Maxl, they are trying to poison me again! Help me, for God's sake, please Maxl, please! The food? Yes, I can see the poison in the food. Shhh, hush, quiet, my dear, they'll hear you!"

7.

As the Mexican delegation made its way to Rome, the staff of the Grand Hotel, apprised of the changed arrival date, scrambled feverishly to prepare accommodations for Carlota's entourage.

The day following Carlota's arrival in Rome, Cardinal

Antonelli, the Pope's emissary, appeared at her apartments. The members of her entourage were dismayed as the Cardinal expounded an entire hour on Maximilian's acts of omission. He especially stressed the Vatican's disappointment that the emperor had not yet restored the confiscated properties to the Church. Asked when Pope Pius would receive Empress Carlota, Antonelli curtly announced, "An interview with his Holiness will not be granted to anyone in this delegation." For three days, Carlota's ministers and the Mexican Ambassador attempted, without success, to obtain an audience with the Pope. Frustrated, the Mexican delegation turned to Austria's ambassador for help; he interceded and obtained an audience for his emperor's sister-in-law.

On the appointed morning, a guide escorted Carlota, veiled and attired in black, to the Vatican throne room. She began quietly, "Holy Father, I'm not here to request money or soldiers of the Vatican States. Nor am I here to attempt to arrive at a concordant with you, although such an accord with the church would win us the support that our reign has never fully enjoyed. I am here only to ask you to use your holy office to persuade Emperor Louis Napoléon to honor the many pledges he made to my husband."

As she told him of Napoléon's intention to recall French troops from Mexico, the blood drained from her face. Señora del Barrio, concerned, stepped to her side to offer support. When Pope Pius realized that Carlota's request would exact no concessions from the Vatican, he chose to continue their discourse in private. Unknown to the Cardinals, the Louis Napoléon advised the Pope that the French troops would soon be recalled from the Vatican States. Without the support of the French army, Pope Pius was in danger of losing the Papal States to the kingdom of Italy.

He waved off his Cardinals and Carlota's advisors and escorted the empress to an adjoining room. The moment they were alone, she fell to the floor sobbing, "Holy Father, I'm so frightened! Louis Napoléon and Eugenie are trying to poison me!"

"What are you saying, my daughter?"

In her panic, she told him that everyone around her was a sinister threat. "Even some of my own entourage are agents of the French emperor. My doctor is giving me venom instead of proper medication—my hairdresser is setting my hair with pins dipped in poison. My ladies-in-waiting report my every move to Napoléon's agents!" Dabbing at her eyes, she whispered, "Only Señora del Barrio can be trusted."

Realizing Carlota was undergoing a mental collapse, the Pontiff summoned Señora del Barrio and advised her to take her mistress back to the Grand Hotel.

The following day, Carlota returned to the Vatican, brushed past Swiss guards and objecting prelates, and made her way into the Pope's private apartments. Once there, she whispered to him that Louis Napoléon's murderous agents hid behind every door in her hotel. They even attempted to invade her suite. To his astonishment, she insisted she be granted permanent sanctuary in the Vatican. The Pope told her that centuries of tradition forbid women to receive the hospitality of the Vatican overnight. But it made no impression on her. No amount of persuasion would make her change her mind. She refused to leave. That evening, the Holy Father at an impasse, relented and instructed an incredulous papal housekeeper to set up two simple cots and two candelabra in an isolated hallway for Carlota and her lady-in-waiting. As Carlota fitfully slept, Señora del Barrio kept a watchful eye over her throughout the night.

The next morning, Pope Pius summoned Señora del

Barrio and demanded that she escort her mistress back to her hotel.

She said apologetically, "Your Holiness, I suspect that my lady's distress has temporarily unbalanced her reason."

"No, madam, it is much worse," he replied gravely. "It is madness, complete madness."

The Pope denied Carlota's tearful pleas to remain forever within the safety of the Vatican. That afternoon she returned to the Grand Hotel and locked herself in her rooms, refusing admittance to everyone but Señora del Barrio. When the servants at the hotel took food to her, she refused to eat until her faithful companion sampled it.

Maximilian, informed of Carlota's condition, cabled instructions to Belgium and Rome that his wife be given over to her older brother, King Leopold II, until he could sail from Mexico to be at her side. Leopold sent Crown Prince Philippe, his younger brother, to take charge of their ailing sister. A week after his arrival in Rome, the prince took Carlota to Trieste, hoping that Miramar, so intimate and familiar to her, might bring his sister's mind back to reality. Carlota recognized her surroundings, but her paranoia did not improve. Under the watchful eye of her grieving attendants, she wandered aimlessly from room to room.

A specialist, called in from Vienna to diagnose and treat her condition, declared her incurably insane at the end of a week's observation.

8.

Late one evening, after retiring to her bed, furtive knocking on her door awakened Señora del Barrio. Opening the door, she saw two of Carlota's young handmaidens wide-eyed and agitated. "Yes Beatrix, Victoria, what is it?"

"Oh, madam, we're so afraid that our lady will hurt herself."

"The empress! In heaven's name, have you left her unattended?"

"Oh no, she's not alone, madam. Jennine is with her."

"Come inside while I get my dressing gown and slippers."

As the two frightened girls hesitantly stepped inside her waiting room, each attempting to shield herself behind the other, the Señora hurried to her dressing room.

"What is the problem, girls?" she anxiously called through the open door. Receiving no reply, she hurried to the waiting room and demanded, "Victoria, speak up!"

"Oh, madam, I don't know how to say it."

The older woman turned her attention to Beatrix, but the younger girl, sobbing, squeezed behind Victoria. Quickly buttoning her dressing gown, the Señora ordered, "If you're both so mute you can't talk, at least take me to the problem!"

Victoria quickly led the way with sobbing Beatrix scurrying, half-crouched, just behind her.

"The empress is in there," said Victoria, pointing at Carlota's bedchamber door.

"Lead the way, Victoria!"

"Oh no, I can't. Please go in, go and see for yourself, madam."

Señora del Barrio, by now extremely concerned, blurted out, "What is it, in heaven's name?"

She hurried past the two handmaidens and pushed the door open. Quickly glancing about as she entered the dark room, she saw Jennine pressed into a far corner of the bedroom, her hand covering her mouth and her eyes riveted on Carlota's bed. Madam del Barrio, seeing for herself what had frightened the three handmaidens, compassionately understood what the others were unable to fathom.

"Jennine," she commanded, "go find Victoria and Beatrix at once! You three wait for me in the hallway. Warn them they are sworn to secrecy on this matter. You are to keep your mouths shut! Remember, you three are all answerable to me!"

"Yes, my lady," answered Jennine, hurrying out of the bedroom.

Soon after Jennine left, a sudden loud knocking at the bedroom door startled the Señora. Opening the door slightly, she was surprised to see the young prince, ashen-faced, framed in the opening.

"What has happened to my sister?"

"Nothing, your Highness. She is in her bed."

"Then why are her handmaidens so distressed out here?"

Attempting to explain as delicately as possible, she answered, "My Prince, the empress is making love with Emperor Maximilian's profile in the Imperial paperweight."

"I don't understand, madam, exactly what do you mean?"

"Oh, dear Mother of God," she thought, "he does not understand what I'm saying. How can I explain it to him? He's so young."

"Well, madam?"

"With your permission, your Highness, I'll confer with the physician when he arrives tomorrow and he can discuss the matter with you, privately."

"Must I remind you that she is my sister, madam! I insist that you tell me now!"

Resigned that there was no other way, she stepped back from the doorway, saying, "Your Highness, please enter my Lady's bedroom and see for yourself."

As he stepped into the darkened bedroom he heard his sister softly murmuring, "Maxl—my love—be gentle with me, please. Oh, my dear—Maxl—Maxl…"

Moving closer to the bed, his eyes gradually adjusting to the dim light, he saw his sister lying in bed, naked, massaging the Imperial paperweight over her entire body.

"My God!" he whispered. For the first time, he realized the extent of her madness.

Turning his face away from the bed he said, almost inaudibly, "Madam, please leave us."

Señora del Barrio stationed herself outside the bedroom door, motioned the three confused handmaidens away and waited for the Prince. After a short time, the door to Carlota's bedroom slowly opened. He stood in the doorway visibly shaken. She waited a few moments and then approached the young man.

Momentarily losing his composure, he asked in a broken voice, "And what will all of you think of my poor sister now?"

Touching his sleeve, she reassuringly replied, "Your Highness, we all love the empress. We are aware of how terribly ill she is. And as to her handmaidens, please be assured that they are loyal and sworn to secrecy."

He stood unmoving, his eyes closed.

She continued, "Your Royal Highness, forgive me for what I am about to say. I speak from the perspective of an older woman, and out of my deep love for your sister. My Prince, what you have witnessed is not shameful; there is no need for embarrassment. Your beloved sister sees us not, nor is she aware of what she is doing. She is in her own private world. In her mind, she is making love to her dear husband."

After a few moments of silence, the young Prince, looking into the older woman's tear-filled eyes, said gratefully, "Thank you, dear Lady."

9.

As Maximilian made final arrangements to sail to Europe to be at Carlota's side, a courier who had arrived on an Austrian ship gave Maximilian a letter from Archduchess Sophie, his mother. Strangely, she wrote nothing about Carlota's condition. Rather, the Archduchess was disturbed that all of Europe was rife with rumors of his possible abdication. She wrote, "I forbid you to leave Mexico. I would rather see you dead than return to the Continent as a piece of fleeing French baggage."

In addition to the harsh admonition from his mother, Mexican monarchists and conservatives besieged Maximilian with begging appeals to remain in Mexico. They feared that the empire would fall if he left the country. With its collapse, they risked their influence, their fortunes and their lives. Torn between going to Carlota or remaining in Mexico, Maximilian acceded to his mother's wishes and to the persuasive pleas of those around him and reluctantly abandoned his plans to sail to Europe.

The world witnessed a remarkable celestial occurrence on November 14, 1866, when thousands upon thousands of bright meteors showered down from the heavens. The Leonide shower of meteors occurs annually on the night of November 14th, but the astronomical phenomenon displayed an unexpected intensity that night. Maximilian, who observed the spectacular occurrence, rejoiced. He took it as a propitious omen.

When Maximilian was just one year old, the royal physicians told his parents that because of his failing health, he would not survive the winter. A month later, on November 14, 1833, the night skies swarmed with thousands of falling meteors. The frightened multitudes who had never before witnessed such an awesome display of shooting stars, feared that it portended the end of the world. But to Archduchess Sophie, who watched her sickly child grow stronger each day following the celestial phenomenon, falling stars became a lucky sign.

Watching the skies for an occasional streak of light became a favorite game for Maximilian's mother and her growing children. They believed that observing a streaking meteor during the evening brought good luck to the sharp-eyed youngsters.

That November night, alone in Mexico City, with his wife's illness and the unending war weighing heavily on his mind, Maximilian took heart from the falling meteors, hopeful that they signified a change in his fortunes. Gently cradling Carlota's Imperial paperweight in his hands, he said to her silvery image, "Carlota, my dear, you will soon be well. We shall win out over our enemies and put this wretched war to rest. I know it in my heart."

The following February, Maximilian, dissatisfied with the lack of progress against the insurgents, traveled to Queretaro to take personal command of an army of nine thousand loyal troops. Unfortunately, his own indecisiveness combined with rivalry among his generals resulted in a disaster; the entire army became trapped within the city. The constant shelling decimated Maximilian's army. As he personally surveyed Queretaro's defenses, he could see the mark of death on the frightened faces of his young soldiers protecting the city's walls. He visited the wounded who were lying on the floors and the rude beds of the make-shift dispensaries throughout the city. The resemblance of his men to the Austrian dead and dying at Solferino startled him. "My God," he thought, "it's happening again! The suffering and horrors are the same; only the uniforms are different. It's Solferino all over again."

After a siege of seventy-two days, Queretaro fell. The defenders capitulated.

During the last hours of the siege, Maximilian's generals, hoping he might avoid recognition and capture, urged him to put on a common soldier's uniform to conceal his identity.

"I don't think it's an honorable thing to do," Maximilian protested.

"Your highness, disguised as a common soldier, you might not be recognized by the enemy. With God's help, you may make your escape and return to the capital."

"How can I abandon my men here in Queretaro?"

"Without you, there is no empire, my emperor. You must make the attempt. You owe it to all of us who are loyal to you."

"Sometimes I wonder if I have anyone's support."

"You have the support of all of us here as well as those regiments in Mexico City. As long as you are free, there is still hope for the empire!"

Maximilian reluctantly donned the uniform, trimmed his beard, and slipped out of his command post.

Early the following morning, while the rebels searched the city for him, Maximilian concealed himself in the mass of captured soldiers herded into the main plaza of the city. Carefully studying the soldiers guarding the prisoners, he found several gaps in their security. Maximilian began to feel that his deception might work. Tonight, he thought, I'll elude my captors under cover of darkness and make my way back to Mexico City. My mission is God-given. I must preserve the empire.

As the rebels searched Maximilian's command post, an abandoned schoolhouse, a corporal spied the green Imperial Paperweight on a pile of dispatches and slipped it, unnoticed, into his shirt. Later that morning, as he showed his prize to his companions, his lieutenant took the paperweight from his hand, and asked, "Where did you get this, Armando?"

"I found it on the street today, Lieutenant. Those pictures inside look like important people."

"Those are the bastards, Carlota and *Maximiliano!*"

"They are?"

"Yes, you fool. Don't you even know what they look like?"

"No, Lieutenant," he replied, embarrassed. Like many volunteers, he came from an isolated village, hundreds of miles away from the events that occurred in Mexico City. Juarez appeared in his remote village one day to recruit him and other young volunteers to "rid our beloved country of the French and Austrian devils."

When the lieutenant left, the corporal's compatriots gathered around the paperweight to study Maximilian's profile. Some of them, like Corporal Armando, saw Maximilian's image for the first time.

Late that afternoon, when the Lieutenant's men took up guard duty in the plaza, one of the soldiers who had viewed the Imperial Paperweight noticed something familiar about one of the thousands of prisoners sitting on the ground.

He caught Corporal Armando's attention and beckoned him to come to his guard post. "That soldier sitting over there looks like that picture in your green glass, corporal."

"Which one?"

"That tall one, over there to the left; the one with the beard."

"Wait," the corporal said, reaching into his pocket for the paperweight. Looking at it and at the profile of the prisoner's face, he said, "Yes, I think you're right! Look at it and look at the side of his face. The beard is smaller, but it's him, alright. It's *Maximiliano!*"

Maximilian noticed the two soldiers looking in his direction, but thought nothing about it until he caught the glint of glass. "What does that soldier have in his hand?" he wondered. "It's green glass. It looks like—can it be Carlota's paperweight? My God, I think it is! How did he get it? Why is he staring at me?"

Corporal Armando pushed his way through the sitting prisoners and asked Maximilian to stand. "Let me see the side of your face, soldier," he ordered. Glancing up from the paperweight in his hand to Maximilian's profile, Armando asked, "You are *Maximiliano*, correct?"

"Yes, soldier," said Maximilian, resigned to his discovery, "I'm the one you seek."

As an armed guard led him away, "Maximilian thought, what an incredible irony of fate to be brought down by Carlota's beautiful paperweight—betrayed by an inanimate object, a piece of glass! That glass ball has struck the final blow to my struggling empire. A mere paperweight! Were that it had never been made!

Looking back at his "celestial prediction" of good fortune the previous November mildly amused Maximilian At a time of great stress he reverted to the superstitions of his childhood. "Imagine," he thought, "to be so naive as to attribute the success or failure of future events to a natural phenomenon, a shower of meteors. I respect science enough to know celestial phenomena cannot influence the course of our daily lives. Desperate times make children of us all."

As a defeated sovereign, Maximilian assumed he would be permitted to go into exile in accordance with the established European precedent. At least he would soon be at Carlota's side. He planned to nurse her back to health at Miramar. But, to his surprise, Juarez denied his request for permission to board a waiting Austrian ship. Instead he imprisoned Maximilian and his two generals, Maja and Miramon in the old abandoned Convent of the Capuchins.

In a vote of four to three, the seven military officers presiding over Maximilian's trial sentenced the fallen emperor and his two generals to death by firing squad. As word of his sentence spread throughout the world, Mexico received hundreds of communiqués from governments around the world requesting a commutation of Maximilian's death sentence. But Juarez remained adamant in his refusal to reverse the decision of the military tribunal. *Maximiliano* must be made to pay for The Black Decree.

Convinced that a reprieve was not in the offing, Maximilian accepted the reality of the court's sentence. In the quiet of the lonely nights, while he contemplated his approaching death, he wrote many letters of farewell to family and friends. In one he said, "How cruelly fate has pounded me blow after blow without letup. Disaster has followed my footsteps, destroying all my hopes. Death seems a happy solution. I shall go to my end as a soldier, a sovereign defeated, not dishonored."

On the morning of June 19, 1867, a beautiful sunrise mocked the day's approaching events. Drums and trumpet flourishes awakened the three prisoners. Puzzled at the unusual commotion so early in the morning, Maximilian asked his two generals if the trumpet and drums announced their execution. General Miramon reportedly replied, "I don't know my emperor; I've never been executed before."

10.

Father Soria, granted permission by the army tribunal to attend the three prisoners during their final moments, reported the details of their execution to his Bishop later that same day.

"I started out before daybreak so that I'd have enough time to celebrate Mass and hear the confessions of the prisoners. As my carriage approached the convent, I searched for the words which might offer some measure of solace to the condemned men. Soldiers stopped me at the iron gate and ordered me to wait until I was sent for. After hearing the sounds of drums and trumpets from inside the convent, they finally admitted me. The corridors were dark and damp, smelling of musty decay and littered with filth.

"I expected to face three mortal men frightened by the prospect of their impending death, but I found, instead, three brave men resigned to their inevitable fate who were prepared to 'walk through the valley of the shadow of death.' I was so emotionally overcome by their expressions of faith that I wept openly as I prayed with them. And then, my Bishop," he related incredulously, "Emperor Maximilian, facing death, embraced me, and Christ-like, offered me his consolation."

"The emperor was a man of understanding and compassion," said the Bishop. "But, I've interrupted you, Father, you've more to relate. Please continue."

"Your Excellency, as I accompanied the three prisoners to the Hill of the Bells, it took all of my will to force my shaking legs up that steep incline. The events that followed reminded me of an old *retablo* I once saw in a small church in Tepatitlan. It depicted the crucified Christ looking down from the cross, forgiving the Roman soldiers standing nearby with their hammers and lances in hand. That old icon was brought to life for me this morning on the hill of death. Emperor Maximilian, like our Lord, giving no thought to his own tragic end, offered his two generals solace, consoled me, his confessor, and forgave his executioners."

As he relived those painful moments, the priest bowed his head. Regaining his composure, he continued, "Before the fatal shots were fired, Emperor Maximilian gave each of the soldiers a gold coin and asked them to spare his face for a funeral of state. A compassionate human being to the last, the emperor yielded the center to General Miramon, knowing full well that a quick, almost painless death was assured to the one who stood in that position. One of the soldiers there told me that those on either side often suffer agonizing wounds until the *coup de grace* is mercifully administered. After all requests were granted and our prayers said, the emperor parted his tunic, and bared his chest. The fatal shots were fired. The generals died suddenly."

The Bishop crossed himself and was about to ask the priest to join him in prayer for the souls of the executed men when the priest began speaking again.

"The emperor, dreadfully wounded, fell to the ground, his body twitching spasmodically. I could hear him softly pleading, 'hombres, hombres...' The officer drew his pistol and fired the final bullet into the suffering emperor's heart."

His eyes welling with tears, the priest fell to his knees and clasped both hands around his crucifix, saying, "My Bishop, the dreadful truth is they martyred a Saint of the Church this morning."

The elderly Bishop, no stranger to death, realized that the young priest kneeling before him witnessed few violent deaths in his life. Father Soria's words reminded him of his own struggles with executions at the same tender age. Placing his hand on the priest's tonsured head, he said, "Father Soria, you've have had a draining experience, one which has cloaked your judgment. The emperor's death, though tragic, does not in any conceivable manner resemble our Lord's agony on the cross. Do not equate the death of a man who assumed high temporal powers with the divinity of the son of God. I'll excuse you now to pray for calm and illumination. When the balm of time has restored your reason, we will talk of these matters once again. Now, Father, rise up and go in peace."

As the young priest took his leave, the Bishop inwardly questioned the purpose of God's plan for Maximilian. "I had such high hopes for the church when he came to Mexico," he thought. "It's all so regrettable that the emperor and the nation had to endure so much suffering, especially since the end of Maximilian's ill-fated empire was ordained before its beginning."

Seven months after Maximilian's execution, the flinty Austrian Archduchess received the remains of her son. The mortician in Mexico took care during the embalming process to preserve Maximilian's corpse. Before shipping his body to Austria, he filled the empty sockets of his deteriorated eyes with glass eyes taken from a wooden statue of the Virgin. To his mother's satisfaction, he died the honorable death of a Hapsburg.

Learning of Maximilian's execution, King Leopold brought his sister back to Belgium. At the young age of twenty-seven, Carlota's rational life ended. Forever imprisoned within her confused mind, she never knew of Maximilian's death. She lived for another sixty years cloistered in the lakeside Bouchout Castle, constantly communing with the shadows that resided in her Imperial paperweight. Often, especially on warm sunny days when her attendants prepared her for an afternoon outing on the water, as they helped her into the boat, she whispered, "Today, my husband, we depart for Mexico."

No longer aware of the passage of time, she remained

eternally young inside, living her life with her beloved Maximilian in that encapsulated universe of crystal, the purple orb which rarely left her hand. In later years, she often asked her ladies-in-waiting the identity of the graying and wrinkled person who looked back at her from the mirrors of her boudoir.

"Cast them into the void of darkness... only death now, the bleak abyss of death..."

11.

When Sgt. Emilio and the other surviving Juaristas returned victorious from the war, Emilio presented the green Imperial paperweight to his wife, Paquita. He won the paperweight weeks earlier from Corporal Armando during a friendly barracks card game. Paquita never once betrayed her intense dislike of the green object to him, although she detested it. It contained the visages of *Maximiliano* and Carlota, whose French mercenaries killed and maimed so many men of the village. The ever-present widows in their black weeds constantly reminded her of the grief caused by the despised monarchs. However, she kept those feelings to herself and prominently displayed the paperweight in their adobe out of respectful regard for her husband's thoughtfulness.

Eleven short months after he returned from the wars, Emilio became ill with *vomito negro*, the dreaded yellow fever. Lying on his cot, he complained to his attending wife, "It must be because I'm not an educated man, Paquita, but I don't see that our lot has improved, even though President Juarez has replaced *Maximiliano*. We still work day and night for the rich *ranchero* only to find that our labors do not keep the children from going to bed hungry. Did my sainted cousin Juancito and my other compatriots strap bandoliers across their chests and die for this? When we marched away from our village to face the exploding mouths of the French cannons, we chanted the hopeful words, 'Country, freedom and liberty'. Where is that hope now? Except for victory over *Maximiliano*, what has all the killing brought us?"

Paquita, gently dabbing the sweat from her husband's face replied, "It has brought us freedom from our enemies, Emilio."

"I'll tell you a secret, Paquita. The French were not our real enemies. Our enemies are still with us—hunger and poverty. Nothing has changed, nothing. Look at us. Almost a year after winning the revolution we are still poor. It was not a victory for you and me."

"There, there," consoled Paquita, as she cooled her husband's brow with a wet cloth, "things will change for the better. It will just take a little time, you'll see."

But Emilio had precious little time left. Two days later, Paquita, alarmed at his worsening condition, summoned a *curandero* from a distant village.

"He must be paid in silver," she was told. Paquita wished that there might be something other than silver to offer the medicine man. She had so little money left; she needed it for food. Casting about for something to offer him, she settled her hopes on the green paperweight. Maybe, she thought, he'll accept it as payment. I'll put it near the window to catch the sunlight. It'll glisten there. Emilio won't fault me for using it to cure his sickness.

When the elderly *curandero* arrived on the arm of a small child, Paquita was shocked to see that the pupils of the man's eyes were white. Mother of God, the *curandero* is blind! What would a blind man want with *Maximiliano's* glass ball? He can't see it. He'll want silver.

As the child led him to Emilio's bedside, the old medicine

man paused and turned his head as if he sensed something in the direction of the paperweight. While he carefully removed a variety of objects from a worn hide bag, he whispered something to his young attendant. The child looked at the paperweight and turned back to the old man. Paquita strained to hear but could only discern a few words in the child's reply, "...shiny...green...round like an eyeball." Apparently they were discussing the paperweight. But how did the *curandero* know it was there? Her question gave way to hope that he might accept it instead of silver.

The child lit candles and placed them in a cruciform pattern around Emilio while the old man muttered inaudible incantations. The healer diagnosed the ailing man's malady with the timeless native practice of ritually rubbing a fresh egg over his entire body. After the child cracked the egg into an earthenware dish, the *curandero* read the pattern of the broken yolk with the tips of his fingers. From its conformation, he gave Paquita a small sewn cloth bag of nostrums to place on her husband's navel and instructed her to apply crushed nasturtium leaves over Emilio's entire body.

The child extinguished the candles, gathered together the healer's paraphernalia, and led the old man to the door where they waited for payment. Paquita asked the curandero if he might consider a small glass treasure from *Maximiliano's* palace instead of silver.

"Is it the green ball over there?" asked the child, pointing at the paperweight.

"Yes."

The old man quickly nodded. But when Paquita placed the paperweight in his hands, his sightless eyes opened wide, his hands shook and the paperweight fell to the earthen floor.

"It's Satan's eye!" he gasped. "Away, away!" he cried to the child, shoving at him to lead him out of the shack. "Silver, only silver!" he shouted as they hurried across the clearing.

"Wait," she called after him, "I'll get your silver."

"No, no!" he shouted, pushing the child ahead of him. "Send it to me! Silver, silver, only silver!"

As Paquita lifted the paperweight from the dirt floor, it felt hot. How can that be? she wondered. Was it the sun? Or was it near one of the *curandero's* candles? No, that couldn't be. She remembered the paperweight was cool when she placed it in the *curandero's* hand. Strange, she thought.

The medicine man's skill proved inadequate for Emilio's worsening condition. Several days later, sensing that the end was near, Emilio summoned Paquita to his bedside. "Place your hand on your heart and swear on your mother's soul that when I die you will bury me deep in the earth."

"My husband, don't speak to me of dying. It frightens me. How can you think of leaving me and the children?"

Emilio, determined to extract the promise, continued, "I still remember those shallow graves we dug after our battles. We ignored the enemy dead; there were so many of our own to bury—they corrupted so fast in the heat. The French carcasses had that ugly—stink of death! The bloated corpses oozed pus out of gaping wounds." After a short pause, he continued, "That putrid smell, after all that time, it still lingers—here in my nostrils." His voice trailed away as his eyes stared into the ugly past. Paquita made the sign of the cross on his forehead and turned away from his cot to attend to the children. She returned to him when he began to speak again.

"Weeks after we defeated *Maximiliano*, we passed those shallow burials again. Rats and wild pigs were digging into the graves of our dead and gorging on them! We tried to beat them off—with the butts of our rifles, but they kept returning to eat the worm infested flesh from the sacred bodies of our honored dead. We couldn't kill all the vermin—we tried. Before leaving we exhumed our brothers' remains and buried them deep in the ground." Emilio's hand reached out and grasped Paquita's arm, "Please, Paquita," he pleaded, "when I die, bury me deep. Promise, Paquita, deep."

As she replaced the nasturtium leaves with fresh ones, she looked at his jaundiced skin, sunken in hollow valleys between his ribs, and remembered how his muscles glistened that sweaty sunny afternoon when he marched off to join Juarez. Paquita felt so much pride that day. Sun-darkened, and taller than most of the village volunteers, the recruiting officer appointed Emilio acting sergeant. Cooling her sleeping husband's hot face with a wet cloth, she whispered quietly, "My dear Emilio, where is your firm flesh, now? Just look at you, a pitiful sack of bones. Dear Mary, mother of God, don't let death take away the father of my children. Please listen to a mother's prayer and make my husband well again."

Four days later the villagers dug a deep grave for Emilio.

"...touched by the evil empress's damned paperweights..."

12.

VALADY - 1866

Monsieur Didierjean became concerned when Empress Eugenie's director of purchases inquired about the proposed delivery date of the third Imperial paperweight. He traveled to the Lorraine factory to inquire about the delay and was shocked to learn that young Pierre Claremont had died.

"Pierre did not even complete the second weight," Kosnar admitted. "The final steps of the second paperweight were executed by Pierre's servitor, old Gaspard." Kosnar confided to

Didierjean that he was at a loss for what to do. He explained that after Gaspard left the factory, no one wanted to attempt the third paperweight. "Furthermore," Kosnar assured Didierjean, "none of my gaffers possess the skills to make that paperweight."

"But, surely, some of your gaffers must have watched Pierre as he worked with the paperweights. They must have seen the process he developed, Kosnar."

"My dear friend, Marcella's curse is a very real threat to the glass families. They truly believe that fearful consequences will befall anyone involved with the Imperial paperweights. The recent tragedies of Carlota and Maximilian have not passed them unnoticed."

Didierjean, who promised to deliver the third paperweight to the palace soon, asked, "What are we to do?"

"Our only hope is Gaspard."

The two directors went to the old man's hut and offered him the position of gaffer if he'd undertake the creation of the third paperweight. After a lifetime in the glass house, doing the bidding of others, a chance to sit at the place of honor, the gaffer's chair, tempted the old man. As they talked, the two directors convinced him that Pierre would have wanted him to create the paperweight, since he alone knew the intricate process. Gaspard agreed to return to the factory to undertake the task, in memory of his young friend Pierre.

With the assistance of three imported Saint Louis glassworkers, Gaspard worked slowly, recalling each of the difficult technical steps that Pierre solved.

The Lorraine community abandoned him the moment he began his struggle with the empress's third paperweight; they feared the evil he created. Only his old friend Tremaine continued to associate with him. He playfully chided Gaspard as they spent evenings together in the local auberge.

"How is that evil child coming, Gaspard?"

"Now I'm having problems with the shield—the colors are cracking in the lehr."

"Are you preheating them before you add the hot glass?"

"Too much the first few times; the colors ran. Now, probably not enough. I've spoiled so many of them, I only have four of Pierre's shields left."

"Some children are difficult, Gaspard. Patience will solve your problem."

"Children! Children! You're as bad as everyone else around here! It's just a glass paperweight! Marcella's been dead for over a year, and they're still frightened of her. They all avoid me like the plague. You'd think I was consorting with demons."

"They'll forget about it after you've finished the work."

"I'm not so sure about that, Tremaine. Even I've started to have some fears about it. I've had strange dreams lately. Marcella comes to me in my sleep and screams at me to stop working on the paperweight."

"You're overly tired, that's all. It's on your mind all day. Your brain just empties it out while you're sleeping."

"Sometimes I wonder. Pierre was such a strong young man…"

Evenings, as Tremaine listened to his friend's struggles with the paperweight's problems, he wondered silently why its birth was so difficult. Was Gaspard being hampered by the curse? Was everyone's fear born of fantasy or did Marcella's evil really exist?

At the end of four months, Gaspard and his Saint Louis helpers successfully completed the third Imperial paperweight. The exertion caused the old man to collapse. Six days later he was laid to rest.

"...Cast them into the void..."

Carlota was already isolated in Bouchot Castle when the third paperweight was delivered to the Tuileries. Eugenie, thinking it unwise to send Carlota an object whose memories might impede her recovery, temporarily placed it in her own collection. She promised herself that she would give it to Carlota after the passage of time dulled the pain of her calamities.

Gaspard's death shook Tremaine, who previously dismissed his friend's growing fears of Marcella's curse. Suspecting there might be some truth about the presence of evil in the paperweight, he went to Kosnar's home to ask the director not to send the paperweight to the empress.

"He is not at home, Monsieur Tremaine; he left for Paris," said Didierjean's wife.

"When did he leave, madam?"

"Over a week ago."

"Did he take the paperweight to the palace?"

"No, to Monsieur Launay."

Tremaine, a life-long Bonapartist, considered it his sacred duty to protect the empire and Napoléon Bonaparte's nephew, Louis Napoléon. I must go to Paris, he thought. I must convince Launay not to give the weight to the empress. If it is evil, it might do harm to the Imperial family. I can't let that happen.

When Tremaine reached Paris, Launay dismissed the old man's fears, saying, "The empress has received the paperweight, already. I've been told that she was well-pleased with it."

That same day, a Cent-Guard stopped Tremaine at the gates to the Tuileries.

"What do you want?" the Cent-Guard asked.

"I must see the empress."

"The empress? Get away old man!"

"You don't understand. There's a threat to the Imperial family."

"Go away!"

"Please, I've got to—"

"Away, idiot! I won't warn you again!"

The following evening, Tremaine bribed a dray driver to let him act as his helper the next time he delivered a load of beef to the palace. Gaining entrance, Tremaine made his way through the kitchens, striding past cooks and servants with a self-assurance that discouraged any question of his right to be there. But when he gained access to the palace proper, a vigilant Cent-Guard apprehended him.

"Hold on, sir!"

"Let me go!"

"What are you doing in here?"

"I must see the empress!"

"How did you get in?"

"Let go of me! I must prevent a catastrophe!"

Unfortunately for Tremaine, the guard caught him invading the palace a week after a bombing attempt on Louis Napoléon's carriage near the opera house. The regime suspected everyone, even someone as old and as obviously harmless as Tremaine. Like many others arrested that week, they led Tremaine away and threw him into a damp cell to languish there until the courts examined his case.

At Tremaine's hearing, the presiding jurist ordered, "André Tremaine, take the stand." He then said, "You were apprehended after gaining access to the palace. Do you admit to the charge?"

"Yes."

"What was your reason for being there?"

"The paperweight is cursed!"

"Paperweight? What do you mean?"

"Marcella cursed the paperweights when Pierre died!"

The chief justice turned away from the distraught old man to quietly confer with the other two jurists. He then asked, "What does a paperweight have to do with your invasion of the palace?"

"It was given to her Imperial Highness by Launay. I must warn her of the—"

"You were attempting to reach the empress?"

"Yes."

"The empress! This is serious!"

"Please, sir, I'm not a criminal. I'm a veteran of Napoléon's Grand Armée. I loved Napoléon and I would lay down my life for his nephew, Emperor Louis Napoléon. Please allow me to explain."

After listening to his agitated reasons for being in the palace, the three jurists conferred in hushed tones and quickly agreed that Tremaine was senile and certainly harmless.

"André Tremaine," the chief jurist intoned, "we've decided to release you. But, be warned! Leave Paris immediately on your release. Do not return! If you are ever seen in the vicinity of the palace again, you'll live out your days rotting in prison!"

Tremaine returned home to add his own anxious voice to Lorraine's Greek chorus. He fully expected any day to hear of tragedy befalling the Imperial family.

13.

PARIS - 1870

Louis Napoléon's apprehension increased daily as Bismarck steadily effected his myopic dream, the gathering together of thirty-nine weak German principalities. Convinced that a short successful conflict would bind the German principalities into a strong nation, Bismarck looked for a way to draw France into a conflict. Spain provided the Prussian Chancellor's answer when she offered her vacant throne to a Prussian prince. Advised of Spain's offer, Louis Napoléon dispatched emissaries to the King of Prussia with a request that none of the King's family accept the throne of Spain. He wanted to avoid Prussian influence on two fronts.

Louis Napoléon's request precipitated a maelstrom of catastrophic events. Bismarck, who intercepted the French couriers, twisted Louis Napoléon's petition into a harsh demand making it appear to be an insult to the Prussian King. The King's reply, also secretly rewritten by Bismarck, insulted the French ambassadors.

Reading the altered dispatch, Louis Napoléon fumed at what he considered an affront to the honor of France. His first reaction was to declare war on Prussia, but he hesitated. Did he have enough troops, guns, ammunition and provisions? Could his forces defeat Bismarck? The Prussians recently proved to be capable on the field of battle against Austria and Denmark. As the emperor waited for an assessment of the state of his military forces, he paced about in his rooms.

"Louis," said Eugenie, "I don't understand your hesitancy."

"I cannot commit to war if my armies are not ready."

"But you've recalled all our armies from around the globe; you'll never be better prepared than you are now. Sooner or later Bismarck will decide to turn his forces on us. If we attack first, we shall have the advantage."

"And if we fail, all is lost."

"If you don't act now, the empire will be forever lost to you and to our son."

"The empire is entrenched in the hearts of our people; they will always support the Bonapartes."

"Don't be so sure, Louis."

"You can see how they rally behind me. Even now they're demonstrating against the Prussian King's provocation."

"That's the point, Louis. You must declare war on the crest of that patriotism. If you don't, your subjects will bring you down and along with you, our son's imperial inheritance."

"I can't commit until I'm sure of the outcome; there is a much broader canvas here than a declaration of war."

"The more you hesitate the more you appear to be weak."

"Weak! Weak? I created this empire, I alone."

"The people see the Prussian insult to France as a point of honor; it's your duty to uphold the honor of the empire."

"Don't press me, Eugenie. I have much more than your concerns about honor on my mind!"

Eugenie strode to her drawing room and returned with the yellow Imperial paperweight. "Look at the image in this paperweight, Louis. This young man lost his regency. He lost an empire and his former subjects executed him. In spite of that, no one in Europe sees him as a failure. He is praised, idolized and held up as a hero, a courageous man. Here is honor! Look at his image and take courage from him."

As she left the room, she made an exaggerated show of placing the paperweight on his desk. Louis Napoléon studied Maximilian's profile and thought about Eugenie's words. "You weren't strong, Maximilian," he said aloud. "You were weak! You didn't resist your executioners; you sat in your cell resigned to your death. Had I been in your place, I would have fought them every inch of the way. They would have had to drag me to the firing squad. I'd have attacked them with my teeth, my feet and my bare hands! I'd have resisted them until the last drop of blood flowed from my body. That's courage, Maximilian, that's honor!"

Early the next morning, buoyed-up by favorable dispatches from his generals, Louis Napoléon confidently declared war on Prussia. Nine days later, accompanied by his son, he boarded a military train bound for Metz to take personal command of the French army. Contrary to the glowing assurances of his field generals, he found his army in a state of chaos. Only two-thirds of the regular troops had arrived at the front lines. Dismayed, Napoléon wired Eugenie, "Absolutely nothing is ready. Our ordinance is in short supply. We do not even have enough troops."

Bismarck, who kept his war machine on constant alert, assembled his armies on the border and quickly gained the offensive. By the eighteenth day of fighting, the war was going so badly for France that Louis Napoléon wired Eugenie, "Situation desperate. Advise my ministers to put Paris into a state of defense immediately."

When the French front began to crumble, Louis Napoléon sent the Imperial Prince to the rear under the protection of trusted aides. Learning of her son's retreat, Eugenie hastily wired the aides, "Stand right where you are, there is more than the Prince's security at stake; there is his honor. I could weep for my son were he killed, but not for running away like a fugitive. For that, I would never forgive him or you."

Realizing the hopelessness of his strategic position, Louis Napoléon overrode the empress's command and ordered his aides to take the Prince Imperial across the channel to England

and safety.

Frightening rumors soon reached Eugenie that the French lines were in danger of collapsing. When the daily communiqués from the front ceased to arrive, it compounded her apprehension; she feared the Prussians had cut the lines. Four days of anxious waiting came to an end when Monsieur Chevreau, Minister of the Interior, requested an immediate audience with the empress.

Rushing in breathless, he said, "Your Imperial Highness, we have just decoded a wire from the front."

"Thank God, word from Louis at last! Give it to me!"

"It's dreadful news, madam."

Quickly scanning the telegram, Eugenie read in disbelief that the Prussians had surrounded and captured the main French Army of 104,000 troops as well as the emperor himself.

The stunned French populace, learning the disastrous news, refused to accept defeat. They angrily blamed Louis Napoléon for the catastrophe. Eugenie could not believe the people had turned against Napoléon, or that she was in danger, even though the Duchesse de Bassano breathlessly warned her, "The emperor's vilifiers are calling him 'Old Mustache,' my Lady. They're shouting that he betrayed them. They've also started to denounce you."

"Don't concern yourself, my dear. The empire has always had a few malcontents—ungrateful republicans."

The people, urged on by the republicans, rejected Napoléon, declared France a Republic and resolved to continue the war against Prussia. The remnants of the French army, recalled by the New Republic, made their way back to Paris, regrouped and, with the help of citizen volunteers, set up a strong defense around the capital. The German forces, meeting little resistance, advanced on Paris and laid siege to the city.

When food and fuel stocks in the capital dwindled, life within the encircled city became extremely bitter. When the people finally exhausted their supply of horse meat, the authorities butchered the two elephants in the Paris Zoo to provide meat rations for the starving Parisians.

By the end of December, the invaders bombarded the forts outside Paris. A week later, shells fell in the city streets. During the final days of the siege, with mobs shouting obscenities against the empress and the captured emperor, Eugenie admitted to herself that she was in more peril from her own countrymen than from the advancing Prussians. Remembering Marie Antoinette's unhappy experiences with her own angry subjects and the guillotine, Eugenie hastily made plans to leave France. With the help of her dentist, she fled the Tuileries, evaded her enemies and escaped to England.

A half year after Louis Napoléon declared war on Prussia, the French authorities requested and were granted an end to the hostilities. Immediately, new fighting broke out in Paris, this time between the New Republic and the left-wing Commune. During the final days of that short conflict, the Communards, realizing that they were losing the war, spread petroleum, tar and gunpowder in many of the government buildings and set them on fire. Among the many structures destroyed in this final senseless act was Eugenie's magnificent Tuileries palace.

Learning of the destruction of her palace, Eugenie grieved, "The Tuileries, all my beautiful things—never to see them again! Was it just a year ago that I was feted at the opening of the Suez Canal? Who would have dreamed of the terrible events that have happened since then? No one—never! The world is turned upside-down. His Holiness, Pope Pius, has lost his Papal States; he's confined to the tiny Vatican. Mother of God, what is God's purpose? It's beyond belief! Our empire, twenty years in the making, gone, gone. It's all gone." Taking a deep breath and letting it out slowly, she picked up a small portrait of Louis Napoléon and said, "Louis is still prisoner in Prussia; my dear son, the Imperial Prince, is exiled with me in a foreign country. How will it all end?"

Seven months after his defeat, Louis Napoléon, "detained" as a guest of the Prussian King in Wilhemshohe Castle, was given his freedom. Eugenie forgot her depression soon after he arrived in England. She found new hope in her husband's upbeat attitude. Undiscouraged by his defeat, Louis Napoléon determined to return to France and regain his empire. To that end, he planned and plotted with Bonapartist sympathizers, laying elaborate plans for his eventual return to power. It gave Eugenie hope that her son would one day inherit the empire from his father. Unfortunately, those plans were cut short. Louis Napoléon died in an English hospital while being prepared for an operation to remove a kidney stone.

"...and those that they love..."

Six years after Louis Napoléon's death, the Imperial Prince enlisted in the English Army as a volunteer to serve in the African campaign against the Zulus. Eugenie felt confident that the Prince's successes in Africa would revive the former glory of the Bonaparte name. She hoped that her son, a Bonaparte, would one day return to France as emperor; it was his destiny.

"What a marvelous adventure war is, Mama!" were his parting words to her as he sailed away to do battle.

To her inconsolable sorrow, Eugenie's dreams of her son's future glory were never realized. Soldiers found the remains of the Prince one oppressively hot afternoon in an African wadi, his putrefying body impaled with eighteen Zulu spears.

Eugenie was so grief stricken at her son's death that she contemplated suicide. "A small draught of poison will bring sweet sleep to my suffering." But she could not take her own life. The consequence of suicide was too horrible to contemplate. Not only would she spend eternity in purgatory, but worse, she believed that such an act would prevent her from ever being with her beloved son in heaven. Instead, she chose to live out her remaining days suffering hell on earth.

In her daily prayers she asked for a short life, always closing with the petition, "And if you have any compassion for me, dear Jesus, take me soon." But Eugenie lived another forty years, nursing her grief. Those at the Verrerie de Lorraine remembered Marcella's graveside curse and knew the exact cause of Empress Eugenie's misfortunes.

"...knives twisting in the weeping chambers of their hearts..."

CHAPTER III.

1.

Three days after spending the evening together at the Art Institute, Matthew paid the first of many subsequent visits to Elizabeth's apartment. She invited him for an Italian dinner.

"I'll make the salad before the pizza gets here," she said, taking a bottle of wine out of her refrigerator. "Why don't you open this Chianti and make yourself at home?"

As he glanced about her small living room he noticed that she had tacked up large travel posters of Venice on the walls. Matthew called out, "You must really like Italy. When were you there?"

"Oh, the posters. Unfortunately, never."

Several art books were scattered on the sofa and coffee table, large folios dealing with Italian paintings and sculpture, Venetian glass and Florentine gold objects. Going to the doorway of Beth's tiny galley kitchen, he said, "You've got a lot of books on Italy out here, too. Bet you've even got one of those Italian tenors on your tape deck."

"Not a tenor, chamber music: 'The Seasons' by Vivaldi. I've been playing the tape for six days."

"Six days! The same tape? C'mon, Beth!"

As she set the table, she explained, "The whole thing is Alex's idea. When I came to Chicago, I complained that my background was full of blank spaces, especially when compared to the European trainees. They're lucky! Just living in Europe, they were surrounded by history and culture—you know, cathedrals, palaces, paintings, sculpture, music. In Iowa, those things are on tapes and in travel brochures."

"You've got to know all of that stuff just to work in an auction house?"

"Sure. Just knowing where something's from and what it's worth isn't enough. If you don't get beyond that stage with objects, you'll never appreciate their true essence. Alex says, you've got to be engaged sensuously, intellectually and aesthetically; you've got to fill out the bleached bones with muscle and flesh. So, every month or so, I choose a period of time in a particular country and then collect all I can about its history and culture. I listen to music and study the arts of the period. Sometimes I tack up posters, like these in here, to help me get the feel of the place. I even bring home catalogues from the office—the ones that have items from the time and place I'm studying. All these trappings help me travel to another place and even back in time."

As Elizabeth returned to the kitchen he followed her, chiding, "So this apartment is a science fiction time machine."

"Hm-hum, I guess you could say that. Sometimes, not too often, I feel like I'm actually there. I really know it's working when I handle pieces from a place I've 'visited' here in my apartment. Alex's says she's done it for years. She said that after a while, I'll identify with a particular time and place. You know, permanently change my apartment from wall to wall, into a definite period, and especially," Elizabeth added, laughing and pointing to both sides of her head, "change from ear to ear! Alex says she's locked into the second half of the 19th century; I guess that's why she knows so much about the missing paperweights."

"She a good boss?"

"Yeah, she's great—a perfect boss!"

"No one's perfect."

"Well, she does have one small fault. No, not a fault, a hang-up."

"Yeah?"

"She's extra, extra neat and clean. Her office has to be spotless. You know, after she reads the mail, or one of our auction catalogs, or after we handle objects or packages, she always washes her hands. She washes them sometimes during the day for no apparent reason at all. Her hands must be raw by the end of the day. She even brings disinfectant from home. Sometimes she uses so much of it in our washroom, I almost gag from the fumes."

"A real antiseptic nut."

"I guess. I get to work early every day just to check her office before she gets there; you know, the desk top, the phone, the window sills. She's so fussy, the cleaning ladies are scared to death of her. You could probably eat off the floor in her home."

"You go to her house a lot?"

"No, I've never been there; she's never invited me. She lives on the edge of the city in a small house with a garden in back. She likes to spend time in it. I've never seen it, but I can picture it in my mind; she's talked about it so often."

"Never invited you there? That's funny."

"Oh, I don't think so. She's real friendly in the office, but she's one of those private people. I doubt if she ever invites anybody."

"By the way, Beth, hear anything more about those missing paperweights?"

"Nothing except that Keith hasn't returned to work."

"Keith?"

"You know, I've told you about him. He's in charge of the receiving department in New York. He's so distraught at being considered a suspect, he won't even leave his apartment."

Matthew walked to the sofa and casually flipped through a few pages of a large book. "Well, I don't know Beth, all of this 'time machine' bit sounds like a waste of time. Couldn't you learn just as much by taking a few college classes?"

Returning to the table with the salad, Elizabeth explained, "But I've taken all of those art, music and history classes. This is more intensive than a classroom assignment. You know, I've even prepared foods that—"

"You mean like tonight, calling a pizzeria on a touch-tone phone?"

"Okay. I admit it's superficial at times. But I've ground corn to make meal for baking. I learned to loom so that I could understand cloth, and rugs, and tapestries—you know, hands-on. I even dug clay, and purified it and made pots and vases in wood-fired kilns and—"

Elizabeth's doorbell signaled the arrival of the pizza.

"And now, *mi amigo, Signore Dolgeri*", she said as she dramatically tore open the pizza box, "because we're dining in old Venice tonight, we're switching off all the electricity and eating by candlelight."

"I wondered why you had all these candles around here."

As they ate, Elizabeth talked about life in early Venice, using the candle-lit travel posters as a guide. She told how the Venetian authorities moved their glassmakers to the nearby island of Murano on the pretext that embers from the factory smokestacks endangered the wooden homes in Venice.

"They were actually moved to that island to hide the glassmaking processes from agents of other glass-producing countries."

"Like today's industrial spies?"

"Right. Venetian glass brought so much money into the treasury that the Doges restricted the glassworkers to Murano. Any worker foolish enough to try to escape the island or to reveal the glass-making secrets was condemned to death. Knowing all of this helps me when I handle an old piece of Venetian glass. I have a better understanding of the period; the conditions in which the glass was made; the involvement of the workers and the Doges in the creation of glass objects and—"

"Okay, okay," said Matthew, raising both hands in mock surrender, "I'm convinced it really helps you in your job."

After the meal, Elizabeth played the tape of Vivaldi as they leafed through the large art books in the candlelit room. As she turned the glossy pages, Matthew felt slight sensations of pleasure each time her arm brushed his, or strands of her fragrant hair swept his shoulder. While she intently described Canaletto's feeling for space and atmosphere and his mastery of the delicate effects of mist, Matthew studied the soft curve of her chin and the fullness of her sensuous lips. She felt him looking at her, but didn't look up; she continued to turn the color plates. He gently touched her cheek with his fingers, and slowly traced the curve of her high cheekbone. Her hand found his for a moment and lingered there. She suddenly closed the book, switched on the lights and went to the kitchen.

Matthew realized that he had gotten too close again. He wondered why she continued to shy away from him. Maybe the chemistry is all wrong, he thought. Probably never meant to be. Or, is she playing hard to get?

"I've got spumoni in the freezer," she called out, dispelling the intimacy of the moment. "Would you like some?"

"Uh-uh, no, thanks, Beth. I've eaten enough pizza and salad for three days." Then glancing at his watch, he added, "Thanks for asking me over tonight; it's been great, but I've got to get going. Dan and I've pulled early shift this week. Got to get up pretty early tomorrow."

As they said good-byes in her doorway, he kissed her tenderly. The slow reluctant parting of their lips stirred long suppressed emotions in Elizabeth. When he turned to leave, she hesitantly touched his shoulder. He turned back and gathered her body to his. Her soft lips caressed his mouth.

"Please Matt," she whispered softly, "stay with me in Venice tonight."

They extinguished all the candles and drifted the night together on the shimmering moonlit waters of Venice.

The next morning Matthew awakened early and carefully removed her arm from around his chest. As she slept, he dressed and quietly left. While showering at the station, he recalled each exquisite detail of the intimacies he and Beth shared. All that morning, his thoughts were filled with her.

At 6:45, the automatic clock-radio began to play soft music, gently nudging Elizabeth from a deep sleep. Lying quietly in her bed, in a half-awake, half-asleep reverie, she wondered aloud, "Were we in canal-laced Venice last night, or was it just a lovely dream?"

Later, as she applied her makeup, she agonized about her decision to sleep with Mathew. It's too late for regrets, she thought. What will he think of me, now? Will he see me now as an easy make? I did ask him to stay the night. He didn't even say good-bye. Did I seduce him? He'll probably never want to see me again. If he does, will he treat me like a tramp?

"I shouldn't have let it happen," she said aloud. "You'd think I'd have better sense. I don't want to go through anything like that mess in New York, ever again."

2.

Elizabeth stepped out of the elevator, hurried down the hallway and entered Sotheby's office. The lights were already on. Alex was there. Taking a few deep breaths, she leaned against her desk, removed her flats and slipped on her heels.

"That you, Beth?" Alexandra called through the open

door.

"Yes, Alex. Sorry I'm late. Just couldn't get going this morning."

"I was worried; it's not like you to be late." Alexandra walked to the reception room smiling, "Your Matthew called."

"Oh, when?"

"A few minutes ago. I told him you hadn't arrived yet."

"Did he say why he called?"

"No, just asked for you."

Later that morning, Matthew stopped by to see Elizabeth. "Thought I'd say, 'Hi'."

"What a nice surprise, Matt," said Elizabeth, relieved that he still wanted to see her.

Recognizing Matthew's voice, Alexandra called from her office, "Good morning, Matthew. Just a social call?"

"Yeah, just passing by."

Walking into the reception office, drying her hands, Alexandra said, "When I heard your voice, I hoped you might have some news about the paperweights."

"No, nothing."

"I was on the phone with New York this morning," said Alexandra, "Some of our people are extremely upset. They're complaining that the investigation is getting in the way of their day-to-day operation."

"If there's a break in the case, you'll probably hear about it way before we do at the district."

"According to what I've been told, except for Keith, the police are very closed-mouthed about any other leads they might have. Someone's coming here from New York about the paperweights tomorrow."

"From the police department?" Matthew asked.

"No, from the insurance company."

Elizabeth explained, "The insurance company doesn't want to get stuck if the mails are at fault."

"Yes," said Alexandra, "they'd love to prove the paperweights were never received in New York. I understand whoever signed for the package scribbled an indecipherable signature on the registration slip."

"Doesn't the mailman remember who signed for it?" Matthew asked.

"Oh, no, Matt." Elizabeth said, then explained, "When I worked in New York, packages came in all day long by all sorts of carriers. They were signed for by anyone in the receiving department or anyone else who was handy."

Early that afternoon, Elizabeth rang Alexandra's extension. "You've got a call from New York; it's Mr. Alschuler."

After finishing the call, Alexandra went to the reception room.

"The paperweights, again?"

"Yes. Sam said that Keith's story checked out. He's no longer a suspect. The money he was spending was really left to Howard by his uncle."

"It was all circumstantial, then."

"Yes it was. Now the police are back to square one. Sam said that that's why they're questioning everyone again. He said that Keith is so distraught, he plans to stay at home until the matter is all cleared up."

"Poor Keith. He may have his faults, but he's no thief. I never believed—" Elizabeth stopped in mid-sentence to answer the telephone. "It's for you Alex, a Mr. Christopher Knott from the Tribune."

"I'll take it in my office."

After the call, Alexandra returned to the reception room, saying, "He's a feature writer. He's coming here this afternoon about the Imperial paperweights. Picked up on their disappearance from a New York newspaper and wants to talk to someone here about their history. The Tribune's planning to do a feature story about them. He was especially intrigued that Oscar Wilde once owned the yellow one."

"The famous playwright?"

"The very same."

"Oh, really? I just assumed that Empress Eugenie kept the yellow one until her death."

"According to what I've been able to learn, it was in Wilde's possession for several years. Like Carlota and Eugenie, he was a serious collector of paperweights."

"What happened to his collection?"

"After he died, it was kept by his two sons, Cyril and Vyvian Holland. Cyril was killed at the front during the First World War. Vyvian eventually sold the paperweights to a Chicago firm, the A. Starr Best Company."

"A. Starr Best. I don't think I've ever heard of them."

"They're no longer in business. They dealt in fine antiques a long time ago. Paperweights were one of their specialties."

"Was Oscar Wilde's collection very large?"

"Oh, yes, about a hundred and twenty-five paperweights of the finest quality. Most of them were from Baccarat, Clichy, and Saint Louis. I've read that twelve of them were extremely beautiful and encased in faceted shells of colored glass. I'm sure the company had no trouble selling off that collection. There are always serious collectors eager to buy top grade pieces."

"Then, that company got the yellow paperweight?"

"No, it wasn't in Mr. Holland's collection. It disappeared years earlier, shortly after Oscar Wilde's death."

"Wasn't he in prison for a time?"

"Yes, soon after he acquired the Imperial paperweight."

"Makes you wonder about Marcella's curse, doesn't it?"

"You're just being silly, Beth."

3.

LONDON - 1892

The aristocratic young man thanked the messenger and closed the door to his apartment. He opened the envelope addressed to 'Lord Alfred Douglas Queensberry,' and read, "Dear Bosie, please meet me at my club at eleven-thirty this morning, Oscar W."

That afternoon, as Oscar Wilde and Alfred Douglas lunched together at the Albemarle, Wilde's guest recalled something he had wanted to tell his companion. "Ross and I happened on a paperweight, one you may wish to add to your collection."

"And where is it, dear boy? Do you have it?"

"No, I didn't purchase it. You're so particular about your likes and dislikes."

"That's because so many supposedly cultured dilettantes equate today's excesses with truly fine art. They'd rather listen to a raucous brass band blaring away in Hyde Park than attend a symphony concert in Albert Hall."

"I don't wish to argue the point, Oscar. I'll only say, though many of us don't possess your impeccable taste, we do show consideration for the opinions of others."

"Oh, Bosie, don't be so sensitive; petulance does not become you. I wasn't referring to you, dear boy. Try to forget what I said and tell me more about that paperweight."

"Well, let me think. The paperweight had a dark blue shell, and through its faceted windows I could see a small umbrella-like structure inside. The top of the umbrella was decorated with concentric rings of long colorful pieces that looked just like Christmas candy."

"That 'umbrella' is called a 'mushroom,' Bosie."

"Oh, a 'mushroom'. Well, as I examined the paperweight, I noticed a solitary black stripe on the outer edge of the—ah—mushroom. It went from the mushroom cap down to the bottom of the stem. It seemed to be out of place to me. I wondered at the time why the design had this odd piece and asked if I might examine it with a magnifying glass."

"Let me guess. The odd stripe was a long thin rod containing the initials 'SL' and the numbers '1848,' right?"

"Why yes, Oscar! How did you know?"

"Bosie, my dear heart, what you and Ross saw was a paperweight made in Saint Louis, France. The 'SL' cane is the company's signature; the numbers '1848' indicate the year it was made—'1848' was the most popular date used by that company. Tell me, where did you see it?"

"Oh, I've piqued your curiosity."

"Indeed you have!"

"It was in that little antiquary shop near Prince Edward Bridge, the one that we've sometimes visited together. You remember, don't you? The proprietor is that gnome-like character, Mr. Wormsley."

"Oh, yes, old Wormsley. Do you remember the condition of the paperweight?"

"It seemed perfect to me, but, of course, no one is as perceptive as you are."

"My dear Bosie, I apologize for anything offensive that you may have felt directed toward you. Believe me, that truly was not my intention. It's that I just can't abide those insensitive clods who posture about as authorities of good taste. Come, my friend, let's proceed to Wormsley's, without delay. If that paperweight is at all as you've described, I must have it."

They hailed a hansom cab, and within half an hour arrived at Wormsley's Curios and Antiquities, a small two-floor Tudor building on a narrow cobblestone street. The upper floor of the structure served as living quarters for the diminutive Wormsley couple. A wall covered with framed paintings and prints divided the ground floor into two rooms: a tiny back room smelling of varnish, spirits and paint, used for repairs, private transactions and storage, and a large showroom containing display cases, tables and shelves crowded with all manner of glassware, porcelain, precious gems, rare woods and metals. An ever-changing display of the choicest items from the proprietor's wares enhanced the shop window.

Peering through the hazy undulating panes of glass, Wilde asked, "Where is the paperweight?"

"It was on that shelf down there to the left."

"I don't see it, Bosie."

"He's changed the window display again. I hope he still has it. Let's go in."

After exchanging greetings, Wilde, anxious to see the object of their visit, said, "Mr. Wormsley, Lord Douglas tells me that you had an attractive paperweight here several days ago."

"Why, yes, Mr. Wilde, it's one which may be of interest to you."

Carefully attaching a pince-nez to the bridge of his nose, the proprietor stepped to the back of the shop. "It's here in this case. I'll bring it there; the light is much better where you're standing."

Wilde accepted the object from the shopkeeper's outstretched hand, walked to the window, and examined it in the sunlight. Turning to his young friend, Wilde said, "Bosie, you were right. It's well made, signed, dated, set perfectly, and has no external damage. Just look at the detail, such a command of glass. It was certainly made by an artist!" Eager to learn more about the crystal ball, he asked the proprietor, "Where did you find this treasure?"

"In a sale of household effects. There were only a few

items of value, small pieces of furniture and this paperweight. When I saw it, I thought it might be of interest to someone who collects them."

"Yes, you were right! Mr. Wormsley, I must have this beauty."

Oscar Wilde considered the find of the beautiful paperweight one of the several fortunate and pleasurable occurrences that lately brightened his life: young Douglas, whom he met just six months before, became his lover; his book, *The Life of Dorian Gray*, sold well; and the rehearsals of his new play, *Lady Windermere's Fan*, progressed to his complete satisfaction. Advance notices of the play already produced ticket sales promising full houses for many performances.

The opening night of *Lady Windermere's Fan* exceeded Wilde's highest expectations. Among the many notable guests in the audience, Eugenie, the former empress of France, traveled the seventy kilometers from her new home in Hampshire to the London theater with a small group of lady friends to attend the premiere.

During the years following her son's death, Eugenie's intense feelings of sorrow slowly abated. She abandoned Camden Place and its sad memories and built a new home, Farnborough Hill, where she gradually gathered up the remnants of her life. Her yearning for human companionship encouraged her to reach outside her solitary existence and invite a few of her former friends to visit her. Eventually, her growing guest list included displaced rulers, princes and members of the aristocracy whom she invited to enjoy her hospitality. Eugenie, by now, ruled over an ever-changing empire of house guests whom she entertained with soirées, concerts, and sumptuous dinners.

During the long second intermission of Wilde's play, the

empress asked her companions if they had any knowledge of the playwright's background.

One of the ladies volunteered, "His father was an outstanding eye and ear physician, your Highness."

"His father was a published antiquarian and a scholar," said another.

"That's true, my Lady, but I have also heard his father sired several illegitimate children."

"That's certainly not a rumor! He actually sued someone for libel. His accuser claimed the doctor was involved in a number of sexual affairs. Dr. Wilde lost the case, and found himself an outcast from genteel society. At the time of his father's scandalous trial, Oscar Wilde, ten years old, suffered great embarrassment when his classmates taunted him about the daily newspaper accounts of his father's adulterous adventures."

When Eugenie asked about Wilde's mother, her retinue answered her query with a flurry of tidbits, each statement giving rise to another.

"Her home is always filled with artists, writers and political agitators. She gives late suppers and disperses spirits lavishly."

"Oh, yes. I was invited to one of her soirées, my Lady. That's where I first saw Oscar Wilde. I was startled to see him outlandishly arrayed in a lilac-colored shirt and a large flowing bluish-red bow tie."

"How garish!"

"Yes, his dress was outlandish, but it paled when his mother made her appearance. Mrs. Wilde is a very large woman. I'll never forget how she was dressed: layers of flowing garments and several red shawls. She had clanking bracelets on her arms and large gaudy brooches on her bosom. There were long unmatched necklaces hanging around her neck, and her facial make-up was plastered on so thickly that it resembled stage makeup."

"Someone said she has touches of genius."

"She is brilliant, but she is also quite eccentric. She's been involved in many sensational literary endeavors. In one of her political pieces, she told the Irish people to build barricades and use their muskets to win their freedom. The editor who published the piece was charged with sedition!"

"Well, with a nonconformist mother and an adulterer for a father, it's a miracle Oscar Wilde has developed into such an entertaining playwright."

One of Eugenie's party, lowering her voice, said, "Gossip has it that Oscar Wilde has a male companion for a lover. I've even heard he's had a string of young male lovers over the years."

"Oh, I don't believe it! He's married and has two small children. He wrote *The Happy Prince* for them."

"*The Happy Prince?* Why, my twins loved that story. I must have read it to them a hundred times."

"He has written wonderful poetry."

On the following day, during their return trip to Hampshire, Eugenie listened as her entourage excitedly discussed Wilde's play.

"Clever dialogue!"

"It was so well written."

"And the satirical jabs at the old-fashioned characters, like some of the stuffy people one sometimes encounters."

"Mr. Dumby reminded me of my own uncle Randolph; his opinions changed like a banner flapping in the wind."

"At times, the play disturbed me. It seemed to cast aspersions on our most cherished institutions; marriage, faith, fidelity."

"But it was all tongue-in-cheek. When Mr. Wilde was

interviewed about his play, he said it was 'just a clever little thing written by a butterfly for butterflies'."

"I truly didn't expect the play to be so charming. It was very different from his novel, *Dorian Gray*."

"The novel and play also seemed unrelated to me at first, but on reflection I see certain similarities in them."

"What can you possibly mean, Sheila?"

"I think each of them illuminate the faults of our society. We live in a society where appearances are everything. In last night's play Mr. Wilde ridiculed that hypocrisy. In *Dorian Gray* he exposed the corruptive side of the same hypocrisy."

"Oh, my dear, I believe you're reaching too far for that comparison!"

"I don't agree with you either, Sheila. But I do know the novel is an evil book. It should never have been published."

"I think we are all reading too much into the play. It was a delightful piece, meant to be enjoyed and not overly analyzed."

Intrigued by Oscar Wilde's effect on her entourage, and especially dazzled by his instant hit, Eugenie decided to invite him to her villa. If she snared the celebrated playwright as a house guest, his visit would be the highlight of the Hampshire social season.

4.

Though Wilde professed a contempt for the pretentiousness of the upper classes, Eugenie's invitation represented a stupendous coup for him. The prospect of visiting a former empress of France thrilled him. Clasping the invitation to his chest, he said to Douglas, "Imagine, invited to the villa of an empress, one who has left her mark in the chronicles of Europe. Her husband's decisions shook the very web of the world's history!"

On receipt of his acceptance, Eugenie dispatched invitations and prepared accommodations to house the many guests who would share Wilde's visit. His arrival at the villa caused a momentary confusion for the empress's household staff. They had expected Mr. and Mrs. Wilde. To their dismay, he arrived with a male companion, whom, with his characteristic flourish, Wilde introduced as, "my dear friend, Lord Alfred Douglas."

Wilde immediately sensed the bewilderment his introduction caused the staff. Upon inquiry he was embarrassingly informed that there are no private quarters available for Lord Douglas, all the other accommodations were occupied by invited guests.

"Oh, it's of no consequence," said Wilde, "Lord Douglas and I will bed down together. We've often shared lodgings in our travels."

The next morning the members of the house staff engaged in guarded whispers about suspicious sounds the upstairs chambermaids had overheard emanating from behind Wilde's locked door.

Two years before he became acquainted with Douglas, Wilde met and fell in love with Constance. In a letter to a friend, Wilde confided his innermost feelings for the girl who would soon become his wife, "I'm going to be married to a beautiful girl, a grave, slight, violet-eyed little Artemis, with great coils of brown hair which make her flower-like head droop like a blossom, and wonderful ivory hands which draw music from the piano so sweet that the birds stop singing just to hear her."

Within a year of his marriage to Constance, a mutual friend introduced Wilde to the young aristocratic Lord Alfred

Douglas Queensberry. Constance approved of Douglas from the start. She saw him as a fragile young man, one who needed looking after. The young nobleman, an aspiring writer, obviously looked up to her successful husband. She felt a special tenderness for her husband who took the time to befriend the young man. With his faded blue eyes, his red-rimmed eyelids, and his thin, cold hands, she worried about the slightly built young man's health.

She told her husband, "You know, Oscar, he idolizes you. Do be gentle with him; he seems so fragile. You have such a powerful personality."

"Yes, he is a sensitive young man. I must admit, I do enjoy his company. It's like having a younger brother. I enjoy rediscovering the world through the young man's eyes. Through him, I'm able to live the young life I never was able to enjoy. My own growing years were so difficult."

"Why don't you invite him to travel with you to Ireland when you go there next month? I would be very content to remain here with the two babies; as a matter of fact, I would truly prefer it."

"I'm afraid he doesn't have the money to travel. His parents are not liberal with his allowance. They're divorced, you know."

"You can afford to take him, Oscar. He would be a pleasant traveling companion for you."

As the two men's friendship deepened, they became inseparable. Douglas accompanied Wilde on a trip to Egypt and on several trips to the Continent where they satisfied their deep affection for each other behind locked doors. At first, almost everyone dismissed gossip of their liaison. But as the rumors persisted, some doubted the "purity" of their relationship.

Wilde made special efforts to keep his sexual relationship

with Douglas from Constance. Although he lived at home with his wife and children, Wilde also occupied rooms at the Albemarle. He asked Douglas to help him keep up their charade when they were in Wilde's home.

"She really doesn't suspect, Oscar?"

"No. She wouldn't understand. She has led such a sheltered life. I do love her; she's my wife and the mother of my children. How can she know the intensity of my desire for you? If she ever found out, I'm certain she'd leave me."

When it happened that Oscar's social or business commitments or Douglas's schooling kept them apart for a period of time, they suffered greatly. During those separations, they posted notes to each other about their feelings of isolation and affection. "...I must see you soon," wrote Wilde. "You are the divine thing I want, a thing of grace and beauty...Why are you not here, my dear, my wonderful boy?"

Wilde, languishing for his young lover, once described Douglas to their mutual friend, Robert Ross, saying, "My Bosie is quite like a narcissus—so white and gold. He lies like a hyacinth on a sofa, and I worship him."

That evening, during Eugenie's magnificent dinner, Wilde was in rare form. When the conversation turned to the escalating prices of fine art, Wilde quipped, "It has been my observation that cynics know the price of everything and the value of nothing." When talk turned to the open indiscretions of the Crown Prince, Wilde came to his defense, saying, "I suppose if the truth were known, most of us walk in the gutter, but a few of us do look up at the stars."

After dinner, the gentlemen retired to the library for cigars, brandy and conversation. There, Wilde made particular jest of the importance men attach to the outward appearance of nobility and morality, and how in the privacy of their personal lives they act in a hypocritical reversal of those ideals. And then to lighten the moment, he added, "I've personally found that the only way to rid myself of temptation is to yield to it!"

His eloquence captivated even those whom he censured.

Early the next day, wandering alone in the villa, Wilde found to his delight that his hostess possessed a modest collection of French and English paperweights. A dazzling yellow overlay that contained within its shell the unmistakable crest of the Hapsburgs especially piqued his curiosity. When he discovered the internal "1864" date and the Mexican eagle, he guessed that the profiles in the paperweight portrayed the ill-fated monarchs, Maximilian and Carlota. Eugenie entered the study as Wilde returned the paperweight to its place on the table. "Oh, Mr. Wilde," she said, "my guests so enjoyed your witty conversation, last night. I suspect they are still talking about you this morning."

"Your highness, I always say there is one thing in the world worse than being talked about, and that is not being talked about."

"How clever, Mr. Wilde." She went to the table and picked up a paperweight, saying, "I see that you were admiring my paperweights."

"Oh, yes, they are a passion of mine. I've collected them for years."

Eugenie was delighted to discover a fellow collector. In a rush, their casual acquaintance transformed into a friendship. They found a common language, and a common interest, one they discussed and enjoyed together.

"Mr. Wilde, when the emperor and I resided in the Tuileries Palace, I had a collection of, oh, so many beautiful pieces. This small collection is but a pale reflection of the number of paperweights I once possessed. During the terrible winter of 1871, when cataclysmic events overtook our empire and the Communards turned against us, I was only a few steps away from the mob's madness. With God's help, I escaped their destructive fury. It all happened so suddenly! I had only moments to gather together a few possessions, including three of my precious paperweights. That large yellow paperweight and two others were the only ones I saved from my entire collection. I don't know what fate befell all of those I left behind. Since coming to England, I've built a collection around the few I was able to rescue."

"Many people lost their lives during that fateful winter."

"Yes, unfortunately, 'from dust to dust.' You know, Mr. Wilde, nine months after I arrived here, the mobs set fire to our Tuileries. Years later, the government took down the few remaining walls of the palace. Nothing remains there now, only gardens. All of my beautiful things were lost to me, forever. I've often wondered about the paperweights that were left behind. If they were not stolen, they were certainly destroyed in that raging conflagration, their beautiful designs melting into unrecognizable shapes."

Wilde thought, how ironic. She sorrows so little for those who died in that terrible holocaust; she grieves more for her lost possessions. Could it be that those with limitless power view the world differently than we mere mortals?" Picking up the large yellow paperweight, he said, "I'm intrigued by this beautiful treasure, your Highness. Are these sulphides the silhouettes of Maximilian and Carlota?"

"Why, yes, Mr. Wilde, how perceptive of you. I'm especially fond of that particular paperweight. You see, I commissioned the Saint Louis factory to create three such paperweights as gifts for Empress Carlota when she and Maximilian ascended the Mexican throne. I presented the first two to Carlota during happier times. This paperweight, the third, was completed after Maximilian's execution. Unfortunately, I was never able to give it to Carlota. She had already entered that world of phantoms. Only heaven knows if any of the past still exists in her confused mind. Poor little Carlota. What do you think of the paperweight, Mr. Wilde?"

"It is the most fascinating paperweight I have ever seen. See how the gold sheen whispers from behind the colors of the shield. And that yellow overlay; yellow is such a rare color in paperweights! Your highness, would you permit me to study it at my leisure during my stay here?"

"Why, of course, Mr. Wilde, I would be most pleased."

Later that morning, in his rooms, Wilde turned the crystal orb round and round in his hands, thinking aloud, "What stories this glass might tell if we could but unlock its mute record." Turning to his lover, he said, "Think of it, Bosie, a life of its own. It would start its story in the primordial mists when quartz slowly weathered into sand. And then it could relate its change from ancient sand into a beauteous glass gem by wondrous manipulations in man's melting fire. After that miraculous transfiguration, it would weave a fascinating story as an attendant to decades of man's history. Even the plainest of paperweights might contain, locked within its shell, a tale to rival the stories of our best poets."

5.

Wilde's second play, *A Woman of No Importance* opened and proved to be an even greater success than *Lady Windermere's Fan*. During the second act intermission, an aristocratic young man delivered a message from Empress Eugenie into Oscar Wilde's hand. It read, in part, "I have asked the bearer of this note to bring you a special gift in heartfelt appreciation of a poem that

I recently discovered in a small volume of your works. The poem touched me deeply and will remain with me until the end of my years. Your words brought tears to my aging eyes and a great warmth to my heart. My son, the Imperial Prince, was my world, and when he died, a part of me died with him."

Looking up from the note, Wilde remembered the poem. He had written it fifteen years earlier when he learned of the prince's death in Africa:

> Eagle of Austerlitz! Where were thy wings
> When far away upon a barbarous strand,
> In fight unequal, by an obscure hand,
> Fell the last scion of thy brood of Kings!
> Poor boy! thou wilt not flaunt thy cloak of red
> Nor ride in state through Paris in the van
> Of thy returning legions, but instead
> Thy mother France
> Shall on thy dead and crownless forehead place
> The better laurels of a soldier's crown...

Eugenie's note concluded, "I remember your fondness for Carlota's paperweight when you visited my villa. I want you to have it. Since I am unable to deliver it personally, I ask that you accept it from the hand of my grandson, Etienne, who comes to you in my stead. I'd like you to know, Mr. Wilde, he is a great admirer of yours and is especially desirous of meeting you. In friendship, Eugenie."

The Imperial paperweight, the ultimate addition to Wilde's collection served as the centerpiece of many of his enthralling dissertations. He often fascinated his guests with tales about Carlota's and Maximilian's tragic downfall, all the while weaving stories around the Imperial paperweight to the delight of his visitors.

"...and, my dear friends," he concluded at the end of his captivating yarns, his eyes fastened on the glittering yellow sphere in his outstretched hand, "one of those three precious Imperial paperweights is this very object which I now hold up before your very eyes!"

Because the success of Wilde's plays made him a public celebrity, his utterances and actions became potential news items for the London tabloids. The new encroachment on his private life presented him with a dilemma. Except for the first year of his marriage, Wilde continually involved himself with a stream of young male lovers. This other life remained so secretive that even his wife did not suspect his sexual involvement with men when he was away from home. And though he and Bosie were now almost inseparable, they both continued their indulgence with other young men. Finding himself on the crest of popularity, Wilde no longer enjoyed his earlier cloak of anonymity. He was obliged to keep his homosexual life carefully veiled, he could not afford to have those private liaisons become known to the public. The law of the realm forbade homosexuality.

During this time, Wilde searched out Somerset Taylor, a homosexual, who procured young men for illicit sexual assignations. Taylor assured Wilde that all of their dealings would be kept confidential; Wilde need not fear exposure.

When Ross and Douglas learned Wilde consorted with Taylor's recruits, they expressed concern for his safety. They warned him that Taylor's young male prostitutes came from questionable backgrounds and that many had records of previous arrests. But he brushed their fears aside, saying, "I'm stimulated by those evil beings. It is like feasting with panthers. The peril is half of the excitement."

6.

"You lying bastards, take that back!" spat the Eighth Marquis of Queensberry. The two men standing with him in the paddock just told him of the scandalous rumors about Oscar Wilde and his son, Douglas.

"Steady on, Queensberry," countered one of the men, "I'm not in the habit of lying to my friends. Look into the matter yourself, you'll see that there's reason for those suspicions."

"To hell with you and your bloody suspicions! Not my son, not my flesh and blood!" he shouted, pounding the fence rail with white-knuckled fists.

"They're always together. Your son practically lives with that bugger."

"By God, I'll find out, and then I'll come back and throw the proof in your faces! I'll force you to recant those filthy lies!"

"Be sensible, Queensberry, what possible reason would we have to lie to you?"

"Why would you even bring it up? Why repeat such dastardly hearsay?"

"Because everyone is talking about your son behind your back and laughing at your expense. We thought if you were made aware of the ugly rumors, you'd put a stop to the situation; that is, if what we've heard is in fact, true."

"If there's any proof to it, I'll personally throttle that bastard, Wilde!"

Lord John Shalto Douglas, Marquis of Queensberry, took leave of his two acquaintances and rushed off to his former wife's residence. His rage had not abated by the time he arrived. Not bothering to greet her, he shouted, "Where the hell is he?"

"What is wrong, John?"

"Answer my question, damn it! Where is Douglas?"

"Bosie?"

"Don't use that stupid baby name! His name is Douglas! Douglas! Where is he?"

"I don't know, John. What is the matter?"

"He's with that Wilde, isn't he?"

"Oscar Wilde?"

"Yes, Wilde!"

"I don't know, John."

"What the hell's been going on around here? I'm the laughing stock of all of London because of him! Don't you watch over him? What kind of mother are you?"

"Bosie is not—"

"Douglas, damn it!"

"Douglas is not a child anymore, John. He does whatever he pleases."

"He's a damn mama's boy. If he'd come with me instead of staying here with you, he'd be a man today! How long has he known that Wilde?"

"About two years, I think."

"Two years? My God! And what in hell have they been doing all that time?

"Don't shout, John. You make me nervous."

"I'll shout around here until I get some straight answers! What's Douglas been up to with that bugger, Wilde? Do you have any damn idea what's been happening to your own son? They're always together! Weren't you suspicious of their relationship?"

"No, not at first, John. Mr. Wilde seemed so erudite, such a perfect gentleman. I even invited him and his wife to tea several times."

"What! You invited him here? Oh, my God!"

"He and Douglas had just met; I hadn't heard any of the rumors yet."

"My God! You suspect them too, don't you! Why didn't you contact me? I'm his father! I'd have split them up!"

Her son's friendship with his charming and learned older companion delighted Douglas's mother, the Marquesa Queensberry at its outset. She took special pride in the fact that Wilde's acquaintances included such notables as the American painter, James Whistler, the actresses Sarah Bernhardt and Lily Langtree, and even Edward, the Crown Prince of the realm. Unaware of their true relationship, she assumed that her Bosie "adopted" Wilde as a surrogate father— the father figure denied to her son when she divorced the Marquis.

Later, when she became aware of the gossip surrounding the relationship of Wilde and her son, Lady Queensberry feared they might indeed be intimately involved. In an attempt to put an end to their relationship, she obtained a position for Douglas with the British Counsel General in Egypt. She dispatched a letter to Wilde insisting that he terminate his relationship with her son at once. She told him she made arrangements for Douglas to leave England and insisted that Wilde honor her wishes and not go abroad to be with her son.

"I even arranged for Douglas to take a position in Egypt," she explained to her pacing husband "but he didn't remain there. He has returned to London. I suspect he spends most of his time with Oscar Wilde. If you can separate them, I'll be eternally grateful!"

The truculent Marquis held no love for his former wife nor any fatherly affection for the two sons he sired. Family life was never important to him; boxing rings, racing stables and young girls concerned him more. After suffering her husband's abuse for years, Lady Queensberry petitioned the court which granted her a divorce on charges of adultery and physical cruelty. Much to his chagrin, Queensberry's sons chose to remain with their mother after the separation. If the truth were known, Queensberry would not have bothered now about his young son except for the gossip attached to his own name. He was fiercely determined to break up the illicit relationship, if it did indeed exist.

Making inquiries, the Marquis learned that Oscar Wilde usually dined at the Café Royale. That evening, Queensberry went to the café and found Wilde and Douglas there. The meal began amicably enough with the three exchanging pleasantries, but as the evening progressed, Queensberry observed that his two dinner companions exhibited an unnatural amorousness toward each other. His skin crawled when they started uttering tender expressions. When they made veiled references to what he perceived to be an unnatural relationship, he threw his fork on the table and left without a word. That evening, he wrote his son, "I demand you break off from this ugly intimacy with that degenerate lecher, Oscar Wilde. If you don't, I shall disown and disinherit you. As of this moment, I am suspending your monthly stipend."

The following morning, Queensberry appeared at Wilde's home. Wilde's manservant answered the furious pounding on the door.

"Where's Oscar Wilde?" Queensberry demanded, pushing his way into the foyer.

The servant's momentary reaction, to grab the diminutive man and throw him out of the door, turned into apprehension as two of Queensberry's hulking brutes came into view. "Whom shall I say is calling?" he asked.

"Tell him that it's the Marquis of Queensberry, and be quick about it!"

"If you gentlemen will wait in the library, I'll see if Mr. Wilde will see you."

As the manservant left the library, Queensberry turned to his two ruffians, saying, "He'd damn well better see me."

When Wilde appeared, Queensberry ordered, "Sit down, Wilde!"

Wilde strode across the room to Queensberry. Staring down into the small man's eyes, he said, "I do not permit anyone to talk to me like that, especially in my own house."

In a rage, Queensberry accused Wilde of improper conduct with his son.

"How dare you accuse me," objected Wilde.

Queensberry shouted, "Your scandalous behavior is gossiped about all over London. I don't care what the hell you do with others, just stay away from my son! I'm warning you, Wilde, if I ever find you and Douglas together again, my two friends and I will thrash you senseless and I'll personally expose you to open scandal!"

"I don't know what your 'Queensberry Rules' are," Wilde replied angrily, "but my rules are to shoot intruders on sight. Now, leave my home at once or I shall summon the police."

After the three unwelcome guests left his home, Wilde instructed his manservant, "The Marquis of Queensberry is the most contemptible scoundrel in all of London. Don't ever allow him to enter this house again."

"What was all the commotion, Oscar?" Constance asked as she entered the library. "I could hear the shouting upstairs. It awakened the children."

"It was Lord Queensberry, Bosie's father."

"What was he shouting about?"

Relieved that she did not hear Queensberry's accusations, Wilde said, "A family matter. He's angry at Bosie for some reason; he didn't say what it was. He's looking for him."

"Isn't Douglas staying near the Albemarle?"

"Yes, but I didn't tell him. Queensberry was in such an angry state of mind, I was certain he intended to do the boy harm. I refused to assist him in any way."

Speculating that Queensberry's efforts might prove unsuccessful, Lady Queensberry made arrangements to send Douglas to Florence on a two month holiday. Much to her dismay, she learned later that Wilde had left for Florence soon after her son's departure.

Wilde journeyed to London six weeks later to attend the opening of his third play, *An Ideal Husband*. When he learned that Oscar Wilde once again inhabited London, the Marquis sent several thugs to harass the playwright. To keep his homosexual relationship with Douglas from his wife, as well as to prevent harm to Constance and the children, Wilde left London with his family and took rooms in Worthing, well away from Queensberry. He explained the move to his questioning wife as a temporary need to be away from the many distractions of London in order to work on a new play.

While residing in Worthing, he wrote his finest play, *The Importance of Being Ernest*. Wilde's latest comedy thrilled London playgoers. At the final curtain they rose to their feet, cheering and calling Wilde to the stage for more than a dozen curtain calls.

Wilde invited Eugenie's grandson, Etienne, who was in the audience, to join him and a few close friends at his home for a critique of the play over a late dinner and champagne. When Etienne arrived, Wilde asked him about a subject that had bothered him since their first meeting. "When you brought me the empress's gift last year, I was puzzled that her note introduced you as her grandson. I didn't know that your father, the Imperial Prince, had ever married."

"It was a private morganatic marriage, Mr. Wilde. I bear

my mother's family name, Mignard."

Eugenie never revealed Etienne's true story, a wrenching pain in her heart, to anyone, not even to Etienne. Her feelings of guilt often overwhelmed her.

Just before the Imperial Prince sailed to Africa to fight in the Zulu War, he approached his mother hand-in-hand with Therese Mignard to ask permission to marry. The shocked empress berated the young girl and accused her of using her extended stay in the villa to "worm her way" into the Prince's affections. Those callous words returned so often to haunt Eugenie that she attempted to ameliorate their harshness by justifying her rejection of the young couple's marriage. She rationalized that her decision was the only course possible at the time; it kept the Imperial Prince's future an open option. As a Bonaparte, he carried her hopes for the glorious return of the French Empire. A marriage which did not join her son to the powerful royal houses of Europe would have been detrimental to his destiny; marriage to Therese Mignard would forever end Eugenie's high expectations for her son's future. She sent the broken-hearted girl back to her parents and the prince off to Africa, little realizing that Therese carried her son's child.

Therese suffered a disastrous homecoming. When the young girl's condition could no longer be hidden, she endured the daily shame of her family's bitterness and of her own disgrace. When her parents told Therese of her young lover's violent death in Africa, she collapsed. Four days later she died giving birth to the Imperial Prince's son. When the little orphan grew strong enough to withstand the long journey, Therese's family sent the baby accompanied by a wet nurse to Empress Eugenie. The short message hastily written by Therese's bitter father read, "This is your bastard grandson. We disavow any claim to him, and wish to never see him, ever again. He is as he was taken from his mother's lifeless womb, unloved, illegitimate and unbaptized."

Eugenie received the tiny child and had him baptized, "Etienne." Although he could never fulfill her dream of a Bonaparte Empire, she accepted him as her grandson and grew to love him deeply; he reminded her of her beloved son. To those who questioned her about her little "grandson," Eugenie explained that Etienne was the offspring of her son's private morganatic marriage.

"As you can see, I am constantly reminded of your Grandmother's generous gift," said Wilde, pointing to the yellow Imperial paperweight prominently displayed on his writing desk.

Douglas added, "You would be amazed at how often Oscar uses that 'little yellow Carlota' to fascinate his guests with Maximilian's tragic story."

"Yes," said Ross, "We've all heard that story so often; I'm sure that any of us could relate it and all its variations from memory!"

"I might be able to add a rather unusual chapter to your 'Carlota' story, if you'd like, Mr. Wilde," offered Etienne.

Wilde beamed, "By all means, Etienne, I'd love to learn more about the paperweight."

"Two years ago, Mr. Wilde, grandmother and I traveled incognito to France. She hadn't seen Paris for twenty-three years. She especially wanted to visit the site of the Tuileries Palace, it held so many memories for her, both good and bad. As we sat together on a shaded park bench, she reminisced an entire afternoon about her years as empress of France.

"Before we left Paris to return to England, we paid a visit to the Saint Louis company sales rooms on the Rue Paradis-Poissonniere to purchase a few decorative glass pieces for our friends in England. As we walked into the shop, an elderly gentleman behind the counter instantly recognized my grandmother. Fortunately, he had the good sense to understand her wishes for privacy. Bowing unobtrusively, he touched her gloved hand to his lips and whispered, 'Your Imperial Highness.' After we made our purchases, he approached us once again and asked, 'Your Highness, do you recall a time about twenty-five years ago when you summoned me to the Tuileries Palace and commissioned me to undertake the creation of three paperweights?'

"Grandmother, replied, 'Yes, yes—', then searched her memory and eventually said, 'You must be Monsieur—ah, yes, yes, Monsieur Didierjean, the director who created those three magnificent paperweights for me!'

"Pleased that she remembered his name, he said, 'Yes, your Imperial Highness, it was a singular honor to have been entrusted with that commission. That was many years ago. I've since left the factory and assist here in the company's sales rooms.' He placed a finger on the side of his nose, closed his eyes, and struggled to ferret out an almost forgotten memory of something connected with those paperweights. Remembering, he drew close to my grandmother and said, 'Your Highness, there was something that occurred during the creation of those paperweights that I must, for your safety, relate to you.'

"It was a strange story, Mr. Wilde, one you might like to use sometime. He said there was a death curse pronounced on the Imperial paperweights by a devil-worshipping sorceress, Marcella of Valady. Marcella's grandson, a glass artist, died as he created those paperweights for my grandmother. The poor old gentleman was certain that the misfortunes that befell Maximilian, my grandfather, and my father, as well as the collapse of my grandfather's empire were due to an evil inherent in the paperweights!"

Wilde clapped his hands, saying, "Marvelous, marvelous! What a splendid story; an evil talisman!" Turning to Bosie and Ross, he asked, "Can you imagine in this age of scientific progress that anyone would still believe in such ridiculous superstitions?"

"Of course," Etienne continued, "Grandmother and I rejected the foolish notion of a curse. We talked about Monsieur Didierjean as we crossed the channel and decided that as a child, he must have been nurtured on the superstitions and witchcraft which the commoners accepted as fact only a few generations ago. He truly believed that the paperweights were cursed."

Lifting the paperweight from the table, Wilde held it to his chest saying, "What foolishness—a curse attached to a piece of crystal. It's a glorious work of art, a paperweight I treasure, and will treasure always."

As Douglas watched his lover, he saw a blood red glow emanating from the glass object in his hand. Startled, he looked around the room to discover the source of the strange illumination, but could find nothing. Did the sinister glow come from within the paperweight, he wondered. Was it his imagination? Douglas shuddered as a cold chill swept through his body.

7.

The Marquis of Queensberry also planned to attend the opening night of *The Importance of Being Ernest*. He told his friends he would expose Wilde by interrupting the play and announcing Oscar Wilde's sordid sexual affairs to the playwright's adoring public. Fortunately, the theater management learned of the Marquis's intention to disrupt the play, and informed the police. On opening night, the authorities, well-aware of Queensberry's proclivity for violence, stationed constables in the lobby and at all the doorways of the Saint James's theater. When Queensberry appeared, armed with a bouquet of rotting vegetables, the officers refused him admittance. Not a man to be put off easily, he ignored the officers' suggestion to leave and attempted, without success, to forcibly enter the theater. He skulked around the theater in the falling snow for two hours, all the while cursing Oscar Wilde, the police and his former wife. Frustrated in his foiled attempt to disrupt the play, the Marquis yielded to the inevitable, threw the rotting bouquet at the stage door and left.

Queensberry remained isolated in his rooms for several days, brooding over his "mistreatment" at the theater. A hot flush rose up the nape of his thick neck each time he dredged up the sickening accusations about his son. How could Douglas submit to the indecencies of that depraved pervert? If he didn't break up the filthy relationship, he could never face his friends at the boxing ring or at the track! He had to do something, and soon. He feared that the shame consuming him would drive him to uncontrollable violence or worse, to madness.

On the afternoon of the fifth day following the incident at the theater, the Marquis went to Wilde's Albemarle Club, and wrote on a card, "For Oscar Wilde posing as a sodomite." He handed the card to the club porter and left. Queensberry was convinced that this denunciation, made in Wilde's own private club, would begin the public exposure which would eventually destroy his son's corrupter.

The club porter placed the accusatory card in an unsealed envelope, wrote Oscar Wilde's name on it, and two weeks later, when Wilde visited his club, gave him it. Reading it, Wilde hurried to his hotel rooms in Piccadilly and immediately sent notes to Ross and Douglas, urgently asking them to come as quickly as possible. When Ross arrived that evening, he found his friend in an agitated state.

"Oscar, what has happened?"

"Oh, Robbie, my dear friend, I hate to trespass on your kindness, but I just don't know where to turn or what to do!"

Never having seen Wilde so distraught, Ross assured him, "If friends can't offer succor in times of distress, they don't deserve to be called friends."

"I'm about to be ruined by that detestable man!"

"Who, Oscar? Stop walking about and tell me what has happened!"

"Bosie's father, Queensberry!"

"What's he done?"

Extending the card in a shaking hand, Wilde choked out the words, "He left this at my club with hideous words written on it. Look what he wrote for all to see!"

"Oh, Oscar, how awful!"

"He gave it to the porter two weeks ago. There's nothing left for me but to take him to court. Am I right? What do you think?"

"Of course you're right, Oscar. How dare he besmirch your character! He must be stopped. You've got a strong criminal case here. I'm certain he'll be imprisoned if you bring him to trial. Have you told Douglas about this?"

"I wrote him a note asking him to come here. He sent word that he'll arrive early tomorrow morning."

"I'm sure he'll want to know what his father's done."

"Robbie, my dear friend, would you do me the kindness to remain with me until Bosie arrives? I have need of both of you to help me decide what course of action I should take."

"But of course, Oscar."

The following morning, Douglas arrived. After reading

the card, he urged Wilde to prosecute his father, saying, "Oscar, my brother and I will gladly give you all the money we have to help you with the expense of the trial." Filled with hatred for his father, the young man rejoiced inwardly at the prospect of his father's imprisonment.

The three friends took a carriage to Ross's solicitors, Humphreys, Son and Kershaw, to inquire about the strength of Oscar's case. Scrutinizing the card, Humphreys pointedly asked, "Is there any truth to the accusation written here, Mr. Wilde?"

Confident that he hid his homosexual affairs well, Wilde replied, "It is a preposterous accusation, Sir. There is not a modicum of truth in the vicious slander!"

"Oscar's a married man with children," added Ross.

"Then, Mr. Wilde, we shall easily win the case."

That afternoon, the barrister applied for a warrant to arrest Queensberry. During the interval between Queensberry's arrest and trial, Queensberry's attorney, Edward Carson, employed several skilled investigators to pursue the slim leads the Marquis had gathered about Wilde. Their probing eventually led them to Alfred Taylor. While illegally searching Taylor's rooms, they discovered the names of young male prostitutes in one of Taylor's notebooks. Notations in the margins appeared to link one of them, Charles Parker, to Oscar Wilde. The investigators searched out Parker and obtained a statement from him attesting that Taylor had procured him for Oscar Wilde. Parker also willingly gave Carson's investigators the names of several other young male prostitutes who intimately involved themselves with Wilde.

While the defense busily gathered information supporting Queensberry's accusation, Wilde and Bosie, unaware of the bizarre turn of circumstances, spent the weeks together blithely enjoying a holiday on the French Riviera.

The prospect of a trial involving Wilde, a noted playwright accused of sodomy, and, Queensberry, a member of the House of Lords, a boxing champion and an outstanding steeplechaser, created a blizzard of gossip in London. On the morning of the trial's first day, long before it began, curious spectators crowded the small courtroom. Queensberry, the first of the two principals to arrive, appeared in a rumpled suit and a blue neck scarf instead of the expected collar and tie. Wilde made his appearance outfitted grandly in a frock coat, sporting a nosegay in his lapel and carrying an ivory handled walking stick.

While Carson, Queensberry's lawyer, questioned Wilde, his repartees brought the courtroom to the point of uncontrollable laughter. That evening, Ross, Douglas and Wilde, encouraged by the progress of the trial's first day, recalled with delight the frustration that Wilde's responses had caused Queensberry's lawyer.

"And when he asked you if you had ever adored a boy madly, and you answered, 'I have never given adoration to anyone except myself,' I thought I'd choke with laughter! You know Oscar, if the judge hadn't threatened to empty the court, they'd never have stopped laughing!"

On the second day of the trial, Queensberry's lawyer began by asking Wilde if he recognized the names: Atkins, Scarfe, Parker or Wood. The lawyer's knowledge of those names startled Wilde.

How did he obtain that information, he wondered. Had Taylor disclosed those names? No, that would have implicated him, also. Was it hearsay or had he actually spoken to the young men? They certainly wouldn't admit to anything; or would they? He had paid them well and they were still on good terms. Wait, wait—that problem four months ago with Charles Parker! It must have been that little thief Parker!

Parker had spent the night with Wilde in the Albemarle Hotel. The following morning as Wilde shaved at his wash stand, he noticed his yellow Carlota was not at its usual place, on the desk. Glancing about the room he saw an unusual bulge in Parker's jacket. Wilde took the jacket from the back of a chair, reached into the pocket and discovered his paperweight. Throwing back the bed sheets, Wilde shouted at the young man sleeping in his bed, "Wake up! Wake up you dirty little thief! Get out of my bed! How dare you steal from me. Don't I pay you enough? Put on your clothes and get out of here. I don't ever want you around here again!"

"What's wrong, Oscar?"

"This paperweight you stole from my desk!"

Parker dressed quickly and went to the door to wait for payment.

"Just open the door and leave!"

"You owe me for last night."

Wilde shoved him out of the room, saying, "I don't owe you anything, you damn thief! Get out of here! I don't ever want to see you again!"

Yes, thought Wilde, that's where Queensberry's lawyer got those names, from that despicable little thief. As the trial progressed, the names of the young men continued to cause him great concern.

At the end of the day, Queensberry's lawyer intimated that on the following day, he would call several young men to the dock who would admit to the shocking acts Wilde paid them to perform.

In a consultation that evening Sir Edward Clarke, Wilde's lawyer, told him that the jury would probably acquit Queensberry.

"Why, in heavens name?"

"It will be almost impossible to convince a jury to convict

a father who appears to be attempting to save his son from the corrupting influence of evil, whether imagined or real."

"You are absolutely sure?"

"Yes, I am. I strongly suggest we withdraw your suit against the Marquis."

"I can't believe what you're asking me to do. Queensberry has already admitted to writing the slander! All that remains now is to conclude the trial. The jury will certainly find him guilty! If I drop the charge, what will everyone think?"

Wilde's lawyer then expressed his most compelling argument for withdrawal. "If we continue, I fear the testimony Queensberry's lawyer is prepared to introduce from those young witnesses might do your reputation irreparable damage."

Realizing the imminent danger to his own name, Wilde reluctantly acquiesced to his counselor's advice. The following day, the judge accepted Wilde's decision, and instructed the jury to return a quick verdict of "not guilty" to the charges of libel against Queensberry.

As soon as the courts released Queensberry from the custody, he wrote Wilde, "If the country permits you to leave, all the better for the country. But if you take my son with you, I'll follow you wherever you go and put a bullet into your corrupt heart."

That same day, Queensberry instructed his solicitors to present the depositions of Wilde's accusers to the Director of Public Prosecutions. The dossier included damning testimony that Taylor procured several young men to engage in immoral sexual acts with Wilde. On the basis of the incriminating information, the courts issued warrants for the arrest of both Taylor and Wilde.

When Wilde's friends learned he was about to be arrested, they rushed to his rooms and urged him to escape to the Continent. Vacillating between fighting the charges in court or fleeing, he hesitated too long. The authorities apprehended Wilde and imprisoned him in Holloway prison.

During his three-week confinement in prison, many of Wilde's acquaintances, fearing they might also become suspect if identified as his friends, avoided contact with him; some took unscheduled trips abroad. The charges devastated his wife. She hadn't believed the terrible accusation until Wilde withdrew his suit against Queensberry. Now, she too began to doubt her husband. Anxious about the effect of scandal on their two small children, she made hurried preparations to take them to the Continent.

Wilde was desolate; everyone had abandoned him. Only Douglas remained steadfast. Of Bosie's merciful daily visits he wrote Ross, "It's not that I'm really alone. A slim young thing, golden-haired like an angel, stands always at my side. His presence overshadows me. He moves in the gloom like a white flower."

On one of those daily visits to Holloway prison, Douglas asked, "Oscar, do you suppose this awful situation might be due to the curse Etienne related to us?"

"Marcella's curse? The paperweight? Oh, such foolishness, Bosie! Don't be absurd. This temporary state of affairs will soon pass. We'll overcome this crisis, you'll soon see." Although Douglas felt slightly ridiculous when Wilde scoffed at his concern, his lover's skepticism did not completely allay his fears. He could not help but wonder about Etienne's story. Was it a coincidence, or had misery attended that yellow object since its fiery creation? Were the misfortunes of Maximilian, Carlota, Louis Napoléon and the Prince Imperial truly unrelated or were they held together by the web of an old crone's curse?

Douglas's told Wilde's attorney that he planned to attend

the upcoming trial daily, in support of his friend.

"Lord Douglas," the attorney said, "I strongly feel that your presence at the trial will be prejudicial to Mr. Wilde's defense."

"I have to show him my support."

"You can best help Mr. Wilde by leaving London. I don't want you to be called to the dock. That will complicate the case for me. It's going to be difficult enough with Taylor's involvement."

Douglas yielded to the attorney's suggestion and reluctantly left for Paris.

In contrast to his impeccable appearance during the Queensberry trial, Wilde, after three weeks detention, appeared in court tired and haggard, his hair uncombed and his clothes unkempt. His confinement had taken its toll.

Mr. Gill, the prosecutor for the Crown, made the opening statement to the jury and began the parade of the Crown's witnesses. Mrs. Ellen, a landlady, who said that Alfred Taylor rented four rooms from her testified against Wilde first. When asked to describe the rooms, she said, "Mr. Taylor sealed off the long windows to the outside with thick dark drapes over which he hung beautiful lace curtains. The rooms were lit up with many candles, and the air always hung heavy with perfume and burning incense."

The prosecutor asked, "Who were Mr. Taylor's visitors, men or women?"

"Only men, very young men, and older gentlemen, too."

"Was Oscar Wilde ever a visitor to Taylor's rooms?"

"I never saw him there, but I certainly have my suspicions about him."

Mrs. Grey, the landlady of another of Parker's rented apartments stated she saw Oscar Wilde visit Parker's rooms.

Questioned by Wilde's lawyer, she admitted she saw him there on only one occasion, and that he stayed for just a few minutes.

The prosecution's next witness, Alfred Wood, testified that he met Wilde through Lord Alfred Douglas and that Wilde performed "acts of indecency" with him many times. Wilde's attorney then cross-examined Wood in an attempt to discredit Wood's testimony by disclosing that Wood had once attempted to blackmail Wilde. Wood came into possession of amorous letters written by Wilde to Douglas and tried without success to use the letters to extort money from Wilde.

On the following day of the trial, Fred Atkins, a witness for the crown, stated he met Wilde through Taylor and accompanied the playwright on a trip to France as his private secretary. He testified that when they were in Paris he observed Wilde on two occasions in bed with young men, and that Wilde even made sexual advances toward him. Although at the outset, his testimony seemed injurious to Wilde, on cross-examination Wilde's barrister also exposed him as a blackmailer—a co-conspirator in Wood's extortion attempt on Wilde.

Edward Shelly, a former employee of Wilde's publisher took the stand next. Shelly testified that soon after he and Wilde became acquainted, Wilde invited him to the Albemarle Hotel. He related that as they dined, Wilde kissed him and suggested they go into his bedroom. He stated that he refused the invitation and left the hotel. He continued to see the defendant after that first meeting, so often that his co-workers teased him about their relationship, calling him "Mrs. Wilde" and "Miss Oscar." Unable to withstand the incessant teasing of his fellow workers, he eventually left his position.

The prosecution called Charles Parker to the dock next. He described how Taylor offered him and his brother, both unemployed, money to meet with some of his male clientele. The following day, Taylor and the Parker brothers joined Oscar Wilde for a late dinner. Parker further testified that after they finished dining, Wilde announced, "Charles is the boy for me." Then turning to the boy Wilde asked, "Will you come with me to the Savoy Hotel?"

"And what was your reply?" asked the prosecutor.

Parker answered, "I agreed to go with him."

"And what occurred there?"

"After a few drinks in his sitting room, Mr. Wilde asked me to accompany him into his bedroom."

"Did you go to his bedroom?"

"Yes."

"Tell us what occurred there."

The young man replied without hesitation and to the gasps of the crowd, "He committed the act of sodomy upon me." He further testified that Wilde paid him for that evening and for many other subsequent evenings. When asked to go into greater detail, Parker turned and stared at Wilde, saying, "I was instructed by Mr. Oscar Wilde to imagine that I was a young girl and that he was my lover. He told me to keep this illusion during our time together. As I sat naked on his knees, he fondled my privates as a man might amuse himself with a girl."

"And then?"

"He sodomized me."

You little thieving whore, thought Wilde, you couldn't wait to expose me to the world. Didn't I always treat you well? And how did you repay me? By attempting to steal from me, and now, by besmirching my name. You small ignorant man, why were you drawn to my little Carlota? You certainly couldn't appreciate its beauty. A shiny trinket to sell to the pawnbrokers for a few pence? If you'd asked for more money,

I'd have given it to you.

On the third morning of the trial, the prosecutor called several witnesses against Wilde, but their testimony proved to be inconclusive.

Prosecution witnesses Antonio Migge, a masseur, and Jane Cotter, a chambermaid testified last that afternoon. According to Migge's testimony, he went to Wilde's room at the Savoy Hotel to give him a scheduled early morning massage. When Migge opened the door, he saw a naked boy in Wilde's bed and Wilde at the washstand, dressing. Wilde dismissed the masseur telling him he decided to cancel the massage that morning. Jane Cotter's assertion that she also saw a teenage boy in Wilde's bed that same morning corroborated Migge's testimony.

On the final day of the trial, Wilde's attorney began his defense of the playwright by pointing out the unjust pillory of his "innocent client" by the English press. He attempted to cast doubt on the testimony of Wilde's accusers by disclosing the questionable backgrounds of the prosecutor's witnesses. He finally placed Wilde on the stand and asked him if there was any truth to the allegations leveled against him. Wilde denied all charges, saying, "There is no truth in any of the allegations, no truth whatsoever."

During Wilde's cross-examination, the prosecutor read excerpts from letters Wilde wrote to Douglas, selecting phrases such as, "You are the divine thing I want." and "Your letters are delightful, they are red and yellow wine to me." Wilde insisted that the prosecutor interpreted his words too literally and his own prurient thoughts influenced his accusation. In reality, Wilde said the passages in the letters referred to much loftier poetic meanings than those inferred by the prosecutor.

As the prosecutor delineated the many charges that the

prosecution's witnesses made, Wilde denied each one in turn. Questioned about his admitted association with so many young men, Wilde replied, "Rather than being a carnal lover of young men, I am in love with youth. A pure love between an older man and a younger man is beautiful, it is fine, it is the noblest form of affection. There is nothing unnatural about it. It is intellectual, and it repeatedly exists between older and younger men, where the older men have intellect and the younger men have all the hope and glamour of life before them."

Alfred Taylor followed Wilde in the witness box. Mercilessly cross-examined by the prosecutor, he offered only supportive evidence in favor of Wilde.

After the closing speeches for the defense and prosecution, the jury retired to arrive at verdicts on the various charges. Deliberating for a full three hours, they finally conceded that they were unable to come to an agreement on any of the indictments levied against the two defendants. Further deliberations, they assured the court, would not result in an accord.

On the application of Wilde's attorney, the court released Oscar on bond pending a retrial.

As soon as Wilde left prison, the Marquis of Queensberry employed several thugs to harass him and anyone they observed giving him food or shelter. Wilde decided to escape Queensberry's hired tormentors by leaving London, but he abandoned that plan; travel was expensive and he was now almost penniless. Wilde's plays and literary works always provided him with a sizable income in the past. But, immediately after his arrest, theaters pulled his plays from the stage and his booksellers dropped his books from their inventory—actions that cut off his income.

His financial situation grew so desperate, the authorities

seized his house and its contents to satisfy his creditors. Mr. Wormsley, who learned Wilde's possessions were to be sold, could not bear the thought of the dispersal of his client's paperweight collection. He decided to purchase all of Wilde's paperweights, telling his wife, "If I'm successful at the sale, I'll keep Mr. Wilde's collection intact and return it to the poor dear man after this distressing business is over and done with."

The paperweights attracted so little attention during the auction that Mr. Wormsley acquired them for a paltry sum of money. Returning to his shop, he carefully wrapped each one in torn strips of sheeting and placed all of them in several boxes for safekeeping.

Learning of Wilde's harassment by Queensberry's minions, longtime friends sent Wilde a message offering him a safe haven. He accepted the invitation and cautiously made his way to their home, remaining concealed there until his retrial. Though his friends encouraged him to flee England, he adamantly refused. He could not in good conscience betray those who had generously provided the money for his bail.

In a long note to Douglas in Paris, Wilde expressed his misgivings about the approaching retrial. "If prison and dishonor be my destiny, I think that my love for you and this idea, this still more divine belief, that you love me in return, will sustain me in my unhappiness and will make me capable of bearing my grief most patiently…if one day, at Corfu or on some enchanted isle, there were a little house where we could live together, oh! life would be sweeter than it has ever been…Our love was always beautiful and noble…the nature of that love has never been understood…Dearest boy, sweetest of all young men, most loved and most lovable. Oh! Wait for me! Wait for me! I am now, as ever since the day we met, yours devoutly and with immortal love. Oscar"

At the opening of the second trial, Wilde's attorney requested that the court try the defendants separately. Since the conspiracy charges of the first trial had been withdrawn, the judge granted his request.

The courts tried Alfred Taylor first. At the conclusion of his trial, the jury found him guilty of indecent behavior on two counts.

The following day, Wilde's trial began with the prosecution's first witness, Edward Shelly. Shelly once again stated that Wilde forced him to commit sexual acts with him on several occasions. During Shelly's cross-examination, Wilde's attorney shed doubt on Shelly's testimony by producing a letter the young man wrote to Wilde in which he stated, "I've longed to see you all week." Wilde's attorney also brought out the young man's irrational frame of mind during the time of the alleged sexual acts by revealing that Shelly physically attacked his own father. That incident led to the young man's arrest. At the disclosure of that occurrence, Shelly admitted, "I could not have been sane at the time, especially since I assaulted my own father."

The court devoted the afternoon of the same day to testimony by Alfred Wood. His questioning produced no new testimony detrimental to Wilde.

The following day, when Wilde's attorney cross-examined Jane Cotter, the Savoy Hotel chambermaid, she admitted that she had a vision problem and was not wearing her spectacles when she thought she saw a naked boy in Wilde's bed.

When Wilde's attorney cross-examined Antonio Migge, the masseur, he asked him whether or not Wilde's door was locked, and whether the person he saw in Wilde's bed was fair or dark. To both questions, Migge answered, "I don't remember." Wilde's counsel confidently assumed the masseur's answers to his questions cast doubt on the reliability of his memory.

During the cross-examination of Oscar Wilde, the prosecutor for the Crown read passages from Wilde's *Dorian Gray* and other literary works, attempting to convince the jury of Wilde's basic immorality. "And in the following passages, your Basil Hallward describes his unnatural feelings for young Dorian Gray. I read now, from your novel, Mr. Wilde, 'Suddenly I found myself face to face with the young man whose personality had so strangely stirred me. We were quite close, almost touching. Our eyes met again.' And later in the book, Mr. Wilde, this passage, 'He defines for me all the passion of the romantic spirit, all the perfection of the spirit that is Greek. Harry! Harry! if you could only know what Dorian Gray is to me! He was made to be worshipped.' And, this passage, Mr. Wilde, 'Crowned with heavy lotus-blossoms, he has sat on the prow of Adrian's barge, looking into the green, turbid Nile. He has leaned over the still pool of some Greek woodland, and seen in the water's silent silver the wonder of his own beauty.' Now I ask you, Mr. Wilde, are those descriptions of the feeling of an older man towards a youth, proper or improper?"

Not waiting for a reply, the prosecutor turned to Wilde's personal correspondence. He read many phrases to the jury. Among them, he focused a great amount of attention on a passage in a letter to Douglas in which Wilde wrote, "Those rose red lips of yours should have been made no less for music of song than for madness of kisses," and, "…your slim gilt soul walks between passion and poetry…"

Wilde replied, "Those selections represent a literary mode of writing and were intended as prose poetry."

"And, Mr. Wilde, in a letter to Lord Douglas in which you wrote, 'Hyacinthus, whom Apollo loved so madly, was you in ancient Greek days,' were you speaking of love between men?"

"What I meant by the phrase was that he is a poet, and Hyacinthus was a poet."

"Always, with undying love?"

"It has nothing to do with sensual love."

In response to the questioning about a young boy in his bed at the Savoy Hotel, Wilde said, "That statement is entirely untrue. No one was there with me."

The list of witnesses exhausted, Wilde's attorney approached the jury and made an eloquent summation in Oscar's defense. He especially directed the jury's attention to the cunning way the prosecutor selected and rearranged portions of Wilde's prose and poetry, reconstructing them out of context in an obvious attempt to prejudice the members of the jury against his client.

The Solicitor-General for the Crown delivered the prosecution's closing remarks. Referring to the letters Wilde wrote to Douglas, he argued, "If such letters were found in the possession of a woman, written by a man, they would be open to only one interpretation. How much worse is the inference to be drawn when such letters are written from one man to another...Any right-minded person would have looked on them as evidence of a corrupt passion." He closed his remarks with a final recitation of each of the Crown's eight counts against Wilde and the testimony offered in their support. Wilde was to write later, "The prosecutor's vicious remarks were like Savanarola's indictments of the Popes of Rome; I was sickened at what I heard!"

The Judge instructed the jury to decide if the Crown had provided evidence of guilt or had only presented suspicion of guilt for each individual charge. After several hours of deliberation, the jury found Wilde guilty of gross indecency on seven counts.

Judge Wills addressed Taylor and Wilde who were standing in the dock. "I had no doubt of the jury's findings. This is the worst case I have ever tried. The evidence in this trial has proven that you, Taylor, kept a male brothel and that you, Oscar Wilde, were at the center of a circle of extensive corruption of the most hideous kind among young men. People who can do these ugly things must be dead to all shame. I shall, under the circumstances, be expected to pass the severest sentence that the law presently allows, although in my judgment it is totally inadequate for such a case as this. The sentence of the court is that each of you be imprisoned and kept to hard labor for two years."

As the words registered in Wilde's brain, his legs began to melt under him. Tightly holding onto the railing he attempted to speak to the judge, pleading, "And I, may I say nothing, my lord?"

The judge, ignoring Wilde's plaintive request, motioned to the bailiffs who took possession of the condemned men and conducted them out of the courtroom to a basement cell, to be held there until their internment in prison.

In a rebuttal to the English press which censured Wilde for his "terrible sin" and applauded his incarceration, Douglas wrote, "I was the young man, the fortunate child who shared Oscar Wilde's love. And for that I was detested and pitied by everyone, including my own father. Had I had the good fortune to live in ancient Athens, my relationship with Oscar Wilde would have resulted in my glory rather than in my disrepute. Why is today so different from ancient Greece? Why can't a man be allowed to love a man rather than a woman, when his nature directs him so? Many noble and gifted men have had similar tastes, Shakespeare, Marlowe, Michaelangelo, Frederick the Great, and many others. And think on this, a man who turns to female prostitutes, who seduces girls or commits acts of adultery and brings bastards into the world does a great deal more harm than the love between an older man and a younger one."

8.

Early one morning, guards arrived at the Old Bailey jail to transport all of the prisoners in basement cells to Pentonville Prison. Reaching their destination, guards led the shackled prisoners single-file down one of the prison's many dingy corridors. The warden stopped before a rusty iron door and signaled for guards to open it. Wilde attempted to close his eyes and block out the prison cell yawning before him, but the horror of his imprisonment and the apprehension of what might happen next, prevented his eyes from closing completely. With his head unmoving and his eyelids narrowed to slits, his half-hidden pupils frantically darted back and forth taking in all the sordid details of the cell. A jailer unshackled Wilde, pulled him out of line, shoved him into the cubicle and slammed the iron door shut. As the key found the rusty slot and turned, the echo of the hard metallic clack reverberated in Wilde's brain, signaling the hopelessness of the pit into which the world rudely cast him.

His entire universe suddenly compressed into a tomb—a constricted, poorly lit, lime-washed, stone block enclosure filled with stale, oppressive air. A small wooden table, a chair, a tin chamber pot and a wooden pallet bed covered with a coarse blanket furnished the painfully sparse cell.

Wilde, like most Pentonville prisoners, was required to unravel and separate oakum in his cell. If he did not meet his daily quota, the guards deprived him of his one hour of silent outdoor exercise in the prison yard that day.

For daily breakfast, the guards gave the inmates oily cocoa and brown bread. The main meal consisted of fatty bacon and beans or a thick mixture of corn meal, water and suet. One day a week they treated prisoners to cold meat.

Stringent prison rules prohibited talking among the prisoners during the entire term of their imprisonment. If caught conversing, the guards severely punished them. In addition, they permitted Pentonville inmates little contact with the outside world. Once every three months, they permitted prisoners one visitor and a single sheet of paper on which to write a letter.

To Wilde's refined senses, Pentonville embodied the depths of hell. During the first month of his imprisonment he moved about in a daze. The prison guards, who took special pleasure in his torment, scorned and jeered at Wilde, who only months before received the adulation of an admiring public. They reduced his diet, which had always consisted of gourmet foods and the finest of champagnes to foul-tasting slop. They denied his chief pleasure, that of eloquently expressing his views by an enforced silence. Wilde, who always enjoyed the companionship of intellectual equals, found himself in the midst of a mute mass of suffering humanity whose only concern was mere survival. Even the ill-fitting prison garb, large, loose and emblazoned with thick prison arrows, pained the sensibilities of one who always dressed immaculately, one who always wore a fine frock coat with a boutonnière in his lapel. The cruel punishment of being limited to one sheet of writing paper every ninety days devastated Wilde, who measured his existence by what he created with his pen; it reduced him to the level of a beast. He wrote later, "Pentonville Prison was a fiendish nightmare, more horrible than anything I had ever dreamed of."

After what seemed an eternity, Wilde received a visit from his wife, the single visit allowed at the end of his first three months of imprisonment. When the prison guard terminated the visit, it was a painful, tear-filled parting for both of them. Just before they took Wilde away, Constance told her husband Mr. Wormsley died of pneumonia and Mrs. Wormsley gave his paperweight collection to Wilde's mother for safekeeping.

Several weeks after his wife's visit, Wilde learned the distressing news that Queensberry served his estate with a bankruptcy notice to recover the costs he incurred in defense of Wilde's libel suit.

When Queensberry's solicitor reminded his client that Wilde was insolvent and there was no hope of recovering any money from him, Queensberry replied, "He's locked away in prison for two years, hidden away from the public eye. I don't care what it costs me, I want him dragged into Bankruptcy court and made a public display. It'll be worth it just to see him squirm again."

Although devoid of assets, the law required Wilde to appear in a public court and make a legal accounting of his finances. The day he appeared, the courtroom filled with those who came to enjoy his debasement. During the long process the court made him go over every item in his finances, while Queensberry, in the company of his friends, gloated over Wilde's degradation. To Wilde, the terrible indignity of appearing shackled in a public court crowned his humiliation.

Through the merciful intervention of sympathetic officials, the authorities transferred Wilde to Wandsworth Prison, and four months later to Reading Jail. His transfer to Reading Jail coincided with a change in its administration, one which placed the institution in the hands of a humane and reform-minded director. Instead of tearing away at oakum, Wilde's labor consisted of gardening, bookbinding and minor duties in the prison library. At the suggestion of the Prison commission, the administration provided him with a generous supply of books to read and writing materials for use during his leisure time.

On the advice of a visiting friend, Wilde started to write about his prison experiences with the intent of future publication. Two major works began to take shape: *The Ballad of Reading Gaol*, a poem, based on a true incident, describing a young soldier's final days in prison and his eventual execution for murdering his wife out of jealousy, and *De Profundis*, a work in the form of a letter containing over thirty thousand words addressed to Lord Alfred Douglas expressing Wilde's private thoughts about the events that led to his imprisonment. The soul searching work placed much of the blame for his misfortunes on Douglas.

On her second visit, Wilde's wife brought him the sad news that his mother died. That Constance made the long journey from Italy to Reading Jail, so that he might receive the sad tidings from "lips that were neither indifferent or alien", deeply touched him. She told him that after his mother's funeral, Wilde's brother brought her the paperweights Mrs. Wormsley left with their mother. Wilde asked Constance to keep them for him and to take special care of the large yellow paperweight. "You remember, Constance, Empress Eugenie gave me that lovely weight. Her magnificent gesture helps me during my moments of darkest gloom."

The remainder of the time they visited together, they discussed the uncertain future of their two children. He advised Constance to consider the aid of a guardian for Cyril and Vyvyan if she felt unable to manage by herself. On her return to Genoa, Constance appointed her brother as guardian for the children, and, to avoid future embarrassment for them, legally changed their names as well as hers from Wilde to Holland, Holland being one of her family names.

Just prior to his release from prison, Constance, who had money of her own, settled a yearly allowance on Wilde with the provision that it be terminated if he ever met with Lord Alfred Douglas again.

On Wilde's release from prison, he attempted to divest himself of the dishonor attached to his well-known name by taking a new name, "Sebastian Melmoth." Late that same night he boarded a ferry and crossed the channel to France, vowing never to return to England again, a land where he had fallen from triumph to utter disgrace.

Several of his friends met him in Dieppe as he disembarked, and offered to help him find a suitable place to live. They searched the French countryside together until they found a small hotel in the tiny Normandy village of Berneval. Pleased with the accommodations, Wilde took up residence there and began to refine his poem, *The Ballad of Reading Gaol*.

With the smell of prison no longer in his nostrils, Wilde longed for the companionship of his family. He wrote Constance asking her to come to Berneval with Cyril and Vyvyan; he hadn't seen his sons for two and a half years. She wrote agreeing to visit him several times a year, but said nothing about the children. Frustrated, he wrote again asking if he might travel to Genoa to see his family, but she wouldn't permit it.

A month later, learning that Constance suffered terrible pain from spinal paralysis, the result of a fall, he wrote her pleading for permission to travel to Genoa to see her. When he read her response, putting him off once more, he tore the letter into bits, exclaiming, "Damn you, Constance! Haven't I suffered enough at the hands of my enemies? Do you take pleasure in punishing me, also? How long will you continue to deny me?"

When, at long last, she consented to see him, Wilde, angry at her previous rebuffs, rejected her invitation. By then, he had decided to forsake his family for Bosie.

Not wanting to be with Bosie where he might be recognized by his wife's acquaintances and thereby forfeit his yearly allowance, Wilde made arrangements to meet secretly with his young lover for a day in Rouen. On Wilde's return to Berneval, he cast about for two weeks accumulating enough money to join Bosie who had gone on to Naples for an extended holiday. When Constance received a letter from her husband postmarked from Naples, she became suspicious that he might be visiting Douglas there. At her request, her solicitor contacted an investigator in Naples who ascertained that Oscar and Douglas, indeed, lived together. She angrily dispatched Wilde a terse letter, saying, "You've violated our Deed of Arrangement! I forbid you to remain there with Lord Alfred Douglas. I forbid you to return to your filthy, insane life! I forbid you to live in Naples. Will you never stop shaming me and the children? I will never allow you to come to Genoa."

Early in December, Douglas left for Paris and secured rooms in a Latin Quarter hotel, where two months later, he was joined by Oscar Wilde. During that winter several editions of Wilde's ballad were published and enthusiastically received. The following spring, in April, Constance went to a hospital for surgery to relieve the painful pressure on her spine. A week later, she died. Devastated, Wilde wrote Ross, "It's really awful. I don't know what to do. If we had only met once again, and kissed each other. But, it is too late, now. How awful my life is!"

"When those they love are wrapped in their shrouds of death, may their suffering be as deep as mine."

Soon after Constance's death, her brother sent Wilde the yellow Imperial paperweight. In the accompanying note, he wrote, "...Constance often spoke of your attachment to this paperweight. She kept it on the night stand next to her bed after you told her of your concern for its safekeeping. It was the last thing my dear sister saw each night before going to sleep and the first thing to greet her eyes when she awakened in the morning. She grew attached to it and shared your appreciation of its beauty. I thought you might wish to have it there with you as a remembrance.

"Your other paperweights are now in the possession of your two sons who asked me to assure you that they will watch after them until you request that your collection be forwarded to you there, in Paris..."

Wilde penned a note of appreciation to Otho for his thoughtfulness. A portion of his closing paragraph read, "...As for the paperweights, it pleases me that my dear sons, Cyril and Vyvyan, wish to keep the collection for me. Please explain to them that in my present state of affairs I do not know what the immediate future holds for me. Quite frankly, I have no long-range plans; I live from day-to-day. I do not contemplate a permanent residence for myself in the near future, but time will surely answer my many unsettled questions. In the meanwhile, Otho, it is my wish that my dear children keep the paperweight collection. intact and consider it one of the few remaining possessions of any value I have to share with them."

When Douglas saw the paperweight on Wilde's desk, he recoiled at the sight of it. "My God!" he exclaimed, "where did that come from?" Not waiting for a reply, he began pleading with his friend, "Oscar, it's cursed!. Please, please get rid of it!"

"It's just a paperweight, Bosie."

"It put you in prison!"

"No, it didn't! I was imprisoned because of those ungrateful whores of Taylor, especially that little thief, Parker."

"That paperweight killed your wife and your mother and old Wormsley! Can't you see it radiates evil?"

"Don't be foolish, Bosie. Listen to yourself. Do you also fear mother's milk? Every child who has suckled at his mother's breast has died, or will be dead in a hundred years. Does that make mother's milk cursed? Those deaths you point to were natural occurrences."

"So close together? I can't believe they were coincidences!"

"My dear Bosie, Wormsley and my mother were elderly. As for Constance, her illness began with a terrible fall."

"Please, Oscar, I've feared that paperweight since Etienne told us about it. It's damned. For heaven's sake, throw it away!"

"Never, Bosie, never! If it ever leaves me, it will be to return to the hand of Empress Eugenie. Just knowing she paid me the supreme compliment of that gift helped to sustain me during my darkest days in prison."

Soon after Wilde received the little yellow Carlota, he and Douglas began to find fault with one another. Wilde's *De Profundis* effectively rent fissures in the deep love that Douglas felt for Wilde. References in the work to Douglas's "shallow nature" and "undergraduate verse" rankled the young man.

"And, furthermore, Oscar," he complained, "you wrote that your association with me wasted much of your time."

"That's absolutely true, Bosie. If it were not for you, I would have used my time much more wisely. I'd have shared it with my little family, with Constance and the boys. Because of you, that door is forever closed to me, now. I shall never be blessed with that happiness."

"But you begged me to be with you."

"I couldn't help myself."

"...and why, Oscar, did you write that I was responsible for your bankruptcy?"

"Until I was imprisoned, my purse provided for everything we did together: trips, food, drink, accommodations. When we first discussed the money necessary to prosecute your father, you said that you and your brother would help me with the expense. When I couldn't raise the money to meet that expense, my possessions were sold to satisfy my creditors. Your father even dragged me, penniless, through debtors' court."

"It's strange you don't remember that when my father was arrested, I gave you all the money my brother and I had, 360 pounds."

The distressful state of their finances became a continuing source of friction. Wilde's income consisted of a small allowance from Constance's estate and the sporadic receipt of his sparse royalties. He augmented those meager resources by whatever he could borrow from friends. Bosie's paltry income came from his mother who provided him with just enough money on which to live, but not enough for the slightest extravagance. Sometimes their hotel bills grew so far beyond their means that, to the consternation of their hoteliers, they secretly gathered together their few belongings and disappeared without a trace.

As their ardor for one another waned, they suffered the remorseful pangs of a deteriorating relationship. And though they made many serious attempts to return to that pre-prison state of affection, more often than not, they angrily separated after bitter disputes over insignificant matters.

Douglas's fear of the "little yellow Carlota" remained a constant source of their tempestuous quarrels. "Oscar, I insist that you get rid of that malevolent paperweight!"

"Bosie, don't be such a silly ass!"

"I refuse to stay under the same roof with that evil thing. If you don't do something about it, I shall leave!"

"Good riddance. It'll be a pleasure to have you out of my sight!"

After a bitter argument which erupted when Wilde accused his friend of not paying his share of their expenses, they parted permanently. When Douglas returned to London and told his mother that the long relationship ended, Lady Queensberry was ecstatic at their separation. Hoping to sever all ties between the two men, including ties of shared indebtedness, she settled all their outstanding accounts. She also sent Wilde funds to settle any bills which might have been overlooked, and money for another three month's rent on his rooms.

Later that year, Wilde learned that Douglas, who inherited eight-thousand pounds on his father's death, visited Paris on a holiday. He invited the young man to dine with him at the Café de la Paix. As they dined, Oscar asked Bosie, now a man of means, to repay the money that he owed him, especially since Wilde was in need. Douglas refused, creating an ugly, embarrassing scene, mocking Wilde and laughing in his face. Wilde rose from the table, and said, quietly, "How dare you treat me like this in public? Haven't I suffered enough because of our relationship? I shall henceforth have nothing to do with you. You've already taken from me any wealth and happiness that I might have had. You've been the chief cause of my grief and ruination. Today, with your shocking display, you've killed any vestige of affection that I had for you. It is my wish to never see you or be in contact with you ever again."

As Wilde walked out of the café, Douglas shouted after him, "You don't love me! You only see me as a repository of money. None of my money is yours. It's all mine, and I intend to spend it only on myself!"

9.

Wilde struggled for the remainder of his life to achieve the means to support himself and his assignations with an ever-changing retinue of pretty young men. That autumn, as he wended his way from Paris to the Riviera, Rome and Naples, his young lovers were many and varied: Icarus, named from a book on mythology; a young actor with "a face chiseled for high romance"; an intelligent Radley school boy; "most beautiful"; a seminary student; a youthful guide; a smart and elegant Adonis; an unnamed muscular Greek boy found in a Venetian garden; and others, many others.

The following spring, Wilde returned to Paris and took up residence in a shabby hotel. The small room, reached by a spiral staircase, offered a single window that overlooked the littered courtyard at the back of the hotel. He thoroughly despised the room's faded wallpaper which was strewn with large ugly magenta flowers. His meager furnishings included a bed, a slatted chair, a washstand, a threadbare settee and a small writing table on which he enshrined his "little yellow Carlota."

Except for correspondence and an occasional article on the need to improve the terrible conditions in English prisons, his creative writing ceased. When Ross wrote him asking about the cessation of his creative writing, Wilde replied, "I feel no desire to write; I don't think I shall ever really write again. Prison destroyed me body and soul. Something is killed inside me."

Evenings, alone in his room, as he fondled his yellow Carlota, Wilde attempted to fight his loneliness by reliving those happier times in London. But those pleasant memories always gave way to questions about the source of his dreadful circumstances. Was it because of my decision to take Queensberry to trial?. Did it begin when I first met Taylor? Or, did it all begin with Parker's attraction to Carlota's paperweight? I should have fled England when I had the chance. In time, it would have all subsided. I could have continued my life as a successful playwright, if not in England, surely here on the Continent or America. They adored me in America. As he dwelt on the events which led to his downfall, a short phrase of Democritus often floated to the surface of his consciousness, a phrase which seemed to have been written especially for him. "Man everywhere blames nature and fate, yet his fate is but an echo of his own character, his own passions, his own weaknesses and his own mistakes."

Ross, who traveled to Paris to visit Wilde, noticed that his friend drank more heavily than usual and that his personal appearance lacked its usual meticulousness; his shirts, coat, trousers and hats showed stains and wear. Wilde complained to his friend that many of his former acquaintances avoided him. Ross suspected that they avoided Wilde because of repeated requests for money, and that others probably shunned him because they felt uneasy in the company of one convicted of such sordid behavior.

"How far I've come down in this world," Wilde lamented to Ross. "I reached such heights with my successes. Look at me now—friendless and enveloped in shame and poverty. Life has become a useless weight; there is nothing left for me but death." As he sat in his dismal room, stroking Carlota's yellow paperweight, contemplating his own death, he added, "When I finally die, I'm afraid there will be no friends left to mourn me; no one shall sing my requiem."

A painful mastoid in Wilde's right ear began to add to his problems. The mastoidectomy, performed to relieve the torturous condition, seemed successful, but within a month, the abscess redeveloped. Fearing that the infection might spread to Wilde's brain, his doctor applied ice packs to his head and administered opiates. Though the drugs were powerful, they couldn't dull the excruciating pain enough to afford Wilde the relief of a much needed rest. Within a week, the doctor sent a telegram to Ross to inform him that his friend had developed cerebral meningitis.

"...EVERYTHING MEDICALLY POSSIBLE IS BEING DONE STOP HE IS FAILING STOP UNLESS DRAMATIC CHANGE MR WILDE WILL NOT SURVIVE THE WEEK STOP."

Ross rushed to Paris where he found Wilde in bed, disoriented and confused. In his delirium, he believed himself happily back on a small Aegean island with Bosie. Ross immediately sent a telegram to Alfred Douglas notifying him of Wilde's grave condition. On that same day, Father Cuthbert Dunne, a local priest, summoned to Wilde's bedside by Ross, made the following entry in the register of his church, "Today Oscar Wilde, lying 'in extremis' in the Hotel Alsace, 13 Rue des Beaux-Arts, Paris, was conditionally baptized by me." Later that week, the priest added at the bottom of the same page, "He died the following day, having received at my hands the Sacrament of Extreme Unction."

"...*suffer the fires of the glory hole while they live*..."

When Douglas received word of Wilde's condition, he immediately left for Paris. To his disappointment, he arrived on the day of the funeral, a day after Wilde's demise. Experiencing pangs of remorse for failing to arrive in time for a reconciliation, Douglas attempted to ease his feelings of guilt by paying for the expense of the funeral and settling Wilde's outstanding medical and hotel bills.

After the brief church service, Douglas, Ross, Wilde's hotel proprietor and a few of Wilde's acquaintances accompanied the casket to the cemetery. There, the handful of mourners huddled together at the open grave, attempting to ward off the savage December wind cutting through their greatcoats and mufflers. While the carriage drivers and their snorting horses waited to return the men to the warmth of the hotel, Father Dunne hurriedly performed the graveside service.

That evening, the hotel proprietor invited Lord Douglas to take possession of Wilde's few effects. The hotelier, candlestick in hand, led the young man up the narrow spiral staircase to Wilde's room, unlocked the door and lit the hanging gaslight jets. When Douglas's eyes adjusted to the soft illumination, the shabbiness of the room shocked him. The hotelier offered, "I'll send the chambermaid with coal to stoke up the fire for you, Lord Douglas. It'll take the chill and dampness from the room."

"Please don't bother, Monsieur, there is little of consequence here; I don't think I'll be very long."

"As you wish, my lord. I'll leave the candlestick for you. The staircase is dark."

Boisie began the task of sifting through the few fragments of Wilde's sparse estate. Many times that evening, the flames of the gaslights rayed into blinding auras as the young man's eyes filled with tears of remorse. *How could I have abandoned Oscar to live out his last days in this miserable room?* His clothes hanging on those nails—they're so threadbare. How he must have loathed to wear them. Why didn't I make life more bearable for him these last few years?

He lifted Wilde's well-worn razor strop from a nail in the wall. Stroking the strop with his hand his eyes focused on Wilde's dilapidated washstand. God, he thought, a corroded mirror and cracked bowl—a cracked bowl! How this wretched room must have offended his sensitivities.

He turned to a small crowded table. On it stood several vials of medicine, a sepia photo of Wilde's two sons, writing materials, and in one corner of the table, a stack of newspapers. Nearing the table, his eyes suddenly caught a glint of yellow glass from behind a stack of letters. "Oh, my God," he cried, "he kept that horrible malignancy!" Recoiling from the sight of the Imperial paperweight, Douglas leaned against the wall, lamenting, "Oscar, Oscar, I warned you, I warned you…" Exhausted from the many emotions of the day, he remained there quietly for a long time, then heaved a sigh and turned to the burden at hand.

On a slatted chair, next to the bed, he found a pile of partially written letters and outlines of literary ideas that Wilde never completed. As Douglas casually paged through the material, he found old clippings of Wilde's London successes as well as newspaper accounts of his court trials interspersed throughout the stack. He placed all of the literary items into a carton, intending them for Ross, who had agreed to act as Oscar Wilde's literary executor. As he gave the room a final look, he wrapped the Imperial paperweight in a silk handkerchief and slipped it into his coat pocket. His task complete, Douglas lit the candlestick and turned off the gaslights. Halfway down the spiral staircase, he paused and whispered, "Good-bye, dear love."

10.

Douglas crossed the English Channel the afternoon of the next day and boarded the first available train to Hampshire where he secured rooms for a short stay. Early the next morning, he sent a message to Empress Eugenie, asking to call upon her.

"It's so good to see you once again, Lord Douglas," said Eugenie. "I've not had many guests this past year. The terrible Boer War has curtailed our social season. So many of our young men are in Africa now. I believe you met my grandson, Etienne."

"Yes, your highness, we became acquainted in London when he visited Mr. Wilde."

"He is in Africa now."

"I didn't know."

"He enlisted eleven months ago. Etienne is a lance corporal, a fusilier with the 11th Brigade. Fortunately, with our recent successes there, the war is coming to an end. The War Department has just announced that Kruger has fled to Portugese East Africa. Now that the Afrikaners are well in hand, Field Marshall Roberts plans to leave Cape Town and return to England. I'm overjoyed that Etienne will be coming home soon!"

"Yes, that's wonderful."

"And how is your friend, Mr. Wilde?"

"I've just returned from his funeral, your Highness."

"His funeral? Oh, I'm so sorry, Lord Douglas, I didn't know he was ill. How terribly sad. He'll be missed. With all that happened to that dear man, he was indeed fortunate to have you as a constant friend. You must have been a comfort to him."

Feelings of guilt swept through Douglas at Eugenie's

words. Noticing the difficulty that the young man was having with his emotions, she avoided the many questions she wanted to ask about Oscar Wilde's demise.

Douglas reached into his coat pocket and took out Wilde's paperweight. As he unwrapped the silk handkerchief from around the yellow paperweight, he said, "Your Imperial Highness, Mr. Wilde once expressed the desire that this paperweight be returned to you if it should no longer be in his possession."

"Why, it's Carlota's yellow paperweight! I gave it to him because he admired it so. That poor, poor man. I hope it brought him some little measure of joy. He had such tribulation these last few years."

Still holding the paperweight, Douglas continued, "Your Highness, for the past two days, this paperweight, this abomination, has presented me with an awful dilemma."

"What do you mean?"

"I was torn between complying with Oscar's wish to return it to you, or to put an end to the malignancy by throwing it into the Channel."

"But, my dear sir, I don't understand why you would consider discarding such a lovely work of art!"

"Because of the evil it possesses, your Highness. It destroys everyone it touches. Your grandson told us about the warning you received when you were in Paris. Since this cursed thing has been in Mr. Wilde's possession, it caused him to be imprisoned; a shopkeeper who kept it for him died; Oscar's wife and mother were put in their graves; and now—" his voice caught, "it has killed—Oscar. Your Imperial Highness, I beg you to destroy it before it settles a catastrophe on you."

Taking the paperweight from Douglas's shaking hand, Eugenie said, "My dear young man, you're tired and distraught. Losing such a dear friend and then traveling this long distance has exhausted you. Please rest here tonight. We can talk about the paperweight in the morning. Tomorrow you'll see things in a different light."

"Thank you, your Highness, but I don't intend to spend another moment under the same roof with that piece of glass!"

"Please, Lord Douglas, do reconsider. Do stay the night. I'll have my physician prepare you a calming sedative so that you may enjoy a night of restorative sleep."

Douglas expressed his appreciation for her kindness but remained adamant in his determination to separate himself forever from the paperweight. As he took leave of the empress, he once again implored her to destroy the crystal.

Nineteen days after Douglas's disturbing visit, Eugenie received two somber military officers who expressed the government's regrets that Lance Corporal Etienne Mignard, a combatant for the Queen, lost his life while engaged in hostilities against the enemy.

Suddenly, everything tumbled into place for her. "The paperweight is cursed! Dear God! Has that monstrous thing I conceived destroyed my entire family? Oh Etienne, forgive me. My poor, poor son—dear Louis!"

Eugenie fainted many times that day, mercifully descending into that protective well of unconsciousness. Revived each time by her physician, she faced her inconsolable grief anew. That evening, Eugenie, weeping, knew that Marcella had found her way into her family, seeking out those whom she loved, to lead them lemming-like into the sea of death. Convinced of the paperweight's evil, she summoned her footman and commanded him to deliver the hellish talisman to the village blacksmith with instructions to destroy it on his anvil.

Clothed in black, Eugenie closeted herself in her villa

until there were no more tears. She resolved to spend her remaining years in self-imprisonment, kneeling in prayer. With the exception of close relatives from Spain, she no longer received guests. Her home, draped in black and purple, became her mausoleum, a silent tomb wherein she ate and slept with her constant companions, despair and loneliness. She waited twenty years for death, a death which finally brought her the sweet peace which had eluded her so long.

"May blood and gall taint their offspring and their own miserable lives..."

CHAPTER IV.

1.

NEW YORK - 1980

Several years before the auction house appointed Alexandra director of Sotheby's-Chicago, she received a transatlantic telephone call from Christa Allen, a friend of many years.

"Hello, Alex? Alex, is that you?"

The agitation in Christa's voice alarmed Alexandra. Fearing bad news, she anxiously asked, "has something happened? Are you and Eric alright?"

"We're okay, Alex. I just had to call you from here. I couldn't wait to write!"

"What is it, for heaven's sake?"

"Eric and I are on holiday here in France exploring out-of-the-way places, trying to uncover some early music."

"Still pursuing old de Machaut?"

"Constantly."

"Isn't Eric jealous that you're hunting for another man?"

"He's caught the bug, too," said Christa, laughing. "Knows as much about Guillame's music as I do."

Alexandra heard Eric in the background excitedly urging Christa to get on with the reason for the call.

"Listen, Alex. We've uncovered a large cache of musty boxes here in Valady, in the basement of the village church."

"Valady?"

"Yes, Valady, a village near Nancy. Anyway, it's not music we've found, but records of the Verrerie de Lorraine!

"A verrerie—a glass house?"

"Uh-huh, the Verrerie de Lorraine!"

"I've never heard of that glass factory, Chris."

"That's why I'm calling you. I remember your obsession with nineteenth-century glass. Eric made inquiries about the company and found that it is virtually unknown. He telephoned a glass scholar in Zurich, but he could only find one short reference to the factory."

"Just one?"

"Yes, a footnote that said it was a small French glass works that closed its doors in 1881 because it couldn't compete with its larger competitors."

"Oh, I wish I could be there with you!"

"So do we, Alex. Glass just isn't our cup of tea. This stuff's really right down your alley, and it looks pretty important! There's so much of it here—loads of it. I knew how much it'd mean to you; that's why I called. Why don't you fly over? We've got another week of vacation. Eric and I could help you go through the material."

"You know I'm dying to, but I really can't, Chris. I've already taken my vacation days, and we're too busy here for any time off right now."

"When could you come over?"

"Not until early next summer, I'm afraid."

"Okay, then, we've got a date for next summer. We'll keep this find under wraps. As soon as you know your vacation plans, write me, and I'll arrange to be here, too. You'll need someone to help dust off those musty records. I remember how much you hate getting your hands dirty. I can open boxes and run interference and relieve you of all the little day-to-day details. That way, you'll be able to spend all your time with the material."

"You'd do that for me, Chris?"

"C'mon, Alex, I'd love to."

"I can hardly wait."

During the late 1960s, Alexandra and Christa shared accommodations while completing their graduate studies at the Boston Academy of Fine Arts—Alexandra in history of art and Christa in medieval music. For her doctoral thesis Christa completed an extensive dissertation on Guillame de Machaut, a fourteenth-century French composer. Alexandra remembered the many large reproductions of medieval vellum that her roommate ceremoniously tacked on their tiny dormitory walls—curiously written music notation of clustered squares, parallelograms, diamonds and rectangles haphazardly arranged on ruler-straight ledger lines. In later years, when Alexandra prepared early music parchments for auction, she recalled with nostalgic amusement Christa's melodramatic descriptions of "ancient, snow-bearded monks with gnarled, ink-stained fingers who spent their entire lifetimes in damp candlelit cells, carefully penning those ligatures, one at a time, on page after page of parchment."

And the music! Alexandra never forgot the eerie hollow sounds of the medieval music that Christa played on their record player.

"Good grief, Chris, some of it sounds like dogs howling!"

"That's because those high voice parts were written for *castrati*; you know, males who were de-balled so they could sing in a high register. Women weren't allowed to perform in public, then."

"Castrati?"

"Uh-huh. If a boy had a great soprano voice, they'd castrate him so that his voice wouldn't change during adolescence."

"How barbaric!"

"It was quite common then. If the operation proved to be

successful, they became popular performers. Some of them were admired like today's rock stars, and became quite wealthy."

"And if it didn't work?"

"Tough luck, I guess."

"But those aren't *castrati* on your record, are they?"

"No, they're male voices, contra-tenors. They're men who can sing in a high register. Those high vocal parts are usually sung by women or by boy sopranos today."

"It sounds so strange—men's voices so high and hollow."

"Well, it's not a vocal quality we're used to hearing."

After leaving the academy, Alexandra and Christa kept in touch. Christa who suffered through several unsuccessful liaisons over the years, fell in love with Eric, a fellow professor at the University of Zurich, and had settled down with him to share a happy life of teaching and research. Alexandra's years after matriculation were troubled ones. She agonized greatly over her mother's long-term confinement in a mental institution, and her mother's eventual death. Alexandra married soon after she lost her mother, but was divorced within a year of her marriage. She experienced several years of extreme depression after her divorce, and subsequently underwent the obligatory sessions with a psychiatrist who lifted many of the debilitating repressions from her psyche. For several years, she held a succession of jobs: working in a Madison Avenue art gallery, editing art books for a publishing house, and teaching art history in a small eastern college. But she felt discontented with each of those positions; they left her unfulfilled. Her life finally came together when she determined to devote her energies and talents to a career at Sotheby's.

As Alexandra and Christa planned, they spent their weeks the following summer in Valady, pouring over the extensive chronicles of the Lorraine factory. Their findings revealed that among the many incredible glass pieces produced by the small glassworks, the gaffers created three magnificent paperweights to satisfy an Imperial commission for the Saint Louis glass company. The description and drawing of the three paperweights piqued Alexandra's imagination.

"Chris, it says here that they were made in 1864 and 1865."

"That's during the Second Empire—Louis Napoléon's reign."

Examining the faded drawing of the paperweights, Alexandra said, "Look here in the margin, a notation: '*pourpre, vent, jaune*'—purple, green, and yellow—each paperweight in a different color! Isn't it curious that the Saint Louis company, one of the premier glass factories of France, would have pieces of such importance created for them by a company so insignificant it only rates a footnote today?"

Alexandra's three week stay in Valady created a resolve in her to uncover one of the three Imperial Paperweights. She agreed with Christa that locating even one of the paperweights one hundred and twenty years after its creation was outside the realm of probability, but still vowed that she would make the attempt. Alexandra theorized that paperweights of that quality were much too important to indiscriminately cast aside; they undoubtedly reposed in some remote corner of the world awaiting discovery. Being of a practical nature, she realized she might never have the means for a search of that magnitude. "I'd have to marry a millionaire," she said.

Christa asked, "If you had the money to hunt for them, where would you start?"

"Well, I'd begin on the assumption that the three weights were given to Empress Carlota. These records have told us that two of them were delivered to Eugenie about the time Carlota and Maximilian left for Mexico. The third one was delivered quite a bit later; that one was probably shipped to Carlota after her arrival there. I'd start searching in Mexico."

"But remember," said Christa, "Carlota returned to Europe and stayed there the rest of her life—in Belgium. They might be there."

"I don't think she would have taken them with her; she planned to return to Mexico as soon as she changed Louis Napoléon's mind."

"Then, if they were in Mexico City when Maximilian was executed, what happened to them? None of Carlota's paperweights have ever come to light."

2.

BUENOS AIRES - 1951

By some unknown route, Emilio's paperweight quit the Republic of Mexico and made its way to Argentina where it comfortably ensconced itself in Evita Duarte Peron's paperweight collection. As the green paperweight made its eighty year journey from owner to owner, the significance of the cameos and heraldic emblem faded into the past. And though a number of knowledgeable paperweight collectors existed in Mexico and Argentina who could have deduced the meaning of its motif, the green Imperial paperweight never came to their notice. If it had, it would have been the object of intense desire.

With the exception of Emilio's paperweight, which she kept in her bedroom, Evita Peron scattered her paperweight collection about her several luxurious residences. The placement of the piece in a Louis XV gilt ormolu cabinet reserved for her most prized decorative objects reflected the importance with which she regarded the Imperial paperweight. She included the piece with her finest Russian enamels, carved gem stones, small gold Incan artifacts and jeweled French boxes.

Evita learned of the piece's alleged curse while on a state visit to Europe. During a stay-over in Trieste, she mentioned to the press that she owned a paperweight that once belonged to Empress Carlota. A descendant of one of Carlota's handmaidens, present during the interview, related an embroidered account of Marcella's curse to Evita. Evita took special delight in acquiring that bit of information which she later shared with Roberta Leon, her personal secretary. And though Evita considered the story an old wive's tale, Roberta, superstitious to a fault, made the sign of the cross and offered up a protective prayer on hearing the details of the sorceress's curse.

Roberta, who escaped her humble beginnings and resided in cosmopolitan Buenos Aires, still carried the residual flotsam of her superstitious background; she continued to utter a curious mix of Christianized-pagan incantations and performed magic rituals to protect herself from "the evil eye." And because Señora Peron often playfully ridiculed her "old village ways," she wore her amulets well-concealed, and carefully avoided uttering her protective spells within Evita's hearing.

Roberta Leon was an only child born to a poor peasant family. Her mother augmented her husband's small earnings by casting spells and reading fortunes in her village. When Roberta's mother was born, the attending midwife forecast her prophetic powers as the infant issued forth from the womb, her tiny features shrouded in a diaphanous veil. After her mother's death, Roberta retrieved the remains of her mother's veil—

particles of dust sealed in a glass vial—and kept them enshrined in her bedroom.

"And what," once asked Juan Peron, "do you suppose the mystical veil was that covered her mother's face when she was born?"

"Probably a piece of torn placenta," laughed Evita. "It's enshrined in her bedroom, in a little glass bottle."

"No!"

"She keeps it on a table like a reliquary, between two votive candles."

"My God!"

Evita Duarte Peron was the youngest of five children fathered by her mother's protector, Juan Duarte, a landowner of moderate wealth with a wife and family,. He established this "other" family with Juana Ibarguren and their five illegitimate children in a small impoverished village, well away from his extensive *estancia*.

As a child, little Evita ran home crying and complaining to her older sister, Elisa, that the village children taunted her. "Why do they call me *bastarda*?" she asked.

"Because, Evita, our mother is not married."

"Are the mothers of the other children married?"

"Most of them are. Señor Duarte is our father, but he is married to another woman."

Little Evita barely comprehended the difficult concept.

Juana's protector died when Evita was seven. For two years, Juana struggled to keep her little brood together, relying on her wits and her bed for the means to feed and clothe the children. Whenever paying customers came to call on their mother, Elisa, the eldest daughter, hurried the younger children out of the adobe.

And when her little siblings asked Elisa, "But why does

she let them do that to her?" Elisa explained, "Because we need the money. They pay our mother for the pleasure she gives them."

Good fortune finally smiled on Juana. One of her regular patrons, an immigrant Italian restaurateur from a larger pueblo forty miles distant, offered Juana a home near his restaurant. The new home, grand when compared to her tiny adobe, was even large enough for her to take in boarders.

To her mother's distress, Evita dropped out of school before completing the elementary grades. Stage-struck at an early age, she lived from month to month eagerly waiting for the occasional visit of small itinerant acting troupes and musicians who performed in the villages throughout the provinces. Her mother warned, "Hanging around those musicians, you'll end up in bars and get pregnant!"

Evita shot back, "I now how to take care of myself. I'll never end up like you!"

When she was fifteen, Evita ran off to Buenos Aires with Augustin Magaldi, a guitarist who promised to help her make her break into the theater. Even though she lacked talent, education, money and theatrical experience, she boasted to everyone that one day she would become the leading actress of the Argentinean stage. Her guitar-playing lover, tiring of her tantrums and her incredible conceit, eventually abandoned her. Stranded in Buenos Aires, Evita barely subsided on the monthly fifteen-dollar salary she earned as an employee in a small radio station.

The next several years she modeled and acted on the stage and in movies, but because of her inexperience, she found those paths too sluggish for her driving ambitions.

Evita returned to radio work determined to capture the attention of the affluent radio sponsors. She would attempt to achieve the success she desired by manipulating those who possessed wealth—a dangerous path taken by starry-eyed girls in the past. Moneyed sponsors made it the usual practice to seduce young hopefuls who approached them for a chance at success. When the rich sponsors tired of them and cast them aside, despair reduced many of the disillusioned girls to poverty and prostitution. Unlike those naive unfortunates, Evita relentlessly pursued her fortune. Using the knowledge she gained by observing her mother's trysts during her early years in the village, Evita moved as a paramour from sponsor to sponsor, improving her lot with each new affair.

But she soon discovered that money and possessions did not satisfy her completely; she developed a thirst for power. Perceiving the power and influence in the hands of the military, she changed her direction once again and began to court the military officers of the ruling group. In a fortuitous happenstance for Evita, she and Colonel Juan Peron spoke at the same rally one afternoon. That chance encounter changed both their lives. Within a few short years after meeting, Evita achieved the highest position of political power in Argentina possible for a woman. She became the wife of the nation's President, Juan Peron.

3.

Sitting up in bed, supported by lace pillows, Evita Peron caressed her Imperial paperweight as she silently reflected on the hardships of her early years and on the past six satisfying years as First Lady of Argentina. Her brother and three sisters, lost in their own thoughts, came that morning to be with her when she learned the results of her latest medical examination.

Elisa, the eldest sister, looked up as President Peron,

followed by two doctors, entered the room. It's not good, Elisa thought as she examined Peron's face. He looks grim. Evita, also sensing bad news, broke the uncomfortable silence, demanding, "Well, learned doctors, what are your findings?"

The words "cervical cancer" drew gasps from her sisters. Peron went to Evita's bedside, took her hand in his and closed his eyes.

Watching Peron, Elisa thought, just look at him, the cheat. It's all an act. He's been escorting that little whore Nelly Madier around for three weeks now. He doesn't fool me. As soon as our Evita got sick, he started sleeping around again. Once a whoremonger, always a whoremonger. If Evita didn't guarantee him the loyal support of her "shirtless ones" he'd have dropped her a long time ago.

Looking up at the doctors, Evita asked, "What's your prognosis?" The doctors hesitated. She glared at them and demanded, "Give it to me straight!"

One of the doctors said, "Señora Peron, it's too early to tell how far the condition has progressed."

Locking her eyes on those of the doctor, she nodded her head slightly as if to ask, "And?"

He quickly said, "With medication and treatment, there is a possibility that an operation may not be necessary."

"You are absolutely sure about your diagnosis? There is no mistake? You are positive that I have cancer?"

"Yes, Señora Peron, we personally attended the biopsy. There is no doubt of malignancy."

At the doctor's assertion, everyone in the bedroom became immobile. All breathing in the room came to a stop. Only the soft sounds of Elisa's stifled weeping could be heard. As had always been her nature, Evita took immediate control of the situation, issuing commands to everyone in the room. "Roberta," she said, holding the paperweight up, "put this back in the cabinet. Juan, you stay here with me. All right, everyone else out of here! I'll send for you two doctors later."

Her brother and sisters instinctively moved toward her but she waved them away. "Out, out! And you doctors, why are you waiting? Didn't you hear me? Out, go, go!"

As they scurried from the room, her husband sat on the edge of his wife's bed, saying, "Why is this happening to us? How can this be when millions of families offer prayers nightly in our name? This calamity is not happening, it's a bad dream!"

She said calmly, "Juan, I've known for some time something is wrong, here inside me. I've been so tired lately, the occasional pain, those irregular discharges. Even you've remarked that I've lost weight."

"We were so elated when the people poured out their love for us at that rally a month ago."

"I'll never forget that night, Juan. My heart almost burst with joy. I thought those thousands would never stop screaming, "Evita, Evita!" And then, when they sang, 'Hear, Mortals, the Sacred Cry of Liberty,' our national anthem—I'll remember that night until my dying breath."

Evita's reference to death gave Peron unsettled feelings; the election was still months away. He vowed, "Evita, I'll send for the finest doctors in the world. They'll make you well again. I need you, I always have."

"Yes, Juan, but now I want you to leave."

"No, Evita!" he interrupted, "my place is here at your side."

"Please leave me now, Juan. Don't deny me this small request. I've sent for Father Benitez and need to rest before I speak to him." Smiling at Peron, she added, "My dear husband, with the help of medication, my pain is bearable. Now that we know what I have, the doctors will know what to do. I have no fear of cancer. We'll beat this illness, just as we've overcome all those other obstacles the past six years."

As the military escort drove Peron back to the Presidential palace, he reflected on their first meeting. A charity invited Juan, an army colonel, and Evita, a radio personality, to speak at a fund-raiser for earthquake victims. What struck him about her was her aggressiveness. In a complete reversal of conventional roles, she introduced herself to him; it didn't matter to her that the man usually made the first approach. He remembered her parting words to him as she left the rally that day, "If, as you said today, the cause of the people is your own cause, then regardless of the extent of the sacrifice, Colonel Peron, I will never leave your side until my death."

Peron's recollection of her prophetic words caused a sudden catch in his breath. As he forced his mind away from Evita's illness, he remembered that within a week of their encounter, she told him, "I love you passionately, my Colonel, and I adore you completely."

Juan Peron, twenty-four years her senior, flattered by her obvious attraction to him, suggested to Evita that they take adjoining apartments in Calle Pasada. Once there, she established herself as his mistress and persuaded Peron, a womanizer, to break-off with his other female lovers.

Evita's affliction intruded once again on Peron's thoughts of happier times. That morning the doctors told him privately that his wife's malady was terminal and that an operation would extend her life only nine to twelve months.

"Then that's what you'll have to do," he told the doctors. "You must keep her alive until after the election."

They cautioned Peron that if he chose that option, the months following the operation would be filled with great suffering for her.

"She's a fighter," Peron said, "she can take it. Just keep her alive until I'm elected."

As the Presidential limousine slowed at the approach to the Palace, Peron said aloud, "How can this be happening to me? Have I worked for six years only to be crushed by her damned illness? With the support of her 'shirtless ones', the election was in my pocket. Everything was going so well. It won't be easy without her; she's been my right arm."

"Excuse me, Mr. President," said the driver looking back at Peron, "did you say something?"

"No, Pablo, just keep your eyes on the road."

4.

Cypriano Reyes, informed that Juan Peron returned to the Presidential Palace, left his office to see him. Reyes, the leader of Argentina's General Confederation of Labor, the CGT, was concerned about Evita. He heard the recent rumors that she was desperately ill but hoped against hope that they were untrue. She had been so instrumental in the creation of the CGT, he could not imagine his organization without her. He always thought her indestructible.

"President Peron, Señor Reyes is here to see you."

"Send him in."

Reyes entered quickly and embraced Peron. "Juan, thank you for seeing me. I'm concerned about Evita. Are the rumors true? Is she ill?"

"Yes she is, Cypriano; she has cancer; it's terminal."

"Terminal?"

"She has less than a year to live."

"Oh, Juan. I'm so sorry. Is she in pain?"

"Yes. It comes in waves. The doctors give her drugs to take the edge off. She tries to mask it from those around her, but the medication can't hide the torment escaping from her eyes."

Reyes, shaken, mercifully shifted their conversation from the painful present to recollections of a happier past. He reminisced about the years when their three lives entwined as they fused the individual workers' unions into a powerful alliance, the General Confederation of Labor.

After a long pause, Peron said, "Cypriano, you must come and see her. I know she would be pleased to see you."

Reyes avoided Peron's eyes, saying, "How can I bear to see her? I'm afraid I'll break down at the sight of her suffering."

"She's become used to seeing those around her cry," Peron assured him. After a long silence, Peron said, "There's been such a change in her appearance in just a month. Her cheeks are sunken and her eyes look out from dark sockets. When she leaves her bed she has difficulty standing upright. Today I noticed how thin her arms have become; she is just skin and bone. Blue veins show through her paper-thin skin like rivers on a map." Peron's voice trailed off as he wearily closed his eyes.

Reyes anguished as he learned the details of Evita's illness. He couldn't decide if he should speak or remain quiet. His throat pained from its constriction as he attempted to hold back his tears. Regaining his composure, Reyes said, "It's so hard to think of her suffering that way. I can't help but remember how radiant she was when she left for Europe such a short time ago."

Peron nodded recalling, "She was so beautiful, so full of vitality."

"Skin of alabaster," added Reyes, "a young blonde goddess. Remember?"

In 1947, as the devastated nations, desperate for food,

recovered from the ravages of the war, Peron sent Evita to Europe as his vendor of Argentina's bountiful larder of beef and wheat.

Unlike Peron's visions of enormous profits, Evita viewed the trip as an answer to a circumstance that constantly rankled her—her rejection by the ladies of Argentina's high society. I'll be recognized as the great benefactor of Europe's starving millions, as well as the benefactor of our poor here, she thought. The Pope will award me with a title of papal marchesa; I deserve it. That'll put me on an equal footing with the snobs here in Argentina. I'll show them.

On the morning of Evita's departure, she said to Roberta, "I'm going to wear my diamond and emerald necklace and earrings. The newspapers will be there. It'll make their eyes pop. Oh, and one of those low-cut blouses—you know the ones."

"The ones President Peron doesn't like?"

"Yes," she said laughing. "He says they make me look like a whore."

"They are very daring, Señora."

"Of course they are. But if I can't wear what I want to, who in Argentina can? I have earned the right!"

When Evita's extensive limousine entourage arrived at the airport, it met with 150,000 Peronistas waving banners and large placards, shouting rhythmically, "Evita! Peron! Evita! Peron!...

Her honey-colored silken hair, combed straight back and gathered into a bun, caught the sunlight and reflected it back into thousands of worshipping eyes. Though it was early morning, Evita embodied a picture of high evening fashion in her long diamond and emerald earrings, precious bracelets and rings, all flashing in the bright crisp morning sunlight. Her ankle-length fur coat, slightly open, revealed a dazzling Van

Cleef diamond and emerald necklace on her milk-white breast. To the cheering men and women, this commoner, born in a condition as desperate as theirs, who came to Buenos Aires at the age of fourteen with all her worldly goods in a tattered cardboard suitcase, was standing before them adorned with trappings reserved for the aristocracy. She demonstrated that it was possible to someday improve their own lot. They saw this promise in Evita.

Addressing her adoring public, she said, "I fly to the old world with a message of peace and hope, as the representative of each one of you, the working men and women of our beloved country. I will be the rainbow, arching from your labor to the hungry people of Europe...in leaving Argentina, I feel a great sadness, for I know that I shall miss you as much as you will miss me. But, because I love you as I do, in going, I leave you my heart."

As her well-wishers began chanting her name, Evita boarded the waiting Spanish airliner.

Generalissimo Francisco Franco and a quarter million cheering Spaniards met Evita at the airport. During her visit, Franco entertained Evita with a continuing round of banquets, receptions, folk dancing, concerts and bullfights. And though it delighted her that he awarded her the highest Spanish decoration, The Great Cross of Isabella the Catholic, she stubbornly held her price of wheat at the highest level.

From Spain, Evita traveled to Italy where the nation warmly received her and the promise of pampas beef. While in Rome, she made a pilgrimage to the Vatican, luxuriously draped in a magnificent white ermine hooded cape. During her audience with Pope Pius XII, she asked him to order the Catholic bishops of Argentina to put their criticism of Peron aside and to openly support his administration. Unsuccessful in obtaining his assurances in those efforts, her disappointment with the Vatican visit was further compounded when she failed to receive the expected marquisate for her work with the poor. Instead, the pope presented her with the customary papal gift, a silver and mother-of-pearl rosary. Argentina's aristocracy gleefully noted the apparent slight to Evita by the religious hierarchy as proof of the Vatican's displeasure with Peron's policies, as well as a censure of Evita's tainted past.

While traveling in northern Italy, Evita made a side trip to Trieste to visit Maximilian's castle Miramar. During a press interview she mentioned she possessed a paperweight which once belonged to Empress Carlota. After the interview, one of the older women on the castle staff related a story to Evita which had been told to her years before by an elderly aunt, a former handmaiden of Empress Carlota. It was a detailed account of a curse placed on three Imperial Paperweights a century before by Marcella, "the witch of Valady." Although fascinated by the tale, Evita could not believe that her paperweight posed any threat to her. With her political sun in such high ascendancy, she couldn't imagine any shred of evil ever eclipsing her success.

By the time she reached Paris, her European junket caught the imagination of the entire western world; she even appeared on the cover of *Time* magazine. One Paris newspaper described Evita as "a stunningly beautiful woman, 5'5" tall, tastefully slim, with long shapely legs, dark brown eyes, honey-colored hair with glints of red, creamy white unrouged skin, dark lipstick and perfect snow-white teeth."

While she toured the French Riviera, her advance team met with representatives of the British government to complete arrangements for her visit to England. The representatives informed Evita, who expected to be a guest at Buckingham Palace, that stays in the palace were restricted to heads of state on "official state visits." Since her tour was considered a private one, the representatives "regretfully informed" her that she should reside elsewhere while in London. Evita, rebuffed, decided to cancel her visit to the British Isles and go directly to Switzerland. England later paid for her treatment of Evita; Juan Peron immediately raised the price per bushel of wheat to England by twenty percent.

The Swiss tour began well, but a few Communists cut the visit short when they threw tomatoes and stones at the Argentinean cars.

"What's the meaning of this?" she demanded of the Swiss representative accompanying her entourage.

"Malcontents, madam."

"How can your government permit this to happen? Is this how you treat your guests? This is an international incident!"

"They don't represent our government, madam. They are communists."

"Your government assured the safety of myself and my people. What are you going to do about it?"

"We're doing all we can."

"Like hell you are!" she snapped. Turning to her political officer, she demanded, "You tell our ambassador to get off his ass and make a formal protest about this incident! Peron'd never tolerate anything like this. They'd all be thrown in jail!"

At the close of her tour, Argentina received laudable recognition by the grateful European community of nations. In an obvious disregard of the communist provocation and "the English misunderstanding," Peron pronounced his wife's tour an unqualified success.

Evita's returning ship was greeted at the harbor by a quarter-million ecstatic workers, chanting, "*Uno, dos, tres, Evita otra vez* [One, two, three, Evita, once again]," and by the pealing of all the church bells in Buenos Aires.

Evita expressed her appreciation to those who gathered to greet her, concluding with a new catechism which she expressed for the first time, one she henceforth repeated often, "Colonel Peron and I are devoted to the very same cause, that of the people. He is large, I am tiny; he is cultured, I am simple; he works with his intelligence, I with my beating heart; he is substance, I am only shadow; he is the master, I am the pupil; he is sure of himself, I am sure only of him. Peron is a God to all of us. We should worship him with every part of our being. He is our sun, our air, our water, our life." Turning to face her husband, she concluded, "Now that I've returned home, I want nothing but to reside in the heart of Peron."

5.

Almost two hours elapsed since Peron left his ailing wife's bedside. Roberta put down her horoscope magazine to answer a soft knock at Evita's anteroom door. "Good afternoon, Father Benitez."

"God be with you, my child. Is your mistress resting?"

"Yes, Father, she's asleep. But Señora Peron gave instructions that I awaken her immediately upon your arrival."

"No, do not disturb her, my child. Please allow her to rest. I'll remain until she awakens; you can summon me then. I shall be in the chapel."

"As you wish, Father."

As the priest sat in the small chapel, he mused, it's as if I met the Perons only yesterday, and yet I've served as their priest and confessor for six years.

He found those years fulfilling. Often called upon to offer prayers and blessings at the dedication of new hospitals, chapels, schools, orphanages and rest homes that the Perons built, he felt truly involved in God's work. And yet, there was a dark side to those years—disturbing rumors of torture and executions. Just last month he heard that soldiers used electric cattle prods on a small group of jailed university students who had demonstrated against Peron—grizzly accounts of electric shocks administered to the breasts and genitals of the young men and women. But he put those rumors aside. Hadn't his bishop told him on more than one occasion to ignore all things political and concentrate only on matters concerning the spirit? After all, he rationalized, they were unsubstantiated rumors.

That morning he told his Bishop, "Your Excellency, for the past month, Señora Peron's vitality has gradually diminished. She no longer leaves her bedroom. Even President Peron who is campaigning for re-election seems to have lost heart in the race—"

A knock at the chapel door intruded on his thoughts.

"Father, Señora Peron is awake." said Roberta. "She wants you to come to her bedroom."

She pleasantly surprised the old priest who expected to find her in bed. Instead, he found her seated in a hooded chair, a fur-lined robe covering her lap and a fine lace shawl over her shoulders. Earlier that week, when he paid her a visit, her pale, hollow-eyed and exhausted appearance dismayed him. Today her eyes seemed bright and her face glowed with a healthy color.

Evita offered the old priest a chair opposite her. As he settled into the chair, she asked, "Father Benitez, would you take tea with me?"

"Why, of course, Evita. You just can't imagine how

pleased I am that you are up and about. Have your doctors completed their tests?"

"Yes, Father, but I'm afraid that my suspicions were correct. They told me that I have a serious malignancy."

Moving his chair closer to her, the priest discerned that the healthy blush on her cheeks and lips was a cosmetic application hurriedly applied over her pallid features. Even the hollows around her eyes were masked with make-up. Aware that Eva generally used make-up sparingly, he realized that she applied it in excess to conceal her deteriorated appearance.

"My dear child, you must not tire yourself on my account. We can enjoy tea together another time, in a few days, when you've regained more of your strength."

As he began to rise from his chair, she said, "Father Benitez, you will stay with me until I've finished. There is a pressing matter I must discuss with you, and I want to do it today. On one of those 'tomorrows' I'll be too involved with my debilitating illness to think clearly."

The old priest, settling back in his chair, realized that Evita harbored doubts about her recovery. A constant observer of her hypnotic influence on the masses and the support her popularity gave Peron, Father Benitez began to feel uneasy about the continued stability of the nation. Bloodshed always resulted whenever Argentina underwent each of her many revolutions. The relative tranquillity the Perons achieved for the nation was a blessing for which he often offered up prayers of gratitude.

"Evita, my child," he said, "nothing is ever final. God in his infinite mercy has effected many miraculous cures. People given up by their physicians—"

"Father," she interrupted, "I doubt God's personal interest in any one of us. If he has such a concern, why does he saddle me with this calamity? Why doesn't he punish our rich countrymen who have never helped the sick or the orphaned? Why doesn't He spare me and give this cancer that's engulfing my body to murderers, rapists and bandits?"

"But my child, God's will and purpose cannot be fully understood."

"Father," she interrupted impatiently, "I seriously question God's purpose! But I don't want to speak about that now, I have another more pressing concern to discuss with you."

Yielding to her strength of will, he avoided a contradictory reply, saying, "As you wish."

"Father, it is apparent that Juan will be re-elected as Argentina's president."

The priest nodded in agreement.

She continued, "After the election, I may not be well enough to assist him with the problems he'll face. It's no secret that many conspire against him. We've stuffed the prisons with his enemies! Our naval officers still hate him for the deaths of those who were killed when the Army overthrew Castillio eight years ago. Furthermore, Father, you are well aware that Juan does not now, nor will he ever have, the support of the upper classes."

"My child, I pray constantly for a reconciliation between—"

"And, Father,' she interrupted, "our greatest regret is that the church leaders embrace the upper classes to the exclusion of Peron who is aligned with the poor."

The priest, wanting to deny her condemnation of the church, struggled to keep his silence, all the while wondering where her discourse would finally lead.

"I attempted to heal the split between our bishops and Peron when I visited the Holy Father in Rome several years ago. It's obvious I did not succeed. My husband's second tenure would be helped immeasurably if he could have the open support of the church." After a slight pause, she continued, "Father, I want you to undertake the task of opening up a private dialogue between your superiors and myself. That's why I've asked you here today. I want you, Father Benitez, to help me smooth a path for an accord between Juan and the religious community. As for my part, I am prepared to generously assist the church in any reasonable way that her bishops might recommend, be it money, buildings or land. Let them know I can be extremely generous."

Stunned by the magnitude of her request, the simple parish priest replied, "With God's help, I will do whatever I can, my child."

"You must make the bishops realize that what I propose is in the best interests of the nation. I'm depending on you, Father. If you and I can accomplish this task, it will mean six more years of continued stability for Juan's administration. We are blessed with rich earth, raw materials and millions of eager working hands. You must remind the bishops that though we have vast potential, we still have large numbers of people who are barely surviving! What we have never truly achieved in this land is a harmonious relationship between the disparate levels of society. Peron has made a beginning; he has started to upgrade the lot of our 'shirtless ones.' And as you well know, he has done this over the protestations of the avaricious factory and land owners. Make them know, Father, that Juan Peron is the only one who has the strength to lift Argentina out of its feudal past!"

Exhausted by her effort, she closed her eyes and leaned back into her chair. The priest waited, but she remained silent, her breasts rapidly rising and falling with each labored, shallow breath. Realizing that she had drained her strength, Father Benitez rose from his chair, crossed himself and quietly prayed to receive guidance for the task that she had given him. Before leaving her bedchamber, the priest placed his stole over her head and gave her a blessing. As he quietly closed the door behind him, Evita's lips silently formed the words, "Godspeed, Father, there is so little time."

Roberta returned to the bedroom after seeing Father Benitez out, and found her mistress slumped in her chair, asleep. Awakening with a start, Evita asked, "Have you been gone very long?"

"No, just a few minutes, Señora. I saw Father Benitez to the door and returned."

"I've just had an odd dream of hollow-eyed priests in black cowls and robes. They were digging graves in the streets. I ordered them to stop but they ignored me. How very strange. I wonder what it all means?"

Roberta, a believer of dreams, felt a dreadful portent in the phantoms that Evita described, but kept her fears to herself, simply saying, "Señora, it's your medication. It was only a dream, it meant nothing. Here, let me pour you some tea."

As Evita's gaze wandered about her bed chamber, it eventually settled on her curio cabinet, her eyes locking on the Imperial paperweight. She said thoughtfully, "If I die, Juan will be left alone to struggle against his many enemies. Lately, Roberta, I've started to understand how Carlota suffered when she feared her husband might be abandoned in Mexico."

Noticing that Evita's attention fastened on the curio cabinet, Roberta inwardly prayed Evita wouldn't ask for the paperweight again. She feared its malevolent power.

"Roberta, please bring the paperweight to me."

Roberta asked, "Don't you worry about the terrible curse that it carries, Señora Peron?"

"Oh, my little village innocent, the old story of that lovely paperweight is only a superstitious yarn. I don't believe a word of it. Please bring it to me."

Roberta opened the cabinet and carefully removed the paperweight from its stand. Keeping her back to her mistress, she unobtrusively crossed herself, silently mouthing, "Sacred veil of my mother, spread your protective folds about me and shield me from the evil of this crystal." Roberta was certain that she felt the paperweight grow hot as she quickly carried it across the room. Did it twist slightly in her grasp, or was it a muscular twitch in her hand? Was it just her imagination? Shuddering inwardly, she placed it in her mistress's cupped hands. In an attempt to screen her fear of the crystal ball from Evita, she casually asked, "Was the paperweight a gift from President Peron?"

"Freyre gave it to me several years ago."

Surprised, Roberta asked, "Señor José Freyre, the Minister of Labor?"

"That's right. Did you know that he was once a glass blower?"

"In a factory?"

"Yes. And like all those in his trade, he worked under terrible conditions. But Freyre was not like those sheep who become resigned to their miserable situations. He had the courage to look beyond his personal lot and find ways to improve the working conditions of his fellow workers. When I learned how Freyre fought the factory owners to organize a glassworkers' union, I was so impressed I told Juan to consider Freyre for the position of Minister of Labor. One afternoon, after he was appointed to that position, I invited him to see the paperweights in my collection; I knew that with his background in glass he would appreciate them more than most. And do you know what? The very next day, he brought me this beautiful paperweight."

"Does he have a collection of paperweights, too?"

"That's what I asked him. He said that this was the only

one he ever owned; it was a gift from an old glassworker. Freyre gave it to his pregnant young wife, but she didn't enjoy it very long. Both she and the child she was carrying died during a difficult childbirth."

"How sad."

"Yes, it was a terrible loss for him. That's all the more reason that I appreciate his gift. It must have meant a great deal to him since he had given it to his wife."

Roberta, remembering the paperweight's curse, knew that Marcella had reached out of the grave, across a century of time, to snuff out the living flame of Freyre's wife and her unborn child. Mother of God she thought, is Carlota's paperweight connected with Evita's illness? She turned away from Evita and crossed herself.

That night, sleep would not come easily to Roberta. Disturbing thoughts of Evita's strange dream and Carlota's paperweight crowded her mind.

6.

For two months following the doctors' diagnosis of her cervical cancer, Evita remained closeted in her bedroom suite. The spasms of pain which came sporadically at first increased in frequency and intensity, progressively sapping the remaining strands of strength in her failing body. At times, even the sheets on the bed pained her skin. Though Peron instructed the doctors and Evita's family to keep her condition secret, her absence from public life nurtured rumors about her failing health a bit more each day.

The warm relationship between Father Benitez and Evita became strained during those two months. She blamed him for failing to arrange a reconciliation meeting for her and the bishops. He prayed and asked for divine guidance in the matter, but the hierarchy ignored his pleas. The bishops remained inflexible in their refusal to consider an accord with the Perons.

One morning, to the dismay of Peron and Father Benitez, Evita announced her intention to attend an upcoming political rally.

"No, Evita, I won't permit it!" protested Peron.

"Juan," she said to her objecting husband, "I mean to be there with you. I'm not going to lie here in bed waiting for death to take me by the hand while the world continues to turn outside. I'll be in my grave soon enough."

"You're in no condition to attend the rally," said Peron. "I won't consider it. It's madness!"

"My child," echoed Father Benitez, "you mustn't go. The rally would be too harmful for you. You must conserve your strength to fight your illness."

"Father," she said wearily, "you always say that God will provide. Put him to the test. Challenge him. Use your prayers to ask for the strength I'll need on that day. Maybe God will be more approachable than your bishops have been." Turning to her husband she repeated in a stronger voice, "I won't change my mind. I intend to—" Suddenly, she forced herself deep into her bed, biting her lower lip as another torturous convulsion erupted within her body. She pressed her open palms down hard on her lower abdomen and writhed in pain. Her suffering, which lasted for a few moments, seemed endless to the two anxious men.

"Those damn doctors," said Peron, "I told them to increase the pain killers."

"I won't let them do it! I don't want to be dead to everything!" she hissed between clenched teeth. "I won't let them make me a zombie!"

Opening her eyes, Eva took in a tremulous breath and passed her limp fingers across her perspiration-beaded brow. Perceiving the concern of her husband and the priest, she assured them, "It's gone, the pain has passed." Setting her jaw, she raised herself on her elbows and said sternly, "I won't listen to either of you. I've made up my mind, and that's settled! I'll live my life as I always have until my last gasp of breath. I will be there beside you on the 17th."

Later, Juan Peron discovered to his consternation that his wife was not content to merely sit quietly at the rally; she intended to speak. All his pleading and protestations were to no avail. Her doctors' heated objections to her self-imposed ordeal were similarly dismissed.

Evita's gaunt appearance shocked the crowds that choked the plaza during the rally. Getting prepared that morning left her exhausted. At Evita's request, Roberta positioned her in a wheelchair near the center of the balcony, just a few steps from the microphones. She sat immobile as officials of the Peronista party made rousing speeches in support of their candidates. Buoyed up by the old familiar speeches and cheers of a political campaign, Evita felt traces of strength slowly returning to her body. She quietly prayed, "Just one more time, God, give me the strength to say what is in my heart."

When Juan introduced Evita, Roberta noticed that many in the plaza crossed themselves. Slowly rising from her wheelchair, Evita traversed the short distance to the speakers' lectern unassisted. A gasp escaped from the multitude when Evita, feeling suddenly weak, put out a hand for help. Roberta, standing nearby, caught her by the arm and helped her to the speakers' dais. As they reached the cluster of microphones, Evita turned to Peron, saying, "I'm unsteady, Juan. Please stay near me."

Peron stepped to the microphones and asked the crowds to listen quietly so that Evita might speak without undue stress. While she spoke, he positioned himself behind her, cradling her frail body in his arms. In a quiet, hesitant but impassioned speech she said, "I've risen from a sick bed to be with you, my 'shirtless ones.' I can never repay the debt that I owe you for honoring and supporting me over the years. I thank you, my comrades, from the grateful heart that beats here in my breast. I know that God will hear the prayers of the humble people of our nation so that I can continue fighting for you until I die. And even if I leave torn shreds of my life on the wayside, I know that you'll gather them up in my name and carry them like a flag to victory."

Pausing to gather strength, she said to Peron, "Just a little longer, Juan."

"My 'shirtless ones,'" she continued, "I intended to talk about many things today, but my doctors have told me not to speak too long."

The end of her speech proved most difficult for her; she had used up most of her reserves. She uttered her last few labored sentences with many hesitations and pauses.

"I pray that—my health will improve—so that I can be with you, once again. But, if because of my health, I cannot, I ask—only one thing of all of you. You must help Peron. Be on the alert—the enemy is always in the background—waiting to ambush us. You must prevent the corrupters from overthrowing our government. Be loyal to Peron—as you've always been—because, in this way, you'll be loyal—to our beloved country—and to yourselves."

Every person looking up at Evita read her meaning; she was preparing them for her death. Men and women looked at each other in disbelief. Many became emotional and wept openly.

As the Peronistas sadly left the Plaza de Mayo that afternoon, they could not help but compare that day's rally to the energized rallies of Peron's first political campaign. Then Juan, coatless, in rolled-up shirtsleeves, and Eva, clothed in the latest fashions, tirelessly toured the poorer areas of the large cities and traveled by train to the provinces to meet with the workers. Wherever they appeared they sealed the loyalty of the lower classes by liberally dispensing food, money and promises.

True to the promises of that first election campaign, Eva, their champion, waged war on those who profited from the labors of the poor. Those who personally benefited from the Evita Peron Foundation, a charity she established, saw her as a benefactor and savior. They assured each other that she provided drink for their thirst, eased their gnawing hunger, and bound up their wounds. The many eulogistic titles her followers bestowed on her testified to the absolute worship she enjoyed: "Lady of Compassion," "Heroine," "Defender of the Worker," "Protector of the Forsaken," "Martyr of Labor," "Argentine Lily," "Lady of Hope" and to the disapproval of the church, "Saint Evita". The latter title especially embarrassed to the Argentinean clergy. They could do nothing to change the fact that their congregations openly worshipped a "former whore of the lowest kind" as a saint.

However much the Peronistas adored Evita, those who owned the businesses and those who belonged to the aristocracy saw her differently. Those affluent citizens who spent their leisure time in the quiet of Buenos Aires's many *confiterias* commiserated with each other over tea and cakes in complaining obbligatos about Peron's draconian oppression and Evita Peron's many extravagances.

"They say she has a cancer in her belly."

"Good. I hope Peron catches it!"

"Careful, my friend, you never know who's listening."

"Her charities for the rabble are bleeding me dry!"

"Speaking of rabble, there was another large crowd of those unwashed scum on the plaza for a rally last night."

"Those stupid animals, they never tire of being herded into the public square whenever Peron wants to make a long-winded speech."

"They've got nothing else to do; they don't work most of the time."

"I know. They just sit around all day drinking *mate* and playing *truco*—ignorant dolts!"

"They may be ignorant, my friend, but they have brains enough to know the handouts will continue if he is re-elected."

"Have you noticed how Peron's bitch always has newspaper photographers around when she distributes her money to those loafers. It doesn't take a genius to see that it's all show. She pockets a hundred pesos for every one she 'generously' gives to the poor."

"What do you mean, 'her money'? It's yours and mine! Last year the government 'requested' my company to donate ten percent of its profits to the Evita Peron Foundation—blackmail!"

"Did you give the money?"

"Did I have any choice in the matter? If I'd hesitated, they'd have cut off my supply of copper or electricity, and I'd have shut down. It wouldn't be the first time they've played that game. If a newspaper opposes them, they cut off the supply of paper or send in their goons at night to destroy the presses. If a factory owner doesn't do their bidding, they cut off his raw materials or his building mysteriously burns down. One of my friends who openly accused Peron's thugs of torching his factory disappeared overnight. No one knows where he is."

"They've become multimillionaires on the backs of the

rich and poor. How else did they amass the fortune to acquire all their residences, her diamonds and her furs. Peron's salary is a mere pittance."

"Where, indeed—corrupt bloodsuckers!"

"Keep your voice down, my friend. We're surrounded by informants. Our waiter could very well report what he overhears to the authorities."

"All the unionists kiss Peron's ass."

"I heard that even the unions and their members are required to donate to Evita's special fund."

"Serves them right. They elected Peron and his harlot."

"Bastards."

"Damn, Bastards!"

"Sh-h-h, not so loud."

7.

After the October rally, the shirtless ones built temporary chapels in plazas throughout the country as gathering places of supplication for Evita's recovery. By the end of the month, her illness became so critical, her physician rushed her to the hospital. Evita's doctors made an urgent call to a world famous American surgeon who flew immediately to Buenos Aires. As the media revealed Evita's worsening condition, crowds gathered outside the hospital day and night to pray for their idol. Crowded churches throughout the nation held masses hourly. Argentine delegations and a flood of telegrams besieged Pope Pius to offer up prayers for her recovery.

After Evita's surgery, the surgeon told Peron that she would live only three to six months. That same week, the people re-elected Juan Peron to the presidency, an office he knew he would serve without Evita.

"Roberta, hurry in here!"

"Señora?"

"I smell smoke. Something's burning. Run! Get help!"

Roberta ran through the sitting room into the hallway to summon the security men. They rushed into Evita's bedroom. One man began beating at an overstuffed chair with his jacket while another ran to get water. Roberta helped Evita into her wheelchair and pushed her into the sitting room. When Roberta returned to the bedroom, one of the men told her, "It was that chair there, near the window. It was smoldering—probably a cigarette."

"No one smokes in here," said Roberta. "Señora Peron can't stand the smell of cigarettes since her illness."

That evening, the security men reported to Juan Peron that after examining the room, they determined that a large green paperweight started the fire. They speculated that the paperweight, which perched on a table next to the window, concentrated the sun's rays on a nearby overstuffed chair.

When Peron explained the cause of the fire to Evita, Roberta remembered there was no sun that afternoon; clouds filled the sky all day. She knew the men were wrong about the sun, although she never doubted that the Imperial paperweight caused the fire. After all, the glassmakers created the cursed thing in Hell's flames. But Roberta kept these thoughts to herself.

Evita made her last public appearance during Peron's second inauguration. She told Peron she wanted to take part in the official ceremonies of his installation. No amount of pleading or reasoning by Peron dissuaded her. She ordered changes to the car so that she could stand with Peron as it progressed up the Avenida 9 d'Julio to the place of inauguration.

Peron asked, "My dear Evita, must you continue to invite your own death?"

"I haven't worked at your side for seven years to just lie here in bed on the day that you will be honored. Don't think that because cancer is devouring my body, it has broken my will. I have a strong heart, Juan. I will see you accept the presidential sash with my own eyes."

On the day of Peron's second inauguration, Eva stood stoically at his side. A metal frame with restraining straps, bolted to the car and hidden by her long fur coat, permitted her to stand beside her husband in the open car. She suffered greatly as she endured the long ceremony. Several times that day she nodded her cadaverous head and slowly raised a bony arm to acknowledge the cheers directed at her.

8.

For months, Roberta endured her own private hell, plagued by the torment of watching her mistress's condition worsen. She was convinced that the evil piece of glass her mistress cherished and handled more and more each day was the source of the cancer. She believed that with each touch, its poisonous corruption nudged Evita's agonized body ever closer to the grave. Roberta reasoned that if a sorcerer could make one ill with small scrap of rodent intestine, the evil power of that piece of glass, created in the searing heat of Hell's flames, must be overwhelming. If my mother were still alive, she thought, she could have cast a spell or made a protective amulet for my mistress. She could have warded off the scourge of that corrupt crystal.

Roberta wondered if she could convince President Peron of the evil inherent in the paperweight. Should she approach him directly? No, he'd think her foolish. He had ridiculed her village ways so many times in the past; he'd just mock her again. She had to reveal the paperweight's deleterious effect to someone, someone who would have the courage to do something about it.

Her desperation settled on Evita's personal priest. Kindly Father Benitez is understanding, she thought. I'll speak to him, he'll listen. He'll help me rid my Evita of that evil abomination. If the good Father won't perform the rite of exorcism on the paperweight, I'll ask him to convince President Peron to take the paperweight away from my mistress. He'll surely listen to Father Benitez.

"The rite of exorcism?" the shocked priest asked incredulously. "You want me to exorcise evil out of an inert piece of glass? Señorita Leon, what must you be thinking?"

"But Father, it has destroyed everyone it touches. It killed Maximilian. I know that it put José Freyre's young wife and her unborn child into their graves, and now it's killing my mistress!"

"My dear child, who put such nonsense into your head?"

"Señora Peron told me of the curse, herself, Father."

"Señorita, be realistic. If she truly believes the paperweight responsible for her illness, do you for one moment think she'd keep it in her possession? Even in her weakened condition she has better sense than to give the slightest credence to such an absurd idea."

"Then, may I make one final request of you, Father?"

The priest nodded impatiently.

"Would you ask President Peron to remove the paperweight from the Señora's bedroom?"

The priest, his patience at an end, vehemently replied, "In God's name, what reason could I give for such a request? You've seen how she fondles that paperweight. During her most terrible hours, that blessed piece of glass seems to give her a few moments of respite from pain. It has become so precious to her that President Peron looks on it as a religious relic. Do you think for one moment he'd take that paperweight away from her? And for what reason? She is dying! What does he care about your foolish imaginings?"

"But, Father—"

"Enough woman! Enough of this talk!"

As she watched the priest walk away muttering to himself, Roberta knew that she had to be the one to help Evita—she had to take matters into her own hands. "When my Evita becomes well, she'll thank me for what I'm about to do."

That evening, when Peron left his wife's bedside for a moment to confer with a waiting aide, Roberta slipped into the bedroom and gently pried back Evita's bony fingers from around the green paperweight. She slowly extracted the object from her mistress's clasp, saying, "Now, you evil thing, I'll get rid of you."

Eva's hand flexed, attempting to close around the missing paperweight. "Where is it?" she asked, opening her eyes.

"My dear one, please close your eyes and rest. I've taken away the venom."

"Roberta?"

"Yes, I'm here, my dear."

"Where—where is my—paperweight?"

"Don't worry, I have it. It is safe with me."

"Give it to me, please."

"The doctor said you must rest. You won't need it any more."

"Juan, Juan, my paperweight is gone!"

"Quiet, dear. He's just outside the door. He'll be back soon. Please try to rest."

"Juan, my paperweight! Juan! Juan!"

"I'm going to destroy this thing. It's killing you! No one

else understands its evil!"

Peron, returned to the room. Seeing his wife thrashing about in her bed, he rushed to his her bedside, asking, "What's happening in here, for God's sake? Evita, calm yourself! Roberta, run down the hall and get the doctor."

"She does not need the doctor, Señor."

"What are you saying? Go get the doctor!"

"This—this is what is causing her illness. It's vile! It's cursed! I'm going to destroy it! That will make my Evita well, again!"

"Give me the paperweight, Roberta!"

"No. You'll just put it back into her hand."

"You crazy woman! What in hell's gotten into you? Can't you hear her begging? She needs it! Give it here, damn you! Now!"

"No!"

"Give it to me!"

"No, I won't!"

In a rush, Peron flew at Roberta, shoved her down and tore the paperweight from her grasp. Viciously kicking her, he screamed, "Get out of here, you crazy pagan bitch! If I ever see you near Evita again, I'll have you killed!"

As Roberta scrambled out of the room, Peron returned to his wife. He placed the paperweight in her palm and gently pressed her fingers around it. Stroking her head, he attempted to console her, "There, there Evita, please stop crying. That bitch won't touch your paperweight again."

Oblivious to what had transpired, Evita continued to sob, "My paperweight, my paperweight, my paperweight—"

"Please try to rest. I'll send for the doctor."

9.

During Evita's last days, she slept the merciful sleep induced by powerful pain killing drugs. Her wasted body weighed only eighty pounds. Outside the presidential residence, throngs of women, aware of her failing condition, prayed on their knees for her recovery. Thousands attended special all-day vigils in the cathedral, to pray for a miracle.

Late, one rainy afternoon, Evita's doctors told Juan Peron that the end was near. Juan summoned her mother, brother and sisters to her bedside as the priest administered the last rites. Juancito, holding the crucifix to Eva's lips, turned to Peron and whispered, "Juan, her lips are moving, I think she's saying something."

Peron pushed Juancito and the priest aside and quickly knelt at the side of Evita's bed. He raised his hand to silence those in the room. Putting his ear close to her moving lips he listened intently.

"...for me? Marcella?—Yes, I see it—A lovely curtain—a glass curtain?—Oh, it's a shroud—It's so lovely—a lovely glass shroud—for me?—yes, it's beautiful—Marcella—my glass shroud. Marcella—Marcella—Marcella—"

Eva's lips moved for the last time. She drifted into a deep coma as her life ebbed away.

"...no sun, no day, no night—only death now, the bleak abyss of death..."

That night the radio stations in Argentina suspended their programs to broadcast religious music. Official announcements interrupted the music every fifteen minutes to state, "It is our sad duty to inform you that at 8:25 this evening, Señora Eva Peron, the Spiritual Leader of the Nation, passed away into immortality." The next day, all the flags in the nation were at half-mast; the government draped public buildings, sign posts, lamps and telephone poles in purple and black.

A deluge of Evita's grieving followers flooded the center of the capital to pay their last respects. The frenzied human mass that seethed around her glass-topped coffin crushed several people to death. In the interest of public safety, Peron called out troops to control the agitated, weeping crowds. For fourteen days, as more than two million people viewed the body of their fallen champion, the state-controlled media eulogized her as "Martyr," "Protector," "Defender," and "Guiding Light."

The public mourning at an end, Juan encased Evita's air-tight silver casket in a white sarcophagus, placed it atop a gun carriage and paraded it to the chapel of the General Confederation of Labor. It remained there pending the completion of the huge mausoleum Peron promised he would build for her remains.

Within a year of her demise, Peron's control of the government began to show signs of deterioration. The Argentineans realized that Evita Peron slightly skewed the political catechism which extolled their leader's greatness. Disquieting rumors circulated throughout the country that Peron despoiled Evita's memory by participating in sexual orgies with teenage girls.

Three years after Evita's death, a powerful coalition comprised of the army, the middle and upper classes and the church, challenged Peron's faltering administration. Without charismatic Evita to rouse the "shirtless-ones" to his side, they overthrew Peron. To ease the concern of those Peronistas who were still loyal to Peron, President Aramburu and the generals who assumed power, allowed him to go into exile.

After he vacated the presidential residences, Eva's many personal treasures, including her paperweight collection, disappeared, never to surface again.

When the military took over, they were shocked to discover Evita's embalmed body still reposing, after three years, in the chapel of the Confederation of Labor Building. Juan never been built her mausoleum. President Aramburu, fearing that Evita's body might become a rallying point for a latent political movement, removed it secretly from Argentina. Officers sealed her casket in a crate marked "Radio Sets," and shipped it to an Argentinean embassy in West Germany. Two years later, a Señora Iroldi arrived in Milan with Eva Peron's sealed coffin, which she claimed contained the remains of Maria Maggi, an Italian widow who died in Argentina. The Señora told the authorities that the body was being returned to Milan to be buried in the Musacco cemetery, near the deceased woman's birthplace.

10.

MADRID - 1972

During his presidential years, Juan Peron salted away enormous amounts of money on both sides of the ocean. After he was ousted from Argentina, he recovered those funds and lived in luxury, first in Paraguay, then in Panama. While in Panama, he met and married Isabelita, an Argentine cabaret dancer. Shortly after their marriage, Peron and his new wife left Panama and established their official residence in Spain.

During the seventeen years that Peron remained in exile, Argentina's government changed hands eight times. Inflation went rampant, corruption persisted in the government, and violence continued unchecked in the streets. Because of the continuing turmoil, an alliance composed of Peron's adversaries and supporters sent a delegation to Madrid to inquire if he might consider returning to Argentina to run for the office of President as a coalition candidate. It was hoped that by this curious marriage of divergent groups, Peronistas, the military, the church, the landowners and the businessmen, Peron might bring order to Argentina's chaotic conditions. Peron eagerly accepted their proposal.

As a further demonstration of their good faith, the military secretly exhumed and delivered Evita's body to Peron in Madrid. When they forced the coffin lid open, Peron and Isabelita gazed down on a body that survived almost twenty years of death without any evidence of corruption. It had been embalmed so well that Evita looked as though she slept.

Isabelita broke their long silence, saying, "She's very beautiful, Juan, after all those years."

"Yes," he replied, attempting to keep his emotions hidden as he looked once again on Evita's features.

Touching Evita's cheek, Isabelita said, glancing at Peron, "But cold as ice."

Sensing a hint of jealousy in her voice, he replied, "You're my wife now, Isabelita. Evita is only a memory."

"Juan, look there. What's shining down there?

"Where?"

"There below her left shoulder."

"Let me see. Oh, it's the paperweight."

"Paperweight?"

"Yes, she loved it. It gave her pleasure, even when she was close to death. I put it in her coffin before it was sealed."

"May I see it?"

"It's just a glass paperweight."

"Please get it for me."

Peron pressed his hand down, deep along the quilted side of the casket, carefully avoiding contact with Evita. He couldn't bear to feel the coldness of death on her body. Reaching the paperweight, he lifted it out. Noticing a strand of Evita's hair stuck to the paperweight, he gently blew it off and handed the paperweight to Isabelita.

"It's dusty, Juan—look. I think it's some of the powder the morticians used on Evita's face," she said, wiping it on her blouse.

Peron turned his face away, saying, "Use a handkerchief!"

Holding the paperweight up to the light, she said, "No need, it's clean now." Twisting it in her hand she said, "It's pretty."

"Yes, and very old."

"The two cameos, who are they?"

"I don't remember, some royalty, I think."

"May I keep it?"

"It's Evita's."

"Please, Juan—such a waste, in a casket."

"Oh, I suppose you're right. Go ahead and keep it. It can't help her anymore." A small door of Peron's memory opened as he recalled Roberta's stark fear of the object and Evita's deathbed ramblings. Did it, in fact, carry an evil curse? Should he return it to Evita's coffin? My God, he said to himself, this is the twentieth century. Crazy Roberta was an anachronism. No one believes in those old superstitions any more.

"What are you going to do with her body, Juan?"

"I'll have Evita interred here, in Madrid."

The Perons returned to Argentina to campaign for the presidency and vice-presidency of the nation. That September, Juan Peron was elected President of the Republic; Isabelita, the former cabaret dancer, became Argentina's Vice President. To the dismay of the nation, Peron developed pneumonia and died of cardiac arrest only nine months after accepting the Presidential sash.

"...winding sheets...shrouds of death..."

When Isabelita assumed the office of the chief executive, the complexity of the task immediately overwhelmed her; nothing ever prepared her for the manifold demands of the presidency. Within three months, the country's economy was in chaos again. Because of her obvious ineptitude, the military began to openly oppose her. Defections occurred in growing numbers within her own party by the Peronistas who rejoiced at her election just a short year before.

Faced with the erosion of support, Isabelita conceived a plan which she felt might win back the support of the Peronistas. When she revealed its details to her advisors, they assured her that it would firmly entrench her in her position.

Accordingly, Isabelita made the startling announcement that she was bringing Evita back home to Argentina. The "shirtless-ones" who had grieved at Evita's disappearance rejoiced that their idol was finally coming back after being lost to them for twenty years. When the casket arrived, a carnival atmosphere filled the streets of Buenos Aires. A military guard escorted her coffin to the capital as the people joyfully received it.

In spite of the positive effect, Isabelita expected Evita's return to have on the nation's stability, political and economic problems continued to worsen. When opposing factions took to the streets, Isabelita's death squads made murder and assassination a daily occurrence.

Two years after assuming the Presidency, Isabelita lost most of her political support. A popular military coup overthrew her. Soldiers escorted her to a chalet in the Andes and placed her under house arrest. Later, charged with the embezzlement of funds belonging to the Evita Peron Foundation, guards moved her to one of Peron's former country homes and detained her there. Released, five years later, Isabelita returned to Madrid.

CHAPTER V.

1.

NEW YORK - 1985

A Sotheby's specialist, evaluating a large group of erotic Japanese ivories that belonged to a deceased collector, found several pieces in the collection with Sotheby's numbers attached to their bases. When he returned to his office, he checked the inventory numbers and identified one of the ivories as an item that disappeared eleven months before. He wouldn't have thought too much about it, since a few minor items went unaccounted for over the years. With thousands of articles handled each month for auction, Sotheby's expected that an occasional loss might occur. They chalked-off those pieces as miscounted lots or mistakes in the initial inventory. But because of the three missing Imperial paperweights, he reported the discovery of the missing ivory to Sotheby's in-house security.

The police went to the deceased collector's home to question his wife.

"Did he attend auctions at Sotheby's?"

"Oh, no, officer. My husband was an invalid. He did all of his buying through auction catalogs and advertisements in antique newspapers."

"Do you know were he bought the ivory?"

"No. They all look the same to me. They're disgusting! He kept records of his collection, though. If you'd like to examine them, they're in the study."

The records revealed that the ivory was purchased from a

New York antique shop. The shop owner, questioned about the ivory, said, "Why, yes, officer, I bought it from Mr. Anderson. He brings in an occasional piece for me; he says he finds them in flea markets and garage sales. They're always nice little pieces."

"Do you have a record of what you've bought from him?"

"Why yes, I'm required to, you know, for tax purposes. I keep a double entry. Let me get my book. Here it is, twenty-seven items from Mr. Anderson during the past four years. Nothing major, but still nice salable pieces. I still have a few that haven't moved yet."

"Where are they?"

"Let's see, item sixteen, a small hallmarked sterling vinaigrette. It's in the case, here, right there on the left. And number twenty-one, a small diamond and emerald lavaliere. Hmm, number twenty-four, a small brass jewel case with enamel portrait; and number twenty-seven, a miniature book, *Bible History* by Shaw, dated 1816."

"Can you describe Mr. Anderson?"

"Of course. He has a dark complexion, good-looking, curly black hair, brown eyes, tall—about six feet. He has a muscular build and a thin mustache."

"We'll be back. Don't sell those four items, they might be stolen merchandise."

"Oh, no!"

At Sotheby's, the officers found that the antique dealer's description of Mr. Anderson fit Nick Amati in Receiving. "Is he here?" asked the policeman.

"No, he's taking a few days off; he doesn't feel well."

"What kind of an employee is he?"

"He's been with us seven years; he's bonded. Is he in any trouble?"

"We just want to talk to him. Do you have his address?"

"Think he might have something to do with the missing Imperial paperweights?"

"That's what we want to find out."

Amati's apartment was in a brownstone converted into four apartments. Ringing his doorbell and receiving no response, the officers rang the other bells. An elderly woman came to her door, opened the door a slit, its opening limited by a security chain.

"Good afternoon, ma'am," said one of the policemen, showing her his badge, "we're from the police department."

"Yeah?"

"We'd like to speak to Mr. Amati, upstairs; but he doesn't answer his bell."

"He ain't home. He's gone away for a couple a days. He in some kind of trouble?"

"No, no problem. We just want to talk to him. Do you know where he went?"

"He didn't say. He asked me to look in on his cats for three days. He said he'd be back Wednesday."

"We want to take a look at his apartment."

"I don't know—."

"Come on, ma'am, we can get a court order if we have to."

"Well, okay; but I got to be there, too."

"That's okay."

The officers' search turned up nothing of value. On their way back to the station, they talked about Amati.

"He's been pilfering from Sotheby's for at least four years, probably waiting for a big score."

"You suppose he's sold to other dealers too?"

"Who knows. He's got to be the one who copped the paperweights. He sure had the opportunity."

"Yeah, and a lot of practice, too."

"Let's report to the lieutenant and then stake out his place until he gets back. We'll collar him and take him down to the station. He's got to be our man; he's the one we've been looking for."

"What if he doesn't come back?"

"Yeah, you're right. We'd better tell the lieutenant to put out an all-points bulletin on him now, just in case he's taken a powder with those paperweights."

2.

PARIS - 1949

The cabdriver tipped his cap and thanked the diminutive passenger for the generous tip. Truman Capote, alighting from the cab, looked about to get his bearings; it had been two years since his first visit. Recognizing a familiar row of shops, he walked quickly in their direction, not wanting to be late for his appointment.

Two years earlier, when Capote hesitantly asked Jean Cocteau to arrange his first meeting with Colette, Cocteau understood his hesitancy. His hostess's world-wide fame reached back to the turn of the century, when her saucy "Claudine" novels caught the attention of the literary world. During her lifetime, the literary community layered laurels on the renowned French authoress like luster on a pearl. At their first meeting, no one knew Capote, a relative unknown. He had just left a job as copyboy to accept a position Random House offered him on the potential he exhibited in three short stories, *A Tree of Night*, *Miriam*, and *Jug of Silver*. And though he gained a small amount of literary success since his previous visit, the celebrated hostess still awed Capote.

Colette lived in an apartment on the second floor of the Palais-Royale, a palace originally built for Cardinal Richelieu by Louis XIII. The building served successively as a residence for the Dukes of Orleans, King Louis Philippe and the descendants of Jerome Bonaparte. After the fall of Louis Napoléon's empire, the Communards torched the building along with many other structures. When Duke Philippe Egalite restored the palace, he added a small row of elegant shops to the ground floor and converted the upper floors into individual apartments.

As Capote reached the courtyard gardens and glanced up at the long narrow windows of Colette's apartment, the many characters of her enchanting stories came flooding in on him: Bel-Gazou, Cheri, Claudine and that delightful courtesan, Gigi. He wondered how much of the seventy-six year old authoress's own life those characters reflected.

Colette's faithful servant, Pauline, accompanied by four curious cats, answered Capote's knock on the apartment door. Looking down at the small young man, she smiled, "Bon jour, Monsieur. Madam Colette is expecting you."

Pauline, preceded by her high-tailed feline escort, led Capote to the bedroom where the French authoress sat in bed, propped-up by lace-edged satin pillows. Extending both hands, she touched his arms, saying, "My wicked little angel, what a pleasure to see you once again."

"Madam Colette," he said, kissing her on both cheeks, "thank you for receiving me."

"My little love, I'm delighted you accepted my invitation. Perhaps you'd like to join me in tea while we visit?"

Pauline left the room and returned with an elaborate tea

service.

"And now, Monsieur," Colette said, stroking a fluffy yellow kitten that had awakened and was nuzzling against her, "we can catch up on the past two years, over Pauline's tea."

While Pauline poured, Capote cast his gaze around the large bedroom and saw that little had changed during the intervening years. He thought, Russia just exploded her first atomic bomb, the world is on the brink of another holocaust, but Colette's world is unchanged. Heavy velvet curtains still hung over the long windows, richly colored oriental carpets rested in the same exact positions on the floor, silk-covered walls glowed with reflected light and the lamps were draped with pink scarves—everything was just as he had remembered from his first visit. As he looked at Colette, he was struck by the fact that his hostess hadn't changed in her appearance, nor did she seem to have moved one inch away from her former position on the bed. Her fuzzy henna-colored hair glowed, her cheeks and lips remained heavily rouged and her sensitive eyes were still carefully lined with kohl. And as before, an ample scattering of cats reposed comfortably about the room, their slit eyes slightly open, lazily watching the movements around them. Even the flowery essence of rose perfume which pervaded the room seemed to have lingered there since his first visit.

"Your apartment is just as I remembered it," said Capote.

"Yes, little has changed since your last visit. The only change has been in my own mobility. It has become very difficult for me to walk about, even here in my own apartment. This is how I spend each day, bed-ridden most of the time. Unfortunately, arthritis has confined my travels to my memories. But, I am never lonely. The world comes to me in letters, in the newspapers, on the wireless and by the occasional guest who stops by to see me." Stirring milk into her tea, Colette asked, "And now, tell me, what have you written lately, my friend?"

"I've just had a novel published, *Other Voices, Other Rooms*. It's a loose autobiography. I also have two small books in the works."

"I must read that new book of yours. I've heard that it caused quite a sensation in America. One of our French reviewers said your book was both wicked and artistically exciting. He quoted a wonderful passage from it. How does it go? 'Love is—hmm, Love is natural and beautiful; only hypocrites hold a man responsible for what he loves. Love is sacred, whatever its form.' That is truly beautiful, my dear friend."

"Some reviewers found my book to be decadent. They objected to it because they said it had an underlying theme of homosexuality. If you'd like, I'll send you a copy when I return to my hotel. You can decide for yourself if it's depraved."

"Please do. I know I'll enjoy it! Tell me, my dear, do you find that writing is easy for you?"

"Not really, although I've been writing since I was eleven years old. It's the process of writing that I don't enjoy. It's pure agony for me; I'm such a perfectionist."

"Did your parents encourage you in your writing?"

"Oh, hardly, madam. I was abandoned by my divorced parents and sent to live with elderly maiden aunts. They had to put up with the annoyance of bringing up a little boy who had no place else to go. I was actually looked after by my cousin. She worked for my aunts as their domestic. She was middle-aged when I was given over to her care, we were children together. You see, she stopped maturing mentally while she was still a child. Because of her, my early years were not completely lonely. She was a wonderful companion. I have such warm feelings of the time we shared together." After a long pause,

Capote asked, "And you, madam, do you have many memories of your childhood?"

"See that large album over there? Please bring it to me; it contains a few reminiscences of my life."

As she turned the first few pages of the thick album, she pointed out stiffly posed photographs of herself and her mother, recalling that her early years with her mother had been idyllic. Her word "idyllic" was like a knife in Capote's heart.

What I would have given for my mother to love me, he thought. Even at the age of four, he could not understand why she left home. On the rare occasions when she came to see her sisters, he remained near her during her entire visit, longing for a kind word or a small sign of approval that never came. His mother did not conceal her resentment of him; he was different. Later, when she became an alcoholic, she rejected him, openly referring to him as a "damn fairy." When he learned she committed suicide, he was inconsolable. Even now, years later, as he looked at pictures of Colette in her mother's arms, a gnawing loneliness pulled at his heart.

Colette paused at a photo of a heavily mustached young man. "That's Willy, my first husband."

At just twenty years old Colette married Henri Gauthier-Villas, a writer and publisher. Villas often locked her in their bedroom and forced her to write stories which he published under his own name. During the difficult early years of their marriage, she felt extremely isolated. Colette missed the sweet chatter of her young friends, and especially the wonderful relationship she had always enjoyed with her mother. Later, Willy devastated Colette when he brought an actress home and insisted that Colette share the same bed with them. After six years of callous mental and physical abuse, she divorced Villas.

Colette turned a few pages and stopped at a photo of two

young women in trousers, standing rakishly and each holding long cigarette holders. Capote recognized one of the two as Colette.

"And who is that with you in the photograph, madam?"

"The Marquise de Belbeuf—Missy." Slowly stroking the photograph, she said, "Oh, how young we were then. After I divorced my first husband, I met this wonderful girl; we became inseparable. We were poor, but happy. To earn money, Missy and I danced and sang in music halls. Those were gay, carefree times!"

When the young women's relationship developed into a passionate love affair, they made no attempt to hide the fact that they enjoyed the forbidden pleasures of Sappho. A theater owner pulled Colette and Missy off the stage and dismissed them when the two young women scandalously shared an extremely passionate kiss on stage during one of their shows.

Colette turned several more pages of sepia photographs and newspaper clippings and stopped, pointing to a frayed photograph of herself and a man holding a tiny girl.

"That's my daughter, named after me, and that's my second husband, Henry Jouvenel."

Colette met Jouvenel, an editor, in 1911. Soon after that meeting she terminated her love affair with Missy and married him. For the next twenty years she wrote steadily, creating many masterpieces with her pen. The collapse of the world economy in the 1930's brought hard times to the Jouvenel family. To raise money, Colette opened a beauty salon, but that venture soon failed. Desperation forced her husband to earn a meager subsistence for his family by selling electric appliances door-to-door.

After a scandalous divorce in which Jouvenal accused Colette of having an incestuous affair with his son, her stepson, she met and married Maurice Goudeket, a writer. Four years after their marriage, France declared war on Germany. The Second World War tramautized Colette; Goudeket had Jewish blood in his ancestry. She realized her worst fears one fateful night when the Gestapo seized Goudeket on the streets and imprisoned him. Fortunately, they released him six months later. For the rest of her life she suffered nightmares about those terrifying months when the "hated Bosch" occupied her Paris.

As Colette began to quickly page through the scrapbook, Capote stayed her hand and turned back to a beautifully lettered certificate. "What's this?" he asked.

"Oh, it's when I received the Legion of Honor."

"The Legion of Honor! How proud you must have been to receive France's highest honor!"

"It was nice, but more for the women of my country than for myself. Most of those medals have been awarded to men. It was time for my country to begin recognizing what our women have accomplished."

Turning more pages, she stopped, saying, "Here is my daughter, Colette, again. She must be almost thirty in this photo. It was taken at the end of the war. Colette has always been the joy of my life," she said closing the scrapbook and leaning back on her pillows.

"Do you write every day?" Capote asked.

"Yes, my dear, but my writing is mostly confined to correspondence now. See there," she said, waving at several unopened letters on the night-stand next to her bed, "I'll read those and answer them this evening. I live for my letters."

"You've been in my thoughts often, Madam Colette. After my first visit here, I scoured bookshops to search out as much of your writing as I could. Your books reveal such a fascinating life."

"Yes, it's all there for the perceptive reader."

Putting down his tea cup, Capote pointed his thumb at Colette's dresser where she kept many of her paperweights on display, saying, "This time, madam, I've come armed with a two-year love affair of those magical baubles."

Smiling knowingly, Colette said, "So, my little gift found nourishment in your soul."

"It certainly did. When you gave me that Baccarat paperweight with the white rose, you knew I'd become obsessed with them."

"Well then, you've caught the blissful illness. I must confess to you, since your last visit, I've borne a feeling of guilt for introducing you to these seductive confections. It was inevitable that you'd be seized with the sweet passion to gather them."

"I've devoured everything in print about them. I especially enjoyed your paperweight chapter in *Le Voyage Egoiste*."

"Yes, *Le Voyage Egoiste*. There's a copy of it over there," she said, pointing to a bookcase.

"There's a marvelous passage near the beginning of the chapter, madam; but wait, let me find it," he said going to the bookcase. He paged through the slim volume until he found the paragraph. "Here it is 'The paperweight—a crystal sphere, a deep abyss, a skillful snare for the imagination, relief for the flagging spirit, a wellspring of unrestrained imaginings—will never cease to mysteriously taunt man!'"

"I derived a great deal of pleasure writing that short piece about my beautiful snowflakes," she said. "They've meant so much to me. When everything else about me generates feelings of hopelessness and despair, they never fail to give me quiet moments of pleasure."

"They do lift the spirits. I've already acquired eleven of

them, all antique French."

"Well, then, I'm afraid I must warn you; there is no cure known to medical science for your malady," she laughed. "You'll just have to live out the rest of your life adoring them."

"How true! But the problem I find is that good examples are rare. And at those infrequent times when I've been lucky enough to find one that I can't live without, it costs me an arm and a leg!"

"They are very dear these days. I collected these you see here, many years ago, at a time when they were not sought after as passionately as they are today. On my excursions to the Marche aus Puces, I sometimes discovered them nestled in among other inexpensive objets d'art. I purchased most of them for only a few francs." She tilted her head back and closed her eyes, then continued, "I have such pleasant memories of those golden days. My dear companion, Germain Beaumont, and I would go together to the flea markets and return with our flat baskets heaped high with small porcelains, pieces of lace, fine books, small paintings and an occasional paperweight." Opening her eyes, she said, "See that large Baccarat on the vanity there, just to your left. Yes, that one. I remember buying it for four francs."

Taking up the paperweight from the vanity, Capote examined its kaleidoscopic bed of richly colored geometric shapes and saw that it was interspersed with a sprinkling of tiny stylized animal silhouettes. He said, "It's signed and dated 1847. A large handsome close-millefiori weight, magnum size, I believe. I bought a similar weight in New York just this year, dated 1848, smaller than this one, for over thirteen hundred dollars! You certainly found a bargain in this paperweight!"

"I never think of them as bargains, *mon ami*, but rather as beautiful touchstones of art left to us by the glass artists who breathed life into them over a century ago." Colette chose a brilliant turquoise Clichy paperweight from among those on her night stand. As she examined the paperweight with her rectangular reading glass, she asked, "In your readings, have you come across the account of the Imperial paperweights Evita Peron mentioned when she visited Trieste two years ago?"

"Yes, right after you gave me my first paperweight. I read it in a newspaper. I was intrigued by her story."

"Did you believe what she said?"

"That they were commissioned by Empress Eugenie? Yes, I suppose I did, because I'm a romantic. I wished with all my heart that what she said was true. She said she has one of them in her collection. If I remember correctly, she said there were several made."

"She said there were three; she has one, and there are two more awaiting discovery, somewhere in the world."

"Hm-m, wouldn't you give almost anything to have one of them!"

"What would you say if I told you that I nearly had one in my grasp some years ago?"

"An Imperial paperweight?" he asked in disbelief. He placed the paperweight on the vanity and returned to the chair next to Colette's bed.

Colette put down her reading glass and told her story. "When my advancing arthritic condition made it too difficult for me to continue my forays to the March aux Puces, my dear Germaine found an astute young man, Claude, who offered to search the flea markets for objects I might like."

"He'd act as your picker," added Capote.

"My 'picker'? Ah, yes, my 'picker'," she echoed, slowly assimilating a new meaning for a familiar English word. "Well, this picker, Claude, has found some very nice things for me. I understand he has expanded his service so that he now supplies other collectors and several antique shops with his finds."

"He must have a good eye."

"An exceptionally good one. Well, one day—it must have been about six years ago—Claude told me that a dealer at one of the flea markets said he had a large faceted yellow paperweight dated 1864, centered with a colorful shield and two white cameos. The dealer claimed the paperweight had once belonged to the English writer, Oscar Wilde. He promised he would bring it to the outdoor market the following week-end and offer it to Claude for sale."

"Oh, Madam Colette!"

"Yes, but when Claude returned to the flea market that weekend, the dealer failed to appear. Claude looked for him on subsequent weeks and even at other Paris markets, but was never able to locate the man. After all this time, Claude still continues to make inquiries, but the dealer seems to have dropped off the face of the earth."

"And you think it was one of the Imperial paperweights?"

"I didn't give it too much thought at the time, but two years ago, when Evita Peron described her paperweight to the press, I remembered the one Claude had described to me. Except for their difference in color, they were exactly the same."

"And the dealer claimed Oscar Wilde once owned it?"

"Yes, he did. It's a matter of record that Wilde had an outstanding paperweight collection. His surviving son, Vyvyan Holland, sold the paperweights just before the outbreak of the Second World War. I've attempted without success to learn if Mr. Holland is still alive, hoping he might be able to shed some light on the yellow paperweight."

"So the trail ends there."

"I hope not. Claude promised to explore even the slightest lead."

"Oscar Wilde, you and I—it must be fate," mused

Capote.

"Fate?"

"Yes, fate, that we three whose lives revolve around writing have been struck by the same strange malady, a desire to possess beautiful paperweights."

Colette thought to herself, more than one strange malady, my little friend.

3.

Colette and Capote continued to communicate with each other through their occasional letters. Fifteen years after his second visit, Capote received a letter from Colette which read, "Since my last letter to you, something unbelievable has happened! Claude's persistence has finally produced wonderful results. He located Carlota's yellow Imperial paperweight, the one which once belonged to Oscar Wilde! Claude learned that soon after the dealer offered him the paperweight, he was killed in a traffic accident. After his death, the man's wife and children left Paris and went to Brittany to be near her family. The dealer's widow still has the paperweight and is willing to sell it. Claude told me he will be making a buying trip near there in several weeks and will purchase it for me. The wait will seem like an eternity!

"I have also located and exchanged several letters with Vyvyan Holland. He wrote me that his father, Oscar Wilde, once owned a paperweight matching the description of my soon-to-be acquired jewel. He said that his father used to call it 'his little yellow Carlota'. According to Monsieur Holland, that magnificent piece was given to Oscar Wilde by Empress Eugenie! It was in Mr. Wilde's possession in Paris when he died, but his son does not know what became of it after his father's death.

"And so, *mon ami*, little yellow 'Carlota' and I will be anxiously waiting to spend a pleasant afternoon with you. When might you be coming to Paris?"

By return mail, Capote replied, "...I will be in Europe in about six weeks on a business matter. I accept with delight your kind invitation to visit with you once again. Be assured I am looking forward to an afternoon of a rapturous *menage a trois* with you and 'little Carlota'..."

In less than a month, Capote, with a heavy heart, flew to Paris to attend Colette's funeral. She died suddenly after a short illness. Upon her death, the French people, deeply saddened, arranged a funeral of state for their premier lady of letters, a funeral attended by dignitaries from around the globe.

During the memorial service, Capote's thoughts wandered back to their mutual quest for the Imperial paperweight. My dear, dear friend, he thought, how ironic for you to have been so close to the prize you sought, and then be denied by death. But, at least, fate allowed you to savor the sweet anticipation of Carlota's paperweight. Few feelings seldom equal the singular joy of anticipation. The actual attainment of an object of desire is not always as pleasurable.

But, unknown to Capote, Colette had held the object of her desire in her hands. When Claude arrived at her apartment with Carlota's paperweight, Pauline told him that Madam Colette was extremely ill. Nurses attended her constantly and a physician visited daily. "But," she added, she's so eager to see the paperweight, Monsieur Claude, I'm sure the doctor won't mind if you see her for a minute."

Pauline went to the bedroom door and spoke to the nurse. Turning to Claude, she motioned, saying, "Come, we may go in. Madam is stirring." As he stepped into Colette's darkened bedroom, Pauline cautioned, "We mustn't stay too long."

"Madame—Madame Colette," said Pauline, softly stroking Colette's cheek, "Monsieur Claude is here."

"Claude?"

"Yes, he has Carlota's paperweight, madam."

"The paperweight?" She attempted to rise up on her elbows. "Help me, help me up, Pauline, please."

As the nurse and Pauline propped pillows behind her, Colette's eyes caught the yellow glimmer of glass in Claude's grasp.

"Oh, it's here—my lovely yellow butterfly."

Claude carefully placed the paperweight into her cupped hands. Her eyes opened wide, then went vacant. The paperweight dropped onto the bed. Colette fell back on the pillows.

"…touched by the evil empress's damned paperweight…"

The nurse quickly felt for Colette's pulse and motioned Claude out of the room. Minutes later, Pauline appeared at the open doorway, assisted by the nurse who helped her to her room. When the nurse returned she told Claude, "Madam Colette is gone. If you'll wait here, I'll bring your paperweight to you, Monsieur."

After Colette's funeral, Capote learned from Pauline that Claude had brought the paperweight to Colette on the day she died, but had taken it with him when he left. When Capote attempted to locate him, he found that Claude and the Imperial paperweight had vanished from the City of Light.

4.

The 1950's were productive years for Truman Capote. His writing included many finely crafted works, among them his brilliant short novel, *Breakfast at Tiffany's*, and the movie script for John Houston's *Beat the Devil*.

As his writing achieved recognition, he found himself in great demand, and quickly became immersed in the rarefied circles of eastern seaboard society. A welcome guest at the best homes and parties, he thoroughly enjoyed his newly acquired status, reveling in the knowledge that he had arrived. And because he only knew loneliness and rejection as a child, he constantly sought out daily assurances of his changed circumstances. To that end, Capote ritually perused the society columns each morning after attending a social affair to read what was said about him.

"Carl, where's my little black bag?"

"Over here on the mantel, Truman. I'll get it for you," said the older man, crushing his cigarette in an ashtray and removing it from its long sterling cigarette holder. Lifting the bag, he complained, "Christ, it's so heavy!"

"Well, what do you expect, honey? Those paperweights are solid glass, heavy as rocks."

"Sure as hell are! A guy could get a hernia."

"Six rocks as big as a man's fist can be pretty heavy, but I don't mind the weight. I've gotten used to cradling them in my lap on long flights."

"Don't you ever get tired hauling them around?"

"No, they're worth the effort. No matter where I settle down for the night—a lonely hotel room or in someone's home—I just open the bag, unwrap them and place them around the room. And you know what? All of a sudden, I'm home. They're so warm and so familiar, just like old friends. Oh, there's the phone, Carl. Would you get it for me?"

"It's the desk, Truman. The limo's here."

"Okay. Tell them I'm ready; I'll be down in five minutes. Ask them to send up a bellboy for my bags. Tell them to send Jimmy, that cute one with the curly red hair."

After the two men embraced and kissed, Capote said, "God, I miss you already, Carl. Wish you were coming with me."

"So do I, but I've got to finish my work here. I promised the gallery the watercolors would be ready for the show by the end of the month. We'll be together soon. Nothing can keep us apart for long. It never has."

"I'll call you when I get to New York."

"Just maybe you will," Carl said. "I won't hold my breath. You know the saying, 'Out of sight—'."

"You'll see."

The following day, Capote surprised Carl with the promised call.

"See there, Carl," Capote laughed, "I didn't forget."

"Well, I can damn well tell you, Truman, you've shocked the hell out of me! Once you settle in New York, you usually forget the rest of the world. I suppose you're going to have another one of those soirées for your 'beautiful' people?"

"Uh-huh. And I've been busy with it; I've already invited some of them."

"The usual crowd?"

"Sure."

"I knew you'd arrange some damn thing as soon as you got there."

"Sounds like you're a little bit jealous. Are you jealous, Carl?"

"Hell no. They're just 'sometime' friends, parasites. You'll see. They'll drop you like a smelly turd as soon as you stop being a celebrity."

"For your information, my love, I'm adored by a lot of people. Princess Lee told me she really enjoys my company. She said I'm always amusing and fun to be with."

"That's just a lot of crap, Truman, and you know it!"

"Hey, listen sweetie, you can just kiss my little rosy-red ass."

"It wouldn't be the first time, would it?"

"Oh, Carl, you're so funny! That's why we get along so well."

Capote's friends could not understand the attraction he and Carl had for each other; they were such opposites in every way. "Truman loves to be with people," they said.

"Yes, doesn't he. He drips southern charm. But that Carl of his is an oddball."

"Guards his solitude and hates people. He actually seems to enjoy offending everyone around him. I don't know why Truman puts up with him."

"And the affected way he holds that long cigarette holder of his—twists his hand, leans his head back and puffs from his wrist."

"Like a Russian Romanoff."

"Betty says that he swishes it around like one of his watercolor brushes."

"Weird!"

Carl never bothered to hide the resentment he felt toward the intrusions made on his and Capote's time together. But, Carl answered a need for Capote. Intimately aware of his lover's wretched childhood, Carl always comforted Capote whenever the younger man lapsed into a depression over his mother's rejection.

Capote, whose many literary and social successes pushed the Imperial paperweight into a seldom visited retreat of his mind, had a sudden reawakening of all things "Colette" when Hollywood made her delightful book *Gigi* into a successful movie. Recalling the letter she had written him just before her death, he decided to initiate a serious search for Oscar Wilde's paperweight. On a flight to Pharos Island, where he and Carl planned a working vacation—Carl to paint seascapes and Truman to complete an article about a trip he had made to Moscow—Capote stopped over in Paris to employ the Au-Courant agency to search for Carlota's elusive paperweight. As the agency reluctantly accepted the assignment, the private investigator told him, "Because you insist, Mr. Capote, we shall undertake the search for you. But since you have so little information about the person named 'Claude' and even less about the paperweight, we cannot offer any assurance of success."

In subsequent years, Capote's desire to possess Wilde's "yellow Carlota" became a curious vacillating obsession, one which went into remission until he received a letter or an invoice from Au-Courant for "services rendered." As he opened the infrequent letters from the agency, all his cravings to possess the paperweight rushed in on him. He thought of nothing else for days until a new onslaught of work or other obligations pushed the paperweight out of his mind once again.

Toward the end of the decade, Capote's work evolved from a poetic style to one that was more simple and direct. The change was a deliberate one. As an established author, he decided to make a break from his earlier work; he wanted to write in a more mature style. To that end, he turned to a style that applied the techniques of good journalistic writing to the non-fiction novel.

A multiple murder in the small Kansas farm community of Holcomb became the vehicle for Capote's charged prose. Using his new style of writing, he crafted a non-fiction masterpiece, *In Cold Blood*, the story of two murderers who killed all four members of the Clutter family. For a period of six years, Capote made frequent trips to the scene of the murders to interview everyone in the community. He also visited the prison where he talked at length with both killers, Perry Smith and Richard Hickock. During those visits and the ensuing trial, he carefully recorded the personal remembrances of those who knew the Clutters, the recollections of the killers and every word and nuance that occurred in the courtroom.

Convicted of the crime, Smith and Hickock appealed their convictions three times, only to have their guilty verdict repeatedly upheld. During the years Capote gathered material for his book, he formed a close relationship with Perry Smith. Present at the hanging, at Smith's request, Capote collapsed and then cried for several days; he lost a close friend.

With the executions, Capote had a complete story. He flew to his retreat in the Swiss Alps and wrote a novel that delineated the terrible tragedy in minute detail: the minds of the killers, the unfortunate farm family, the crime itself, the trial, the appeals and the eventual hanging of the criminals. Carefully selecting from his voluminous collection of facts—six thousand pages of notes—he skillfully illuminated the text from the commission of the crime to the eventual punishment of the murderers. Capote's book received immediate acclaim as a modern masterpiece and became an instant best seller.

Capote, a multimillionaire from *In Cold Blood* royalties, purchased a United Nations Plaza twenty-second floor two-bedroom apartment where he lived next to such neighbors as

Johnny and Joanne Carson, Robert Kennedy, Lee Radziwell and Jacqueline Bouvier. In addition to the New York apartment, he acquired a chalet in Verbier, Switzerland, a home in California and a large piece of property with two adjacent homes on Long Island—one for Carl and one for himself. For the next few years, Capote enjoyed an incredibly fulfilling life as he mingled with many of the well-known eastern seaboard elite.

Carl placed a long distance call to Kansas where Columbia Pictures employed Capote to "insure the integrity" of the filming of *In Cold Blood*.

"Mr. Capote's suite, whom shall I say is calling?"

"Tell him it's Carl."

"Just a moment, please."

As Carl waited, he inserted another cigarette in his sterling holder and lit up.

"Hi, Carl."

"Hi Truman. Who's the queen that answered the phone?"

"That was Nathan. I met him several days ago at a concert in Kansas City."

"Is he staying there with you?"

"Yes, he and his three friends are resting here for a few days between concerts. He's such a lovely young man, and very talented, too."

"I'm not interested in what he does to turn you on, Truman."

"No, no, Carl. You don't understand, although, come to think of it, you old fart, he could teach you a thing or two. What I meant was that he's a fine musician. He plays the viola beautifully—he studied at Juliard."

"Oh, a musician."

"Yes, he's a professional; he's the violist of the Allegro

String Quartet. They're all young musicians. The music critics really praised them here—great reviews. We've become close in just a few days. And guess what, Carl; the four of them came to my suite last night to give me a personal concert. Imagine, a concert for an audience of one!"

"They're all pretty young men, I suppose."

"Why Carl, there's that jealous streak again. As a matter of fact, Dorothy, the second violinist and Richard, the cellist are husband and wife. Anthony, the first violinist is also married and has twin babies."

"And you're paying for their keep, right?"

"Yes, I am. They're between concerts for six days. I asked them to stay over, here in the hotel."

"You're supporting all four of them for six days? Christ, Truman!"

"I can afford it. It's none of your damn business what I do with my money. Anyhow, it's so boring here, I welcome the diversion."

"Yeah, I suppose you do," Carl said. After a few long puffs on his cigarette, he asked, "They played for you last night?"

"Uh-huh, and it was wonderful! One of the pieces they played for me was a quartet by Ravel, Maurice Ravel. During the first movement, when Anthony and Nathan played the second theme together, I actually wept. It was like seeing reflections of Venice through floating gauze. The warm velvety voice of Nathan's viola communing with the high clear song of the violin—it was so hauntingly beautiful, so full of longing. It was almost too much to bear. If only my writing could evoke such engulfing feelings. You know, Carl, I really miss you."

"I doubt it, especially with that young viola player there to keep you amused." Receiving no reaction from Capote, Carl continued, "Anyway, Truman, the reason I'm calling is to tell you that a letter came for you today from that agency in Paris."

"From Au-Courant?"

"Yeah. I didn't think you'd want to wait until you return to New York to read it."

"I haven't heard from them in two years!"

"I knew you'd want to know what they had to say, so I read it."

"What'd they say?"

"One of their investigators on the trail of some of King Farouk's missing jewelry uncovered the fact that he once owned one of those Imperial paperweights."

"Oh, my God, and?"

"According to what they found out, when he died, he still had that paperweight in his possession."

"Where is it now? Did they say?"

"They don't know. But they wrote to ask if you want them to forget about Oscar Wilde's paperweight and start looking for King Farouk's, instead."

"Yes, by all means! Listen, Carl, I'll call Paris from here and tell them to go ahead. You know, I've had dreams about those paperweights. If only they could find one."

"This just might be it, Truman."

"God, I hope so."

"How much longer do you think you'll be in Kansas?"

"The shooting'll be finished in three weeks. I've really missed you. We'll have some great times together when I get back."

"Just the two of us?"

"Yes, just you and me, you'll see. Thanks for calling, Carl."

"See you in three weeks, Truman."

"Bye, Love."

Replacing the receiver on its cradle, Capote gazed at the young statuesque Adonis standing silhouetted at the shuttered window. After a few moments, he settled himself deep into the blankets and quietly suggested, "Take off that towel, Nathan, and come back to bed. I have such a strong desire to put my arms around your beautiful body."

On his return from Kansas, Capote, flush with success, gave a lavish ball in the New York Plaza Hotel for more than five hundred "friends"—a mix of some of the most influential and celebrated people on the east coast. The New York tabloids called Capote's black and white masked ball the "Party of the Decade." Rumors had it that the fabulous soirée cost him over seventy-five thousand dollars.

In 1970, while living on the west coast, Capote completed *The Dogs Bark; Public People and Private Places*, a collection of personal reminiscences. One of the short stories in the collection was his paean to paperweights, "The White Rose." It described his first visit with Colette, and her gift to him of a Baccarat paperweight containing an exquisite white rose.

"I just had to include Colette in my book," he told Carl. "It's my small contribution to her memory. If I hadn't met her, I would never have known these glass jewels. I owe her so much."

"I liked that story, Truman. Did Colette really say that to you when you objected to accepting the paperweight?" Carl asked.

"That's right. Her very words were, 'My dear, really there is no point in giving a gift unless one also treasures it oneself.'"

During that same year Capote began to write his announced major opus, *Answered Prayers*. Although secretive about its subject matter, he assured everyone that the new novel would establish him as the Proust of American letters.

Impressed by his announcements, Random House gave him an advance of $800,000 for the book; Twentieth Century Fox paid him an advance of $350,000 for movie rights without seeing one word in writing.

Capote, constantly sought after by everyone, became involved in a perpetual round of travel, TV interviews, and socializing. Because of his many appearances on television, the public came to recognize this oddly assembled individual on sight: his large head, his small chunky body slouching on a sofa, and his legs, too short to touch the floor, dangling childlike in the air. His hallmarks were his nasal whine and the nervous flailing of his hands. He soon became a sought-after media celebrity, delighting his hosts and viewers with his curious appearance, strange mannerisms and especially with his outrageous statements.

5.

Ever the recluse, Carl continued to avoid contact with Capote's friends and refused to participate in any of Capote's expanding activities. Their life together became so modified that Carl spent most of the year isolated in Capote's Swiss chalet, well away from New York. Those infrequent times when they were together, they found they had little to share with each other. After much soul-searching, Carl and Capote admitted to each other that the intense love they once felt for each other had faded. Capote tearfully told Carl that he had lately contemplated taking a new lover.

"I understand," said Carl, "but promise me that we'll always be friends. You have been the focus of the most important time of my life, my passionate years. My advancing years have put those carnal cravings behind me now. My feelings for you have toned-down to a warm glow. You're still young and vital and need someone who can satisfy your desires. Remember, Truman, I've always been and will always be your friend."

Soon after Carl left for Verbier, Capote met Lenny and became involved in a torrid love affair. The new sexual partner in his life, a young garage mechanic, abandoned his wife and children to become Capote's constant companion. Everything was "just great" to Lenny. Not a complex person, he preferred beer to champagne and fried catfish to caviar. He was not "into books," instead, he avidly perused comic books and girlie magazines. Capote was convinced that when they first met, his young friend did not know who he was nor that he wrote for a living. Capote wrote Carl, "All he knows is that I like him and that I have lots of money."

Capote's friends found Lenny dull, a one-dimensional adult whose entire universe of information consisted of RPM's, gears, transmissions and engines. But, to Capote, Lenny was the compatible companion that Carl had never been. The new man in his life gave him no arguments, offered no recriminations, and voiced no criticism of his friends, his socializing or his drinking. He was simply a willing lover.

Returning to his apartment one afternoon, Capote found Lenny juggling three valuable antique paperweights high into the air. "For Christ's sake, Lenny, don't do that!"

"It's okay, Tru," he said unconcernedly, "I've been juggling for years. Toss me another one, and I'll try to keep all four going at once."

Capote lowered his voice and calmly said, "Just put them down, Lenny, please." As Capote returned the paperweights to the cabinet, he realized the young man had no conception of the value of the objects scattered about in the apartment. The shiny glass balls just served as convenient substitutes for apples and oranges.

To Capote's dismay, their idyllic affair was short-lived. While traveling together in Europe, Lenny unexpectedly asked for permission to fly back to America. After arriving in New York, Lenny terminated their relationship and returned to his family. Capote, deeply distressed at his abandonment, went through an extended period of despair. Dredged up memories of his mother's rejection further compounded his distress.

During the next few years, as Capote broke-up with one homosexual lover after another, he sought solace in pills and alcohol. Detoxification was the usual stressful consequence at the termination of each of his many affairs.

After three years of disappointing love affairs, Capote began a relationship that lasted eight years. Justin, whom he first met in a gay bathhouse, was separated from his wife and three young children. Capote, taken by the man's muscular build, asked the bathhouse manager, "Who is that good-looking guy standing over there, Conrad?"

"That's Justin Hall."

"I've never seen him here before."

"That's because you come here nights. He usually comes early in the morning, works out with weights, steams, and goes to work."

As Capote drank in the man's physique, Conrad continued. "He's just getting started as an interior decorator with Crayden and Spindel."

Capote knew the firm's name; it was an exclusive decorator shop in Manhattan. He's middle-aged, sort of old to be starting a new job as a decorator, Capote thought.

Capote introduced himself to Justin and learned that he had recently sold a floundering family antique business. Using his knowledge of fine furniture and decorative objects, Justin obtained a position with Crayden and Spindel.

With an ambitious eye toward the future, Capote's new acquaintance offered to help him decorate his residences, speculating that if his work was successful, he might be asked to decorate the homes and apartments of Capote's many wealthy friends. Capote soon convinced Justin to give up his new position and accompany him on an extensive trial honeymoon which he tactfully explained to everyone as a "sojourn to collect decorative items for my homes and apartment."

They flew to Greece and then to Istanbul. From Turkey, they took the Orient Express to Venice where they enjoyed a three week honeymoon before flying to Switzerland. On their return to New York, Capote, deeply in love, doubled Justin's salary.

When Justin discovered his new employer's interest in paperweights, he began to familiarize himself with Capote's "other passion." It was not long before he learned enough about the crystal baubles to carry on an intelligent conversation about them. That he now had a lover with whom he could share more than a bedroom interest elated Truman.

Justin's sixteen years in the antique business served as an added bonus for Capote. It afforded him a valuable link to New York antique dealers. He was especially pleased that his new lover obtained paperweights at "dealers price," a trade euphemism that translated to substantial discounts for him.

When Capote's friends first met his erudite companion, they felt Justin a great improvement over Carl and Lenny. However, their opinion of him changed when they discovered how abusive and crude Justin acted when he drank too much.

To add to their irritation, Capote's new lover soon appointed himself chatelaine of Capote's telephone, screening all calls to his lover and deciding who could speak to Capote and who could not. When Capote's friends complained to him that Justin isolated him from them, Capote was secretly pleased. He reveled in the assumption that Justin acted out of jealousy—a jealousy born of his intense love for him.

In time, Justin's persistent possessiveness wore on Capote. That Capote and Carl continued to remain friends particularly perturbed Justin. He constantly urged Capote to break off with his friend, but Capote refused to do so. They bickered constantly.

Justin, now secure in his relationship, began to viciously berate Capote in public. On one occasion he threw a drink into Capote's face. The turbulent relationship finally came to an end when Capote broke with his truculent lover. Depressed, Capote went on an alcoholic binge, collapsed and was rushed to a hospital. On his release, he and Justin reconciled, promising that they would be more understanding of each other. But, their arguments soon began anew. Their life together became a recurring scenario of reconciliation's, new rows and break-ups. After each separation, Capote entered a hospital to endure yet another alcoholic detoxification.

6.

In June of 1975, the first of four fragmentary installments of *Answered Prayers*, Capote's unfinished opus, appeared in *Esquire*. The selection, "Mohave," met with instant praise. Capote rejoiced. Its success confirmed his belief that despite his personal problems with alcohol, drugs and Justin, the quality of his craft did not diminish.

When the next installment, "La Cote Basque," appeared in the October issue, Capote shocked his rich and famous friends. The selection contained explicit stories in which their protégé detailed their most intimate affairs. And, although he concealed the real names of his characters in his *roman à clef*, it was obvious to most readers who his characters were. He infuriated the east coast elite, who had welcomed him into their exclusive circle. He betrayed their privacy and their trust. They considered him a traitor.

Their reaction stunned Capote. "How could they turn on me like that, Justin? God, I only wrote what I saw and heard. They were so open about everything. It's all true; I didn't fictionalize any of it."

"No one wants their dirty linen exposed, especially those high-brow friends of yours."

"But, I'm a writer! I have only my own experiences to draw on. This work was something I've worked all my life to be able to do. Writing is an art; I'm an artist. Everyone knew what I was doing. Don't they realize that 'La Cote Basque' is a significant chapter of an important sociological work?"

"They don't see it that way, Truman. They think you used them. Quite frankly, when I read it, I felt I was spying on them during their most private moments."

"I didn't use their real names; no one knows who they are."

"The reviewers guessed who they were; their identities are no secret, Truman."

"Oh shit, that's all you know about it!" Pouring himself another tumbler of bourbon, Capote complained, "I don't know what to do. No one lets me explain myself. They won't answer my messages. No one's bothered to call me for days. I feel deserted."

"And they won't call you, either. Don't take it so damn

hard. They're just a bunch of jerks.". Watching Capote down the glass of bourbon in a swallow, Justin warned, "I'll tell you something else, Truman. That heavy drinking you've been doing lately doesn't help much, either. You don't want to end up in the hospital again, do you?"

"It softens the hurt of their rejection. Anyway, Justin, don't be so damn picky. I don't see you joining the AA's. You do your share of drinking around here, too, you know."

"Well, don't say I didn't warn you about your fair-weather friends. You can see how much they value your friendship, now."

"Oh, dry up! You've turned into a fuckin' hermit, like Carl! You never did like my friends! You're nothing but a pain in the ass, afraid to be around happy people!"

"At least I haven't deserted you like your 'happy people' have."

"Go to hell!" Capote angrily responded, pouring himself more bourbon.

While Capote still suffered the agonies of rejection, Neil Simon offered him an acting part in the movie, *Murder by Death*. He asked him to play a role that parodied himself. Simon told Capote, "It'll be easy for you to do; just be your natural self."

Capote gleefully accepted, gloating to Justin, "Those hypocrites who dropped me will just crap when they hear about the movie! I'll show them, you'll see."

The filming proved to be an excruciating ordeal for Capote. Justin awakened him at six each morning and drove him to the studio. Once there, Capote remained in a private trailer until summoned for wardrobe and make-up. After preparing for the part, he returned to the stultifying confines of his trailer to wait until he was needed for a take, a take that often was not filmed until hours later. He then returned to his hotel for the night to begin the ordeal again at six the following morning. The demanding routine left him exhausted.

When the movie was released, the critics panned Capote's acting. They said he hadn't portrayed himself well; he overacted.

Early the next year, in need of money, Capote signed a fifty-thousand dollar contract for a speaking tour of thirty colleges and universities. The pace drained him, traveling from place to place and sleeping in a different hotel each night. He found solace in the alcohol that he consumed, and in the several paperweights he placed about himself in his hotel rooms.

Disastrous years followed *Esquire's* publication of "La Cote Basque". Since Capote no longer enjoyed the adoration and popularity that once nourished him, he decided that he and Justin would leave New York and take up residence in Palm Springs. "It'll be great, Justin. It's always summer there. I don't need these New York bitches! I've got friends out there. The change'll be good for us. I know we'll get along better out there, too. You'll see."

Contrary to his prediction, the move to California did not ease their stormy relationship.

"Damn it, you've been in my mail again!"

"I'm just trying to help, Truman.".

"You're throwing my letters away before I get to see them."

"There's so much junk mail and so many people writing you, I only sort out the dross. You ought to be grateful."

"Bullshit! You're just plain nosy. Anyhow, it's an invasion of my privacy!"

"Oh, come on, Truman. After sharing a bed together all

these years, we don't have any secrets from each other, do we? What's really chewing at you?"

"I'm not getting all of my important mail, and I know it. I got a call from Carl last night. He asked me why I haven't answered his letters."

"That persistent old bastard! He's still trying to break us up. Is he still sucking on that cigarette holder of his? He acts like it's a tit!"

"Don't change the subject! Damn it, Justin, in the future, I want you to keep your big nose out of my mail! And, another thing, I'm sick and tired of hearing you've turned away the few friends that still speak to me."

"Speak to you? They're parasites! Carl has been sponging off of you for years. He's even taken over your chalet in Verbier. He acts like he owns it!"

"That's none of your god-damned business! I've always been generous with my friends. And, for your information, Justin, I gave him his cigarette holder."

"Still sticking up for him, taking his side! What'd he do with it, shove it up your ass when you were making love?"

"You son-of-a-bitch, you don't know the meaning of real friendship. I'm warning you, Justin, from now on, keep your nose out of my business!"

"Christ, Truman, I'm only thinking of you. The junk mail eats up your precious time. You need time for your writing."

"My writing? I'm a better judge of my writing needs than you are. I wrote *In Cold Blood* before I ever met you. I didn't need your help then and I sure as hell don't need it now. I've had it up to here with your interference in my personal affairs!"

"Oh, dry up, Truman, and stop whining. Damn it, I don't ask for much around here. God knows I earn my keep, scrounging around antique shops, house sales and dirty flea markets finding things for you."

"The hell you do. You haven't found a good paperweight in months. I haven't forgotten your trip to Paris, acting the big man, squandering away my money on your damn friends!"

Earlier that year, Justin flew to Europe on a supposed quest to locate Carlota's Imperial paperweight. He convinced Capote he could easily locate the Imperial paperweight for him. He said, "After all the money you've thrown down the drain looking for that paperweight, you can afford a few thousand dollars to send me to France to find it for you."

"But Au-Courant scoured Europe for years hunting for it."

"Truman, they're not in the business of antiques. They don't know the first thing about where to look. I've got connections with a lot of antique dealers over there."

Capote later learned Justin spent the entire time in Paris lavishly entertaining old male friends. What hurt Capote was not the money or the lying, but that Justin abandoned him for the company of others—especially so soon after Capote's friends in New York dropped him.

"You just use me to live high on the hog. You don't fool me, Justin! I happen to know you get kickbacks whenever I buy from your dealer friends."

"Oh, so we're down to the real dirt now, are we? The real truth is you need me to satisfy all your little dirty desires. You know what, little man, you don't realize that you need me a hell of a lot more than I need you!"

"You don't love me, Justin. You just hang around for whatever you can get out of me."

Their arguments continued unabated. Justin sometimes became so frenzied during their disputes that he physically attacked Capote. On several occasions, Truman sought sanctuary from Justin's violent outbursts by escaping to friends' homes.

"He gets so frenzied when he's drunk," Capote told his psychiatrist, "I fear that my very life is in jeopardy."

"Then why continue living with him? Nothing is worth that kind of stress and danger!"

"How can I explain it? There are times, less often now than before, when he's had just a few drinks and he's just a little bit mellow, Justin becomes the sweetest, most tender lover I've ever known. During those times together I can forgive him anything."

Justin's violent eruptions eventually escalated to such an intensity that Capote, fearing for his own safety, decided to make a complete and final break from his lover. Dreading a personal confrontation, he left California and flew to New York. Once there, he telephoned Justin and told him of his decision. He said he had sold the house in which they had been living, and because the new owner intended to take immediate possession, Justin would have to vacate the premises at once. The finality of Capote's resolve left Justin stranded in California. He was forced to find temporary shelter in an unheated garage. For toilet necessities he used a lavatory in a nearby filling station.

Once in New York, Capote became involved with the Warhol set. But, the east coast proved to be more disastrous to Capote than the west coast had been. Beginning on a Himalayan high at the outset of each new homosexual affair, he sank into progressively deeper depressions after each break-up.

"I just can't stop taking tranquilizers," he complained as he admitted himself into one rehabilitation clinic after another.

"I'm drowning," he told a psychiatrist, "and all I ever grab is another sinking anchor."

When interviewed by the media, he presented a tragically pathetic picture, disoriented and obviously under the influence of narcotics and alcohol. He often declared, "I'm an alcoholic, I'm a drug addict, I'm a homosexual; but, I'm also a genius."

During an interview on a popular talk show he was so thick-tongued that the host became concerned about Capote's condition. Capote's lapses of thought and his long pauses upset his worried host, who asked him if he would prefer to come back another time, giving the intense heat of the television lights as a convenient excuse. But Capote preferred to stay, replying, "I feel—perfectly—fine," and remained to continue the almost incoherent interview.

7.

NEW YORK - 1981

Carl, awakened from a sound sleep by his telephone, fanned the air above the night stand until his hand found the receiver. He hoarsely answered, "Hello."

"Carl, Carl, love—"

"Truman, is that you?"

"Yes, Carl. Thank God you're there! It's so wonderful to hear your voice again."

"Damn it, Truman, I was sleeping. It's the middle of the night here!"

"I know, Carl, I'm sorry, but I desperately need your help."

"I can't do much for you; Switzerland's a long way from New York. You don't really need me. Why don't you call one of your pretty friends, Lenny or Justin.". Focusing his eyes on the luminous clock dial, Carl said, "Jesus Christ, it's four in the morning! I'm going back to sleep."

"No, wait! Please, Carl, don't hang up! Hear me out, please."

"Oh, Christ!" said Carl, sitting up and reaching into his night stand for his cigarette holder and a cigarette. Lighting the cigarette, he plumped up his pillow, leaned back and asked, "What do you want?"

"Carl, I got a call from Paris, from the Au-Courant agency. They called the day before yesterday. They think they've located one of Empress Carlota's paperweights."

"Not Farouk's paperweight, again," said Carl, remembering Capote's eternal search and all the fruitless leads.

"No, not that one. They think they've found another one."

"Another one?"

"Yes. Listen, Carl, they said that there's going to be an auction in Buenos Aires with some of Evita Peron's things in it. From the description they gave me, it sounds like lot 94 is one of the Imperial paperweights. It's not Wilde's yellow one. It's the green one that belonged to Evita—Evita Peron."

"And what the hell do you want from me?"

"If there's the slightest chance of getting it, I've got to try. I've got to fly down there. Carl, you know how long I've searched. I planned to go by myself, but I'm not completely well; I'm still a little weak. And I get disoriented so easily."

"Same old problem?"

"Yes, Carl. But I've gotten help for myself, I'm much better now, really."

Perceiving that Capote indeed sounded rational and sober, he asked, "Then, why do you need me?"

"I need someone to go with me, someone to help cut through the red tape, make arrangements and get me to the auction on time. I need someone I can depend on. Oh, Carl, would you do it for me? I've no one else to ask."

"Where the hell is your wonderful friend, Justin?"

"I broke up with him a long time ago. I think he's still in California."

"I didn't know."

"I need your help, Carl. I'm all alone. You're the only true friend I've ever had. Please, don't turn me down. Why don't you take a few days off and fly over here. I'm staying at the Regency—you know—on Park avenue. My flight leaves for Argentina on Wednesday afternoon. Please say you'll go with me."

The poor little son-of-a-bitch, thought Carl, as he crushed his cigarette into the ashtray. He's had such a rough road. I do owe him a hell of a lot. Maybe, just maybe, he's starting to climb out of that box he's been in.

"Carl, Carl, are you there?"

"Yeah, Truman."

"Please say you'll go with me?"

"Okay, I guess I owe you that much. I'll take a flight out of here and get to New York the day after tomorrow, sometime in the morning."

"Oh Carl, how can I ever repay you? I'll make it up to you somehow. Just think, the paperweight's almost in my grasp."

When they arrived in Buenos Aires, the hotel clerk apologized that he could not provide accommodations for them on the same floor. He explained that they should have made reservations ahead of their arrival.

After they unpacked, Carl and Capote took a cab to the auction house to preview the paperweight. Capote puzzled Carl by making no effort to examine the paperweight. He had talked about nothing else since they left New York. "Don't you want the clerk to get it for you, Truman?" he asked.

"I'll just look at it in the case for a while. I don't want to seem too eager; it might encourage others to bid against me tomorrow afternoon."

When the clerk finally handed the paperweight to Capote, he examined it carefully, but with a casual air, hoping not to attract the attention of the other bidders crowded around the cases.

On their way back to the hotel, Capote was ecstatic. "Evita's paperweight! I actually held it in my hands! An Imperial paperweight! I've searched for one of those treasures for thirty years! I'll bid the moon to get it! It's going to be mine, Carl. God, I can't believe it's happening."

The next morning Carl's call to Capote's room would not go through the switchboard. He took the elevator to Capote's suite and knocked on the door. Receiving no response, he went to the lobby and had a late breakfast and a cigarette in the coffee shop.

An hour later, he went to the desk and asked the clerk to ring Capote's rooms.

"I'm sorry Sir, but we were asked not to disturb Mr. Capote's suite. He left specific instructions not to ring him nor clean his suite until after he takes leave of the hotel this afternoon."

Carl, imagining that Truman was having a private *tete-a-tete* with an 'instant' friend, asked, "Did he give you an approximate time when his room could be cleaned?"

"Yes, he said after one o'clock. He said he would be requiring the services of a taxi at that time also."

Carl looked at his watch and saw that Truman would not have to leave for the auction for another hour. He asked, "When did he make the request?"

"Late last night."

Yes, Carl thought, I was right, Truman found an 'instant'

friend to share his bed last night. Carl left the hotel for a walk and returned at twelve- thirty. He went directly to Capote's suite. Knocking on the door and receiving no response, he returned to the hotel lobby. Worried now, he told the desk clerk he feared something might be wrong with Mr. Capote. The day manager, Carl and hotel security hurried to Capote's suite. Unlocking the door they found Capote on the floor, delirious.

The manager turned to the security officer, saying, "He looks pretty bad. Get on the phone and call the house doctor. You'd better call an ambulance too!"

Three days later, when his doctors allowed visitors, Carl went to see Capote in the hospital.

"Well, Truman, you made it. I thought you'd bought it when we found you. Mixing alcohol and amphetamines is deadly, my friend."

Recognizing his visitor, Capote was able to whisper, "Thanks—to you, dear—friend, I'm still alive. I survived—once again. But," he softly said, "the—paperweight— it's gone."

"I'm sorry about the paperweight, Truman, I know how important it was to you. I thought of going to the auction, but you were so bad off, I decided to stick around, just to make sure you pulled through okay. Now that you're on the mend, we'll be flying back to New York, soon."

"When?"

"The doctor said you'll be released a day after tomorrow."

"Would you—do me one—last favor—before we—go back to New York?"

Looking down at the sunken eyes of the pitiful, small man, he said, "Of course, Truman, if I can."

"Would you—please—find out—who bought the Imperial—paperweight?"

During his visit the next day, Carl told Capote that the auctioneer would not divulge the name of the successful bidder on lot 94; the purchaser requested anonymity. The Argentinean said that an attractive woman, a *Norte Americana*, bought the paperweight, but nothing else.

"It's gone. Oh Carl, if only I could turn—the clock back. I should have listened. You were so right to try to get me help—for my problem, years ago."

"That's all in the past, Truman. What you must do now is get well and stay well."

"I know, Carl."

Capote produced no significant writing during the final years of his life. He continued to appear on talk shows, where audiences looked upon him not as an author, but as a media curiosity. His television hosts never knew whether he would arrive or not, nor what his condition would be if he did appear. More than likely, he would be inebriated or incoherent from the effects of drugs. Capote declared, during one of these interviews, "My life is over. I can no longer do what I always could, I can't write. But I believe that I have written one great masterpiece, *In Cold Blood*. In fact, I know I have! I've also written eight or nine short stories as good as any in the English language."

In 1983, he entered various hospitals and clinics sixteen separate times. His addiction made him so unintelligible and disoriented that his few remaining friends began to avoid him. Learning of Capote's growing problems and disintegrating condition, Carl left Verbier and flew to New York. Finding Capote confused, sick, unattended and lying in bed in his own excrement, he cleaned and bathed him and took him to a hospital. When the hospital released Capote, Carl delayed his return to Switzerland until he was satisfied his friend was sufficiently recovered to take care of himself.

The following year Doctors treated Capote for a cerebral concussion when he fell and struck his head. That same year, he entered the hospital to have clots cleared from his lungs. In August he overdosed, collapsed and was rushed to Southampton Hospital. Continuing to hallucinate, even after his release, he flew to California. The first night there was a fitful one for him. The next day he felt calm and had a quiet restful day.

The afternoon of the following day, Carl called him from Verbier. "I couldn't reach you in New York. I thought you might be there, at Joan's."

"I called Joan from the hospital. She said I could stay here until I felt better."

"How do you feel now?"

"I had a good day yesterday, Carl. But today I'm so tired. My heart keeps racing, then it slows down. It's a strange feeling."

"Your heart's racing?"

"Yes, off and on."

"Let me speak to Joan."

"She's not here. She's away for the weekend. When do you think you'll get here? We've got to get to Buenos Aires."

"Buenos Aires?"

"Yes, the auction—Evita's paperweight."

Oh, my God, thought Carl, he's hallucinating! The auction was three years ago. Won't he ever get over his damn mother's rejection?

"And if you could get here in time, Carl, we'd fly to Argentina together."

"Now listen, Truman," said Carl, "get on the damn phone and call Joan's doctor right now! I'll catch the first plane out of here and come to California."

"No, I'm not calling him. He'll just want to put me through that horrible detoxification again. I'd rather die first. I never want to go to another clinic or hospital again. More than anything else in the world, I would like to have you lie down with me for a little while. You've always been such a comfort."

Carl immediately telephoned a mutual friend in Los Angeles and asked him to look in on Capote until he could reach California.

Later that afternoon when Carl's friend arrived, he was shocked to find that Capote was not breathing. He quickly summoned the paramedics, but they were unable to revive him. Drugs and alcohol had ended his life.

...I curse all those who—will ever touch those unholy paperweights..."

When Carl arrived at Joan's home to gather up his friend's personal effects, he saw that Truman had not died alone. The little black bag was there, next to the bed. Six antique paperweights which Capote placed about the bedroom—his most constant companions—kept their faithful vigil.

CHAPTER VI.

1.

Since the summer she and Christa inspected the records at Valady, the three crystal treasures of the Lorraine factory were never far from Alexandra's thoughts. Four years after that summer, Alexandra assumed the directorship of Sotheby's-Chicago. During a social function to raise funds for a local PBS station, she disclosed her Valady findings to Charles Edmire, a wealthy retired Chicago industrialist. Alexandra and Edmire were not strangers to one another; he was an avid paperweight collector. While employed in New York, she occasionally acted as his private agent, assisting him in the acquisition of several fine paperweights.

Tantalized by her account of the Imperial paperweights, the elderly collector asked, "Who else knows about those records, Alexandra?"

"Only my two friends, Christa and her husband."

"Good," he said, and then added, "If you and your two friends would promise not to share those findings with anyone else but me, absolutely with no one else, I'd gladly underwrite such a search. I wouldn't want to lose those paperweights to another collector."

His insistence on secrecy was not a problem for Alexandra. Christa already suggested they keep the Lorraine discovery under wraps until Alexandra published the results of her research.

Edmire's offer was exactly what Alexandra needed. She planned to find one of the paperweights for him, and then convince him to lend it to the Art Institute of Chicago for display. The only return she desired was recognition for accomplishing an important piece of glass research.

Alexandra always felt that her efforts never received the acknowledgment they deserved. She was convinced that the glass fraternity deliberately snubbed her since she crossed over to the "crass" business side of antiques. She imagined that the act of marketing art objects made her an outcast to others—a priestess of Mammon who tainted the purity of art with commercialism. She especially singled out museum staffs as her antagonists. Alexandra once remarked to Elizabeth, "Museum people build protective walls around their esoteric world; they deny access to anyone not connected with a museum. Like members of medieval guilds, they refuse to recognize the serious work that occurs outside their own limited domain."

Once, when a client donated an outstanding collection of fine French gold and enamel snuff boxes, originally intended for auction at Sotheby's, to the Art Institute of Chicago, Alexandra told Elizabeth, "It makes my blood boil the way those curators curry the favors of advanced collectors. They're so deceitful. They do it to plunder the choicest pieces from private collections. They look on the pieces they appropriate and imprison in their cloistered galleries as their personal coups."

Mr. Edmire arranged a bank account specifically for locating the Imperial paperweights. Wasting little time, Alexandra employed researchers in France to ferret out all extant references to the Verrerie de Lorraine. Others were employed to investigate French museum records for references to Imperial decorative glass objects of the Second Empire. She also forwarded funds for a page-by-page duplication of the boxed Lorraine records in the basement of the Valady church.

After exhaustive inquiry, Alexandra's researchers unearthed evidence that Empress Eugenie commanded the three paperweights be created as a gift for Empress Carlota. From the moment of that astonishing discovery, Alexandra became so preoccupied with her search that much of what occurred in her daily existence seemed like passing shadows.

The investigators finally traced each of the paperweights to their last known owners: Empress Carlota, Oscar Wilde and Eva Peron. In spite of additional months of probing, the paperweight trails ended with those three individuals. Nothing else surfaced; there were no further leads.

Becoming impatient, Edmire suggested that Alexandra contact her Sotheby's connections in Belgium, France and Argentina and engage them to monitor promising estate sales as well as local auctions on the meager chance of uncovering one of the Imperial paperweights.

"Do you really want to do that?" she asked. "It'll be costly, without any guarantees. They're all experts; they won't come cheap."

"Look, Alexandra, I've spent lots of money for the past three years and all I have to show for it is history: where the paperweights were made and who had them last. We haven't the slightest idea where to look or if they still exist! I don't want to keep spending money without any hope of finding them. That's just throwing money down a well!"

Alexandra knew that if he withdrew his funding, she would never find the paperweights. She'd do what he wanted, but it was hopeless. Oh God, she prayed, something has to turn up!

"We'll try my idea for a couple of months. If that doesn't turn up anything new, we'll just quit the search. I know it'll cost a bundle, but we might as well try it for a while. We're no closer to those paperweights than we were three years ago."

To their amazement, his suggestion brought an almost

immediate response. One of Alexandra's searchers in Argentina discovered the listing of a large green paperweight in a catalog of an auction to be held in Buenos Aires. He telephoned Alexandra, "...and the auction is rumored to contain a few of Eva Peron's former possessions."

"Is there a picture of the paperweight in the catalog, Lazaro?"

"No, but it is described here. It's in Spanish. Let me translate the description for you. 'An encased paperweight, light-green, dated inside the glass, '1864'. It contains two cameos facing a shield surmounted by the Mexican eagle. The entire design is surrounded by, hmm, *un anillo*—hmm, oh yes, by a circle of millefiori canes, all over a dark green background.' I think it's what you've been looking for, Miss Saint George."

"Do you think I'll have any trouble at the auction house, Lazaro? I don't speak Spanish too well."

"No, Miss Saint George. Buenos Aires is a cosmopolitan city. The clerks in the auction house speak many languages: German, Italian, French, English. But, if you think you might need someone to help you after you've visited the auction house, please telephone me and I'll accompany you."

Armed with the certainty that her Argentine informant uncovered Eva Peron's Imperial paperweight, Alexandra flew to Argentina. When she previewed the items to be auctioned, she was astonished that the green paperweight in the case was, indeed, one of those that she had searched for, for so long.

"May I see that paperweight, please?" she asked, her voice shaking with emotion. "No, not that one—that one there, the large green one."

The clerk took the paperweight from the case and placed it before Alexandra on a padded piece of black velvet.

Oh, my God, she thought, I've found it; I've found one of

Empress Carlota's paperweights! Alexandra wanted to pick it up to examine it more closely but feared her shaking hands might drop it. Instead, she stood for a long time immersed in its history, all the while, gently stroking the paperweight. Then, finally picking it up and cradling it in both hands, she carefully examined its internal design. It's so much more beautiful than I ever imagined, she thought. It contains all the glass skills known to man. But it's much more than that; it embodies the essence of a refined era before automation replaced the creative imprint of the human hand. Just look at it catching the light! It's so beautiful! It has an ethereal beauty, a beauty born of man's spirit, that ineffable quality of all great art. It speaks to the senses, to the intellect, to the emotions; it's the quintessential glass masterpiece.

"Please, Señora," the waiting clerk said impatiently, pressured to help the many clients clamoring to examine other auction pieces, "if you've quite finished with item —94, I'll return it to the case."

"Oh, yes," Alexandra replied, embarrassed that she kept the others waiting, "thank you."

The few lampwork and millefiori paperweights in the auction elicited little interest from the bidders that afternoon. When the auctioneer placed the Imperial paperweight on the block, there were only two counter bids to Alexandra's initial bid. Its anonymity enabled Alexandra to acquire it for less than the cost of her air fare. Had paperweight collectors the world over known the importance of her prize, they would have flocked to Argentina *en masse*, and the bidding would have set a record.

After paying for her prize, Alexandra hurried to her hotel, intending to have dinner in the dining room, but changed her mind and remained in her suite. She could not bear to be parted from the paperweight. Alexandra hardly touched the room service meal she ordered. She nibbled at her food as she sat at the desk drinking in the beauty of the paperweight.

Later that evening, she telephoned Edmire from her hotel room. "We finally got it, Mr. Edmire! We got one of the Imperial paperweights, Evita's green one!"

"Fantastic, Alexandra! I can't wait to see it!"

"It's absolutely exquisite!"

"I'll bet it is. How soon can you get back to Chicago?"

"My flight gets into O'Hare at 4:45 tomorrow afternoon."

"Good. I'll send André with the limo to pick you up. He'll bring you directly here. Plan to have dinner here with me."

"I can't wait to call Zurich and tell Christa and Eric about our good luck!"

"No, let's wait, Alexandra. Let's keep it under wraps for a while. As long as we keep it quiet there's a chance we might find the other two paperweights before anyone else knows they exist."

"Alright, Mr. Edmire. See you tomorrow." After she hung up the phone, she said, "God, finding one of the three was a chance in a billion. We'll never find the other two. Oh well, it's his money."

When Edmire examined the paperweight, he was certain the Saint Louis factory created it. He told Alexandra that all the millefiori canes in the paperweight bore fourteen cogs on their periphery—a characteristic of Saint Louis canes. To help ascertain the source of the paperweight, Alexandra brought along a black light on her next visit. Turning off all the illumination in the study, they exposed the paperweight to black light. She and Edmire were startled when the paperweight glowed a deep blood-red, a color they had never seen before in any paperweights.

"Just look at that red, Alexandra," said the amazed collector, "It's not the Saint Louis fluorescence I expected!"

"No, it's certainly not Saint Louis's coral-pink. In all the work I've done with glass, it's a color I've never seen before. This strange fluorescence proves that the paperweight came from an obscure factory. It had to be made in the Lorraine factory."

"Yes, I think you're right; just look at that red glow, Alexandra. It sits there like a huge ember. It's almost hypnotic."

Seven months later, the second Imperial paperweight, Wilde's "little yellow Carlota", came to light in London. The brother of a picker who had tragically drowned in a boating accident sold it to Spink & Son, Limited. He told Spink's buyer his deceased brother, Claude, found the paperweight a generation ago for an elderly French authoress. But she died.

It remained in Spink's showroom for five months before its description appeared in one of their advertising brochures. Not recognizing the historical significance of the piece, Spink's offered it for 875 pounds. Receiving a brochure from one of her paid contacts, Alexandra made a transatlantic call to verify the paperweight's availability. Two days later she flew to London and purchased it for Edmire.

2.

With the acquisition of the second Imperial paperweight, Edmire became obsessed with finding the third paperweight. "Our search is incomplete, Alexandra," he complained. "They were originally created as a set. I won't rest until they're together again, here in my study!"

During the years Alexandra searched for the Imperial

paperweights, she heard a recurring rumor that King Farouk of Egypt sent emissaries to Belgium during the late 1940's to search for the Imperial paperweight which once belonged to Empress Carlota. She often wondered how Farouk gained knowledge of the Imperial paperweights three decades before she and Christa discovered the record of their creation in the dusty Lorraine documents. Even now, as she became involved in her search for the third paperweight, the existence of the Imperial paperweights still remained unknown to the paperweight fraternity.

It was no secret to her that the deceased King of Egypt collected paperweights. When Farouk ruled Egypt, his agents often swooped down on major paperweight auctions, and to the consternation of all those present, outbid everyone for the choicest pieces. Money was no object when the king's desire was caught by the glitter of an outstanding paperweight.

Alexandra had often perused an old auction catalog of Farouk's paperweight collection. It was an exercise she performed with catalogs of all major paperweight collections dispersed at auction. Reflecting on Farouk's rumored search for the Imperial Paperweights, she decided to leaf through the well-worn office copy once again, on the off-chance that she had overlooked something that may have seemed insignificant on previous readings. She carefully read the individual descriptions of every lot, but found no hint alluding to the third paperweight. Closing the green paperback catalog with a sigh, she placed it on her desk, saying aloud, "Well, Alexandra, still no Imperial paperweight in here, but what a splendid collection! Every time I look at this catalog I'm amazed that he acquired so many exquisite examples."

Leaning back in her office chair, she lifted the thin book to eye level and looked at the title on its well-worn cover: *The Palace Collections of Egypt—Catalogue of the Extensive Collection of Fine*

French Paperweights and Ornamental Glass by Emile Galle—The Property of the Republic of Egypt—and now sold By the Order of The Government.

Alexandra often speculated about the accumulated treasures of Farouk; the catalog in her hand represented only a minute portion of his far-ranging collections. How thrilling it would have been to have attended the auctions in Farouk's enormous four-hundred room Koubbeh Palace. It was general knowledge at Sotheby's that the dispersal of his coins, stamps, paintings, jewelry and objects of art earned the Egyptian Government well in excess of $200,000,000. And that was thirty years ago, she thought. I wonder what his collections would bring at today's prices.

There was so much political unrest in Egypt during the early months of 1954, following Farouk's dethronement, that the cognoscenti who traveled to the Land of the Nile to acquire Farouk's treasures experienced many anxious moments as dangerous political and military confrontations swirled around them. During the two days devoted to the disposal of Farouk's paperweights, the prospective bidders warily witnessed the clamorous street demonstrations directed against General Naguib. In spite of the political turmoil and a general strike, a small group of thirty bidders—collectors, agents and dealers—courageously traveled to Cairo to bid for Farouk's crystal treasures.

As Alexandra returned the catalog to the files, she remembered an old issue of the *Bulletin of the Paperweight Collectors' Association* that described the auction in Cairo. The article noted that Paul Jokelson, the founder of the Paperweight Collectors' Association, attended the sale. Alexandra impulsively decided to make a long distance call to him, hoping he might recall a clue or an obscure fact which might assist her in her search.

"What an exciting experience that must have been, Mr. Jokelson," said Alexandra.

"I remember it as if it were yesterday. I purchased several fine paperweights at that auction. You know, Miss Saint George, during the auction, the taxi drivers were on strike in Egypt. In order to return to my hotel, I had to be transported back to the city in an army vehicle!"

"Can you recall anyone who might have been actively involved with Farouk when he built his collection?"

"He got many of them at auction. He also bought weights from Spink's in London, from Delomosne & Sons and, I think, from Arthur Ackerman of New York. I also heard that some of his paperweights came from Roger Imbert in Paris, although of that, I'm not sure."

"I'm especially interested to know if there was anyone there in Egypt who was involved with Farouk's collection before the auction."

"Before the auction?"

"Yes, when he was making purchases, or even someone who might have assisted the Egyptian authorities at the time of the auction."

"At the time of the auction? Yes, yes, there was someone. While I was there I met a Mr.—ah, Salhid. Yes, Salhid. He assisted the Egyptian Military Government in assembling Farouk's glass collections for sale. I found him to be fairly knowledgeable about paperweights. Later I heard he left Egypt and settled in England. I believe he took a position with the Victoria and Albert Museum. If he is still there, he has held that position for many years."

Mr. Jokelson's recollections offered Alexandra a new lead. Slim, she thought, but she would pursue it, no matter how spare it seemed. Her transatlantic call to London confirmed that Mr. Youseef Salhid was indeed with the Victoria and

Albert Museum, employed as curator of glass antiquities. And, yes, he told Alexandra, he knew something about the purple Imperial paperweight. He graciously agreed to see Alexandra the following weekend, even offering in a friendly gesture to meet her flight at Heathrow Airport.

3.

He's been in England for over forty years, Alexandra mused as she cleared British customs. I wonder if this displaced Egyptian assimilated English ways? Will he touch his forehead and chest in an Islamic greeting or will he greet me with a lilting "Cheerio, love"?

Alexandra hadn't expected to be met by a fez-capped Egyptian in flowing white robes, but she was surprised to find a tall, dark, elderly patrician in Harris tweeds awaiting her arrival. As he politely shook her outstretched hand, he merely said, "Miss Saint George, welcome to London." Taking her flight bag and opening his large black umbrella, he continued, "I'm afraid I must apologize for our damp weather this morning. We'll have to share my umbrella."

As they taxied to her London hotel, Youseef Salhid related a curious story—one which gave Alexandra new hope.

"I first became aware of the Imperial paperweights soon after Evita Peron's Rainbow promenade through Europe, Miss Saint George. When the Argentine entourage stopped near Trieste, Mrs. Peron mentioned during an interview that she owned one of three paperweights created for Empress Carlota by command of Empress Eugenie. I read the account so often that I can quote it word for word '...a beautiful paperweight with a coat of arms, and cameos of the two young monarchs who came to such a tragic end...Another of the three paperweights was in the possession of Empress Carlota, but disappeared after the empress died. A third paperweight was made, but other than that fact, nothing else is known about it...'

"You know, Miss Saint George, to most readers of Evita Peron's daily adventures, her mention of the paperweights was an unimportant bit of trivia buried in an otherwise fantastic chronicle of her tour. But to King Farouk, that seemingly insignificant bit of information exploded out of the newspaper into a shower of desire. The possible existence of the Imperial paperweights whetted his appetite."

"Yes, I know how his agents used to outbid everyone at paperweight auctions," said Alexandra.

"But of course they did, Miss Saint George. King Farouk's treasury was a bottomless well; his slightest whim was always immediately satisfied. After Farouk read the account of the Imperial paperweight, he summoned Dr. Abdallah Moustafa, the director of our national museum and asked him to send several of his curators to Belgium to seek out Carlota's missing paperweight. In spite of the fact that those of us on the museum staff were schooled in archeology and not in investigative detective work, the director mutely complied with our King's request. However, not wanting to deplete experienced museum personnel to satisfy what he considered to be a passing whim of the King, Moustafa sent to Belgium, two neophytes, Mohammed Kassim and myself. Dr. Moustafa directed us to begin by interviewing the descendants of the Bouchout Castle staff who had served Empress Carlota during the final years of her life. He surmised that Carlota's paperweight might have been given as a remembrance to someone who attended her during her final days. And because a keepsake from the empress would have been considered a gift of great importance, he concluded the treasured paperweight would have been considered an heirloom by the recipient's descendants.

"With the helpful intervention and the limitless resources of the Egyptian embassy in Belgium, Mohammed and I painstakingly traced the descendants of Carlota's retainers: doctors, nurses, ladies-in-waiting, cooks, coachmen, housekeepers and chamber maids. At the end of eleven months, having exhausted every possible lead, we finally gave up the search and flew back to Cairo.

"On our return, Moustafa sent word to King Farouk that an extensive search for the paperweight had been made, but no trace of it was found. Dr. Moustafa then returned us to our former positions: Mohammed resumed his work in the restoration department of the Cairo Museum, and I went to dig for Pharaonic glass near Ad Diwan."

The taxi's arrival at Alexandra's hotel interrupted his story. After Alexandra registered, she invited Salhid to be her guest at lunch in the hotel dining room so that he might continue his story.

"Oh, I couldn't accept."

"Now listen, Mr. Salhid, my sponsor is a wealthy man; I'm on an expense account. If he were here, he'd insist that you be his guest for lunch. Anyhow, I've flown all the way to London to hear your story; I can't wait another day for the ending!"

"All right then, Miss Saint George, since you insist, I'll wait here in the hotel lounge while you accompany your bags to your rooms."

A year after the two young curators returned to Egypt, the king summoned Moustafa to the Koubbeh Palace. The director sensed, but did not understand the reason for Farouk's apparent displeasure. Rising from his chair, the King said, "Dr. Moustafa, its been almost two years since I asked you to locate a certain item for me, only a small piece of crystal. And as yet, you, Dr. Moustafa, you deny me, your King, this simple request."

Allah, preserve me, thought the director, he's talking about that paperweight! I assumed the paperweight matter closed. Arms outstretched, Moustafa offered, "Your majesty, my curators could unearth no trace of the paperweight, although they searched for almost an entire year."

"Don't waste my time telling me what I already know. What have you done about my request since then?"

Moustafa felt the sweat beading on his ample torso. In a moment rivulets began to run down his belly and the folds of his back. Farouk had absolute power to bestow as well as revoke directorships in Egypt's many national institutions; Moustafa's continuing position relied on Farouk's good will. Choosing his words with care, he answered, "Your Majesty, since I received no reply to the letter I sent you a year ago, I assumed you decided we should abandon our fruitless search."

Holding his breath during the interminably long silence that followed, Dr. Moustafa averted his eyes from the King's steely gaze. He thought of suggesting to his King it might have been more practical to send private investigators who were more experienced in inquiries of that nature, rather than museum personnel. But, because such a suggestion might have been construed as a criticism of the royal judgment, Moustafa kept that thought to himself. Fully expecting a scathing redress, he was surprised to hear the King's next utterance spoken softly and sounding almost friendly.

"My brother, never presume to assume anything about your King. That borders on arrogance. Now, I suggest you return to your museum and make arrangements to send to Belgium those same searchers you sent before. Tell them you will not tolerate failure this time."

"Yes, my King."

"Don't disappoint me, again, Dr. Moustafa."

Comprehending the hidden message in the King's command, the director struggled to find the words for a reply, but before he could utter a word, Farouk closed Moustafa's audience with, "Peace be with you."

The shaken director bowed deeply as the King turned and left the room.

Twenty minutes after taking leave of Salhid in the hotel lounge, Alexandra stepped out of the elevator.

"Ah, there you are, Miss Saint George," he said. "I took the liberty of reserving a table. They are waiting for us."

"I'm sorry I took longer than I thought I would; I had to freshen up a bit."

"My dear Miss Saint George, an apology is not necessary."

As they dined, Salhid took up his story once again.

"About a year after we returned from Belgium, Dr. Moustafa summoned the two of us to his office and told us Farouk desired that we return to Belgium to resume the search for Empress Carlota's paperweight. We protested, reminding the director we searched eleven months without uncovering a single clue.

"Taking up a letter opener from his desk, he pointed it at us, saying, 'You are to go back and find it. Excuses are not acceptable. It is the King's command!'

"'We'll just be going over old ground again,' Muhammed complained. 'Empress Carlota's been dead for over half a century. And besides, Belgium has gone through a World War since she died. It's hopeless! Anyhow, it's bone-chilling damp up there, even in the summer. The sun never shines. It was so cold during the winter, I thought I'd die!'

"Director Moustafa slowly rose from his chair and locked his eyes on Muhammed's, saying hoarsly, 'You don't understand, Muhammed, my boy. Shall I make it clear to you? If you don't find it, your failure will result in dire consequences for the both of you! Don't bother to return to the museum without that paperweight!'

"Seven months later, we finally traced Carlota's paperweight to a destitute Belgian family, one which eluded us during our first search, and for good reason. The DeGroots, descendants of one of Carlota's ladies-in-waiting, prospered for many generations through the benevolence of the Crown. But the family fell on hard times. We learned that the DeGroots served King Leopold II during his unpopular cooperation with occupying German forces during the Second World War. After the Allies liberated their country, many Belgians viewed their King as a Nazi collaborator. Their resentment quickly flared into unrest. With the threat of a major uprising, Leopold relinquished his throne in favor of his son, Baudouin, thereby avoiding a civil war. With Leopold's abdication the DeGroots and others who profited from his unpopular support were left without the patronage of the crown. The members of the outcast family suddenly found themselves *personae non gratae*. Shunned by the royal house, the DeGroots had reached the nadir of their fortunes, barely surviving, when we approached them. They gratefully accepted what they felt was a windfall when they sold us the old purple paperweight."

Alexandra asked, "And then it was added to King Farouk's collection?"

"Yes, of course."

"But," said Alexandra, "it wasn't included in the 1954 auction. I know, I've checked the catalog of the Koubbeh Palace auction many times."

"You are quite correct, Miss Saint George. You see, when

King Farouk was forced to abandon the monarchy, he gathered up many of his prized possessions and sailed across the Mediterranean to Italy. Since the paperweight was quite rare, he apparently chose not to leave it behind."

"I seem to remember seeing a photo of him in a magazine—I don't remember which one. It might have been in one of my mother's *Life* magazines. The photograph was taken on the Riviera soon after he lost his throne. I must have been ten or eleven years old at the time."

Her memory dredged up some details of the picture. She remembered that his picture repulsed her at the time; he looked so grotesque. He was walking on the beach wearing a bikini, dark sunglasses, sandals and a floppy white hat. Two spindly legs supported his huge gourd-shaped body. She asked, "He was never liked, was he, Mr. Salhid?"

"Oh, on the contrary, Miss Saint George. When he was young, the prince was adored by everyone in Egypt as well as by many here in England. He was six feet tall, slim and handsome, with fair hair and gray-blue eyes. You know, Miss Saint George, the English people liked him so much they affectionately called him 'Prince Freddy.' The English press wrote that he was the most perfectly brought-up boy in the world."

"He spent time in England?"

"Yes. His father, the old king, sent him here to complete his studies when he was just a boy, only sixteen."

"Why to England?"

"My country was still under British influence at the time. English military and political advisors propped up Egypt for many years. Old King Faud quite naturally sent his son to be schooled in England. He hoped that the prince's close association with British classmates, future English notables, would reinforce political ties between the two countries in later years. Unfortunately, the death of his father cut young Farouk's English education short. He was here less than a year when our old King Faud died. The young prince returned to Egypt. Fifteen months later, when he became eighteen years old, he was crowned King."

"How was the young king received by the people?"

"We could hardly wait for him to reach the age of majority. You see, during the many months before his investiture, the ruling Provisional Council met with one failure after another. It had alienated most of the people. When the young prince became our king, we rejoiced. After his coronation, he took long trips up and down the Nile to pray in the mosques with the common people, visiting village after village and spending many hours listening to his subjects' requests and complaints. And then, to give the villagers the feeling he kept in constant touch with them, even when away in far-off Cairo, our young king installed radio receivers with loudspeakers in the village centers to carry his messages throughout Egypt. I can assure you, Miss Saint George, he was extremely popular with the people during his early years on the throne."

"Was he just being a shrewd politician?"

"I truly believe that he was sincere during the early years of his reign. You know, Miss Saint George, during those first few years, Farouk attended a Mosque every Friday without fail. And there was never an occasion when he was seen drinking in public."

"The Islamic prohibition of drinking."

"Yes. The people were especially pleased that he always appeared in public in a *tarboosh*."

"A *tarboosh*?"

"A fez, a *tarboosh*," he laughed. After a short pause, he continued, "The people called him 'Farouk the Pious'."

"Then, why did they turn against him?"

"There were many reasons, I suppose. His first wife, Farida, was very popular with the people. She bore him three beautiful daughters, but, alas, no sons; she produced no heir for the royal throne. That was unfortunate for Egypt, and especially for Farida."

"I remember that he divorced her."

"Yes, over the unspoken objections of many of the common people. But he did remarry. There was also, the matter of his later life style. The people did not object to the luxuries he acquired. After all, he was their king. But they strongly objected to his open amoral affairs with women, young girls and even young boys. But then, later, his popularity suffered greatly when he openly turned to excessive gambling; gambling is forbidden in the Koran. I suppose the reason that most of the people turned against him was the terrible defeat we suffered at the hands of the Israelis. In just six days they destroyed our entire Egyptian army. Everyone blamed Farouk for that debacle. Three years after that rout, General Naguib Muhammed led young officers in a coup against Farouk. Very few Egyptians mourned his downfall."

Quickly calculating the dates, Alexandra said, "That was in 1952, two years after he acquired the Imperial paperweight. You know, Mr. Salhid, there is a century old belief that those paperweights carry a curse which brings terrible misfortunes to those who possess them."

"We Egyptians are quite familiar with such curses, Miss Saint George," he said smiling. "Most of our Pharaonic tombs carry hieroglyphs promising the direst of consequences to those who dare to break the necropolis seals. That paperweight, as you say, may have been unlucky for Farouk, although it seems to me he brought about the fall of his dynasty by his own hand."

"You don't seem to be very sympathetic about his downfall."

"You're quite right, Miss Saint George. But that is another story involving a personal hurt that occurred to me many years ago. It's of little interest to anyone but myself."

Alexandra's curiosity prodded her to ask about Salhid's "personal hurt," but she decided not to. It seemed to her he wished to avoid the subject.

When Salhid learned that Alexandra's flight was scheduled to leave for Chicago in two days, he suggested they lunch together at his favorite Egyptian restaurant the following afternoon. Looking forward to what she hoped might be an exotic culinary adventure, Alexandra accepted his invitation.

That evening in her hotel room, as she reviewed the day, Alexandra felt satisfied that her visit with Youseef Salhid had garnered many significant clues on the path to the third Imperial paperweight. She now knew that Salhid purchased Carlota's purple paperweight in Belgium in 1950 and took it to Egypt. King Farouk returned it to the Continent in 1952. She would direct her researchers to concentrate their efforts on Farouk's final years in Europe. She was close. Just the thought of it sent shudders of pleasure through her entire body. If only it could be found. She would publish her research and astonish the world of glass with her announcement of the discovery of the three Imperial paperweights! Mr. Edmire would be pleased when he learned of her progress.

4.

The next day, as Alexandra and Sahlid neared their destination, the Arabic characters on several shop windows heightened her anticipation. The boxy black hackney finally slowed, turned a corner and came to a stop on a narrow street. When Salhid helped her out of the cab, Alexandra was distressed at what she saw. Instead of the exotic surroundings she anticipated, her eyes met the unclean gutters and debris-strewn sidewalks of an old neglected London neighborhood. My God, she thought, if the restaurant is as filthy as this street, I won't be able to eat! What'll I do? I'll have to feign illness.

Sensing her slight hesitation, her host apologetically offered, "I'm afraid that this neighborhood is not as elegantly fashionable as the West End, Miss Saint George. But I'm sure you'll find the cuisine in this restaurant to be quite delectable."

Embarrassed for having revealed her apprehension, Alexandra quickly replied, "Oh, I'm really looking forward to our luncheon," and then, in an attempt to set them both at ease, added, laughing, "but, I did expect an oasis with a tent and a camel or two, not a quiet London side street."

As he opened the door to the restaurant, her escort quipped, "Alas, not even the rotating fans of the Casbah."

"Nor a *tarboosh* in sight!" she added.

When the door closed behind them, she became aware of the dulcet babble of the Arabic tongue, its melodic lilt ebbing and flowing, softly filling the large room. From behind the open doorway to the kitchen she could hear the plaintive arabesques of oriental music punctuated by the occasional clang of a cooking utensil. A thick aromatic scent of roast lamb, pungent garlic, oregano, and hints of lemon, nutmeg and cinnamon filled the room. Other unrecognizable scents wafting through the restaurant piqued her curiosity. When her eyes adjusted to the meager artificial light of the restaurant's dim interior, she was relieved that, though the furnishings were plain, everything appeared to be scrubbed clean. The wooden floor, chairs and simple tables were so well scoured that the wood had a satiny sheen.

"Good afternoon, Youseef," smiled the plump proprietor, fan in hand.

"Good afternoon, Khalid. May we have the table in the corner, there?"

"Of course, my friend."

The strategic location of their table afforded Alexandra a sweeping view of the restaurant and its aged male patrons. Oriental rugs of various sizes decorated the restaurant's walls. The wall over the entryway bore a dozen or more identically-sized framed pictures. She recognized those of Sadat, Nasser and Farouk. The others, unrecognizable, with long black twisted mustaches and hard-set eyes, she assumed to be the notables of Egypt's Islamic past. Scanning her surroundings, her eyes were drawn to a small table crowded with water pipes in the far corner of the room. She wondered if they were decorative or still in use by the restaurant's customers. As her senses drank in the exotic strangeness about her, she turned to her escort, saying, "It's so different in here. It must remind you of Egypt."

"Oh, my dear Miss Saint George, to my way of thinking, this restaurant is more Western than Egyptian. It's the food and conversation that draw me here."

"It doesn't seem very Western to me, Mr. Salhid."

My dear lady, he thought, *this quiet corner of London with its arrow-straight streets in no way resembles the crowded bustle of the bazaars or the smells and sounds of the twisted alleyways of the old Cairo of my youth.*

"When I think of Cairo and the coffee houses I used to visit when I was young, I have such a feeling of nostalgia, Miss Saint George. Hundreds of them literally crowded in the side streets and the back alleys of the city. At that time only males frequented the coffee houses; that's still a Middle Eastern tradition in the villages and in the older sections of the large cities. When I was a child, the men in the coffee houses reclined on wooden pallets for hours discussing politics, history and religion while drinking coffee, and smoking their favorite tobacco in bubbling *shishas*. Our social and intellectual activity centered on those coffee houses. In some of them, especially those in the unsavory areas of the city, one was able to get hashish and to even gamble."

When he first arrived in London, Salhid thought he would return one day to live out his life in Egypt when he retired, but discovered on a recent visit there that too much changed. Cairo acquired a startlingly new look during his absence. Modern hotels, public buildings, fast-food restaurants, Western and Japanese cars, shiny new bars, department stores and clothing stores dealing in the latest English fashions all displaced his childhood haunts. Disappointed, he made his way to the old city wall where horse drawn carts, bazaars and mosques—the fading echoes of his youth—could still be seen. The ancient men he encountered continued to wear the *tarboosh* and to carry on the old ways. But with the passing of those few elders, Salhid inwardly lamented the lost world of his sweet memories—the nurturer of his childhood. It grieved him that those last few vestiges of his formative years would soon disappear and exist only in his memory. He left Egypt realizing, sadly, that he was a stranger to the place of his birth as well as to his adopted country.

Khalid brought water and towels to their table for the ritual cleansing of the hands. How civilized, Alexandra thought as she washed her hands and then unconsciously used the towel to clean her silverware. Returning to the table a few moments later, their host pointed to a large well-worn blackboard nailed above the door to the kitchen on which were chalked the selections of the day. He asked, "And what is your pleasure this afternoon, Youseef? And for the English lady?"

Alexandra turned from the Arabic squiggles on the blackboard to Youseef, saying, "Would you please choose for me; I can't possibly read the menu."

As they began their meal, Salhid said, "I notice you are left-handed, Miss Saint George."

"Yes, a small curse visited on me through my mother's genes. Strange that you should notice."

"Those of us who are raised in Muslim countries are accustomed to eating only with the right hand. When I first came to England many years ago, I was startled to see an occasional person use his left hand for food. I've become used to it over the years, although it still catches my attention."

After their meal of roast lamb, unleavened bread, stuffed grape leaves and beans in oil, Khalid brought them pastries and demitasses of cloyingly sweet thick Turkish coffee generously laced with cardamom. The coffee was so thick, Alexandra mused she could easily stand a teaspoon in it. The baked rich pastry consisted of a filling of chopped walnuts, cinnamon, sugar, butter and honey layered between paper-thin sheets of crisp dough.

"I've had this pastry in Chicago, in Greek restaurants."

"Yes, Miss Saint George, it's common to all Near Eastern countries."

"Hm-mm, full of calories and so sinfully delicious!"

Their conversation now flowed easily, affording Alexandra the opportunity to inquire about Salhid's allusion to the "personal hurt" he had made on the previous day.

"Something you said yesterday piqued my curiosity. I hope you don't feel I'm prying into your personal affairs. Quite frankly, if you prefer, I'll respect your privacy in the matter."

"My dear Miss Saint George, I honestly do not recall

what it was that I kept from you."

"You mentioned a hurt of many years when we spoke about King Farouk."

Pouring more slow-flowing coffee from the long curved spout of the brass *ibrik* into their small cups, the elderly Egyptian replied, "Oh that. I suppose I over dramatized a simple case of prejudice that happened over forty years ago."

"To you"?

"Yes, when I was just a neophyte in my profession. You remember, Miss Saint George, I told you yesterday that Kassim and I found the paperweight for King Farouk."

"Yes, of course."

"Well, when we returned from Belgium with the Imperial paperweight, Dr. Moustafa was ecstatic. He immediately rushed us to the Koubbeh Palace and personally presented us to King Farouk. You can't possibly imagine how thrilled we young Egyptians were to be ushered into the presence of our King. Farouk received the paperweight from my hands and promised that Kassim and I would be well rewarded for successfully fulfilling his request.

"Two months later Kassim was promoted to a relatively high position in the Department of Conservation. The Director had leap-frogged him over several senior museum professionals."

"King Farouk's promise?"

"Of course. When we returned from Belgium, Dr. Moustafa sent me back to my former position as the junior member of the dig at Ad Diwan. I waited there five months, each day expecting to receive word of a promotion, especially after learning of Kassim's good fortune. When our expedition returned to Cairo, I went to Dr. Moustafa and asked him when I could expect my share of the reward promised by our King. He was impatient with me. I still remember his words as clearly as if he spoke them yesterday. 'You don't expect me to bother the King about your status, do you? He has more important matters to attend to.' When I reminded him of Kassim's promotion and asked why I hadn't yet benefited from King Farouk's promise, he said, 'That's obvious enough, Salhid. What did you expect? You are a *Copt*.' And when I reminded him that he himself was present when the King said I'd be rewarded, he snapped, 'Well, I've decided you're not ready for a promotion, yet!'"

"The ugly truth was difficult to accept. I realized that my young friend, Kassim, a follower of the Islamic faith, would continue to rise in our profession as long as he enjoyed the favor of the King. I, on the other hand, would always be denied my full recognition, no matter the level of my competency. My ambitions and accomplishments would always be tempered by the discrimination of those above me because of my religious beliefs. Can you imagine the agony of a twenty-two year old on the brink of a career facing such a stumbling block? I was crushed!"

Alexandra, emotionally caught up in Salhid's story, offered a sympathetic, "I'm so sorry."

"My dear Miss Saint George, that was over forty years ago. I've put it behind me. On rare occasions when it finds its way into my consciousness, I bury it quickly. I must admit, however, that during that first year, the ache was difficult to put aside, especially when I learned later that Kassim was appointed as one of the curators to the King's personal treasures and given residence near the Koubbeh Palace."

"That had to be very difficult for an ambitious young man to accept."

"Yes, it was. But when Farouk fled Egypt, to be followed soon by Kassim, I naively thanked my God for the retribution they had both received. Later, when the military cast about for someone to catalog and arrange Farouk's collections for auction, I gladly volunteered my services. I enjoyed every moment of their dispersal. I felt a deliciously sweet revenge as I helped sell off Farouk's treasures." Laughing, he continued, "Of course, I was young then. And later, much, much later, I did suffer a few pangs of Christian remorse for having enjoyed myself so much at the time. Soon after those auctions I was offered a position in the museum here. At least in London, my faith has not been a handicap to my career."

They both fell silent for a few moments. A question began to form in Alexandra's mind. She finally said, "You are a *Copt*." Being unsure of the term she added, "I don't think I know very much about your religious beliefs."

"Well, I suppose the easiest way to describe my faith is that it is the Christian Church of Egypt and Ethiopia. It's closest in present day worship to the Greek Orthodox Church. The major difference is that we are monophysites."

"I'm afraid that I don't understand that term, either."

"It merely means that we believe that Jesus Christ has only one nature, a divine nature. You see, Miss Saint George, over fifteen hundred years ago, in 451 A.D. to be exact, the Roman Pope declared all believers of monophysitism to be heretics because they would not accept the Council of Chalcedon's edict that Jesus Christ had two natures, human as well as divine. We Copts had no choice but to withdraw from the authority of the Catholic Church and establish our own religious hierarchy."

"Is it a large denomination?"

"Not any longer, I'm afraid. During the seventh century there were many followers. At that time, all of Egypt and Ethiopia embraced the faith. Today, there are only about four million of us in the entire world. We continue to maintain several monasteries which were built during the Middle Ages, as well as more recent churches here and there in Egypt. We have dwindled in numbers so that today we have less than a dozen bishops to manage our shrinking congregations."

The next day, Youseef accompanied Alexandra to Heathrow airport. Before she boarded her plane, he offered, "I will attempt to contact Kassim to learn if he has any knowledge of the present whereabouts of Farouk's paperweight."

"Do you see him very often?"

"No, Kassim and I lost contact with each other many years ago, but I may be able to locate him through mutual acquaintances."

"My sponsor will undoubtedly show his appreciation for any help in his quest for that 'holy grail'."

"Surely, Miss Saint George, with the curse which attends it," he said, laughing, "you must mean, 'unholy grail.'"

When Alexandra returned to her office on the following Tuesday, a cablegram from Youseef was already awaiting her.

"LOCATED KASSIM STOP HAD KNOWLEDGE OF MISSING GRAIL STOP PRESENT OWNER MOST WILLING TO SELL STOP PLEASE ADVISE STOP YOUSEEF SALHID."

CHAPTER VII.

1.

For days following the acquisition of the third Imperial paperweight, Alexandra floated on an exhilarated high. She had never in her life experienced such elation. After nearly six years of Herculean research, last minute flight schedules and countless false leads, she rejoiced at her unbelievable achievement. Never mind that the three paperweights belonged to Edmire; that was a temporary condition. As in Carter's discovery of Tutankamen's tomb, Edmire, like Lord Carnarvon, would be incidentally recalled as the financial backer of her discoveries. Students of historical glass would forever remember her as the one who uncovered those wondrous glass masterpieces.

But Alexandra's euphoria was short-lived. To her dismay, Edmire decided to temporarily withhold the discovery of the Imperial paperweights. He elected to relish their beauty like favorite concubines, closeting them in his mansion, where, he told Alexandra, they would remain hidden away, for just a little while. When she expressed her disappointment at his decision, Edmire consoled her with the promise that he would soon announce the existence of the paperweights to the public and then offer them for display to the Art Institute. He assured her he would identify her as their discoverer at that time. Placated by his promises, she agreed that he earned the right to enjoy them privately for a while. In his own way, he shared in her search too; he experienced the same disappointments, the same frustrations and the same false leads. They certainly cost him a great deal of money; she would bide her time.

But as time passed, the old man's possessiveness of the paperweights intensified. He continued to welcome Alexandra to his mansion to share them with him, but steadfastly ignored her frequent suggestions to reveal their existence to the world. As the months wore on, he remained inflexible in his refusal. Although frustrated by the firmness of his resolve, Alexandra elected to wait him out; searching for the paperweights taught her patience. She'd wait until he relented or until his demise. The latter consequence did not seem too far off to her; Edmire's advancing years and deteriorating health lately required the services of a full-time nurse.

Their visits together settled into a routine. Alexandra arrived at his mansion after dinner and accompanied him to his study, where they spent the evening meticulously examining the many outstanding examples in his extensive paperweight collection. The first few months, they compared the Imperial paperweights to his other paperweights, carefully observing the similarities and differences in their construction. But, as time passed, they turned away from the other paperweights and concentrated only on the Imperial paperweights.

Alexandra's long hours with the three paperweights began to lend themselves to fantasies. During the early days of her research she uncovered the curious fact that Empress Carlota died on the same day that her own mother was born. That coincidental date, January 16, 1927, found a fertile niche in Alexandra's mind as she continued to commune with the Imperial paperweights. When away from the mesmerizing influence of the crystal globes, the strange fantasies she experienced in Edmire's study troubled her. She wondered if those illusions took root with the discovery of that common date. Or were they the result of a residual psychosis from the trauma she suffered at the break-up of her early marriage?

Worse yet, had she inherited a defective gene, the same gene that caused the dreadful mental aberration in her own mother?

Whatever the source of her growing fantasies, Alexandra's imaginings took on a bizarre reality for her. The notion that Carlota's essence passed from her eighty-seven year old body, at the moment of her death, to enter Alexandra's mother at the precise moment of her mother's birth, did not come in a sudden, blinding revelation. It slowly seeped in from some murky corner of Alexandra's mind. She felt certain that she now understood the reason for her mother's insanity; Carlota's attempt to dominate her mother's psyche caused the madness. Stranger yet, she came to believe that Carlota's spirit struggled inside her mother until it escaped from its confinement, nineteen years later, to unite with Alexandra at birth. In Alexandra's convoluted consciousness, the paperweights, though created during another century, were made expressly for her.

Edmire's heart eventually deteriorated to such an extent, he no longer left his mansion. He confined most of his activities to the living quarters on the second floor. The ailing old man continued to cling tenaciously to the Imperial paperweights; they became the center of his shrinking universe. Fearing for their safety, he took them out of his display cabinet and locked them away in a small wall safe. He still permitted Alexandra to examine them during her visits, but only when he handed them to her. Although she felt constrained, she had no choice but to abide by his wishes, for to Alexandra, the standing invitation to view the three paperweights was her only contact with Maximilian, whom she now imagined alive and residing in the three crystal spheres.

Alexandra's growing need to possess the three paperweights eclipsed her earlier expectations of recognition. If they were hers, she wouldn't be subject to Edmire's whims—she could be with Maximilian forever, residing inside them with him.

Convinced that there was only one solution to her problem, she tentatively broached the idea of marriage to Edmire. "It must get very lonely in this large house with only a household staff," she said.

"I do miss my two sons. I don't see either of them often since Bradley transferred to San Francisco. Benjamin has been in Philadelphia seventeen years now. They're busy with their own businesses and families. There was a time after my wife Stephanie died that I went to the club to spend time with my old friends and business associates, but most of them have died off, too. Loneliness is the bitter reward of living a long life."

"It must be frustrating not to be able to share all of your lovely things with someone. Have you ever thought of taking a companion to share your many interests?"

"You mean a woman? Marry again?" he asked incredulously.

"Yes, why not? To someone who'd enjoy your companionship."

"Oh, Jesus, no!"

The old man felt such a strong attachment to his departed wife that the idea of marriage seemed like a betrayal. On the rare occasions he fantasized taking a nubile bride to his bed, he hastily put the thoughts aside, fearing the physical demands of a nuptial night might end his life. Lonely as he was, life still tasted sweet. And though the thought occasionally crossed his mind that Alexandra might be a good companion, he was too accustomed to his solitary existence to encumber his life with the demands of a new wife.

2.

Edmire's failing heart eventually imprisoned him in a wheelchair. His illness became so severe that he required daily visits by a physician.

Whenever Alexandra arrived for the evening, Edmire waved off his nurse and asked Alexandra to wheel him into the study. Sitting in the darkened room under a single bright lamp, Edmire caressed his crystal beauties, turning them this way and that, examining them with a large ivory-handled magnifying glass. After a while, he reluctantly shared them with Alexandra, making certain only one paperweight left him at a time, tightly cradling the other two against his chest. Accepting the paperweight, Alexandra held it quite still and focused her attention on Carlota's cameo, descending down, down through the layers of glass until she was deep inside the crystal with Maximilian. She quietly resided there, luxuriating in the feelings of security and warmth until the old man nudged her arm, took the paperweight from her grasp and handed her another. Well into the evening, his rheumy eyes filled with tears of effort, Edmire gathered all three paperweights to himself, propelled his wheelchair to the wall safe and locked them away.

As always, a biscuit jar and a selection of teas were waiting on a server in the adjoining bar, placed there earlier by Edmire's manservant. Alexandra excused herself, went to the other room, chose a tea—Edmire no longer had a sense of taste—switched on the water heater, added the tea at the right moment, let it steep, and then wheeled the cart into the study where she served the tea and biscuits. They followed this ritual religiously.

One evening, Alexandra sensed an unusual restlessness in

her host. He seemed troubled and disturbed. Later while having tea, he said, "Alexandra, I've decided not to exhibit my paperweights in the Art Institute as I originally promised you I'd do."

Alexandra did not protest; she had heard as much many times before. But she was not prepared for what followed.

"They've become so important to me" he said, "that I don't ever want to be parted from them. When I die, they'll be broken-up and the pieces put in my casket. They'll be sealed with me in my family crypt forever."

Alexandra recoiled at this words. Waves of emotion swept through her body. She asked, "But why destroy them?"

"Because, sooner or later, everyone will find out about them and realize their real worth. They'll break into my mausoleum, pry open my coffin and take the paperweights away from me. They're worthless broken; nobody would want them. Anyhow, they're mine, I spent a lot of money for them. I'm not going to leave them to anybody; I especially don't want to leave them to those insensitive dolts who lope through museums. I don't want everyone staring at my beauties."

Half-hearing his reasons, Alexandra involuntarily sucked in huge gasps of air. As feelings of vertigo came over her, she held onto the arms of her chair. Gaining control, she finally said, "I wish you'd give some thought to your decision. You must surely realize that the Imperial paperweights are far too important to be destroyed."

"I've made up my mind, Alexandra, and that's that! When I die they'll be broken up and put in my coffin! I've left word for my attorney about my intention to add a codicil to my will."

"When is he coming?"

"Sometime after next week. He's on a fishing trip in Canada. I told his secretary to have him come and see me as soon as he gets back. I'll have him put it in my will then. He doesn't know we found the Imperial weights. No one does. I don't want them to go to the Art Institute along with my other paperweights. I've got to make sure he makes my will read that way."

Alexandra pushed her chair away from the desk and stood.

"Going already, Alexandra?"

"Yes. Sorry I can't stay any longer, but I must get home. I have some important paperwork I must attend to before tomorrow morning."

She hurried to her car in a state of panic. Buildings, store fronts, street lamps and automobile headlights all flashed in a blur past her side windows as she sped home. He can't destroy my paperweights. If he does, I'll never be with Maximilian again. It's another one of Louis Napoléon's evil plots. That devil! Won't I ever rid myself of him? Don't worry Maximilian, I'll save you. I won't abandon you! I'll find a way for us to be together forever!

That night, she struggled endlessly, probing the irrational areas of her raging mind. "He's sick, he'll die before his lawyer returns from Canada; no, he'll stay alive to spite me. He'll have his own way! I can't let him destroy them. What will become of Maximilian? I'll kill him—I might get caught—I can see through his disguise—I must stop him—How long will he continue to torment me? I'll steal the paperweights! Maybe he'll change his mind. Oh, God, what'll I do?"

Confused, she returned again and again to the obvious solution to her dilemma. To save the paperweights from destruction Edmire must die before adding the codicil to his will. But how? At daybreak Alexandra's twisted mind conceived a way to prevent the destruction of Carlota's paperweights. "His heart! His heart! Yes, I can do it! It'll work. That's the way. Brilliant, brilliant!"

As she drove to work the following morning, she marveled at the simplicity of her plan. Garden magazines had, over the years, given her a casual knowledge of plant pharmacopoeia. She would rely on the deleterious effects of a common garden plant—the digitalis-producing foxglove. She knew the easily available plant would have a devastating effect on old Edmire's weak heart.

That afternoon she left the office early and stopped at a local garden shop to purchase six healthy foxglove plants. When she arrived home, she stripped all the leaves from the plants and dried them in her microwave oven. She crushed the dried leaves, scooped them into an envelope and placed it in her purse.

That evening Edmire's worsening condition caused his physician considerable concern. Dr. Karnes was at the point of recommending hospitalization for his elderly patient when Alexandra arrived. Edmire annoyed Judy, his nurse, when with the wave of his hand, he cavalierly sent her away.

As Alexandra wheeled the old man into the study, she reviewed her simple plan, satisfied it would deliver the paperweights and her beloved Maximilian from their imagined enemy, once and for all.

That evening, immersed in the paperweight she held in her hands, she murmured, "Be patient, my dear husband. It won't be long now. He'll tire soon. He won't destroy the paperweights. I'll see to that."

"What was that, Alexandra? Did you say something?" Edmire asked.

Startled back to reality, she answered, "Just thinking out loud."

When Edmire took the last paperweight from her, Alexandra went to the adjoining room to prepare their tea. Once there, she checked her purse for the envelope with the crushed leaves. As she washed her hands, she said, "Everything is ready now. If I can get the foxglove down him before he puts the paperweights in the safe, I'll just slip them into my purse. We're the only two who know they're here. No will ever guess." She emptied the dried foxglove leaves into an infuser and steeped the powerful digitalis in Edmire's teacup. "The old fool can't taste a thing," she said aloud. "He'll never know what hit him." Alexandra then steeped raspberry tea in the teapot for her cup. She'd take the precaution of adding some of it to his cup after his death.

When she returned to the study, Edmire had already returned the paperweights to the wall safe. Damn, she thought, they're locked away. Well, at least they won't be destroyed.

The foxglove brew was extremely effective. It began to over stimulate Edmire's feeble heart. "Alexandra," he said, hoarsely, "something is wrong. I feel hot. Oh, Jesus, my heart is going like a triphammer! I'm dizzy! I can't breathe. Oh, the pain! Please, please Alexandra, I need help! Get Dr. Karnes. Hurry, Alexandra, hurry!"

Alexandra sat unmoving, quietly sipping her raspberry tea. Edmire, clutching at his chest, fell out of his wheelchair onto the floor.

"...open up the ground..."

After finishing her tea she felt for his carotid artery and found no pulse. She flushed the foxglove residue down the bar sink, rinsed his cup and partially filled it with the raspberry which she intentionally dropped next to his body, spilling tea on the Tabriz. She filled her cup again and leisurely enjoyed a sugar wafer with her second cup while Edmire remained splayed face-down on the floor. After finishing the tea and wafer, she knelt next to his body and felt for a pulse once again.

Finding it quiescent, Alexandra hurried out of the room, making a show of excitedly summoning the doctor. After a cursory examination, Dr. Karnes assumed that the inevitable finally happened to his elderly patient. Satisfied that Edmire's weak heart had finally given up, he filled out a death certificate giving heart failure as the cause of death.

After the reading of Edmire's will, his lawyer told Edmire's sons of his intention to give his paperweight collection to the Chicago Art Institute. The lawyer felt that, though not stated in the will, the family might want to consider Edmire's intention. His sons, advised of the Imperial paperweights' existence and value by Alexandra, decided to convert the three paperweights into cash and keep the balance of his paperweight collection in the family. On the pretext of making arrangements for their auction in New York, Alexandra took possession of the three Imperial paperweights.

3.

Having rescued the paperweights from destruction, Alexandra put a scheme into motion to gain permanent possession of them. She began with a telephone call to Dominic Amati, a former lover who worked at Sotheby's New York. "Dominic, I need your help! Tomorrow I'm going to mail a registered 'dummy' package with three insignificant sulphide paperweights in place of the Imperial paperweights you're expecting. I want to be sure that you personally open it, so I'll wrap the package in brown striped paper."

"I don't get it, Alex. What the hell's going on?"

"Hear me out, Dominic, please."

"Guess I'll have to, but it sure sounds screwy to me."

"Listen, Dominic. While I was packing the three Imperial paperweights for shipment to New York, I accidentally knocked two of them together and bruised their basal rims. I've made arrangements with a glass conservator in Lockport—near here—to restore them before sending them on to you in New York. Once I get them back from him, I'll personally bring them there. It will be easy for you to slip them into Sotheby's and exchange them for the three 'dummy' sulphides. No one will be any the wiser."

"What if somebody else gets to the package first?"

"That's why I'm putting three other paperweights in the package. I can always claim that we made a shipping error."

"But, Alex honey, why all the mystery?"

"Just stop and think about it, Dominic. How can I admit to New York that I was careless with those priceless paperweights? Please, help me, for old times sake. I'll make it up to you."

"I don't know, Alex."

"I'll pick them up in a week or so; just as soon as they're restored. They won't be needed there for the catalog work-up for another six weeks. I promise, as soon as I get them, I'll bring them to New York and personally place them in your hands. We can meet in that motel on the west side, you remember the one."

"Yeah, I remember—the one you forgot about when they offered you the Chicago job. We had a pretty good thing going until you decided to take off."

You bastard, she thought, that's why I took the Chicago job—just to get away from you!

"Alex, you still there?"

"Yes, Dominic, forgive me, I was distracted for a moment. Please say 'yes' for old times sake."

"Will you spend the night with me?"

"Yes, if that's what you want. Just say you'll cover for me."

"Okay, Alex. I'll do it for you. I wouldn't do it for anybody else. You know I'll be putting my job on the line."

"There's absolutely no risk involved, Dominic. I'll get them to you long before they're needed there."

"You'd better!"

"I will, I will. Thank you, Dominic! You won't be sorry, I promise." After hanging up, she spat, "Sure, you'll do it for your usual pound of flesh, you filthy bastard!"

When news of the missing paperweights spread throughout Sotheby's, the turmoil that ensued frightened Amati. He made an anxious telephone call to Alexandra. "Alex, I got to have those paperweights right away! There are cops up to our butts here!"

"How did they discover they were missing, Dominic? The auction is over three months away."

"It's that fuckin' Keith! He was suckin' up again. He got the bright idea of writing a historical background about those damn paperweights for the catalog. He needed them to work up their descriptions. He had free time on his hands and decided to work on them before the weights would be needed for the catalog photos."

"And he couldn't find them."

"Yeah, the stupid jerk!"

"Keith called me about them a day before yesterday. He was in a panic."

"Hey, forget about that fruit cake! How about me?"

"I'm sorry that I got you involved, Dominic."

"Forget about that fuckin' 'sorry' business, damn it! You get those paperweights to me, and I mean right away!"

"I'll do it as soon as I can. I'll call you back tomorrow morning after I talk to the glass man about the repairs."

"Don't screw me up on this, Alex. You got me into this mess, now get me out of it!"

"I'll take care of it, Dominic, I promise."

"You'd better!"

Fearing that her calls to Amati might be traced back to her own telephone, Alexandra took the precaution of making all her subsequent calls to Dominic from public pay phones, usually from the drug store on the ground floor of the Prentiss Building. Worried that Amati might divulge her deception to the authorities because of the pressures he experienced, Alexandra quickly made preparations to meet with him. She'd have to put her plan into motion sooner than she expected.

4.

Late the following Monday night, Alexandra telephoned Elizabeth at home to say she was taking several personal days to fly to San Francisco. "I'm going to see that old friend who is desperately ill—the one I told you about two days ago. I'll be taking an early United flight out of O'Hare in the morning."

"When will you be back, Alex?"

"Thursday or Friday."

"Is there a number in San Francisco where you can be reached?"

"I don't know where I'll be staying. If I find I'll be away for more than three days, I'll get in touch with you."

"Okay, Alex. Have a safe trip."

The next day, Alexandra drove almost seven-hundred miles to Easton, Pennsylvania, where she spent the night. Early the next morning, she had a hearty breakfast and drove to South Hackensack where she drank several cups of black coffee and had her car filled with gas. Before crossing the George

Washington Bridge, she telephoned the motel and asked for "her husband, Mr. Amati."

"Dominic, it's Alexandra."

"Alex! Where the hell are you?"

"I'll be there in half an hour."

"You got them?"

"Yes, all three of them, right here in my shoulder bag."

"Okay, Alex. Remember, you promised to sleep with me tonight."

"You won't be disappointed, I intend to keep my promise."

"You owe me. I took a big chance covering for you. We're still up to our asses at work with cops and investigators."

"I know. Where do I find you, Dominic?"

"Room 115, on the ground floor. I'll leave the door unlocked, just walk in."

"I won't be long Dominic."

"I'm hot for you Alex, hurry!"

Forty minutes later, she arrived at the motel, parked the car and took her revolver out of the glove compartment. After twisting the silencer on the .32, she slipped it in her shoulder bag. Seeing no one on the lot, she left the car, hurried to unit 115 and stepped into Amati's motel room. Closing the door behind her, she killed Amati with a single shot. A few moments later, she looked out of the window to make certain no one was nearby and quickly slipped out of the room. When she opened her car door, Alexandra suddenly felt ill and vomited. She wiped her mouth. "Oh, how disgusting," she said, repulsed at the sight of vomit and lipstick smeared on the back of her glove. "I just bought them! I don't need them anymore," she said, pulling them off and dropping them onto the parking lot.

As she turned onto the expressway marked "West", she felt confident that she had covered her tracks completely. The only person who could connect her with the missing weights was dead. She set her cruise control and relaxed into her seat to begin the miles back to the paperweights and Maximilian in Chicago.

When she planned Amati's murder, she imagined that a single bullet fired from her .32 would leave a clean, neat hole in his heart, followed with a closing of his eyelids and a collapse to the floor—a quiet passing, like Edmire's. She hadn't contemplated the recurring images of Amati's death. Mile after mile, try as she did—singing, playing the radio, reciting poetry—she could not put the grisly details of his death out of her mind. The images began with his face brightening in anticipation as she entered the room. He didn't notice that she had taken the silencer-tipped revolver from her shoulder bag. Approaching her naked, with arms outstretched, he stopped momentarily as Alexandra brought the gun up to the level of his chest. His expression, quizzical at first, turned into disbelief, and then changed into a mask of terror. She intended to shoot the bullet straight into his heart—his filthy heart—but he startled her when he lunged at her. Her arm flew up as she jerked the trigger. The bullet smashed into his right eye. He lurched back and fell with a dull thud to the floor, his one remaining eye staring, unseeing, at the ceiling, his mouth open in a silent scream. Looking down at his naked body, Alexandra saw that his extremities were twitching. She lifted her gaze from Amati's body and focused on a curious mass of wet organic matter on the wall of the room. The explosion of her bullet, bursting through the back of Dominic's cranial cavity had spewed blood, bone, flesh, pieces of hair and brain onto the wall. Exploded bits of matter and blood slipped slowly down the wall and fell to the floor. Each time she recalled that image, Alexandra unconsciously activated her windshield wipers to wash off the blood and matter that seemed to be sliding down her windshield.

As she turned for a final look before leaving the motel room, she saw two liquid pools spreading out from his naked body: red blood flowing from the back of his skull and yellow urine escaping from his relaxed bladder.

"You had it coming, you bastard," she said aloud, stamping on the accelerator, "stringing me along for three years—taking advantage of me—using and abusing me, then dropping me for some young red-headed bitch!"

"...may blood and gall taint their miserable lives..."

5.

The distraught night manager unlocked the door and admitted the police to the motel room. He stood at the door, running his fingers through his thinning hair, mumbling, "Oh, Jesus, Jesus, all that blood; the poor guy, Jesus—"

"Anybody touch anything in this room?" asked the sergeant.

"No sir, nobody."

"How'd you discover the body?"

"Yesterday morning, when he checked in, the guy left a 7:30 wake-up call with the day clerk. He didn't answer my call this morning, so I told the maid to go over and wake him up. When she opened the door and seen him laying there on the floor she started screaming like mad."

"Where is she now?"

"Huh?"

"The maid, where is she?"

"Back there, in back of the office, lying down."

"I'll want to talk to her. Anybody see or hear anything?"

"I don't know. Some of the guests checked out already."

"Early birds. Okay, I'll need all their addresses. In the meantime, I've got to question everybody who's still here." Pointing at the corpse, the sergeant asked, "You know who this guy was?"

"Mr. Amati, Dominic Amati."

"Where's he from?"

"From here, from New York."

"You ever seen him before?"

"Yeah, he used to come here pretty often a couple a years ago. He always had dames with him."

"How about this time?"

"No, he was by hisself this time."

"Know anything about him?"

"Not much. Except, he told me once, he had a big job in New York. It's the first time he's been back in a long time."

"And the last time, too."

"Huh?"

"Nothing. Now listen, you and this officer go to all the rooms still occupied. I want those people to report to your office. Like I said, I'll also check your register for the names and addresses of all those who checked out already."

"Yes, sir."

"Paul," the sergeant said, turning to the other officer, "you'd better get on the horn and tell the department to get someone from forensics out here. They've got to go over this room while it's still hot."

"Okay, Sarge."

The next morning in the ready room of the Ninth New York Precinct, the captain stopped an officer to ask, "Anything on that motel case yet, Ross?"

"Yeah, Captain. He's that light-fingered guy we put out

that all-points bulletin on. Remember, he's the guy from Sotheby's that was selling stolen goods to that antique dealer. He's been swiping from them for years. He's got to be the one that stole those three paperweights."

"Doesn't take a genius to figure that out. Any leads on who stiffed him?"

"Only suspect we got so far is that guy, Parker—Keith Parker. He's the guy we brought in for questioning last week about spending all that money. He had a blow-up with the stiff over those missing paperweights; threatened to kill him. We just picked him up again. Andy and Ted are questioning him now. Claims he's got an alibi for the time the stiff got it; he was home with his live-in boyfriend."

"A guy?"

"Yeah."

"Oh, one of those. Think he did it?"

"No, uh-uh. He's probably telling the truth. But, at least, it looks like we're doing our job. Keeps the papers off our butts for a while."

"It won't last. You can't fool them very long. Keep me informed, Ross."

Later that day, the captain called Sgt. Ross to his office. "How's the lab coming with the slug and those gloves you guys found on the parking lot?"

"Still working on 'em, Captain."

"What about the couple that saw the license plates and the car?"

"Them people don't remember enough to help."

"When you get the report from the lab, call Chicago and give them whatever you find out."

"Check."

CHAPTER VIII.

1.

Matthew sped to the 18th District, skidded his Toyota to a stop, sprinted up the back stairs and punched in nine minutes late. As he paused leaning against a desk to catch his breath, Sgt. Dobrinski slapped him on the shoulder, warning, "You clocked in late again, kid. You're gonna get into trouble with Mulcahy! It's bad enough he's on my butt again. You don't want him on yours."

"What'd you do this time?"

"Two cops on a stake-out seen me at a bookie joint yesterday when I was supposed to be on duty. Damn! It would happen!"

"They didn't turn you in, did they?"

"Hell no, they'd never do that. But they were laughing about it in the duty room yesterday afternoon. They think Mulcahy listened at the door."

"Oh, no!"

"Yeah, a real kick in the nuts! I don't know what he'll do to me now. He's had it in for me for a long time."

"Why'd you take such a chance?"

"Who knows. I'm stupid, I guess. I could of called in my bet, but no, I had to go to the bookie joint, myself."

"Think they'll bust you?"

"Shit, worse than that! Might even get thrown off the goddamn force—lose the pension I've worked for all my life."

"Jesus! Did you see Mulcahy, yet?"

"Saw him this morning."

"Did he bring it up?"

"Nope."

"Maybe he didn't hear them."

"He heard 'em, okay. I can tell the way he looks at me. Tell you kid, what bothers me most is I'm afraid Josie might leave me. She left me once before when I gambled away a lot of money. I used to be a compulsive gambler—cards. I learned to keep my habit under control with a bet now and then on the horses. If I lose my job over this, she'll leave me for sure; that'll really kill me. Damn Lieutenant! If I had a name like O'Malley or O'Brian, he'd keep off my ass, for sure. Those damn Irish, they all stick together. And, wouldn't you know it. The one time I was lucky enough to hit the daily double. Damn!"

"The daily double?"

"Yeah, won over four hundred. A lot of good it'll do me now. He'll burn me for sure, the asshole." Glancing at the clock on the wall, Dobrinski asked, "How come you're so late gettin' in, kid?"

"Had trouble getting through traffic; it's really piled up."

"I been waiting for you to get here. There's a break in the paperweight caper."

"Caper? Where do you come up with those dumb words? Reading those old detective novels again?"

"Oh shit," laughed Dobrinski, "I thought it sounded okay. I guess I heard it on an old TV movie the other night."

"What about the paperweights?"

"Chewing on his already soggy cigar stub, Dobrinski said, "Well, there's this Dago, a guy by the name of Amati, Dominic Amati, who worked at Sotheby's in New York. They found him wasted in a motel."

"They tie him in with the paperweights?'

"Yeah, sort of. He was one of the honchos in the receiving department in New York—you know, where all that stuff come into the auction house. He's one of the guys that sign for the packages that come in, and tag them with inventory numbers. They think Amati is probably the guy who signed for the three paperweights when the package came into the auction house. It wouldn't be the first time he's copped something."

"Yeah?"

"Seems he's been stealing things out of there, regularly."

"Sticky fingers. How'd he get it?"

"Plugged right through the eye. Blew out the back of his skull. Splattered his damn brains all over a motel wall. Whoever did it used a .32."

"How'd you find out?"

"Got a call from New York this morning, early. Talked to a guy, name of Sgt. Ross. He said it happened day before yesterday."

"And they think that this guy, Amati, had something to do with the paperweights?"

"Like I said, the stiff probably signed for them when they came in and snuck'em out. Now they're gone and he's on a slab in the morgue. They think his accomplice wasted him and took the paperweights. And you haven't heard the best part yet, kid. They think it was a broad that did it! The motel manager said that some broad telephoned the motel asking to talk to the stiff. She claimed he was her husband. Thing is, he ain't never been married."

"Then, the paperweights are still missing?"

"They sure are. I don't think they'll ever find 'em now."

"Did they go through the room for fingerprints? I suppose they looked for clues."

"Come on, kid, they know their job! It's not the first murder in The Big Apple. Right now they probably got a couple forensic guys in the motel combing every inch of the stiff's room. They won't miss a thing. What the hell do you think, no one is as good as the Chicago P.D.?"

"Yeah, guess you're right, Dan."

"Hey, I got an idea, kid. Let's take a ride over to Michigan avenue later this morning. Them two gals probably knew this guy Amati when they worked in New York. The Saint George dame is worried about those paperweights. She'll be glad to hear there's some movement in the case. Besides, you'll be able to see your girlfriend, too."

"Beth'll be there, Dan, but Alex might still be away."

"She's gone?"

"Yeah, she took a few days off and flew to San Francisco. Beth said she went there to see a friend who's pretty sick."

2.

When they walked into Sotheby's reception room, Elizabeth stretched up from her desk and gave Matthew a quick kiss on the cheek. Removing his soggy cigar, Dobrinski pointed its misshapen end at her, saying, "Hey you kids, that's no way to act in a Michigan avenue office!"

Elizabeth laughed, "I know, Dan, but we haven't seen each other since last night."

"Your boss still in 'Frisco?" asked Dobrinski.

"As a matter of fact, she's back. Flew back last night. She got up late this morning and came in about half an hour ago. She's exhausted. Did you want to see her? She's in her office."

"Yeah, tell her I've got some information on those paperweights."

Elizabeth hurried into Alexandra's office. They both appeared instantly. Alexandra asked, "Have they found the paperweights, Sergeant?"

"No, not yet. Do either of you remember a guy by the

name of Amati in New York?"

"Why, yes," answered Elizabeth, "both of us knew Dominic; we worked with him in New York. Alex, you dated him, didn't you?"

Alexandra's heart beat furiously. Damn it, Beth, she thought, you would tell them that! Keeping her voice under control, she said, "yes, we had a few dates. It was just a casual acquaintance, nothing serious."

Elizabeth knew Alexandra and Dominic had been deeply involved for several years and wondered why she lied. She felt guilty herself, because of her own involvement with Dominic after Alexandra transferred to Chicago. Elizabeth had gravitated to him because she felt they both shared a mutual loss when Alexandra left New York. When the older man showed an interest in her, she was flattered. It all started innocently enough, at first, with an occasional luncheon date, a movie and walks in Central Park. He took advantage of her obvious inexperience and eventually took the naive young girl as one of his lovers.

Each time he made Elizabeth submit to him, she felt violated. He always placed her in the superior position, just high enough so that her nipples brushed against his bare chest. Growing passionate, he'd grab her buttocks and force her down on him, entering her completely, thrusting himself in a frenzy until he was spent. After his spastic-like convulsions subsided, he'd always push her off and say, "That was great, wasn't it?"

When she became pregnant, he berated her for her ignorance of contraception. He lied, angrily telling her he was married and insisted she abort the fetus. Elizabeth became confused after the abortion when Dominic stopped seeing her. Later she discovered he was unmarried and had taken another young Sotheby's girl as a lover. When Alexandra asked Elizabeth to come to Chicago, it was as if she had been lifted out of a dark pit. She never told anyone about her affair with Dominic; it was an episode in her life she pretended never happened. She certainly did not want Matthew to know, ever.

Alexandra's query interrupted Elizabeth's thoughts, "But, Sergeant, why did you ask if we had worked with him?"

"He was found dead in a motel yesterday."

Elizabeth gasped.

"Oh, my God!" exclaimed Alexandra, feigning shock.

"He's dead?" asked Elizabeth in disbelief.

"Yeah, the coroner said that it happened day before yesterday, in the morning."

"Did anyone hear the shot?" Alexandra asked.

Dobrinski said, "No, they think the gun probably had a silencer. Has anyone from your New York office called you about Amati, yet?"

Making a show of weakness, Alexandra sank into a chair, saying, "Oh no, Sergeant, we had no idea. How horrible! He was such a nice person. Do they know who committed this dreadful crime?"

No, they're still checking it out. As soon as we heard about it, we thought you should know." Putting on his hat, Dobrinski said, "Come on, Matt, the lieutenant wants us to look into a break-in on Wabash."

As they stepped into the elevator, Matthew asked, "A break-in on Wabash?"

"Had to get out of there. Didn't you catch what that dame said? I didn't tell them how he died. How'd she know he was murdered? All I said was that he was dead. She even asked about the gun shot. I didn't say nothing about a gun. You know, I saw her eyes dilate when she said she knew the stiff only casually. It all ties in, Matt: the dame pretending to be his wife, the Olds with the Illinois plates, and the gloves. They must have been in it together, Amati and that dame. She mails the paperweights to the auction house in New York; he slips them out of Sotheby's. They meet in a motel to divide up the loot; she wastes him and then takes the paperweights back. Smart cookie. She's in the clear because she mailed them to New York. Pretty neat!"

"Wait a minute, Dan. What was that you said about an Olds with Illinois plates, and the gloves?"

"Look kid, I didn't tell you about the car and the gloves because I didn't think too much about it at the time. When that Sgt. Ross called this morning, he said that when they questioned some of the people at the motel, an old geezer from Illinois said he noticed a dark brown Olds with Illinois license plates parked in the motel lot. Seems he always looks for cars from Illinois whenever he and his wife travel. Anyway, he saw the car pull out of the lot and speed away sometime late Wednesday morning. According to the motel register, there wasn't anyone staying there from Illinois. It was about the same time that the Amati guy was bumped off. A broad was driving the car, but he only saw the back of her head. The New York cops couldn't follow up on that lead because the old guy didn't remember nothing else about the car or driver. They also found a pair of woman's gloves on the parking lot. One was smeared with puke and lipstick."

As they left the elevator, Matthew asked, "If you suspected Alex, why didn't you question her on the spot?"

"Oh no, not yet. Got to check out a few things, first. She's not going anywhere. Don't want to jump the gun. It's all circumstantial, so far. I could be wrong, but I got a pretty strong feeling about this one. Anyhow, if I'm wrong, I don't want nobody from Sotheby's running to the department and bitching about me. I'm in enough hot water already." When they reached their car, Dobrinski stopped, and said, "Listen Matt, I want you to talk to your girlfriend and get some information for me without letting on that I suspect her boss."

"Like what?"

"Make sure the Saint George dame actually flew to 'Frisco; and if she did, when and on what airline? If her name's on the manifest, then I'm wrong about her."

"Okay, Dan."

"And try to find out what make car she has, and its color. Don't let on why you're pumping her. Hey, listen, I got an idea. Why don't you take your little blonde for lunch today, it's almost noon. I'll drive back and cover for you at the station. Let me know right away what you find out!"

"Got it—the flight, the airline, the make of her car and its color."

"Right!" responded Dobrinski as he squeezed behind the steering wheel.

3.

Matthew and Elizabeth walked to Water Tower Place and rode the escalator up seven floors to Kaplan's Delicatessen. After ordering corned beef on rye and coffee for two, Matthew said, "I'll bet it's pretty hectic when Alex leaves you in charge."

"Not really. I'm able to handle most inquiries. I can usually reach her for anything that requires her expertise. Even when she takes trips, I have a detailed itinerary. It's no problem getting in touch with her in an emergency."

"Do you make her travel arrangements?"

"Most of the time."

"You always use the same airline?"

"I try to. She flies United whenever she can; she likes to pile up credit on their Mileage Plus program."

"Then, you arranged her flight to Frisco?"

"No, as a matter fact, I didn't. She wasn't exactly sure when she'd be flying there; she had to wait until her friend improved enough to receive visitors. She didn't know until the last minute when she could go. She booked the flight herself."

"When was that?"

"Monday night, yes, late Monday night. She called me before she left—after the ten o'clock news. It must have been around eleven or eleven-fifteen."

"Then she took a United flight to Frisco on Tuesday."

"Uh-huh, early Tuesday morning. Why all the sudden interest in Alex?"

"Oh, no reason. Just wondering, I guess," he said casually.

Walking back to Elizabeth's office after lunch, Mike attempted to learn about Alexandra's car. In a sudden inspiration, he told her that he and Dan had often argued over the merits of foreign and American-made cars. "He's one of those 'buy USA' nuts. He called me un-American. He said I was putting American workers out of work when I got my Toyota. I don't think most people notice if their friends have foreign or domestic cars, do you? You probably don't know what your boss drives."

"It's American."

"What make is it?"

"I've only seen it a couple of times; she usually takes a commuter to work. I think it's an Olds."

"Are you sure?"

"It might be, but I'm not sure."

"What color is it?"

"Oh, it's dark brown."

Beth stopped walking and caught Matthew's left arm, saying, "Wait a minute." Turning him to face her she said, in measured tones, "Matt, you're asking questions about Alex, again. What's going on?"

"Nothing, honey," he answered, removing her hand from his arm.

As they began walking again, Beth demanded, "Stop evading my question."

"I don't know what you mean."

"Yes you do. You've been quizzing me about Alex. Don't deny it!"

"Come on, honey, it's just your imagination."

Reaching the Prentiss Building, Matthew stopped to kiss her on the cheek. Irritated, she pulled away saying, "Don't put me off with a peck on the cheek, Matt. What's going on?"

"Beth, I can't tell you. Just don't say anything to her about it. It's very important she doesn't know we're checking up on her. I'll come by your apartment to explain, later tonight. Got to go. Got to get back to the station. Dan's waiting. Bye, honey."

"What's it all about?" she called after him.

As he quickly walked away, ignoring her question, Beth paused at the entrance to the building, puzzled that Matt took such a convoluted path to draw out those few seemingly unimportant bits of information. She realized his sudden invitation to lunch was a ruse to question her. Elizabeth felt especially hurt that he used their relationship to pump her about Alex. Alex, of all people, she thought. And why did he ask me not to say anything about it? If it's a police matter, Alex could be in danger. How can I possibly keep it from her? I owe her so much. If it hadn't been for Alex, I'd still be stranded in New York.

4.

When Elizabeth entered the office, she saw Alexandra furtively searching through the file cabinets.

"Alex, I'm back. Can I find something for you?"

"Oh Beth, I'm glad you're here. I can't find the musical instrument catalog from the June '85 London auction. Would you please try to find it? I have a client on the phone. He's asking the hammer price for item 73. It's a 1784 Gragnani violin."

"I'll get it," said Elizabeth, tossing her purse on her desk.

Elizabeth hurried to the files as Alexandra returned to her office. She retrieved the catalog and took it in to Alexandra who was chatting with the client on the phone. Pointing to the entry, she wrote on Alexandra's note pad, "It sold for $24,640."

While Elizabeth mechanically performed the functions of her job that afternoon, she vacillated between her loyalty to Alexandra and her strong feelings for Matthew. She felt certain Matthew's request for secrecy did not originate with him, it was his cigar-chewing partner's idea. Several times that afternoon she left her desk and walked to the door of Alexandra's office, but each time she hesitated and returned to her desk, mute; her love for Matt bridled her impulse to tell Alexandra.

Later, when Alexandra returned the musical instrument catalog to Elizabeth's desk, she said, "I just couldn't find it, Beth. I looked under—"

"It was in the pending drawer. Remember? We're waiting for two more music catalogs so that we can send them to the binders."

"Oh, that's right. How could I have forgotten. I've been so absent-minded lately. It must be the missing paperweights." Noticing that the young girl seemed troubled, she asked, "Is everything all right, Beth?"

Averting her eyes, Elizabeth replied, "I'm okay, I guess."

"Problems with your handsome Matthew?"

"Yes, sort of."

Alexandra walked back to her office, saying, "You know the old aphorism, Beth, 'The course of true love—"

"Alex," Elizabeth interrupted.

Alexandra paused at her office door, "Yes?"

"Never mind."

Moments later, overcome with guilt, Elizabeth buzzed Alexandra's office.

"Yes, Beth?"

"Alex, I don't know if it's really important, but Matt has been asking questions about you. I think it's a police matter of some kind. I suspect it was his sergeant's idea."

Alexandra's heart began pumping furiously. She switched off the intercom as she attempted to bring her short gasps for air under control. Regaining her composure, she signaled Elizabeth, saying, "Sorry, Beth, my hand inadvertently hit the intercom switch. Why don't you come in here? You've really piqued my curiosity." She fixed a smile on her face, picked up a sheaf of papers, and assumed a pose of amused curiosity."

As Elizabeth stepped into her doorway, Alexandra asked, "What in all the world would your young Matt want to know about an old middle-aged divorcée, twice his age? Did I forget to pay a parking ticket, or something?"

"I feel foolish about it, Alex, but I just can't keep it from you."

"I'm sure it's not very important, either, but you've really caught my interest."

"He asked me which airline and which flight you took to San Francisco. He also wanted to know the make and color of your car."

Alexandra felt her hands suddenly become cold. Carefully controlling her voice, she flippantly asked, "Is that all he wanted to know?"

"Yes, Alex. I asked him why, and he wouldn't tell me. I can't imagine what it's all about."

"Well, I can't either. Don't concern yourself about it. It can't be very important."

Only a few minutes elapsed after Elizabeth returned to her desk when Alexandra appeared in the reception room, pulling on driving gloves. "Would you please hold down the fort for the rest of the afternoon, Beth? While you were at lunch, I made an appointment to look at a collection of old icons. A Greek dowager, Tula Tsoukalakis, called to say that she might decide to put them up for auction."

"Will you be back today?"

"No, I don't think so. Her home's on the North Shore."

"Do you have a phone number for me?" asked Elizabeth, as Alexandra opened the door to the hallway.

"No," she said irritably.

"What if there is an emergency—"

Alexandra cut her off, snapping, "God! Just take the message, Beth!"

"Okay, Alex. See you in the morning."

As Alexandra hurried out of the office without a reply, Elizabeth thought how unlike her it was to leave the office without giving a number where she could be reached. She couldn't remember that it had ever happened before. What surprised her more was the way Alexandra spoke to her. "Boy," she said, "this is not my day. First Matt uses me and now Alex snaps at me for no reason. What else can go wrong?"

When Matthew left Elizabeth, he took a cab to the district. Dobrinski was not there. He had just left to interview a victim of an apartment robbery. Later that afternoon, as

Matthew told Dobrinski what he learned, the older officer's eyes brightened. His suspicions of Alexandra were beginning to flesh out.

"She didn't suspect anything, did she, kid?"

"Yeah, I'm afraid she did."

"Damn it, Matt," Dobrinski complained, clamping his teeth down hard on his cigar, "the last thing I told you was—"

"Yeah, I know. I tried."

"Think she'll tell her boss?"

"She might. They're pretty close."

Resigned to his junior partner's bungled attempt, the older officer said, "Too late to worry about it now. By the way, when you were having lunch with your girlfriend, that Sgt. Ross called again. The lab tested those gloves they found on the parking lot. There's gunpowder on the left glove, the same glove with the puke and lipstick on it. They're sure that the dame that plugged that Dago was a southpaw."

"Yeah?"

"You know, kid, that long-legged Saint George dame is left-handed. Listen, I'm going to call United to find out if she was on a manifest to Frisco this week. If she collects mileage, they'll have her flight on record, too. I'll have them check both ways: real-time processing on reservations and those computer tapes they use for monthly mileage statements. While I'm doing that, why don't you run her name through the DMV and get an official description of her car."

As Matthew waited at the teletype, he could hear Dan's voice rising in pitch and agitation. From the bits of conversation Matthew could hear above the station's background noise, he gathered that Dobrinski was hearing exactly what he suspected.

"...Alexandra Saint George. Her last name? It's S-T-G-E-O-R-G-E...Yeah, yeah. No, I'll just wait, that's right. I thought so, Monday, Tuesday. Uh-huh, uh-huh. You sure? ...during the...yeah, yeah!...What?...accumulated mileage...no, I'll wait...Frisco? How about anywhere else? No mileage. Okay, I'll wait. Uh-huh...When? Yeah, yeah, Thanks, thanks! What? Yeah, thanks, good-bye."

By the time Dobrinski joined Matthew at the teletype, the machine was spitting out information on Alexandra's car. Looking over Matthew's shoulder, Dobrinski saw that Alexandra's car fit the puzzle.

"That's it kid, it all checks out! United checked their reservation tapes and their Mileage Plus records; there's no record of her flying to Frisco or back! While I go talk to Mulcahy, you call your girlfriend and make sure that her boss is there. I want to make an official call on that dame."

Matthew tore the printed sheet off the machine, walked to his desk and dialed Elizabeth's number.

"Good afternoon, Sotheby's-Chicago, Miss Field speaking."

"Beth, honey, it's Matt. Sorry I wasn't completely honest with you at lunchtime. It wasn't my idea."

"I just knew your partner put you up to it. You know, you used me, Matt."

"I know, honey. Forgive me?"

"What else can I do? I love you."

Glancing around the station room, Mike lowered his voice saying, "I love you too, honey. Listen, Beth, I'm calling to tell you we're coming up there again. We're going to question Alex. She's still there, isn't she?"

"No, Matt. She left to see a client about a half-hour ago. She'll be back tomorrow."

Turning to the approaching Dobrinski, Matthew said, "She left for the day."

Dobrinski banged the desk with his fist saying, "Ask her

if she told that dame we're checking on her."

"Beth, did you tell Alex what I asked about?"

"Yes, Matt, sorry."

Turning to Dobrinski, he said, apologetically, "She knows, Dan."

Dobrinski removed his cigar stub, threw it on the floor and ground it with his foot, saying, "Damn! You can bet your ass she's on her way home to get rid of the murder weapon! Let's get over there and stop her! Hang up, kid! Get her address off the DMV sheet! C'mon, let's go!"

Beth's connection suddenly went dead. Her mind couldn't fully comprehend what she overheard. Did Dobrinski say 'murder weapon'? Alex, a murderess? No! An uncontrollable shaking seized her body. Beth went to the lavatory, splashed cold water on her face, patted it dry, and stared into the mirror, all the while attempting to steady her shaking legs against the vanity.

What happened in San Francisco? The police must be wrong! Did I really hear something about a murder weapon? Alex a murderess? No, I can't believe that. He must have said something else. But they're going to her house. Why? Why? I've got to warn her!

She ran to her desk and quickly punched in Alex's phone number, pulled off her earring and put the receiver to her ear. "Hurry! Hurry! What's taking so long? Oh God, it's finally ringing. One, two...ten, eleven." She hung up the receiver. "There's no answer, she's not home yet! She's still looking at those icons. Oh, God! How can I reach her? I've got to help her! I've got to get to her house before she gets back from the North Shore! No matter what Dobrinski thinks, Alex is not capable of harming anyone, let alone of committing murder! I'll drive to Alex's home. I've got to be at her side when they confront her with their terrible accusation."

5.

When Alexandra hurried out of Sotheby's, she drove home, terrified. They're setting a trap for me, she thought as she activated her windshield wipers to clear off Amati's blood. Her confused mind juxtaposed several threads of time in her consciousness. She saw herself being threatened simultaneously by Louis Napoléon and Sgt. Dobrinski. Even the Imperial paperweights began to close in about her. No longer three beautiful works of art, they became restricting prisons in her hallucinating mind. By the time she reached her driveway she was determined to escape her pursuers by freeing herself and Maximilian from the confines of the faceted paperweights.

"I'll free us. I'll break them open, and then, my love, we'll escape to Miramar."

Flinging open the car door, she ran to her house. Her hand shook as she fumbled at the lock. Suddenly, from inside her house, she heard her phone ringing. She stood absolutely still, key in hand, counting the rings, "...three, four...ten, eleven. The phone stopped ringing. They know I'm here! They're calling on the phone!"

Finding the slot, she unlocked the door and rushed into the living room. Scooping up the three crystal balls and cradling them against her breasts, she frantically rushed from room to room, not knowing what to do. She finally stopped in the kitchen, out of breath, and placed the paperweights on the counter. As she stood there, unrelated thoughts raced about her mind in senseless chaotic patterns. Steeling herself, she clenched the edge of the counter top with both hands and forced her mind to narrow its focus on the three glass objects lined up before her. "How will I get us out of these prisons?" she asked Maximilian's profile in the nearest paperweight.

While mentally casting about for a tool to penetrate the

crystal, her senses became acutely aware of both real and imagined stimuli around her. As she stared at the paperweights, they began to expand, slowly at first, and as she watched, they ballooned at a quickening pace. She shut her eyes tightly in an attempt to stop their frightening growth. Finding comfort in the darkness, she chose to keep her eyes closed. Then, far off, on the furthest edge of her hearing, she perceived the ticking of a clock, a ticking that increased in intensity with each new beat. Suddenly, the whirring refrigerator burst in on her senses when the compressor kicked in. It pounded like thunder against her ear drums. In an effort to shut out the din, she covered her ears, but found the refrigerator noise replaced by the racing beats of her own heart. When she finally removed her hands from her ears and opened her eyes, every sound in the room had vanished. Her eyes caught a glint on the floor. Is that blood? Amati's blood? She ripped a banner of paper towels from the roller and knelt on the floor to mop up the tell-tale blood; but the blood had disappeared! As she remained kneeling, the hollow silence pressed hard against her ears. That's odd, she thought. She strained to hear anything at all. As she listened, a faint alien rustling, barely perceptible at first, developed into ominous stretching and crackling noises, rapidly growing in intensity. Her eyes searched the room to discover the source of the bizarre sound. Startled, she hoarsely whispered, "My wallpaper is moving!" Alexandra watched incredulously as growing vines on her flowered wallpaper pressed against the stretching, complaining paper. Suddenly, their tendrils broke through the restricting paper. They're writhing like snakes. Look, look, they're starting to move across the ceiling! I can hear them growing! They're squeezing through the tiny openings between the foliage and stems, and coming into the room!

    As she watched the twisting vines, she heard them

making faint wet squeaking sounds. "If they reach the paperweights, we'll be trapped. We'll never escape! Hurry, hurry!"

In her panic, Alexandra returned to the three paperweights, breathlessly murmuring, "I've got to do something soon or we'll be locked forever in a prison of vines!" Alexandra's eyes narrowed as she searched out the few rational areas of her memory. "Yes, yes, I know! I can do it! Sudden changes in temperature will shatter glass! That's it! Oh, yes, that's it! Maximilian, my love, we've outwitted them!"

Tearing a deep copper pot from its hook on the wall, she filled it with water, turned the gas jet to high, placed the pot on the stove and dropped the green Imperial paperweight into the heating water.

"When the boiling water heats it clear through, I'll throw it into cold water. That'll crack it wide open! Ice water, yes, ice water! I'll make ice water!"

She emptied two trays of ice cubes into a tall glass pitcher and added water. Placing the pitcher next to the two remaining paperweights, she went back to the copper pot to wait for the water to begin boiling. "Boil, damn you, boil!"

Just as tiny bubbles began to form on the sides of the pot, her ears caught the sound of a car coming to a stop in her driveway.

"Our enemies are here, Maximilian! Don't worry my love, I'll protect you."

Alexandra ran to her bedroom, rummaged through her night stand and found her revolver. She hurried to the living room and stood motionless next to a window, concealed from the officers' view. As she watched Dobrinski and Matthew get out of their car, she whispered, "Napoléon's henchmen have found us, but we'll escape those monsters."

6.

Matthew closed the squad car door, saying, "You know, Dan, I've been thinking, maybe the reason United doesn't have a record on her is because she took another airline."

"Hell, I thought of that, too, but I doubt it. If that's the case, she can tell us when we question her. Look, there's her car, a brown Olds!"

The older policeman removed his cigar stub as he walked around Alexandra's car. Tossing the stub into the foundation plantings, he called to his partner, "She must of been in one hell of a hurry when she got here. Look at this, she left her car door wide open!" Shaking his head he added, "You check this car over for a .32 while I go to the house."

The sound of squealing brakes grabbed Dobrinski's attention as Elizabeth's car skidded into Alexandra's driveway and braked inches behind the police car.

"Jesus Christ, Matt, what the hell's she doing here?"

Matt muttered, "Oh no, not Beth."

The oil sticker on Alexandra's car momentarily diverted Dobrinski from her arrival. He noticed that the date on it was just six days old. Quickly checking its mileage against that of the odometer, he shouted to Matt, "Hey, kid, look here! This car's traveled almost eighteen-hundred miles in the last five days!"

That last bit of evidence satisfied Dobrinski that he had found a key piece to the puzzle. "That's it." he said, with a satisfied finality, "She did it. She didn't fly to Frisco. She drove to New York, plugged that guy in the motel, took the paperweights and drove back to Chicago. If we can find her gun, ballistics'll wrap-up the case."

Elizabeth grabbed Matthew by the arm, demanding, "What's going on here?"

"Honey, we think Alex killed Nick Amati."

Her eyes widened, her mouth stopped open in the midst of an intake of air. "You're both crazy," she shouted incredulously, "she was in California!"

"We think she was in New York, honey."

"Oh, no! You're wrong! Alex wouldn't hurt anyone! I've worked with her for years; she couldn't commit such a terrible crime. She's a warm and caring person!"

Dobrinski turned to face her, and said scornfully, "Warm and caring, hell! You only see what you want to see. You don't see the warts and blackheads in your boss's brains."

"You're wrong, damn you!" she shouted, glaring at the older man.

"Look cutie," he continued, his tone less harsh, "I've seen it lots of times before. Losers always seem to wear halos to their family and friends. A young punk's mother won't believe that her kid'd rip off a neighbor's house. All she sees is the little curly headed boy who used to sit on her lap while she read him stories."

Elizabeth covered both ears, shutting out Dobrinski's voice. Matthew moved close to her and tenderly enfolded her in his arms. Her defenses collapsed and she broke into tears.

"Matt," Dobrinski said, "as soon as your girlfriend settles down, you come to the house. I'm going there now."

"Okay, Dan. Take care!"

"God," sobbed Elizabeth, "I can't stand that ugly man."

"He's just doing what he has to do, honey."

As Alexandra watched Dobrinski approach, her resolve grew with his every step. "I killed him once!" she said, aloud. "What's he doing here, walking across my lawn, naked?"

Dobrinski rang the doorbell. Without hesitation, she opened the door, quickly raised her weapon, fired, slammed the door, dropped her handgun and ran back into the house.

Dobrinski sank to the ground, shouting, "Matt I'm hit! Get on the horn! Officer down!"

While Matthew rushed to the squad car to call for help, Elizabeth went to Dobrinski's aid. Matthew ran up just as the old officer, holding his right arm, assured Elizabeth, "It's just a flesh wound, kid, didn't hit the bone. Man, it hurts like hell!" Turning to the young officer, he said, "You're not going in there, Matt. Get back on the horn and tell'em to bring a wagon and some tear gas. We'll smoke her out."

Alexandra, confused and gasping for air found herself in her bedroom. Then, remembering the paperweights, she ran to the kitchen, reached into the pan of boiling water, grasped the paperweight and plunged it deep into the pitcher of ice water. Unable to stabilize under the extreme and sudden changes of expansion and contraction, the tremendous forces of internal stress tore the molecules of the glass apart. She felt it crack and snap in her tight grasp. Like hard-crack-stage syrup, she thought. Through the side of the pitcher, she observed spider web cracks form over the entire surface of the paperweight and descend down in planes into its core.

"The glass walls are crumbling, my dear. We'll soon escape!"

Alexandra withdrew her hand from the ice water and placed the crackled paperweight on the counter. The crystal came apart, falling into three large pieces. Taking up the largest segment, she became fascinated by the rainbow hues reflecting from the many cracked internal planes of its new interfaces. As she played the prismatic colors in the sunlight, it slowly dawned on her that she and Maximilian were not free, they were still imprisoned! There were two more glass cells preventing their escape. They had to be destroyed!

Suddenly, the inhibiting effect of the ice-cold water

surrendered to the desperate signals of Alexandra's scalded nerve cells. In a rush, excruciating pain enveloped her left hand. She shrieked and dropped the broken piece of paperweight. Clutching at her throbbing hand, she leaned against the kitchen cabinets and slipped slowly to the floor.

"Oh, my hand! Help me!" she moaned in agony. "Someone help me! Mother! Maximilian, please! Oh God, the pain is unbearable. Please, someone, help me!"

Hearing Alexandra's anguished cries for help, Elizabeth started for the door. Dobrinski, struggled to his knees, demanding, "Hey, stay put! Where the hell do you think you're going?"

"Wait, Beth, wait!" Matthew shouted as he caught her arm, "She'll shoot you too!"

"Let go of me, Matt! She's crying for help! She needs me," she yelled, violently wrenching away from his grasp. She shoved the door open and ran in the direction of Alexandra's wails, calling out, "I'm coming, Alex. Where are you? Alex? Alex?"

Matthew drew his .38 and started after her.

"Watch yourself, kid!" Dobrinski shouted as Matthew disappeared into the house.

Elizabeth, reaching the kitchen, found Alexandra sitting on the floor, moaning.

"What's wrong?" she pleaded as she dropped to her knees beside her friend. "Oh, Alex! Your poor hand!"

Matthew, entering the kitchen a moment later, quickly assessed the situation and holstered his '38. He began to struggle with Alexandra in an attempt to clamp a pair of handcuffs on her wrists. Elizabeth could not believe that he was trying to restrain her suffering friend with manacles.

"What are you doing, Matt? Stop it! Can't you see she's terribly hurt?"

Fending off Elizabeth's pounding fists, while trying to control Alexandra's flailing arms, he managed to clamp the handcuffs onto Alexandra's twisting wrists. Damn, he thought, they'll just have to be locked in front of her until I get some help.

As Matt began to read Alexandra her rights, she struggled to her feet and strained in vain to break the strong chain connecting her two wrists. Staring wild-eyed at both of them, she snarled knowingly, "I'll destroy you both! I know who sent you, it was that bastard, Louis Napoléon. You'll pay for your deception. Once I see the Holy Father, we'll free Maximilian and come after you."

Elizabeth tearfully turned to Matthew, saying, "Oh Matt, she's hallucinating. She's sick. What's happened to her?" Moving toward her suffering friend, she attempted to assure her, "Dear Alex, we'll get you help. You'll be better soon, I promise.

"Don't you touch me," Alexandra viciously warned as she backed away from her. "You think I don't see through you! Edmire and Amati didn't fool me, either. They tried to keep me from my Maximilian, but I got rid of both of them." She bared her teeth and drew her lips taut against her gums as a hoarse demonic laugh emanated from deep in her throat. A sudden stab of excruciating pain in her hand cut her laughter short. She fell to her knees, moaning.

Two police cars with wailing sirens screeched to a halt in the street. Car doors slammed. Sgt. Dobrinski, holding his arm, appeared in the kitchen doorway accompanied by four officers with drawn weapons.

"What's going on in here, Matt?" he demanded.

"Everything's under control, Dan."

"Good," said Dobrinski, collapsing into the nearest kitchen chair.

"Dan," said Matthew, "Alexandra said that she did away with Amati. She also said she got rid of Edmire."

"Mr. Edmire," Elizabeth said, "is the one who owned the three Imperial paperweights! Alex was with him the night he died."

Glancing at Alexandra Dobrinski said, "You sure were a busy lady." Noticing the handcuffs on her wrists, he said, "What the hell, Matt, you cuffed her in front! Cuffs go in back! She could of grabbed your gun that way!"

"Christ, Dan, the way she was struggling, I was lucky to get them on her at all! Anyway, you'll be glad to know we also found the three missing paperweights. They're over there on the counter; one of them is in pieces."

"Busted?"

"Yeah, the green one. There's a piece of it on the floor."

Dobrinski turned to one of the officers, ordering, "Wilkens, turn off that gas stove. And, Burke, you take charge of those paperweights. Make sure you get all the broken pieces, too. Be careful with them, they're valuable evidence!" He asked Matthew, "Why the hell is she sitting in the corner moaning like that?"

"She scalded her hand, bad. But that's not the worst of it. She's gone off the deep end."

"Off her rocker?"

"Yeah. She's not making much sense."

"We got her .32 just inside the door," said Dobrinski. "She dropped it after she plugged me. Burke's got it in a plastic bag. Matt, you turn it over to ballistics while these guys take me and the prisoner to the emergency ward. Mulcahy can decide what to do with her when you turn in the report."

"May I go along with Alexandra, Dan?" asked Beth.

"Sure kid, you come along. You're probably the closest thing to a family she's got."

Suddenly, Alexandra charged forward in a desperate attempt to grab the two undamaged paperweights with her bound hands, but she was pulled back by an alert officer. Struggling against his tight grasp, she hissed, "Don't touch those paperweights, they're mine." Her face changed into a sardonic smile, as she growled, "Leave them alone or you'll be swallowed up by the fires of Hell!"

Alexandra's adrenaline suddenly flowed, creating such superhuman strength in her body that she tore free of the officer's grasp. Laughing strangely, she started for the paperweights again. "Got to throw them into the boiling water!" she howled.

"Stop her!" cried Dobrinski.

The startled officers lunged at the maddened apparition.

"Jesus, she's got sharp claws," one of the policemen cried out as Alexandra raked her nails across his ear. One of the officers managed to grab her in a tight bear hug from behind. Alexandra squirmed in his tight grasp. "I'll kill you, I'll kill you", she growled as spittle dripped from her parted lips.

As suddenly as her explosive violence began, she suddenly became quiescent, her muscles rigid and her eyes staring straight ahead.

"Be careful, Burke," cautioned Dobrinski, "she's playing possum."

"I don't think so, Sergeant. She's hardly breathing, she's stiff as a board."

"Don't let go of her."

"I got her, Sergeant."

"Dan," said Beth tremulously, "I think she's in a catatonic state."

The old officer replied, "Whatever it is, it's a hell of a lot better than before. Wilkins," he ordered, "get out to the wagon and get a straitjacket. She'll be a lot easier to handle with it buckled on." He shuddered as he caught sight of Alexandra's left hand. "Christ, look at her hand, she scalded the hell out of it!"

Alexandra was no longer aware of the intense pain. Her shattered mind had once again entered the world of the Imperial paperweights. She whispered, "My darling Maximilian, I've come back to you. But we must be very careful. Our enemies are all around us. If we remain quiet, they won't find us. Close your eyes, my dear. See, like this, and they can't see us. There, isn't that better? Quiet and dark, my love, quiet and dark. Don't move, quiet, quiet, sh-h-h-h—"

"What's she saying, Burke?"

"I don't know, Sergeant, but she's anchored to the floor like a rock."

The officer returned with the straitjacket. Dobrinski, holding his bleeding arm, instructed, "Get those damn manacles off, but watch your step! You'd better get hold of her arms first. Matt, you get it on her before she goes nuts again!"

"...destroy their reason..."

With the straitjacket buckled on, the policemen attempted to escort Alexandra out of the kitchen, but she refused to budge. They struggled, attempting to pull and shove her along the way.

"We'll never get her out of here like that. We're going to have to strap her on a stretcher and carry her out."

"No, wait," said Beth. Facing her resisting friend she quietly said, "Please come along with us, we've come to escort you to Miramar."

Alexandra's tense body relaxed. She assumed a regal bearing and slowly walked, straitjacketed, through her home to the waiting police van, all the while acknowledging imagined subjects to her right and to her left.

"Ain't that a bitch," said Dobrinski, shaking his head. As they walked through the living room, he said, "You two kids were in such a damn hurry coming in, you probably didn't notice this room."

Elizabeth saw, for the first time, that the room was a step back into time. Alexandra had carefully searched out period lamps, elaborate picture frames, heavy tasseled drapes, flowered wall paper, carved tables, overstuffed settees and oriental carpets to furnish her little Victorian world. She, in fact, lived the later half of the nineteenth century in that one room. It was a space where the personages and events of the Victorian Age had come to be more real to her than the world outside. By the time she was apprehended, everything and everyone outside of that room were merely intruding shadows. Discussing it later, Elizabeth told Matthew that when she saw the room, it was as if she had stepped into a stereopticon slide of a Victorian drawing room.

Matthew agreed saying, "It was a real time machine, wasn't it?"

7.

The first day that Dan Dobrinski was well enough to return to work, he went directly to Lieutenant Mulcahy's office.

"I'm reporting for duty, Lieutenant."

"You got a written release from the doctor?"

"Yeah."

"Okay. Now listen up, Dobrinski. Get your ass up to Captain Barootian's office at 10 a.m. sharp!"

"What's the problem, Lieutenant?"

"Just be there on time!"

Dobrinski returned to his desk to wait for the two hours to pass.

When Matthew punched in, he was pleased to see that Dobrinski had returned. "Glad you're back," he said. Noticing that his partner seemed downcast, he asked, "Everything Okay, Dan?"

"Captain wants to see me. Mulcahy probably made out a report on the day I was at the bookies. That son-of-a-bitch is just itching to see me take a fall. Didn't even ask me about my arm."

"Don't jump the gun, Dan," said Matthew, trying to ease his partner's obvious distress.

"It'll be termination from the force, for sure. Oh, Christ, what'll I tell Josie? It don't matter the years you put in. Screw up once, and it's crap all over your face!"

"Loosen up, Dan, it might be something else."

"Like what? A cup of coffee? Or the weather? Come on, kid, Captain Barootian never wastes time with small talk. It's the ax, for sure."

"You don't know what he—"

"Oh, for Christ's sake, Matt, shut up! What the hell do you know? You're just a punk rookie, still wet behind the ears!"

Matthew left and went to the squad room where he busied himself with reports. It's best to leave Dan alone right now, he thought. He returned a few minutes before Dobrinski's meeting with the captain. The old sergeant was at the mirror, attempting to flatten a curled-up shirt collar.

"Damn thing won't stay down," he said. "Oh, shit! Well, I'd better get up there."

"Good luck, Dan."

"Yeah, thanks. Hey, kid, I'm sorry I blew up."

Later that morning, Dobrinski, grinning, told Matthew,

"Man, those paperweights really saved my ass!"

"You're off the hook?"

"Yeah, ain't that great! You know what? The Captain didn't even mention the horses. You won't believe this—he put me in for a commendation! He said the superintendent called him and asked him to personally thank me for breaking the case. I guess old Edmire's name still has a lot of clout around City Hall."

"What about Mulcahy?"

"He won't bother me any more. Now that I've got Barootian on my side, I'm set till I retire."

8.

"Good morning, Sotheby's-Chicago, Elizabeth Field speaking."

"Hi, Miss Field, this is Christa Allen. I'm calling you from Zurich—Zurich, Switzerland."

"Oh, yes. Alexandra spoke of you often. You two went to school together."

"That's right, roommates in Boston. Miss Field, my husband and I are extremely concerned about Alexandra. It's been four months since the awful tragedy; we've not been able to learn anything more about what happened to her since her arrest. Can you tell us what's happened and how she is?"

"Oh, sure. I attended her hearing. The court determined that Alex was suffering from an acute case of schizophrenia. She's been institutionalized in a mental facility. They're trying to help her."

"I hope they can. The papers here in Europe carried the details of the theft and the two murders, but dropped the story soon afterward."

"The media played it to the hilt here, too. I guess it was good copy. Just last week there was a thirty minute special on TV reporting the complete details of the stolen paperweights and their one-hundred twenty-four year old story."

9.

NEW YORK - 1986

"Sold, four-thousand, two-hundred and fifty dollars."

The sharp rap of the auctioneer's wooden hammer terminated the bidding on lot 191.

Leafing through the auction catalog, Matthew quietly said, "Getting close now, Beth, only three pages away."

"I know. Can't you just feel the tension?"

As the slide of the next paperweight appeared on the screen at the front of the large room, he said, "Bidding's really slacked off. Just a couple of bids on that last one."

"Probably didn't make the reserve."

He nodded in agreement, "The heavy bidders are waiting for the two big ones."

At Elizabeth's insistence, the young couple changed their plans for a honeymoon in Nassau to attend the auction at Sotheby's New York. They were not there to buy; they were there to witness the disposition of the two Imperial paperweights which played such an important part in their lives.

Shortly before their wedding, she pleaded, "Please, Matt, we've got to go to the auction. I'm sorry I didn't think of it sooner, but I wouldn't have met you if it wasn't for those paperweights. They're the reason for our happiness! Please, honey."

The changes were costly: additional money for the travel agency and his promise to work the holiday duty schedule for the balance of the year. His only thought was to please her; he couldn't deny her anything.

On the balmy June morning they arrived in New York, the day before the auction, Elizabeth took a cab to Sotheby's to view the paperweights while Matthew enjoyed a swim in the hotel pool. When she returned, he asked, "Well, did you see them?"

"I sure did! God, they're beautiful—like jewels, rare jewels!"

"Lot of people there?"

"Oh, yes! Had to elbow my way just to get near the display cases. Publicity's really pumped up the excitement. At first I couldn't imagine that there were that many paperweight collectors in the whole world. But after listening to some of the people around me, I realized most of them were there because of the murders."

"Morbid curiosity."

"Uh-huh. And when I finally got close to the display cases, I heard this one guy say that the paperweights were made out of plastic! Imagine, plastic!"

"Oh, no!"

"And get this. He told the people near him that he used to make paperweights by pouring liquid plastic around spiders and flowers. I couldn't believe my ears when he pointed to a case of crystal weights, and bragged, 'It took a lot of patience and a special knack, but mine turned out as good as those.' And you know what? Some of the people shook their heads accepting what that idiot was saying!"

"Like Dobrinski always says, honey, 'There are a hell of a lot more horses' asses than horses in the world.'"

She smiled in agreement.

"See anyone you know?"

"Uh-huh. I ran into Keith. He said the first day the Imperial paperweights were on display, so many people came to see them that the lines extended way out to the sidewalk!"

The auctioneer hammered down lot number 192, "Sold, six-thousand, five-hundred dollars."

A sudden rustle filled the large room as several hundred bidders turned to the next catalog page.

Matthew turned to Elizabeth and whispered, "Bet the crap really flew around in here last year."

"When the paperweights disappeared?"

"Yeah."

"You haven't forgotten we had our share of excitement over them too, have you, honey?"

"Marcella's evil curse at work," he whispered, his eyes widening in mock fear.

As the sale continued, Elizabeth's awareness of the auctioneer's silken voice slowly faded. Her mind wandered back to the previous year, to the turbulent events that effected the course of so many lives.

Finally, item 207 was placed on the auction block. The room stilled. A large image of the paperweight appeared high on a screen at the front of the auction room. The intense color emanating from it filled the room with purple shadows. The sound from the assembled bidders, like air expelled from an air hose, was followed by agitated murmurings. Other images of the purple Imperial paperweight were flashed in quick succession: a side view, the bottom, close-ups of the shield, the sulphide profiles and the flower-bedecked date canes. The noise in the room rose in a steady crescendo with each new frame. The changing views finally came to rest with the original slide.

"Here it comes, Matt," Beth whispered as she gripped his hand.

The auctioneer paused waiting for respectful silence. The room quieted. His velvety voice, polished and subdued began, "The next lot, lot number 207, created by the Lorraine factory, is one of the two extant paperweights commissioned by Empress Eugenie of France for Empress Carlota of Mexico. It is a light violet double overlay containing the Hapsburg crest, surmounted by the Mexican eagle. The shield is enameled in colors over gold. Sulphide silhouettes of Emperor Maximilian and Empress Carlota of Mexico appear on either side, facing the coat of arms. The internal date, 1876, which appears below the design, is embellished with vines, leaves and miniature flowers. The entire design, encircled by a ring of canes, appears on a dark purple ground. I have a starting bid of $125,000 on lot 207. Are there any additional bids?"

Is that all he's going to say about it? thought Elizabeth. How can he squeeze out all the romance, tragedy and significance from that ineffably beautiful masterpiece and reduce it to a few dry sentences? He makes it sound so ordinary.

Scores of bidding paddles erupted into the air. The lights suddenly flickered in the room, dimmed, brightened, then went out. When they came back on again, the projected image of lot 207 had disappeared.

"One moment, please, ladies and gentlemen, there is a slight problem with our projected image."

In the commotion that followed, pseudo-frightened whispers of "Marcella's curse" could be heard throughout the auction room.

"What's happening, Matt?" Elizabeth asked.

"I think the bulb blew on their projector. Probably caused

a short in their circuit."

"We will resume the auction," continued the unruffled voice of the auctioneer, "as soon as we can once again project the image of lot 207 for you. Thank you for your patience."

"That'll knock a few bucks off the price of the paperweight."

"No, it won't, Matt. If anything, it'll heighten the excitement of the auction."

"You don't think it was done on purpose, do you?"

"Oh, come on, Matt!"

The paperweight's image suddenly appeared again at the front of the room, blurred at first, then quickly focused. The mellifluous voice of the auctioneer began, once again, "Thank you for your patience ladies and gentlemen. We can now proceed with the bidding on lot 207. Our opening bid is at $125,000."

As the bidding moved quickly into stratospheric levels, numbered paddles reluctantly descended throughout the large room. The bidding gradually slowed, teetered, and finally came to rest with paddle number 17 still raised at $425,000.

"Are there any additional bids? Are you finished?" After a slight pause the auctioneer banged his crystal gavel on the desk, declaring, "Lot 207, sold to bidder number 17 for $425,000."

Lot 208, the yellow Imperial paperweight, also began with a $125,000 initial bid. In this instance the bidding was much more spirited. But inevitably, all the raised paddles throughout the hushed room dropped, one by one, until at $375,000, the bids came from just two locations. The second paperweight was finally hammered down to paddle number 115 at $475,000.

Sources later revealed that agents representing two renowned paperweight collectors—Maurice Lindon of France and Arthur Rubloff of Chicago—purchased the Imperial paperweights.

When questioned in Paris about Marcella's curse, Mr. Lindon said, "It makes a very fascinating story, but it no doubt added an extra half-million francs to my bidding cost."

Lawrence Selman, Mr. Rubloff's agent, scoffed at what he considered an "old wives' tale." Asked about the continuing influence of Marcella's curse on the Imperial paperweights, as evidenced by the problem with the projector, he replied, "I don't believe in Marcella's curse. But if, in fact, the curse still exists, it has certainly lost its power over the years. I don't consider a blown-out projector bulb very intimidating."

EPILOGUE

"Chicago Police Department, Central District, Officer Porcelli."

"Robbery detail, please."

"Thank you, ma'am. I'll transfer your call."

"Robbery, Officer Brown."

"Oh, hi Glenn. This is Beth. Is Matt in?"

"No, Beth, he's out making a report. He should be back before lunch."

"Would you have him call me here at work as soon as he gets back?"

"Listen Beth, if it's an emergency, I'll put out a call. He can phone you from where he is."

"No thanks, Glenn, it can wait. But please don't forget."

When Matthew returned to the station, he dialed Elizabeth's number. "Hi, honey. Glenn said you called."

"Yes. Have you heard about Arthur Rubloff?"

"No, what happened?"

"Hold on to your hat; he died last night!"

"Yeah?"

"I heard it on the radio this morning on the way to work."

After a slight pause, Matthew said, "I know what you're thinking, don't I?"

"Well, it's only been five weeks since he bought the paperweight!"

"And you're suggesting that Rubloff was the victim of Marcella's evil curse?"

"It can't be a coincidence."

"Sure it is. I don't believe in superstitions, and neither do you. Honey, he was pretty old. Anyhow, you remember that there were two of those paperweights auctioned off that afternoon."

"I wouldn't want to be in Mr. Lindon's shoes right now."

"Oh, come on, Beth."

Eleven days later, Elizabeth received a call from the New York office.

"Morning Elizabeth, this is Keith. May I speak to Douglas?"

"Good morning, Keith. Douglas is in conference. Can you wait?"

"Yes, if it's not too long. I've got to talk to him about those three Flemish tapestry panels he sent us."

"For the September auction?"

"Well, of course! The two large ones have a reserve, but I don't have a reserve for the small panel. Do you happen to know if the consignor put a reserve on it?"

"No, I'm sorry. You'll have to speak to Douglas about that."

"Off the record, how are you adjusting to your new boss?"

"Douglas is very nice." she said, adding, "He's not new to me anymore; he's been here eleven months."

"Just between us, Elizabeth, I still can't understand why they had to import some limy from the London office to replace Alexandra. There are plenty of us here in New York who could have handled the job in Chicago."

Elizabeth thought, poor Keith, still perturbed at being passed over for a second time.

"Any news of Alexandra?"

"I visited her last week. The skin graft is coming along fine. But mentally, she seems much the same to me, although her psychiatrist says she's beginning to respond to medication and treatment. I hope they can help her."

"They work miracles in some cases. Oh, by the way, Elizabeth, we just heard that Maurice Lindon died."

"Oh, my God!"

"...wrapped in their winding sheets, their shrouds of death..."

CODA

It is reported at the writing of this book that both Christie's and Sotheby's are attempting to initiate negotiations with the beneficiaries of the deceased collectors' estates to once again offer the Imperial paperweights at auction.

NOTE

For readers who desire to know which of the characters in this novel are not fictional, they are listed below in the order of their appearance in the book. All other characters are fictional and do not portray any persons living or dead.

—*George N. Kulles*

CHAPTER I.

Richard J. Daley—former Mayor of Chicago
Maximilian—Emperor of Mexico
Guiterrez de Estrada—an Official of Louis Napoléon's Court
Carlota—Empress of Mexico/PAPERWEIGHT COLLECTOR
Comtese Castiglione—a favorite Courtesan of Napoléon III
Louis Napoléon/Napoléon III—emperor of France
Eugenie Montijo—Empress of France/PAPERWEIGHT COLLECTOR
Georges Haussmann—Architect who reconstructed Paris
General Forey—French General in Mexico
J. Launay—Manager of Hautin-Launay Company/dealer of glass
Eugene Didierjean—Manager of Saint Louis Glass Factory
Comte Bacciochi—Court Chamberlain of the Tuileries Palace
Duchesse de Bassano—Chief Lady-in-waiting to Eugenie

CHAPTER II.

Arthur Rubloff—Real-estate developer, PAPERWEIGHT COLLECTOR
Leopold I—King of Belgium, Carlota's father

Emperor Franz Joseph—Emperor of Austria
Victoria I—Queen of England, PAPERWEIGHT COLLECTOR
Adelina Patti—Nineteenth century opera star
Elizabeth, "Sissy"—Empress of Austria
Sophie—Archduchess of Austria
Pius IX—Catholic Pope
Benito Juarez—President of Mexico
General Bazaine—French General in Mexico
General Arteaga—Commander-in-Chief of Juarez's army
Augustin—Maximilian's adopted Mexican son
Señora del Barrio—Carlota's Chief Lady-in-waiting
Leopold II—King of Belgium, Carlota's brother
Philippe—Crown Prince of Belgium
Father Soria—Maximilian's Priest at his execution
Generals Miramon and Maja—Maximilian's Mexican generals
Prince von Bismarck—Unified German states into a nation

CHAPTER III.

Oscar Wilde—Playwright, PAPERWEIGHT COLLECTOR
Alfred Douglas ("Bosie")—Son of Lord Queensberry
John Shalto Douglas Queensberry—Marquess of Queensberry
Constance Wilde—Oscar Wilde's wife
Robert Ross—Wilde's friend and literary executor
Lady Queensberry—Alfred Douglas's mother
Sir Humphrey—Ross's and Wilde's solicitor
Edward Carson—Queensberry's lawyer
Sir Edward Clarke—Wilde's lawyer
Charles Parker, Fred Atkins, Edward Shelly, Jane Cotter, Mrs. Ellen, Mrs. Grey, Antonio Miggi, Mrs. Perkins—witnesses against Wilde
Sir Frank Lockwood & Charles Gill—Crown's prosecutors

Otho—Constance Wilde's brother
Cyril and Vyvyan Holland—Oscar Wilde's sons
Father Cuthbert Dunne—Wilde's priest at his death

CHAPTER IV.

Evita Duarte Peron—Wife of Peron, PAPERWEIGHT COLLECTOR
Juan Peron—President of Argentina
Juana Ibarguren—Evita's mother
Elisa, Juancito, Herminda—Evita's siblings
Augustin Magaldi—guitarist who befriended Evita
Father Benitiz—the Perons' personal priest
Cypriano Reyes—Leader of Argentina's Labor Confederation
Generalissimo Francisco Franco—Dictator of Spain
José Freyre—Minister of Labor and former glassworker
Isabelita—Peron's wife and president after his death

CHAPTER V.

Truman Capote—Author, PAPERWEIGHT COLLECTOR
Colette—French authoress, PAPERWEIGHT COLLECTOR
Pauline—Colette's servant
Henri Gauthier-Villas, Henry Jouvenel, Maurice Goudeket—Colette's Husbands
Marquise de Belbeuf ("Missy")—Colette's lover
Colette Jouvenel—Colette's daughter
Perry Smith and Richard Hickock—Murderers
Johnny and Joanne Carson, Robert Kennedy, Lee Radziwell, Jacqueline Bouvier—Capote's neighbors
Neil Simon—Playwright

CHAPTER VI.

Farouk—King of Egypt, PAPERWEIGHT COLLECTOR
Paul Jokelson—Founder of the Paperweight Collectors' Association, author, PAPERWEIGHT COLLECTOR

CHAPTER VIII.

Maurice Lindon—PAPERWEIGHT COLLECTOR
Lawrence Selman—Paperweight dealer, author and agent for Arthur Rubloff collection

ABOUT THE AUTHOR

George Kulles has studied paperweights for twenty-six years. He is a respected expert in the field who has lectured and written voluminously on the subject publishing two books *Identifying Antique Paperweights—Millefiori* and *Identifying Antique Paperweights—Lampwork*. Kulles is a knowledgeable conservator of paperweights and he has appraised pieces for museums and private collections.

Kulles' other passion is education. He worked as an administrator for the Chicago Board of Education for 31 years. He possesses a bachelor degree in music from Augustana College and a Master's degree in art from De Paul University.

Kulles currently resides in Illinois with his wife, Jean.